Robert Goddard was born in Hampshire and read History at Cambridge. His first novel, *Past Caring*, was an instant bestseller. Since then his books have captivated readers worldwide with their edge-of-the-seat pace and their labyrinthine plotting.

FOUND WANTING

On his way to work, London civil servant Richard Eusden is intercepted by his ex-wife, Gemma, and told that his old friend Marty Hewitson is dying, and needs one last favour — today. Eusden agrees, but the seemingly simple errand turns into a race for life — his *and* Marty's. He travels across Belgium, Germany and Denmark and into a mystery that connects Marty's late grandfather with the Russian Royal Family who were murdered ninety years earlier. Eusden finds himself in a battle with ruthless people who would kill to steal the secret they believe Marty and he hold. Eusden's every move seems to be a step closer to disaster. But move he must if he is to escape the clutches of history. It's his only hope . . .

Books by Robert Goddard
Published by The House of Ulverscroft:

IN PALE BATTALIONS
TAKE NO FAREWELL
HAND IN GLOVE
CLOSED CIRCLE
BORROWED TIME
OUT OF THE SUN
BEYOND RECALL
SET IN STONE
SEA CHANGE
DYING TO TELL
PAST CARING
DAYS WITHOUT NUMBER
SIGHT UNSEEN
PLAY TO THE END
NEVER GO BACK
NAME TO A FACE

ROBERT GODDARD

FOUND WANTING

Complete and Unabridged

CHARNWOOD
Leicester

First published in Great Britain in 2008 by
Bantam Press
an imprint of
Transworld Publishers
London

First Charnwood Edition
published 2009
by arrangement with
Transworld Publishers
The Random House Group Limited
London

British Library CIP Data

Goddard, Robert.
Found wanting
1. Suspense fiction.
2. Large type books.
I. Title
823.9'14–dc22

ISBN 978–1–84782–689–3

Published by
F. A. Thorpe (Publishing)
Anstey, Leicestershire

Set by Words & Graphics Ltd.
Anstey, Leicestershire
Printed and bound in Great Britain by
T. J. International Ltd., Padstow, Cornwall

LONDON

1

The sky over Whitehall is doughy grey, the air chill and granular. It is a Monday morning in early February, yet winter has seemingly only just begun after a dank, extended autumn. The cold is almost a tonic for Richard Eusden as he emerges from the Churchill Café, mug of strong black coffee in hand, and sits down at one of the pavement tables. He drops his briefcase beside his chair, sinks his chin within the sheltering collar of his overcoat and lets the warmth of the coffee seep into his palm as he surveys the familiar scene.

The traffic is thinner than usual, but slow-moving nonetheless, thanks to the pelican crossing adjacent to the café. It beeps and blinks in service to the dark-suited men and women crossing in both directions who are bound for their desks and work places in the ministries either side of Whitehall. Many already have their security passes dangling round their necks, their identities surrendered and declared, their working weeks about to begin in variations on an institutionalized theme.

Richard Eusden's security pass is still in his pocket. He will take it out only when he is most of the way down King Charles Street and turning into the Foreign Office staff entrance. The delay is a small assertion of his individuality, pitifully small in all conscience, but one of the

3

few open to him. A civil servant closing fast on fifty with an index-linked pension no longer an unimaginably distant prospect cannot afford to cock a snook at the government machine he is undeniably part of. But there is no need to rush to take his place within it this morning. It is not yet 8.30. His train was neither late nor overcrowded. He is feeling less than usually travel-worn. He sips his coffee and tries to savour the moment. He knows he should put it to more obviously practical use, if only for the benefit of any of his colleagues who may pass by. There are file notes in his case he intended to study — but did not — in the course of the weekend. He could profitably cast an eye over them now. Staring into space is perhaps not the wisest image to project in the ever more image-conscious culture that has engulfed his profession. But still he goes on staring, through the plume of steam rising from his coffee.

The truth, he recognized long ago, was that he should never have become a civil servant. Deep within his soul he lacks the vital capacity to think the conventional thought — and to believe it. Having become one, he should have quit once he realized his mistake. He should have dropped out, travelled the world, searched for something else — anything else — to do with his life. But he had just married then and assumed he would have children, who would need the comfort and security his career could supply. And by the time that and a number of other assumptions about his marriage had been confounded, he had persuaded himself it was too late to make the

4

break. More accurately, it was too easy to refrain from making the effort. Now it really is too late. Life, he is well aware, is what you make of it. And this is what he has made of his. He is smartly dressed and well-groomed. He is not losing his hair or running to fat. His blue eyes still glisten. His brain is still sharp. By most people's standards, he leads an enviable existence. He tries to remind himself of this as he contemplates the predictable day and unsurprising week that lie ahead of him. He needs a change, but he does not expect to get it. He takes a deeper swallow of coffee and sets the mug down on the table.

His fingers are barely free of the mug handle when three short blasts on a car horn snap his attention to the other side of the street. A pea-green Mazda is cruising slowly through the pelican crossing as the light flashes amber. The driver's window is opening and a face coming into view that Eusden senses he is on the brink of recognizing, only for a dirty red slab of bendy bus to cut off the view.

The bus slows for traffic ahead and merely crawls forward. It is an open question to Eusden whether he will see the Mazda again. It may already be past the Cenotaph and heading towards Trafalgar Square. He knows nobody who drives such a car. He has no concrete reason for supposing the horn was sounded for his benefit. The incident seems about to de-spool into the ebb and flow of the morning.

But it does not. The Mazda completes a fast and illegal U-turn into the bus lane as the blockage to Eusden's view finally removes itself. The car jolts to a halt at the pavement's edge, the driver waving through the windscreen to attract Eusden's attention. He starts with astonishment. The driver is Gemma, his ex-wife. He has not seen or spoken to her for several years. They have, she memorably assured him the last time they met, nothing to say to each other. The clear implication of her manner on that occasion was that they never would have. Something has changed her mind — something urgent, to judge by her behaviour.

'Richard,' she shouts through the open window. 'Get in.'

Eusden grabs his case, jumps up and strides across to the car, stooping to engage Gemma at eye-level. She looks, if anything, younger than he remembers. Her hair is shorter, her face slightly thinner, her skin clear, aglow with health. She is dressed in a black tracksuit and trainers. She appears what she is: fit, energetic, intent.

'Get in,' she repeats.

'I'm on my way to the office,' Eusden objects, though with little force. He already badly wants her not to drive away without him.

'Sod the office. Will you please just get in the car?' Her tone is impatient, but her gaze is pleading. She needs him. For once, she really does. 'Please, Richard.'

A double-decker is bearing down on them along the bus lane. Something has to give. He hesitates, then opens the door and climbs into the car. Gemma accelerates away, tyres squealing.

6

'Sorry,' she says, though whether she is apologizing for her driving or her unannounced reappearance in his life is hard to tell.

'What's going on, Gemma?' Eusden asks, buckling his seat belt as they swerve into Parliament Square.

'I was looking for somewhere to park when I saw you. We have to talk.'

'What about?'

'Marty.'

Marty Hewitson. Eusden's childhood friend. Gemma's other ex-husband. Of all the subjects under the sun, Marty should be the last she wants to broach between them.

'He's asked me to do something for him.' She keeps to the right, circling the square, looking ahead, avoiding any danger of meeting Eusden's eyes. 'I want you to do it instead.'

Surprise gives way to disbelief. *Why the hell should I?* is Eusden's instinctive response. But all he actually says is, 'Really?' Certainly he can imagine no reason why he would even consider helping either of them. Then Gemma supplies such a reason. By answering the question he has not asked.

'He's dying, Richard.' She shoots a glance at him. 'Marty's dying.'

2

'Dying?' Eusden repeated incredulously as they drove along Birdcage Walk through the visibly unaltered but transformed workaday morning.

'An inoperable brain tumour,' said Gemma, sorrow deepening her matter-of-fact tone. 'He's got a few months at most. But it could happen sooner. It could happen any time.'

'Have you seen him?'

'No. And I don't want to. I don't think I could handle that, Richard. But I'd have to see him to do this favour he wants. That's why . . . '

'You thought of me.'

'You and Marty were friends long before I came into your lives. You shouldn't let him die without . . . patching it up between you.'

'Shouldn't I?'

'No. Of course you shouldn't. You know that.' Her sidelong glance caught him unawares, his expression doubtless revealing more than his words. 'Don't you?'

★   ★   ★

Nearly forty years had passed since Richard Eusden's first meeting with Marty Hewitson. Carisbrooke Grammar School, Newport, Isle of Wight: a cool day in early September, 1968. They were of the last generation of boys on the Island to take the eleven-plus and found

8

themselves standing next to each other when the first year intake was corralled in the windy school yard that morning. Of such chances are friendships made. They were both intelligent and inquisitive, intellectually ambitious as well as mildly rebellious. They stuck together through seven years at Carisbrooke, Richard thriving on exams, while Marty, the more naturally gifted of the two, kept pace with him effortlessly. Then on to Cambridge, where their fateful shared infatuation with the bewitching Gemma Conway began.

It took more than two decades for the tragicomedy of their triangular relationship to play itself out — insofar as it had. After Cambridge, Richard joined the Civil Service, Marty went into TV journalism and Gemma studied for a Ph.D. They were all based in London. Marty seemed to have won the contest for Gemma and Richard tried to accept defeat graciously. But Marty was already beginning to hone a serious drug habit which Gemma could not tolerate. She left him for Richard. They married while Marty was ITV's Man in the Middle East. Gemma secured a teaching post at Surrey University. They moved to Guildford. Suburban conformity beckoned. But Gemma recoiled from it. Marty returned from the Middle East, Lebanese girlfriend in tow. They began to spend time together as a foursome. Gemma landed a post at the LSE. Soon, she was back with Marty, despite the drugs, though Richard did not find out until the Lebanese girlfriend told him. Divorce followed. Gemma married Marty. They moved to Italy, where Marty was supposed to be writing a novel while Gemma taught at the University of Bologna. There was a kind of rapprochement. Richard visited them several times. Everyone behaved in a very civilized way. But it was not clear if they had their hearts in it. Naturally no novel was written. Cocaine became more important to Marty than Gemma. She left again — for a fellowship at Cambridge. Marty drifted back to London. His greatest attribute — the impossibility of holding a grudge against him — was unimpaired. Richard knew better than to try holding one anyway. Winning back Gemma was a different matter. He could not stop himself trying to do that, with some success, at least for a while. But too much had gone wrong too often. Their relationship finally fizzled out around the time Marty copped an eighteen-month prison sentence for drug dealing. The experience did not prove salutary. He was on remand for a second offence when he skipped the country. Richard, who had put up his bail money, had neither seen nor heard from him since, bar one cryptically apologetic postcard from Uruguay. The triangle was broken at last. Or so it had seemed.

★ ★ ★

'Where are we going?' Eusden asked as Gemma took off from the lights by Buckingham Palace.

'Hyde Park. We can talk there.'

'OK.'

10

He opened his briefcase and took out his phone. 'I'd better call the office and let them know I'll be late.'

'Say you can't make it today at all.'

'Why not?'

'That favour I mentioned. It's now or never.'

'What d'you mean?'

'I'll explain. I promise. Just wait till we're out of the traffic and I can concentrate.'

★ ★ ★

Memories gather poignancy like dust. They confer on the past a magical unattainability. Schooldays on the Isle of Wight; student years at Cambridge; married life in Guildford; evenings in pubs with Marty, rivalry for Gemma sharpening their arguments about politics and economics and the future of the world: Eusden mourned them all now as lost interludes of contentment, even though contented was not what he had felt at the time. Marty Hewitson was the best and closest friend he would ever have. And he would never love another woman as he had loved Gemma Conway. Those were facts of his life. He could not alter them. He could not wish them away. Even if he wanted to. Which of course he did not.

★ ★ ★

There had been plenty of spaces in the car park by the Serpentine. Joggers and dog-walkers were thin on the ground at this hour. The bare trees

11

were skeletal against the gunmetal sky. Some geese were still asleep, heads tucked under wings, denying the day had begun. Only the coots were active, corvetting noisily around as Gemma set a brisk pace past the boathouses, the hotel blocks of Park Lane rearing ahead like the buttes of a sunless desert.

'Where's he been these past few years?' Eusden asked, breathing hard from the effort of keeping up with her.

'Amsterdam, mostly. He doesn't think the police have been trying very hard to find him. But he doesn't want to risk arrest by coming back here.'

'So, what's the favour?'

'He phoned me last week. I was too shocked by his news to realize how . . . difficult I'd find it to see him again. He wants something taken to him.'

'In Amsterdam?'

'No. He's coming to Brussels to meet me off the Eurostar this afternoon. I'm hoping you'll agree to go instead. It's just a day trip, Richard. You'll be back this evening. The Foreign Office can spare you for twenty-four hours, can't they?'

'Why is it so difficult for you to see him again?'

'Because I've got over him. I don't want to see him looking ill or old. I don't want to be reminded of what we once had — and what he threw away.'

'You can't bear to see him because you loved him once. But you *can* bear to see me.'

'You're not dying.'

'Actually, we're all dying, Gemma. Just at different rates.'

She stopped and looked at him. 'Are you going to do this?'

'Depends what *this* is.'

'A package of some kind. I'm to collect it later this morning from a Bernie Shadbolt.'

'Who's he?'

'Someone Marty met in prison. Someone he trusts.'

'Why doesn't he trust him to take the package, then?'

'He said Shadbolt couldn't spare the time. For what it's worth, I suspect it's a ruse. To see me again. Maybe to . . . try to persuade me to go back to him . . . for as long as he's got left.'

'When did that possibility occur to you?'

'When Monica pointed it out to me.'

Ah, Monica. Eusden had wondered how long it would be before Gemma's Cambridge housemate found her way into the conversation. He had tried hard not to ponder the true nature of their relationship. Naturally, he had failed. 'Did she also point out that carrying a package through Customs for a convicted drug dealer isn't the smartest of moves?'

'For Christ's sake, Richard.' Gemma looked genuinely disappointed that he had asked such a question. 'No one's trying to set you up. Marty lives in Amsterdam. He doesn't need to smuggle drugs over from the Isle of Wight.'

'The Isle of Wight?'

Gemma sighed. 'The package is a family keepsake of some kind. Something he wants to have with him . . . in the months ahead. However many months there are. Shadbolt picked it up for him from Aunt Lily.'

Marty's aunt lived in a chocolate-box cottage beside the village green in St Helens, one of the Island's more picturesque settlements. She was, as far as Eusden knew, Marty's only living blood relative. It was plausible enough that she should be storing something for him. But that fact did not banish every hint of a set-up. It merely rendered the set-up, if there was one, more arcane. 'So, Shadbolt could spare the time to look up Aunt Lily, could he?'

'He had business on the Island, according to Marty.'

'Friends in Parkhurst to visit, maybe.'

'Maybe.'

'Is there something you're not telling me, Gemma?'

'No. It really is very simple. One of us has to go. We can't just . . . abandon him. I'd be grateful if you went. I think it might be good for you. And Marty. But I can't force you to go. It's up to you.'

★   ★   ★

The café at the eastern end of the Serpentine had just opened when they reached it. Gemma did not object when Eusden suggested going inside for a coffee, even though she already had what she wanted from him. He had agreed to take the package to Brussels, as she had doubtless been confident he would.

They sat by a window table, looking back up the Serpentine to the bridge they had driven over twenty minutes earlier. They sipped their coffees, a silence looming towards awkwardness.

'When I first set eyes on you,' Eusden said at last, 'you had blonde hair and an Alice-band. And you were wearing a dress with a flower pattern on it and a petticoat showing beneath the hem.'

'Are you making some point, Richard?'

'Just reflecting . . . on your change of style.'

'Well, no one could accuse you of changing.'

'Would it really be so hard for you to see Marty again?'

'Yes. It would. OK?'

'OK.'

'Have you got your passport with you?'

'What do you think? I wasn't planning to leave the country today. I wasn't planning to leave the office.'

'I'm sorry for the short notice, all right?' Gemma's mouth tightened. 'I hardly slept last night. I was still intending to go myself when I went to bed. Tossing and turning, I eventually realized . . . I couldn't.'

'You could have phoned me.'

'I had to get on the road. Besides, I thought you'd react better . . . face to face.' She sighed. 'My mistake.'

'I've agreed to go, Gemma. Isn't that enough?'

'I suppose it'll have to be.' She drank some coffee, glanced at her watch, then drank some more. 'We need to collect your passport before we meet Shadbolt. And the train's at twelve

15

forty. So, I suppose we should start moving.'

'If you say so.'

'The flowers on the dress were forget-me-nots, by the way,' she said as she stood up. 'It went to Oxfam years ago. I don't have any dresses now.'

3

The round trip to Chiswick to collect Eusden's passport took the best part of an hour. It was nearly eleven o'clock by the time Gemma drew up in the yard of Shadbolt & Daughters Ltd, Car Repairs and Servicing, Blue Anchor Lane, Bermondsey. Trains into and out of London Bridge were rumbling overhead along a weed-pocked yellow-bricked viaduct, three arches of which, plus two aged Portakabins, constituted Bernie Shadbolt's business premises. And business seemed to be brisk, to judge by the number of cars on view in various stages of dismantlement and the flashes of an arc welder that periodically floodlit the cavernous recesses of the archways.

They headed for the Portakabin with a fluorescent striplight shining through its chicken-wired windows and entered a paraffin-heated fug of cigarette smoke. The smoking was being done by a preposterously busty blonde in a low-cut T-shirt and straining jeans, currently engaged in a telephone conversation. The space was shared by a younger, slimmer woman wearing jeans that were under much less stress and a capacious cardigan over a higher-necked T-shirt. She had dark, shoulder-length hair and a pale, anxious face. She looked up from a computer screen as they entered and smiled. There was a sisterly resemblance despite their many dissimilarities.

17

Eusden took them to be the eponymous daughters.

'Can I help you?'

'I've an appointment with Bernie Shadbolt,' said Gemma. 'My name's Gemma Conway.'

'Oh, yeah. He's expecting you. Hold on.' The daughter reached up to a wall-mounted telephone, took it off the hook and pressed a button.

A bell started ringing somewhere in the vicinity. The response was swift. Eusden could hear the growled '*Yeah?*' from where he was standing.

'They're here, Dad.' Eusden did not catch the response to that, but the daughter supplied one as soon as she replaced the receiver. 'He'll be right with you.'

It was odd, Eusden thought, that she had said 'They're here' so naturally, almost as if his presence had been foreseen, an idea he found far from comforting. His gaze strayed to a noticeboard just inside the door. Amidst various flapping print-outs of health-and-safety regulations and fire precautions was a postcard, held by a single drawing-pin. The picture looked uncannily like an Amsterdam canalside scene. He was about to prise it back for a sight of the handwriting, when the door opened behind him.

'Mornin',' said Bernie Shadbolt. He was a tall, wiry man of sixty or so with crew-cut grey hair and a boxer's face, sea-grey eyes regarding them cautiously over the flattened bridge of his nose. His clothes — Crombie, polo-neck, tailored trousers and stout-soled shoes — were in varying shades of black. He looked like a man who

18

meant business even when he was not engaged in it.

'I'm Gemma Conway,' said Gemma.

'Got any ID?'

'Do I need any? I thought you were expecting me.'

'I was. But you can't be too careful.'

To Eusden's trained eye, Gemma was finding it difficult not to be riled. But she managed it. 'My passport's in the car.'

'Can I take a look?'

'All right.'

As Gemma headed for the door and Shadbolt stepped back to make way for her, he turned his attention to Eusden. 'Who are you?' He was clearly not a man who wasted time on niceties.

'My name's Eusden. Richard Eusden.'

'Ah. Right.'

'Heard of me?'

'Yeah. Packing your passport too, are you?'

'I am, yes.'

'Good.' Shadbolt gave a taut little smile and waved him on ahead.

★   ★   ★

Passport inspection was a cursory affair. Shadbolt did not seem seriously to suspect they were impostors. 'Sorry about that,' he said when he handed them back. 'Just playing safe.'

'Richard's an old friend of Marty's, Mr Shadbolt,' said Gemma, who evidently felt some kind of explanation was called for.

'Call me Bernie.' Shadbolt grinned at her

19

wolfishly, then looked at Eusden. 'Marty told me all about you, Richard.' His instant familiarity was disturbing. 'He reckoned it was fifty-fifty you'd go along for the ride.'

'You've got what we're here to take?' asked Gemma, who had clearly decided against mentioning that only Eusden would actually be going.

'Yeah. It's in the boot of my car. But look . . . ' Shadbolt glanced at his watch — a chunk of pseudo-Rolex. 'Why don't we hop round the corner for a drink? You've got time before your train.' Marty had obviously briefed him well. 'It's only twenty minutes from here to Waterloo.'

Gemma frowned. 'I think we should probably — '

'Great,' Shadbolt declared. 'Let's go, then.' He grinned. 'My shout.'

★ ★ ★

The pub round the corner was the kind of place Eusden was happier visiting on a Monday morning than a Friday night. Signs advertised karaoke and meat raffles. The island bar was reached through a sparse array of utilitarian tables and chairs. The only upholstery in sight had been ripped, the foam innards spilling out like a fungus. It was barely ten minutes past opening time, but they were not the first customers. A couple of elderly derelicts had already started on pints and cigarettes.

The landlady's wary face lifted marginally at

the sight of Shadbolt, who ordered himself a Scotch and a packet of crisps. The crisps, it transpired, were for the pub dog, much the friendliest of its inhabitants. Gemma's request for a Perrier and Eusden's for a half of bitter elicited a frisson of disapproval.

'Cheers,' said Shadbolt, starting on his whisky. Eusden reciprocated half-heartedly. Gemma said nothing. 'I couldn't let the two most important people in Marty's life come and go without at least standing them a drink.'

'The two most . . . '

'That's right, Richard. You and Gemma. It's what he called you when he filled me in on this little fetch-and-carry operation.'

'Really?'

'I'm not telling you anything you don't already know, now am I?'

'I suppose . . . '

'You're with the FO, right?'

'Er, yes.'

'Any chance you could put me wise on that dodgy dossier, then? Only, I've got a nephew in Iraq. He'd be interested in exactly how you Whitehall wallahs managed to get it so wrong. If you did get it wrong. Know what I mean?'

'It's good of you to have done this for Marty,' said Gemma, taking pity on Eusden.

'Well, I owed him one.'

'What exactly is the package?' asked Eusden, feeling no keener to discuss the nature of Shadbolt's debt to Marty than the calibre of government intelligence.

'Don't you know?' Shadbolt shot back at him.

'No. How could I?'

'You're his childhood chum. I reckoned you'd know all about it.'

''Fraid not.'

'So, what is it . . . Bernie?' asked Gemma, smiling tightly. 'The package.'

'Some old attaché case. I mean, really old. Locked. Marty's got the key, natch. You could force it open easily enough. But that wouldn't be playing the game, would it? Marty didn't say what was in it. I guess he's keeping us all on need-to-know.'

'Didn't you ask his aunt?' Eusden put in.

'According to Vicky, she didn't know either. Or, if she did, she wasn't — '

'Who's Vicky?' queried Gemma.

'My daughter. You were just speaking to her.'

'So, you didn't go yourself?'

'Nah. Too busy. Besides, I thought Vicky'd go down better with the old biddy. Plus it gave her a break from all that secondary smoking Jules inflicts on her.'

'We ought to make a start for the station,' said Gemma, polishing off her Perrier. 'You're supposed to check in half an hour before the train leaves.'

'No worries,' said Shadbolt, passing his glass to the landlady for a refill. 'I'll drive you. You can leave your car at the yard. Want the other half, Richard?'

'No, thanks. I . . . '

'I'm not going, Bernie,' said Gemma, uncomfortably but emphatically. 'It's just Richard. So, I'll drive him to Waterloo. Thanks all the same.'

22

Shadbolt smirked at her. 'I must have misunderstood.'

'Like you, I'm rather busy at the moment,' she said defensively.

Eusden smiled grimly. 'Whereas I have all the time in the world.'

★ ★ ★

'Crying shame about Marty,' said Shadbolt during the short walk back to the yard.

'So it is,' agreed Eusden.

'Tell him from me if there's some specialist he needs to see who could pull off a miracle cure, he doesn't have to worry about the money.'

'That's very generous of you,' said Gemma.

Shadbolt beamed at her. 'That's what friends are for.'

★ ★ ★

He led the way across the yard to his car — a vintage Jag polished to a fine sheen. Eusden caught a glimpse of Vicky watching them through the window-mesh of the Portakabin as her father unlocked the boot and swung it open.

'There it is,' he announced.

And there it was. A battered old leather attaché case. Very old, as Shadbolt had said. Probably Edwardian, Eusden judged. But he had an advantage in dating it. There were initials stencilled on the lid: CEH. And he knew what they stood for.

'Seen it before, Richard?' Shadbolt asked.

'No.'

'Funny. You look as if you have.'

'I've never seen it before.' Eusden looked Shadbolt in the face. 'But I recognize the initials.'

'Reckoned you might.' Shadbolt raised an index finger across his lips. 'But don't tell, hey? If Marty didn't think I needed to know, we'd better keep it that way.'

4

'I recognized the initials as well,' said Gemma as they drove away from the yard.

'I suppose you would.'

'I guess they confirm what Marty told me. A family keepsake.'

'Strange Aunt Lily doesn't know what it is, then.'

'Maybe she just pretended not to know.'

'Yeah. And maybe she's not the only one.'

'You think Shadbolt was holding out on us?'

'I'm certain he was.'

'Why would he?'

'I don't know. But Marty can explain everything when I see him. He's bound to tell me the truth, isn't he?'

'You're getting this out of proportion, Richard.'

'I hope you're right.'

'I am. Give me a call when you get back. You'll see things differently then.'

'I wonder.'

Gemma's return ticket was for the six o'clock train from Brussels, due into Waterloo, thanks to the time difference, at 7.30. If everything went according to plan, Eusden would be back home an hour later, his simple task accomplished. And he would have seen his old friend Marty Hewitson, probably for the last time.

The attaché case passed unremarked through the X-ray machine at the Eurostar terminal. Eusden was momentarily tempted to ask the operative what he could make out of the contents. The weight, about equal to that of his own briefcase, suggested they might be documents of some kind.

He waited in the departure lounge for boarding of the 12.40 to be called. It was a quiet day for Eurostar. Most business travellers would have caught an earlier train. And it was a slack time of year in the leisure market. He sat alone, flanked by his two items of luggage: his briefcase and the battered old attaché case.

CEH was Clement Ernest Hewitson, Isle of Wight police officer, father of Denis and Lily Hewitson, grandfather of Marty. He had lived into his nineties and was more than twenty years dead. A long departed relic of a bygone age. But not forgotten by any who had known him. Which included his grandson's childhood friend, Richard Eusden.

★   ★   ★

Eusden had based a school project on the life and times of Clem Hewitson. He was, in a sense, the only biographer the man had ever had or was ever likely to have. Clem was already over eighty when young Richard first met him. A widower of long standing, he lived alone in a spotlessly clean terraced house in Cowes, just up the hill from the floating bridge. His grandson's home was socially a world away — a mock Tudor residence set in half an acre of land at Wootton Bridge — but it was only a short bus ride from Cowes. Most Saturdays would see Richard and Marty meeting at the Fountain Arcade, where Richard's bus from Newport arrived, for several hours of aimless wandering around the town that usually ended with tea at Clem's.

The old man was a natural storyteller, whose life had given him a seemingly inexhaustible fund of entertaining recollections. Born in 1887, the year of Queen Victoria's Golden Jubilee (as he never tired of pointing out), he followed his father into work at White's shipyard, but rapidly tired of the physical toil and exploited a family connection with the Chief Constable (Clem's uncle had served under him in the Army) to get himself taken on as a police constable. He rose through the ranks to become a detective chief inspector, in charge of the Island's modest CID, and clocked up more than forty years in the force, inclusive of four in the Army, braving shot and shell on the Western Front during the Great War (as he always referred to it).

Richard had plenty to choose from when it came to selecting incidents from Clem's career for inclusion in his project: suffragettes, German spies, drifting mines, burning ricks, suicide attempts, escaped prisoners — Clem had tackled them all, along with a varied assortment of burglars, arsonists, fraudsters and the occasional murderer. Hard though it was to believe, in view of the almost total uneventfulness of life on the

Island as experienced by the average schoolboy in the late 1960s, Clem could look back on excitements galore — and was happy to do so.

Richard was not blind to the possibility put to him by his father, when he relayed some of Clem's stories, that they were exaggerated, if not entirely invented. Reluctantly, he concluded that this might well apply to the old chap's single most startling claim: that he had saved the two eldest daughters of Tsar Nicholas II from murder by an anarchist in Cowes in the summer of 1909. As Clem told it, the Grand Duchesses Olga and Tatiana went shopping in the town during a visit by the Russian imperial family to Cowes regatta that year. Clem stopped, disarmed and arrested a gun-wielding would-be assassin who was in the process of entering the rear of a millinery shop where the two girls were idly debating a hat purchase. This brave and timely intervention earned Clem the personal thanks of the Tsar. 'Pleasant fellow,' said Clem of Nicholas. 'Probably too pleasant for his own good, though, considering how things turned out for him.'

As it transpired, the story was too good to be true. Richard took himself off to the County Records Office in Newport after school one day and looked up the *Isle of Wight County Press* for the relevant week. The Tsar and Tsarina and their children had indeed been in Cowes in August 1909, or, more accurately, *off* Cowes, in the moored imperial yacht. And the two eldest Grand Duchesses had definitely gone shopping in the town. But no assassination attempt thwarted by a PC Hewitson was mentioned. The four days of the imperial visit had passed without incident.

Richard was too embarrassed to challenge Clem on the point, but Marty was not. And Clem had a ready answer. It took no great effort for Richard to retrieve a clear memory of the old man as he was that day: tall, bald, lean and stooping, eyes twinkling, mouth curling in a smile beneath his yellowy-white handlebar moustache, studying Richard across the tiny front parlour of his house, the room smelling of pipe smoke and stewed tea, sunlight streaming through the window on to the brightly patterned tiles flanking the fireplace and the framed photograph above it of Clem on his wedding day back in 1920, when his moustache was lustrously dark and his back was ramrod-straight.

'You've been checking up on me, boy? Well, we'll make a detective of you yet.' The laugh merged with a cough. 'It comes down to politics, see. They couldn't have it said the Tsar's daughters weren't safe on the streets of England. So, it was hushed up. I should have had a formal commendation by rights. But that's the way of the world. Might be best if you didn't put it in your project, though. It could still be a state secret for all I know.'

Richard did not believe him, much as he wanted to. But absolute veracity was hardly to be expected from such an inveterate yarn-spinner as Clem Hewitson, whose claims of secondment to Special Branch during the Second World War and missions abroad he was still not free to talk about were as tantalizing as they were dubious.

Certainly his son, Marty's father, Denis Hewitson, had no time for the old man's 'romances', as he called them. Denis ran a ship-design business in Cowes which he took very seriously, as he did his golf and his garden. His outrage when pop festival-goers slept on his lawn one summer's night in 1969 kept Richard and Marty — and Clem too — laughing for weeks. Richard's father was equally strait-laced, as befitted a deputy county surveyor. At heart, Clem was younger than either of them. That plus the distant reach of his memory — he often recalled watching Queen Victoria's funeral cortège, the mourners led by the new King Edward VII, and his cousin the Kaiser, when the grand old lady's body was conveyed from Osborne House to the waiting royal yacht *Alberta* on a sparkling winter's afternoon in 1901 — made him an object of fascination as well as fondness.

The boys eventually outgrew that fascination. They naturally saw less of him after they left for Cambridge in the autumn of 1975, though no return to the Island was complete without at least one visit to the old man. He never accused them of neglecting him. Somewhere, Eusden had a photograph taken by Gemma of the three of them — Richard, Marty and Clem — standing together on the Parade in Cowes, with the *QE2* visible out to sea, cruising up the Solent towards Southampton. Clem had just passed ninety then, but looked as spry as ever.

Eusden remembered borrowing a photographic history of the Island from Newport Library once in an attempt to imagine the

Cowes of Clem's youth. The town had a pier then; women wore long dresses and wide-brimmed hats; the men boaters and high-collared jackets with waistcoats. The sun seemed always to be shining, pennants fluttering from the massed yachts on regatta days, watched by parasol-twirling ladies. Ironically, Eusden would need an equivalent volume for more recent decades to re-imagine his own youth now: the ice-cream days of summer, when he and Marty took buses to distant parts of the Island, supplied with sandwiches and orange squash by their mothers, free to roam and explore. Alum Bay, Tennyson Down, Blackgang Chine, Culver Cliff: the places were all still there; but the times were gone, beyond recall.

Over the years, Eusden's visits to the Island had become fewer and farther between. His sister Judith still lived there. She and her husband ran a garden centre at Rookley. Physically, his mother was still there too, vegetating in a nursing home at Seaview; mentally, though, she had left long since. Judith occasionally rebuked him for neglecting his nephew and niece. He found it impossible to explain to her just how painful it was for him to return to the sights and sounds of his childhood and adolescence. 'When you went off to Cambridge, I thought you'd be back for Christmas,' she said to him in a soulful moment after their father's funeral. 'But you know what, Richard? You never did come back. Not really.'

When Clem Hewitson died, in the summer of 1983, aged ninety-six, Marty was in the Middle

31

East. He did not attend the funeral. Neither did Eusden. He had often regretted his absence, though he doubted Clem would have held it against him. The old man was as hard to offend as he was to forget.

★   ★   ★

As the train drew out of Waterloo station, Eusden gazed up at the attaché case lodged in the luggage rack above his head. The mere sight of those initials — CEH — had plunged him into helpless reminiscence. This had made him wonder if Marty wanted whatever the case contained to reconcile himself to his past in some way; to make peace with the times and the places — and the people — he had effectively fled from. It was hard to conceive of any other reason why he should be so eager to retrieve it. But there might be such a reason. Eusden realized that. And in two and a half hours, he would find out whether there was or not.

BRUXELLES

5

The Belgian countryside and the outskirts of Brussels had looked grey and bleak through the train window. But there was nothing to be seen of the outside world on the concourse of Bruxelles-Midi station. Eusden was in a man-made realm of platform buttresses and garishly lit retail units: fast food and quick fashion amidst the tidal swash of travellers. There was nothing to be seen of Marty either, at the spot where he had told Gemma he would be waiting: Sam's Café, adjacent to the escalator down from Eurostar Arrivals. This did not worry Eusden unduly. The train had got in ahead of schedule and Marty had never been on time for anything in his life. Eusden changed a tenner into euros at the Western Union next to the café, bought himself a coffee and sat down at one of the tables out front.

★ ★ ★

Ten minutes later, he was beginning to grow a little anxious. Marty was not a well man. It was easy to imagine some disaster had overtaken him. Eusden decided to check the arrivals screen for trains from Amsterdam.

He had risen from his chair with that in mind when a figure appeared at his table from inside the café: a tall, broad-shouldered, middle-aged

35

man in a dark suit and an elegant bottle-green overcoat. He was lantern-jawed and sharp-nosed, with grey quiffed hair and pale blue eyes, sparkling behind gold-framed spectacles. He stood, decisively it seemed, in Eusden's path.

'Excuse me,' he said in a clipped *Mitteleuropa* accent. 'You are Richard Eusden?'

'Yes.'

'May I join you?' He set the cup of coffee he was carrying down on the table and extended a hand. 'I am Werner Straub.' The edges of his mouth curled in the faintest of smiles. 'A friend of Marty.'

'Really?'

They shook. Straub's grip was hard and cold. 'Yes. Shall we sit?'

They sat. Straub's glance fell instantly on the attaché case, propped next to Eusden's briefcase in the chair next to him. The clamour of the PA and the gabble of passing travellers seemed suddenly distant, as if an invisible bubble had formed round the table.

'Perhaps you are surprised that I know who you are,' said Straub, his voice quiet but distinct. 'Marty told me that his ex-wife would come.'

'There was a change of plan.'

'I know. She phoned him . . . after the change.'

'Ah. Right.' This was a surprise. Gemma had not said she meant to warn Marty of the substitution. Eusden would have thought her keen to avoid explaining herself.

'Then Marty phoned me. I was already on my way, you understand.'

'Where *is* Marty?'

36

'Cologne. He travelled there yesterday from Amsterdam. To meet with me.'

'And your connection with him is . . . '

'We are business partners as well as friends.' Straub sipped his coffee. 'Not such old friends as you and he, of course.'

Eusden's surprise was turning to confusion. Straub looked about as unlike someone who would befriend Marty — or indeed do business with him — as it was possible to imagine. 'Why did Marty send you rather than come himself?'

'Sadly, he is unwell. A bad headache. You know about the . . . tumour?'

'Yes. I do.'

'So unfortunate.' Another sip of coffee. 'You must have been distressed to hear of it.'

'I was.'

'He is resting at the hotel. He will be better by tomorrow, I think. The headaches . . . come and go. It is a pity you will not see him. I know he is sorry about that.'

'So am I.'

'But it cannot be helped. You have brought . . . the article he wants?'

'Yes.' Eusden lifted the attaché case on to his lap, feeling strangely glad of the excuse to take hold of it. 'Here it is.'

Straub studied the initials for a moment. 'CEH. His grandfather, no?'

'That's right.'

'Good. So, I take it from here. And you are free to go home.' Straub smiled and extended a hand, seemingly expecting Eusden to surrender the case there and then. But Eusden made no move. Straub's smile took on an edge of puzzlement as he slowly withdrew his hand. 'You are . . . unhappy about something, Richard? I may call you Richard, I hope. I am Werner. We are both friends of Marty. We are both . . . obliging him.'

'Look, I don't want to appear suspicious, but . . . I don't know you.'

'No. Of course not. I understand. And there is no hurry. My train is not for an hour. We can talk. We can get to know each other.' Straub snapped off a piece of the small biscuit that accompanied his coffee and ate it, regarding Eusden with apparently amiable curiosity as he did so. Then he flicked a crumb from his fingers and continued: 'You are Marty's oldest friend. I am probably his newest. You can tell me about his past. I can tell you about his present.'

'So tell me.'

'He is one of those people who . . . adds enjoyment to other people's lives. I first met him on a matter of business. I liked him from the start. I became his friend. I will miss him if the doctors are right and he dies as soon as they say he will.'

'Do you think they might not be right?'

'No. But . . . there may be hope. That is where our business comes in. Do you know what is in the case, Richard?'

'I've no idea.'

'Yet you knew his grandfather.'

'And I've still no idea. Certainly none about how something belonging to a man who died

38

more than twenty years ago could help Marty now.'

'It is, as usual in this world, a matter of money.' Straub leant forward, lowering his voice still further. 'There is a doctor in Switzerland who may be able to relieve Marty's condition. Not actually to cure him, you understand, but to give him more time. A year or two, rather than a few months. He runs a special clinic in Lausanne. It is very exclusive. Very expensive. Marty could not afford to go there.'

'How expensive do you mean?'

'Several hundred thousand euros.' Straub shrugged. 'Doctors used to bleed their patients. Now they bleed their patients' bank accounts. Progress, no?'

'Are you saying . . . the contents of this case are worth several hundred thousand euros?'

'To the right buyer, yes. And I have found such a buyer. That is my profession. I broker deals in the collectables market. I negotiated harder for Marty than I would for most clients. And we have a result. Marty can go to Lausanne as soon as I deliver the article and take payment. I am waiving my commission, Richard. We must get the best treatment for our friend. Do you not agree?'

'Of course.' Eusden looked down at the case, its leather scuffed, its metal catches pinpricked with rust. 'It's just . . . hard to believe Clem owned anything so valuable.'

'It is worth what someone is willing to pay for it.'

'And what is it, Werner?' Eusden shaped a

smile. 'What is the article?'

Straub grimaced. 'I wish I could answer your question. But Marty said . . . you should not be told.'

'Why not?'

Another grimace. 'I think that amounts to the same question. You should ask Marty, not me. I am only his . . . representative.'

'Why don't I do just that? Give me his number and I'll call him now.'

'He said he was going to take a pill and sleep off the headache. We should not disturb him. He will have switched off his phone anyway.'

'You won't give me his number?'

'It would be pointless, Richard. He would not answer.'

'That leaves me in a difficult situation, Werner. I've never met you before. From what you tell me, this case means a lot to Marty. You're effectively asking me to hand it over to a stranger with no guarantee it'll ever get where it's supposed to go.'

'You do not trust me.' Straub frowned in disappointment. 'That distresses me.'

'I'm sorry, but there it is.' Eusden tried to look and sound calm, though he did not feel it. Straub might be telling the truth. Or he might not be. Eusden had so little hard information to go on that it was impossible for him to judge. He was sure of only one thing: as matters stood, he could not surrender the case to Straub. Their encounter was going to have to end without a handover. Fortunately, they were in a very public place. Eusden was free to stand up and walk

40

away with the case any time he chose.

'Perhaps you should call Marty after all.'

'Perhaps I should.'

'Allow me.' Straub slipped a phone out of his pocket, tapped in a number and passed it to Eusden.

There were several rings, then an automated voice announcing the call could not be taken. Eusden did not leave a message. He looked across at Straub. 'Voicemail.'

'I did warn you.'

'Give me the number of the hotel.'

'He may have blocked incoming calls.'

'I'll risk it.'

'Very well.' Straub recited the number. Eusden tapped it in.

The answer was prompt. 'Hotel Ernst.'

'I'd like to speak to one of your guests,' said Eusden. 'Marty Hewitson.'

'Your name, please.'

'Richard Eusden.'

'Hold on, please.'

'They're putting me through,' Eusden said to Straub, whose face betrayed not the slightest reaction.

A delay followed. Then the receptionist was back on the line. 'There is no answer from Mr Hewitson's room.'

'Is he in?'

'I do not know. Do you wish to leave a message?'

'Yes. Ask him to call me.' Eusden dictated his mobile number. 'You've got that?'

The receptionist read it back and added: 'Is

there anything else I can do for you?'

'Possibly.' Eusden thought for a second, then said, 'Do you have any rooms for tonight?'

'Tonight? I'll check.' A moment later: 'Yes, we do.'

'Good.' There was a reaction now from Straub, though not much of one. He raised his eyebrows about a quarter of an inch. 'I'd like to book a room.'

The booking was swiftly accomplished. Eusden ended the call and handed the phone back to Straub.

'You're coming with me to Cologne, Richard?' he said.

'What else can I do? Without being able to speak to Marty.'

'The pills he takes are rather strong. I suppose the phone ringing would not be enough to wake him.'

'Either that or he's feeling a lot better and has gone for a stroll.'

'Unlikely.'

'Well, we'll find out when we get there, won't we?'

'We will, yes.' Straub smiled. 'And it will be a pleasure to have your company on the train, of course.' His smile broadened. 'So, that is settled.'

'Yes.' Settled at a price, Eusden thought. The train fare to Cologne; a €250 room at the Ernst; another day's leave at zero notice: Marty was suddenly having an impact on his life it was hard not to resent.

'I think I will have another coffee,' said Straub. 'Can I get you one?'

'No, thanks.'

'Excuse me, then.'

He stood up and headed for the counter, empty cup in hand. As he took his place in the queue, Eusden slipped his phone out of his pocket and dialled Gemma's number.

'Hello.' Eusden swore under his breath. It was Monica who had answered. At least he assumed it was Monica, though they had never actually spoken before. She had just the gratingly chirpy voice he would have imagined.

'Is Gemma there?'

'Is that Richard?'

'Yes.' Another silent obscenity.

'Hi. I'm Monica.'

'Of course. Hello. Look — '

'Gemma's taking a shower. London's so dirty, isn't it? Well, maybe you don't notice, living there all the time, but — '

'Did she speak to Marty earlier?'

'Sorry?'

'Did she speak to Marty earlier?'

'I don't know, Richard.' Eusden wondered if her use of his name was intended to be as irritating as he found it. 'Is it important?'

'Very.'

'Well, I'll have to get her to call you back.'

'OK. She's got my number.' Eusden glanced into the café to check on Straub's progress. He had reached the head of the queue. It looked like his coffee was already being prepared. And, while he waited, Straub was also making a phone call.

'What's the slimy bastard up to?' Eusden murmured.

'What did you say?' asked Monica.

'Nothing. Sorry.' Having Gemma call him on the train, with Straub staring, sphinxlike, at him from the seat opposite, suddenly seemed like a bad idea. 'On second thoughts, tell Gemma I'll call her.'

'When would that be? Only, we're going to a five o'clock showing at the cinema. Have you seen *Notes on a Scandal*, Richard?'

'*What?*'

'Well, never mind. I just mean it might be a better idea if you leave phoning again until you get home.'

'Until I get home.' Straub had ended his phone call and was paying for his coffee. 'Yeah, that's a great idea.'

KÖLN

6

Avec Thalys, découvrez le plaisir de voyager à votre rythme en Europe. So the blurb declared in the timetable that Eusden had received along with his ticket to Cologne. But pleasure and rhythm were a long way from his grasp. Reassurance and logic, which he would have settled for, were also nowhere to be found. As the high-speed Thalys bulleted them east through the late afternoon and early evening, he struggled to get the measure of his companion — without success.

Extracting information from Werner Straub was as easy as grabbing an eel. The man had a gift for turning every question back on the questioner. There was little doubt in Eusden's mind by the time their journey ended that Straub had learnt far more than he had revealed, particularly about Clem Hewitson, despite Eusden's efforts to be as reticent as possible.

Nor had a message left on his phone by Gemma done anything to relieve his difficulty. Guessing she might ignore his request to wait for him to call her, he had switched it to voicemail and run a check during a visit to the loo. Sure enough, she had been in touch, though not to much purpose.

'*What's going on, Richard? Monica said you sounded anxious. Sorry I didn't tell you I was going to call Marty and warn him you'd be there instead of me. I actually only did it on the spur of the moment. Anyway, I didn't get to speak to him. But he must have told you that himself. I suppose he did get my message, didn't he? Of course he did. Otherwise you wouldn't know about it. You must be on your way back by now. Call me when you get in.'*

★ ★ ★

It was a bone-cold evening in Cologne. They exited the station on to a wind-swept piazza beneath the soaring, spired mass of the cathedral. According to Straub, the Hotel Ernst was only a short walk away and for that Eusden was grateful.

It looked as swanky a place as its room rates implied. The glitter of the lobby suggested there would be plentiful creature comforts to compensate him for the inconvenience of being there. Marty was obviously not in the business of saving his pennies — or his cents. But then, as Eusden sombrely reminded himself, his friend did not have much of a future he needed to worry about.

'I will go straight up and see how Marty is,' said Straub, steering him gently away from the reception desk. 'Wait in the bar, Richard.'

'I may as well check in.'

'Do that later. If Marty is feeling better, he will want to see you right away.' Straub smiled. 'He will probably want to buy you a drink.'

Eusden was too weary from their verbal fencing match on the train to argue. And he certainly needed a drink. He headed for the bar, while Straub made for the lift.

★ ★ ★

Five minutes elapsed while Eusden made swift inroads into a large gin and tonic, which he fully intended to charge to Marty's room. The bar was low-lit and wood-panelled, the atmosphere soothing. He began to devise a suitably barbed greeting for his friend. Then Straub walked in — alone.

'How is he?' Eusden asked as Straub sat down beside him. Straub gave an enigmatic little smile. 'I do not know.'

'What d'you mean?'

'Marty is not here, Richard.'

'Not here? Are you saying . . . he's gone out?'

'Not exactly.' The waiter appeared. Straub ordered a drink, then returned his attention to Eusden, dropping his voice to a confidential murmur. 'I will explain the situation to you, Richard. But I must ask you to remain calm — and quiet — while I do so. Marty's welfare depends on you doing that.'

'*What?*'

'I am serious.' The intensity of Straub's gaze left no room for doubt on the point. 'Marty needs you to behave sensibly. His life is at stake. You understand?'

'No, I don't understand. What the hell — '

'*Calm and quiet.*' Straub propped his elbows on the table and steepled his fingers, cocking his head slightly as he looked Eusden in the eye.

49

'Are you going to be?' The question was suffused with a threat that was all the greater for being unspecified — and uttered *sotto voce*.

'I'm listening,' said Eusden levelly.

'Good. Now — ' Straub broke off as his drink arrived: a blood-red Campari. Coasters and complimentary nuts were adjusted by the waiter in a pregnant hush. Then he glided away. And Straub resumed. 'Marty did not come to Cologne yesterday, Richard. I travelled here alone. I booked in under his name. I brought his phone with me. That is how I knew you would be waiting for him in Brussels.'

'How did — '

'Please.' Straub silenced him with an emphatic, chopping gesture. 'We do not have much time. I will tell you everything you need to know. Marty is in Hamburg. He is locked inside my mother's apartment. He is tied to a chair with his mouth taped. He has been there' — Straub consulted his watch — 'for nearly twenty-four hours. My mother is away on holiday, you see. She will not be back until the middle of next week. So, no one will find Marty in time to save him from death by dehydration.'

'You . . . must be joking.'

'I am not. You can save him, Richard. In fact, *only* you can save him. I have a key in my pocket that will open a left-luggage locker at Hamburg central station. Inside the locker is a set of keys to the apartment, with a tag tied to them. The address is written on the tag. There is a train to Hamburg at twenty-one ten. It will arrive at one fifteen tomorrow morning. You should be on it.

50

If your friendship with Marty means anything to you, you will be. Naturally, I require something in return for the key. I require the attaché case.' Straub sat back and raised his glass. 'Prost.' He took a sip.

Eusden stared at him, unable for the moment to formulate a response. The man surely had to be mad to go to such lengths. Though perhaps he had not gone to such lengths. There was always a chance that this was merely a ruse to trick Eusden into surrendering the case. But why? What could the case possibly contain that made sense of all this?

'Perhaps you do not believe me,' said Straub, reading his mind with discomfiting accuracy. 'If so, you will find this interesting.' He took his phone out, pressed some buttons and held it out so that Eusden could see the screen. 'A captured image that will dispel any doubts.'

Eusden squinted at the screen. And there was Marty, older and gaunter than he remembered, but still instantly recognizable by his mop of curly hair and the jut of his brow. He was dressed in jeans, sweatshirt and trainers and was sitting in an upright wooden chair, his ankles roped to the legs, his shoulders pulled back, his wrists bound out of sight behind him. There was a shiny smear where his mouth was covered by a strip of tape and a length of rope stretched taut from the back of the chair to an anchoring point out of shot. The setting appeared to be some kind of domestic interior. And the picture came complete with a timer display that proved it had been taken the previous night: *22:32, 04.02.07.*

Straub withdrew the phone and slipped it back into his jacket. 'The case, Richard. I must have it.'

'You won't get away with this.'

'I think I will. Marty will not want you to go to the police. Take my word for that. Better still, ask Marty when you see him.'

'He's not a well man. You know he isn't. How's he going to stand up to the ordeal you're putting him through?'

'Go and find out.'

'You're a cold-hearted bastard, aren't you?'

Straub looked as if he found the accusation faintly flattering. 'The case, Richard. I will have it now, please.'

Eusden hesitated for a moment. But the simple if unpalatable truth was that he had no choice. He picked up the attaché case and handed it over.

'Thank you.' Straub laid it on the table in front of him. From his pocket he took a small key and unlocked the catches. Eusden could see nothing of the contents when he raised the lid. There was a sound of papers being riffled through, then Straub gave a frowning nod. 'Good,' he said, closing the case and relocking it. He smiled. 'Excellent, in fact.'

'You have your . . . collectable?'

'I do.'

'I hope you think it's worth what you've done.'

'There is no doubt that it is.' Straub delved in another pocket. When he reached across the table and opened his hand, Eusden saw a different key resting in his palm, larger and

52

chunkier than the one that had opened the case. 'Locker number forty-three, Richard. Time you were going, I think. You need to catch that train. They empty the lockers after twenty-four hours. I engaged it this morning at eight o'clock. So, you need to be there before eight o'clock tomorrow morning. The twenty-one ten is the last train tonight. You cannot afford to miss it. I suggest you start for the station. Now.'

HAMBURG

7

Eusden was unsure in retrospect how he endured the four-hour journey to Hamburg. The train was old and slow and grubby, the route a grim haul through industrial towns and stretches of countryside veiled in darkness. Most of the passengers looked about as happy to be aboard as he was. They were travelling, like him, because they had to.

Eusden had been sorely tempted to call Gemma and offload some of the concern he felt for Marty and the anger that filled him at being put in such a position. But there was nothing Gemma could do except worry. And it was not her fault that Straub had laid a trap for one of them to walk into. Eusden suspected it might at least partly be Marty's fault, however, a suspicion he intended to voice once he was sure his friend had come to no harm. All he could do meanwhile was stare out at the night-blanked North German Plain and stifle his frustration.

★   ★   ★

Hamburg central station was thinly populated at 1.15 in the morning, a deadening chill invading its cavernous, empty spaces. Eusden, drained by sleeplessness and anxiety, tracked down the left-luggage lockers as swiftly as he could and

57

opened number 43.

The keys were there, as Straub had promised. And so was the tag. The address written on it in bold block capitals meant nothing to him. He could only hope a taxi driver would be able to find it.

The night he walked out into was still and numbingly cold. He clambered into the lead cab in a short queue of more or less identical cream Mercedes and proffered the tag to the driver. A glance and a nod was all he received in return. Then they were on the move.

★   ★   ★

A ten-minute surge through a deserted city centre and they were there: Brunnengasse, a pedestrianized link-route between a main road and a residential side street. Modest but reputable apartment blocks lined the route, prettied up with window-boxes and Juliet balconies. The address on the tag was number six: a single door serving twelve flats, each equipped with electronic bell-pushes, speaker-phones, and mailboxes next to the entrance. There was, however, no way of telling which flat belonged to Straub's mother.

Eusden let himself in with one of the Yale keys and started checking the names displayed alongside the front doors of the flats. He had reached the third floor before he found what he was looking for: FRAU B. STRAUB. He rang the bell. There was no response. He tried again, pressing his ear to the door. Was that a muffled

58

groan he heard? Maybe. Maybe not. He unlocked the door and pushed it open.

★ ★ ★

The picture on Straub's phone had prepared him for what he would see. But what he could actually see was very little. The flat was in darkness, a wedge of amber lamplight from the street illuminating only a portion of carpet in a room ahead of him. There was that groan again, apparently emanating from the same room. Eusden groped for the light switch and pushed it down. Nothing happened.

Another groan, louder this time. He headed for the wedge of amber and entered what various hummocked shadows suggested was a lounge, with a pair of windows affording a view of the flats opposite. As his eyes adjusted to the gloom, one shadow resolved itself into a figure lying on the floor. It was Marty. He had toppled the chair over at some point, but was still tied to it, slumped on his left side.

'It's me, Marty,' said Eusden, stooping over him. He caught a pungent whiff of stale sweat and urine. Marty turned his head and rolled his eyes. 'Hold on.' Eusden located one end of the strip of tape and pulled it free as gently as he could.

'Good to see you, Coningsby,' said Marty in a hoarse whisper. The use of Eusden's college nickname was reassuringly spirited. It was a reference to his family's supposed descent from the eighteenth-century poet laureate Laurence

59

Eusden, sometime rector of Coningsby, in Lincolnshire. The pair had driven up there from Cambridge one Saturday in pursuit of the poet's shade, but had only succeeded in becoming so drunk in the village pub that they had had to stay overnight before driving back. 'Not that . . . I can actually see you.'

'The lights don't work.'

'Werner turned them off at the mains. Just as well the block's centrally heated, otherwise I'd have frozen to death. The fuse box is in the hall cupboard.'

'OK. Hang on.'

Eusden retreated into the hall and opened the cupboard. After collapsing an ironing board on himself, he succeeded in feeling his way to the fuse box. He pushed up all the switches. Overhead lights came on in the hall and lounge. He hurried back.

The scene was stark. Marty lay trussed and crumpled. There was far more grey in his hair than when they had last met. And he had lost weight. He looked like an old man, lying where he had fallen. But he still sounded like the younger version of himself Eusden recalled. 'If you're still as good at untying knots as you were in the Scouts, it'd be quicker to fetch a knife from the kitchen.' A nod pointed Eusden in the right direction.

The kitchen, like the lounge, was fitted out in an old-fashioned style. Frau Straub did not appear to be an enthusiastic modernizer. Eusden discovered several formidably bladed knives in one of the drawers, however. He chose what seemed the sharpest.

'For Christ's sake be careful,' croaked Marty as Eusden set to work. 'I don't want to bleed to death after surviving twenty-four hours bound and gagged in this hellhole.'

'I *am* being careful. There.' He released Marty's wrists and started on his ankles. Once those ropes were also free, he pulled the chair away and watched Marty roll slowly forward, groaning and grimacing as he gradually straightened his arms and legs. 'How d'you feel?'

'Oh, tip-bloody-top, thanks.' Marty gasped as blood coursed back into starved limbs and joints. 'How do I feel? How do you think I feel?'

'Sorry.'

'No need. At least you came. Where would I be if you hadn't?'

'What's this all about, Marty?'

'Didn't Werner tell you?'

'Hardly.'

'No. I suppose he wouldn't.' Marty coughed and sat up gingerly, supporting himself against the chair. 'Any chance . . . of a drink of water?'

'Of course. I should've thought.'

Eusden filled a glass from the kitchen tap. Marty gulped the contents down and handed it back for a refill. 'I'd never have thought German tap water would taste so good.'

'You shouldn't drink too much too fast.'

'OK, nurse. I'll sip the next one.' Marty ran a hand along the rope that still fastened the chair to a radiator pipe. 'Then I might think about standing up.'

Eusden refilled the glass. Obediently, Marty

drank slowly this time, the glass shaking in his hand as he did so. He gave Eusden a pained smile. 'Sorry about the state I'm in, Richard.'

'Don't worry about that.' Eusden sat down in a nearby armchair. 'We'll soon get you cleaned up.'

'Gemma talked you into taking her place, did she?'

'Yup.'

'Thought she might.'

'You did?'

'I can read her like a book. You too, come to that. You gave the attaché case to Werner, I assume.'

'I wouldn't say *gave*. It was his price for the address of this place. And the keys. I didn't have much choice.'

'You could have told him to go to hell. I'm a dying man, Richard. Didn't Gemma mention that?'

'She mentioned it.'

'So, saving my life is ... a temporary achievement at best.' Marty raised a trembling hand. 'Don't get me wrong. I'm glad you came. See what was in the case, did you?'

'No.'

'But Werner opened it in front of you?'

'Yes. He seemed satisfied with what he'd got.'

'I'll bet. Was he alone?'

'Yes. Shouldn't he have been?'

'There was a hired heavy waiting when we came here on Sunday night. Ill or not, I might have got the better of Werner on his own. Maybe he took the bloke on for just the one job. You should be grateful he didn't add roughing you up to the contract. Not that he needed to, of course. I guess he was confident whichever of you and Gemma showed up would cooperate. Leaving Werner in the clear.'

'We should report what's happened to the police, Marty. You were assaulted, for God's sake. And I was robbed.'

'Forget it.'

'*Forget it?*'

'I mean forget going to the police. Werner knows I can't do that.' Marty swallowed some more water. Then he braced himself against the chair and rose unsteadily to his feet.

'Careful.'

Eusden was at his side. But Marty signalled to be left alone and smiled stubbornly at his success in standing upright. 'What happened after you handed over the case?' he asked, rubbing his sandpapery chin.

'I caught the train here.'

'I didn't know there were through trains from Brussels.'

'We were in Cologne. We travelled that far together. Straub said you were waiting for us at the Hotel Ernst. That's where he . . . presented his terms.'

'Cologne? Well, I guess that makes sense. An hour from Frankfurt airport on the high-speed line. He'll make an early start.'

'You think he's planning to leave the country?'

'No. He's planning to meet someone off a flight from the States. Someone I was supposed to be meeting with him. Looks like I've been

63

. . . iced out of the deal.'

'What *is* the deal, Marty?'

'You don't want to know.'

'After the day I've had, yes, I do.'

'Sure about that?'

Eusden nodded emphatically. 'Absolutely.'

'OK. Tell you what. I'll take a shower. The water'll probably be cold, but at least I'll smell sweeter. You didn't bring a change of clothes with you by any chance?'

'I came straight from the office.'

'I should've guessed from the way you're dressed. Never mind. Maybe Werner's mother hasn't chucked out everything that belonged to his father yet. You could check that while I shower. And see if the old bat left any food in the fridge when she jetted off for her fortnight in the sun.' Marty set out at a totter across the room. 'When I'm clean and less hungry, I'll tell you what you think you want to know.'

8

Marty's instinct about Frau Straub's disposal policy was sound. There was a wardrobe in the main bedroom filled with suits, shirts, sweaters and trousers that could easily have come from a German equivalent of John Collier *circa* 1970. Eusden laid out a hopeful selection on the bed and headed for the kitchen. The pickings there were thinner: a few rye crackers in a tin, an unopened pack of Emmental and several bottles of Löwenbräu. He opened one of the beers for himself and went back to the lounge.

As he entered the room, the telephone started ringing. At 2.25 a.m. he thought the caller was unlikely to be Frau Straub's sister in Stuttgart. Maybe it was a wrong number. On balance, he hoped so.

After ten to twelve rings, it stopped. Then, a moment later, it started again. He picked it up.

'Hello?'

'Check the mailbox.'

'What? Who is — '

But the line was already dead. Eusden replaced the receiver and gazed out through the window into the night. Then he crossed to the light switch and flicked it to off, plunging the room into darkness. He returned to the window and peered down into the street. There was no sign of life. After a struggle with the latch, he succeeded in opening the window. He leant out for a wider view. But there was nothing to see.

The shower was still running in the bathroom. Marty could not have heard the telephone ring. Eusden debated with himself what to do. The message could be a trick, devised to lure him or Marty outside, but Straub would surely not have given up his only set of keys. If his 'hired heavy' was the caller, he was probably equipped to let himself in. Besides, he could have waylaid Eusden when he arrived if he had wanted to. And they would have to leave sooner or later anyway. Eusden headed for the door.

★ ★ ★

His confidence had ebbed somewhat by the time he reached the ground floor. Through the window beside the main door he could see nothing beyond an empty stretch of paving, the light of the porch lamp leaching away beyond that into velvety shadows. He took several deep breaths to calm himself. By rights he should be at home in Chiswick, sleeping soundly after an undemanding day in Whitehall. Instead he was in Hamburg, behaving like a Cold War spy making a pick-up from a dead-letter drop in the middle of the night.

He finally tired of his own apprehensiveness and yanked the door open. Nothing moved on the street. No shadow in human form loomed into view. The mailboxes were only a few steps away. He reckoned the smallest key on the bunch would fit the lock on Frau Straub's box. And so it proved.

Inside was a thickly filled brown envelope. He lifted it out, closed the box and retreated indoors. There was neither name nor address written on the envelope. It had clearly been delivered by hand. It had also been left unsealed. Eusden pulled back the flap. A chunky wad of banknotes met his surprised gaze. The topmost note was €100. So were the next few. He gasped, shoved the envelope into his pocket and started up the stairs.

★   ★   ★

'Where the hell have you been?' demanded Marty when Eusden walked back into the flat. 'I come out of the shower and you've vanished into thin air.' He cut a bizarre figure in white shirt, hound's-tooth-patterned sweater and twill trousers that finished an inch or two above his trainers. He had a beer in one hand and a hunk of cheese in the other. His hair was still wet and he had a towel looped round his neck to catch the drips. 'Plus you switched the lights off. Are you trying to spook me?'

'We had a phone call. Announcing a special delivery.' Eusden took the envelope out of his pocket. 'I've just been down to collect it.'

'What is it?'

'Money. Rather a lot, by the look of it.' Eusden dropped the envelope on to the coffee table. 'See for yourself.'

Marty sat down in the armchair and plonked the bottle of beer on the table. He put the cheese in his mouth and devoured it as he fanned the wad of notes, then counted them. 'Bloody hell,' he said when he had finished. 'There's ten thousand here. What did the caller say?'

''Check the mailbox.' Nothing else.'

'It has to be from Werner.'

'You think so?'

'No one else owes me a cent, Richard. This is my pay-off. A pittance compared with the profit he's hoping to make. But enough, he's calculated, to persuade me to give up and go home.'

'And will you?'

Marty took a swig of beer and sat back in the chair. 'It'd make the time I've got left more comfortable than it's likely to be otherwise. And it'd make my landlord a happy man.'

'But it wouldn't pay the Swiss specialist's bill, would it? Not from — ' Eusden stopped. The incomprehension on Marty's face told him what he should already have guessed. 'There is no clinic in Lausanne offering a revolutionary treatment, is there?'

''Fraid not. Nice idea, but . . . no.'

'Straub said that's what you needed the money for that you were going to make from selling the contents of the case.'

'Just as well he was lying, then. Since this is all the money I'm likely to see now.'

'Are you saying you'll settle for that?'

'It'd be the smart move, I guess. What he put me through here was the stick. This is the carrot.'

'You're going to let him get away with it?'

'Sit down, Richard. You look like a man with a mission. It doesn't suit you.'

Eusden sat down. 'You promised me an explanation, Marty.'

'Yeah, but this money . . . changes everything.'

'How?'

'It means I don't have to go away empty-handed. Terminal illness alters your perspective on life, take my word for it. I could have my own fortnight in the sun now. Several fortnights, in fact.'

'And that's enough?'

'What d'you want me to say? At heart, I've always been a hedonist. It makes no sense to put you in the picture if we're not going to do anything about it.'

'We?'

'I can't go on alone, that's for sure. All in all, it's probably best to end it here. Take the air fare back to London out of this lot. You'll be behind your desk again by Wednesday morning, sipping a coffee freshly brewed by your curvaceous PA, glad your excursion to Hamburg is just a brief, bad memory. Then, in a few weeks, if you feel like it, come over to Amsterdam and we'll spend some of Werner's dosh on a pub crawl.'

'You seem to have forgotten you owe me most of this in bail money.'

'Ouch.' Marty's expression suggested he really had forgotten. 'OK. It's a fair cop. You have first call on it, no argument. Help yourself. Don't worry about me. Dying penniless is a piece of cake.'

'I'm not interested in the money, Marty. I'm interested in the truth. You surely don't think you can get away with stonewalling me like this, do you?'

'Why not? You're not planning to tie me up again, are you?'

'I knew Clem almost as well as you did. What did he have that a creep like Straub could sell now for a small fortune?'

'Not so small, in all likelihood.' Marty smiled wryly. 'Sorry. It really is best if I say nothing.'

'How did you meet Straub?'

'Our research interests . . . coincided.'

'Research into what?'

Marty's smile assumed a pained fixity. He did not reply.

'Clem came to Hamburg once, didn't he?'

'Did he?'

'You know he did. While I was on the train, I remembered him talking about it. One of his hush-hush Special Branch missions, some time after the War. We used to think he made them up. I'm guessing he didn't make this one up.'

'Guessing? You certainly are.'

'Tell me I'm wrong, then.'

More silence. Marty's smile faded into blankness.

'Why did you come to this flat on Sunday evening?'

'Werner said there was something here that might interest me. He was lying, naturally.'

'But why were you taken in?'

'I'm a gullible guy.'

'Come on, Marty. You thought it was likely to be true. Why? Something to do with Straub's father, maybe? What did he do for a living?'

'Journalist. Worked on the local daily. The *Hamburger Abendblatt.*'

'At the time of Clem's visit?'

'Probably. If there was a visit.'

'What was in the case?'

'You're not going to give up, are you?'

'No, I'm not.'

'Oh God.' Marty rubbed his face and took another gulp of beer. He gave Eusden a long, studious stare. 'You'll regret getting involved in this, y'know, you really will.'

'I'm already involved.'

'No. Affected by it. But not involved. There's a big difference. I'm not chasing a quick buck, as Werner seems to think. I'm chasing . . . meaning, I suppose. When the doc told me I was on the way out, I considered how I ought to spend the small amount of time I have left. More of the same in Amsterdam. Or something . . . different. That's when I remembered Clem's attaché case.' (Marty had always referred to his grandfather as Clem, making him seem more of an old friend than a relative.) 'It ended up with Aunt Lily after he died. When I eventually got round to visiting her, she said I ought to have it. She thought I'd be able to make sense of the contents. I took a look. I couldn't work out what they amounted to. So, I . . . asked her to hold on to the case for me. She made a point of locking it and giving me the key. She had an inkling, I think, that it was . . . important. I couldn't see how at the time, but I do now. So does Werner.'

'What did it contain?'

'It's a long story. And I'm dog-tired. Neither

71

of us is thinking straight. There might be a way, if you help me, to get at the truth, despite losing the case. I'm just not sure. The Foreign Office would have to do without you for a while, though. You'd have to . . . make a commitment. So, sleep on it. There's a single bed in the spare room. As the invalid, I'm claiming old Mother Straub's double. Let's get a few hours' kip. Then, in the morning, if you still feel the same way I'll tell you everything.' Marty summoned a weary grin. 'Every last incredible detail.'

9

Eusden woke with a start. Dawn had broken, grey and grudging. Its dusty light revealed the anonymous furnishings of a room he did not immediately recognize. For a moment, he could not even have said where he was. Then the events of the previous day avalanched back into his mind. And the prevailing silence expanded ominously.

He threw on his clothes, calling Marty's name as he did so. But the call went unanswered. The flat was small. It took only a few seconds to confirm he was alone.

Then he noticed the envelope full of money still lying on the coffee table in the lounge. If Marty had taken any of it, he had certainly not taken much. Was that, Eusden wondered, his idea of an honourable parting? A debt settled. But a secret kept. He could only repeat what he had said when his friend had jumped bail, forfeiting his surety. 'Fuck you, Marty.'

'Nice greeting,' said Marty, coming through the front door just as Eusden spoke. 'A simple 'Good morning' would have sufficed.' He was wearing a parka and carrying a travel bag. Though pale, gaunt and unshaven, he looked absurdly cheerful and was munching a pretzel. 'You didn't think I'd run out on you, did you?'

'It wouldn't be the first time,' Eusden responded defensively.

'What it is to have a reputation.' Marty hung up his coat and strolled into the lounge.

'Where've you been?'

'The hotel I was supposed to check out of yesterday morning. Werner had paid my bill, considerate fellow that he is, and had them pack my stuff to await collection. So why don't you make coffee while I put some of my own clothes on? After breakfast you can take second turns with my toothbrush and shaver. Can I say fairer than that?'

* * *

A mug of black coffee was ready and waiting for Marty when he entered the kitchen five minutes later, in clean sweatshirt and jeans and eagerly peeling the cellophane off a pack of Camel cigarettes. 'Don't look at me like that,' he said, catching Eusden's wince. 'I'm not going to die of lung cancer, am I?' He lit up, sat down at the formica-topped table and took a sip of coffee. 'Why can't I smell bacon frying?'

'Because there's none to fry. The menu's cornflakes — without milk.'

'OK. We'll breakfast out. Meanwhile — '

'Meanwhile you've got some talking to do.' Eusden sat down at the other end of the table, theatrically fanning away the cigarette smoke as he blew on his coffee.

'Does that mean you're in?'

'I guess so.'

'I'm looking for something more definite than that, Richard.'

74

'What did you have in mind?'

'Phone the office and say you're taking the rest of the week off. Personal emergency. Compassionate leave. Your budgie's died. Whatever. Tell the FO to FO.'

'There won't be anybody in yet. They're an hour behind, remember.'

'Leave a recorded message. All the better. No need to explain.'

'I'll have to explain eventually.' Somewhere deep in Eusden's brain, a series of calculations was under way. He had to find out what Clem Hewitson's secret was. He knew himself well enough to understand that he would regret failing to do so for a long time, possibly for ever. Too much of his own past was tied to his memory of the old man for him simply to walk away. He was also aware that part of him had been excited by the intrigue and uncertainty of the previous twenty-four hours. He had felt more alive during them than he had in months — if not years. Creeping back timidly to his desk in Whitehall was in truth not even an option. 'OK. I'll make the call.' He rose and headed for the spare bedroom. 'My phone's in my bag.'

'No.' Marty grabbed his arm as he passed. 'Use the land line.'

'What?'

'I'm serious. Turn your mobile off and leave it that way. We need to be untraceable from now on.'

Eusden looked at his friend disbelievingly. 'Come off it, Marty. It can't be — '

'But it is.'

'This had better be good.'

'Or bad. Oh, yes. It is. One of those. Or both. You can be the judge.'

*   *   *

'Lorraine, this is Richard. More apologies for you to make on my behalf, I'm afraid. I'm dealing with a . . . family crisis. I'm going to be away until the end of the week. I have unused leave, so it should be no problem. I'll call you when the situation's clearer. 'Bye.' Eusden put the phone down and returned to the kitchen. 'It's done,' he announced.

'Unused leave? That sounds sad.'

'Can we get on with it?'

'Actually, no. This flat gives me the creeps. I've spent far too long staring at its puce-coloured walls. Why don't we pack up and clear out? There's a café round the corner that was just opening when I went past in the taxi. We can get some breakfast there and much better coffee than this stuff you scraped out of a jar.'

'When are you going to stop stringing me along, Marty?'

'When I've lit my first postprandial cigarette. Which, if you shift yourself, won't be long.'

*   *   *

Eusden washed and shaved in short order. When it came down to it, he had no more wish to linger in the flat than Marty. They made no effort to clear up after themselves. ('That's

76

Werner's problem,' declared Marty. 'He's got a week or more before *Mutter* gets back from Majorca.') They slammed the door behind them and strode away without a backward glance, studiously avoiding eye contact with a neighbour walking her dog.

There was a broad, paved square a few minutes away. The Café Sizilien stood in one corner. Assorted Hamburgers bound for work were bracing themselves for the experience with coffee and croissants and certainly the morning was cold enough to warrant a good deal of bracing. Marty opted for two boiled eggs and several thickly jammed and buttered bread rolls. Eusden joined him, surprised by how hungry he felt. The coffee, as Marty had promised, was a vast improvement on Frau Straub's instant.

★ ★ ★

'No sign of Werner's heavy,' said Marty, scanning the customers from their window table as he licked raspberry jam off his fingers. 'He's betting I'll take the money and run.'

'Instead of which . . . you're just taking the money.'

'You'll get your share.'

'That's not what I meant.'

'No, I guess not. Sorry.' Marty lit his second Camel of the day. 'So, where to begin?'

'How about the beginning?'

'Easier said than done. But I'll try.' Marty pulled out his wallet and fished something small

77

and flimsy from its depths. He laid it in front of Eusden. 'What do you make of that?'

It was a fragment of an envelope with two stamps stuck to it. The smaller had a king's head on it beneath the word DANMARK. The larger depicted a ploughman struggling to control his horse as a plane flew overhead. Beneath the ploughman appeared the words DANMARK LUFTPOST. A single postmark covered both: KØBENHAVN LUFTPOST 17.5.27.

'What am I supposed to make of it?' Eusden queried.

'Danish, right?'

'Obviously.'

'Twenty-five øre King Christian the Tenth with twenty-five øre airmail supplement. Part of my dad's collection. I never actually looked through it until he died. I mean, philately? Do me a favour. But ask yourself: where'd he get it from?'

'No idea.'

'Yes, you have. Who would a stamp-mad schoolboy cadge something like that off?'

'His father?'

'Exactly. Clem.'

'So, Clem had a letter from Denmark.'

'Yes. Which he must have hung on to, since Dad was only six years old in 1927. He didn't get into stamp collecting until his early teens.'

'OK. But — '

'Did you know Clem spoke Danish?'

'What?'

'Well, *spoke* might be an exaggeration. But he certainly read it.'

'You're having me on.'

'No. You asked me what's in the attaché case. The answer is a collection of letters, written to Clem over a period of ten years or more in the nineteen twenties and thirties. In Danish. Now you can see why I couldn't make head or tail of the contents of the case.'

'Who were the letters from?'

'A guy called Hakon Nydahl. Captain — or *Kaptajn* — Nydahl, as he signed himself. Ever remember Clem mentioning the name?'

'No.'

'Nor me. What about Copenhagen? Did he ever admit to going there?'

'Not sure. There weren't many European cities he didn't claim to have visited at some point.'

'True. But we know he was corresponding with someone in Copenhagen, so it seems a good bet, doesn't it? As to what they were corresponding *about*, you'd need a Danish translator to tell you that. Werner's probably contacting one even as we speak.'

'Why's it so important?'

'Ah, that brings us to Werner's father: Otto Straub. Thanks to him we know Clem came to Hamburg in the spring of 1960. It's not something I ever remember my parents talking about. Maybe he didn't tell them where he was going, or even that he *was* going. But yes. Clem was here. And why? To testify in a court case Otto was covering for his paper. Clem let us believe he came just after the War, if you remember, before he retired from the police. But that was eyewash. He'd have been

79

seventy-three in 1960.'

'What was the court case about?'

'Anastasia.'

'Sorry?'

Marty chuckled. 'You heard.'

10

Anastasia. A legend in her own death-time. Eusden knew what history said of her. Born 1901, fourth and youngest daughter of Tsar Nicholas II. Murdered by Soviet revolutionaries in 1918, along with her parents and siblings. He also knew of the persistent legend that she had survived the climactic massacre at Ekaterinburg. A woman claiming to be Anastasia popped up in Berlin a few years later and spent the rest of her life convincing many and failing to convince others, notably most of Anastasia's surviving relatives, that she was indeed Her Imperial Highness the Grand Duchess Anastasia Nikolaievna. Opinion was still divided when Anna Anderson, as the woman came to be known, died in 1984. But it hardened in the 1990s, when the remains of the imperial family were excavated from their burial site near Ekaterinburg and verified by DNA analysis, a test which Anna Anderson's remains subsequently failed. Seventy years' worth of books, films, lawsuits and conspiracy theories foundered on a simple matter of genetics. The claimant to Anastasia's identity was found to have been a fraud.

This much Eusden remembered, though he was aware there was also much more he had forgotten. He had read a book on the subject, seen a couple of television documentaries purporting to tell the full story, flicked through several magazine articles probing the mystery and scanned various newspaper reports of twists and turns in the affair. He well recalled swapping theories with Marty after they had speed-read a sensationalist work called *The File on the Tsar*, published while they were at Cambridge, even though he could not recall what those theories were. Their interest had been heightened by Clem's airy claim to have met Anastasia — the real Anastasia — during his brush with the Russian imperial family in Cowes in August 1909. He had supposedly visited the imperial yacht to receive the thanks of the Tsar and Tsarina for saving their eldest daughters, Olga and Tatiana, from assassination and Anastasia had briefly spoken to him. 'A forward little girl', was his later summation. She would have been eight years old at the time, so perhaps it was not surprising he had no more to say about her than that.

But perhaps, Eusden was now forced to consider, Clem's dismissive attitude was a smokescreen. It was otherwise hard to account for his presence in Hamburg in the spring of 1960 as a witness in Anna Anderson's civil action for recognition as sole surviving child of the last Tsar of All the Russias.

★ ★ ★

'I had no idea trying to find out who Clem's mysterious Danish pen pal was would lead to Anastasia,' said Marty as he lit a third Camel from the end of the second. 'I was just looking for something to take my mind off . . . well, death, frankly; specifically, my own. Anyway, I went to Copenhagen to get the goods on Hakon Nydahl. He was a Danish naval officer who graduated to a number of confidential court appointments. Gets a shortish write-up in the Danish DNB. Born 1884, which makes him just a few years older than Clem. His bit-part in history comes in 1920, when the Tsar's mother, the Dowager Empress Marie Feodorovna, arrived back in her native Denmark, where she was known by her original Danish name, Dagmar. She'd been in the Crimea when the Soviets started rounding up royals after the October Revolution and was evacuated on a British warship. Her sister was Edward the Seventh's widow, Queen Alexandra. After staying with her for a while, Dagmar headed for Copenhagen and moved into a house in the seaside resort of Klampenborg, which she and Alexandra kept as a holiday home. King Christian the Tenth, her nephew, appointed Nydahl to manage her affairs. And that's what he did, dutifully and diligently, until her death in 1928. Anna Anderson had gone public with her claim to be Anastasia by then, but Dagmar dismissed her as an impostor without even bothering to meet her. There's not much more to say about Nydahl, if you trust the official accounts. He died a bachelor in 1961, aged seventy-seven.'

'How come he was in touch with Clem, then?' asked Eusden, when no explanation was immediately forthcoming.

'That's what I wondered, obviously. There's no apparent connection. But clearly there was one. Why else would Clem go to the bother of learning Danish?'

'Why would he anyway? A courtier like Nydahl must have spoken English.'

'Secrecy, maybe? Clem could be sure no one in our family — or in Cowes, come to that — was going to be able to read letters written in Danish.'

'But what was there to be secret about?'

'That's what I tried to find out. I hit a brick wall at first. Then I did what I should have done earlier: look for Nydahl on the Web. He gets a single mention, in one of the hundreds of Anastasia-related sites. Needless to say, there are a lot of people out there in cyberspace convinced she was the genuine article and the DNA results were faked. I put out some feelers and Werner responded. It was my name that did it. He'd been trying to discover who Clem Hewitson was for years because of his father's account of Clem's mysterious participation in the Anna Anderson court case. Apparently, the judges wanted to hear testimony from Nydahl about Dagmar's attitude to the claimant. Nydahl said he was too ill to appear, but suggested Clem could tell them all they needed to know. Otto Straub, like most other observers, couldn't understand what this retired British police officer had to do with it. And they never found out. Because, when Clem came over, he was heard in camera. To this day, no one has any idea what he said.'

They left the café and, at Marty's suggestion, walked up to the ring road skirting the city centre, on the other side of which, beyond a stretch of landscaped greenery, stood Hamburg's courts complex: three mansarded neo-Gothic blocks, with modern extensions. The view was blurred by mist and sleet, dampness deepening the prevailing chill, the stud-tyred traffic rumbling rhythmically past.

'That's where it all happened in the Anna Anderson trials,' said Marty. 'I expect you've forgotten the ins and outs of her story. I certainly had. She burst on to the public stage in 1922 and spent the next ten years or more badgering members of the Romanov family for recognition and living off supporters who were either genuine believers or after what they hoped to get out of her. Berlin, Paris, New York, assorted German *Schlosses*: she was always on the move, charming and convincing some, offending and alienating others. She also fitted in a lot of physical and mental illness. There were several interludes in hospitals and asylums along the way. Finally, in 1938, she instituted legal proceedings in Berlin to claim any money left by the Tsar in German bank accounts. There was certainly some, possibly a lot. If she'd succeeded, she'd no doubt have moved on to other countries. The Bank of England, for instance, was rumoured to be holding a sizeable sum deposited by the dead but officially merely missing Tsar.'

'I do remember that,' said Eusden. 'The Tsar's missing millions.'

'Yeah. Well, pounds in the bank or pie in the sky, we'll never know now. The case was chucked out. Anna's lawyers appealed. The appeal was suspended because of the outbreak of war. The court papers ended up in the Soviet sector, which effectively blocked all progress. Her lawyers eventually decided to sue the Romanovs for recognition. The chosen defendant was a great-niece of the Tsarina, Barbara, Duchess of Mecklenburg, who happened to live in Germany, making her a convenient target. Hamburg suited all parties as a venue. The case opened in January 1958 and dragged on, thanks to various delays, adjournments and illnesses, for three years. In the end, Anna's claim was dismissed. Her lawyers appealed — again. Another three years passed waiting for the appeal to be heard and yet another three actually hearing it. It was finally turned down in February 1967. All this time, Anna had been leading the life of an eccentric recluse in a chalet in the Black Forest with half a dozen dogs and two dozen cats. She never came to court. One of the judges went to question her during the first trial, little good that it did him. A year after losing the appeal, she shoved off to the States and married an oddball well-wisher called Jack Manahan, Professor of East European history at the University of Virginia. She spent the rest of her days as Mrs Manahan in Charlottesville, Virginia. A lot of people, including her husband, went on believing she was Anastasia. But the DNA experts tell us she was actually a Polish factory worker called Franziska Schanzkowska, who exploited a physical resemblance to Anastasia to reinvent herself as a Russian princess — with astonishing success.'

'Did Clem ever say whether he thought she was genuine or not?' asked Eusden.

'Not that I can recall.'

'Do you think he told the judges what he thought?'

'Must have, I suppose. If they asked him. But we don't know what they asked him.' Marty squinted across at the court building. 'Or what he said in reply.'

★ ★ ★

They retreated through the smart shopping streets of the city centre to the Jungfernstieg, on the shores of Hamburg's answer to Lake Geneva: the Binnenalster. Marty steered Eusden into the imposing Hotel Vier Jahreszeiten for mid-morning coffee and cake. He was still making up for his enforced fast, he explained, as he forked down a gooey slice of torte. 'Besides,' he went on, 'this is where Anna's legal team put up prize witnesses and either licked their wounds or toasted their minor triumphs. I don't know if Clem stayed here. Depends who was paying his bill, I suppose.'

'And who might've been?' asked Eusden.

'Good question. According to Werner, his father said Nydahl's testimony was called for after the Danish government turned down a request from the court for access to a document known as the Zahle Dossier. Herluf Zahle was Danish ambassador to Germany when Anna first came forward. King Christian instructed him to establish whether she really was Anastasia. I imagine he was trying to decide what line to take on his aunt Dagmar's behalf *if* there was any substance to the claim. Anyway, Zahle seemed to think Anna was the real deal at first. He covered all her medical expenses — she was seriously ill with TB for several years — and helped her out on numerous occasions. He only backed off when the Schanzkowska allegation surfaced in a Berlin newspaper and even then he made it obvious he didn't believe it. The dossier contained all his papers relating to the case. Crucial material, which the Danes held back. Who knows why? Nydahl was a friend of Zahle's and the courtier charged with looking after Dagmar's interests. He must have known what was in the dossier. Hence the attempt to get him to testify. But he pleaded illness, which may have been genuine, since he died the following year. Clem was his chosen substitute. A bizarre choice on the face of it. Strings must have been pulled somewhere, though, to ensure he was heard in camera. Clem obviously *was* the natural choice. For reasons you and I can only guess at. Werner, on the other hand, will probably know what those reasons were, as soon as he has the letters translated. Unless he's done a crash course in Danish on the sly and can read them himself, which I wouldn't put past him.'

'Who's he meeting off the plane at Frankfurt?'

'An eccentric American millionaire who's distantly related to Jack Manahan and is prepared to pay through the schnozzle for evidence that Jack's wife was the true-blue Anastasia.'

'But she can't have been. The DNA evidence ruled that out. You said so yourself.'

'Ah, Richard, you always were too much of a determinist.' Marty gave him a benignly superior smile. 'She can be whatever people persuade themselves to believe she was. The DNA technique they used back in the early nineteen nineties has been discredited now, anyway. It produced far too many false positives *and* false negatives for comfort. Besides, why trust DNA results which you and I, and everyone else bar a couple of boffins in lab coats, haven't a hope of understanding over hard physical, *visible* evidence? Anna Anderson was the wrong height, shoe size, *ear* size, to be Franziska Schanzkowska, but right for Anastasia. She had a scar on her shoulder exactly where Anastasia had a mole removed. She had the same deformity of the big toe as Anastasia and her sisters. Besides, everyone who met her agreed she was an aristocrat, a difficult trick for a Polish factory worker to pull off. And let's not get into all the things she knew that only Anastasia could know. A graphologist testified at the trial that there was no doubt Anna's handwriting and Anastasia's were those of the same person.'

'Fine. But why didn't they have the same DNA?'

'How should I know? The excavation of the

remains at Ekaterinburg was a suspect business anyway. The authorities had obviously known where they were for years — if not the whole time since 1918 — before they chose to dig them up. And DNA only proved they were Romanovs. It was down to pathologists to say *which* Romanovs. The Tsar and his family, obviously. But unfortunately they weren't all there. The Tsarevich and one of his sisters were missing, almost certainly the youngest sister, Anastasia, despite attempts by the Russians to prove it was Maria. As for Anna Anderson's DNA, they extracted that from an intestine sample they found at the hospital in Charlottesville where she'd been operated on a few years before her death. Nobody could say it was exactly tamper-proof.'

'What are you suggesting, Marty? The KGB crept into the hospital and planted a false sample?'

'I'm not suggesting anything. I only got involved in this because . . . ' Marty broke off. He groaned and pressed one hand to his forehead.

'What's wrong?'

'Nothing. I . . . get these pains from time to time.' He grimaced. 'They'll get worse, apparently, as the tumour grows. It could affect my vision, hearing, speech. It could trigger fits and God knows what. Oh, there's a lot to look forward to.'

'Listen, Marty, I — '

'It's all right, Richard. It really is all right. I'm dying. But not today. Or tomorrow. Probably not

90

this week. Or even next.'

'Even so . . . '

'Yes? Even so *what*?'

'Why don't we forget Werner and his machinations? You've got your pay-off. Why not spend it . . . having fun?'

'It's spoken for.' Marty smiled. 'A debt to a friend.'

'Forget that too.'

'OK. If you insist.'

'I do.'

The smile broadened. 'We'll see. But Werner? No. I can't let that pass.'

'What can you do?'

'Try to put a spoke in his wheel.'

'How?'

'I've got an idea. And you promised to help me, as I recall. It's time we were moving.'

'Where're we going?'

'A department store, to start with. I can't be seen with you in that suit, Richard. It's bad for my image. Besides, I assume you'll want to put some clean clothes on eventually. After that, the station. We have a train to catch.'

11

'Why Århus?' asked Eusden, glancing down at his ticket. He and Marty were sitting next to the fruit machine in a small bar above the platforms at Hamburg central station, lunching on beer and bagels in the half-hour at their disposal before they boarded the slow train to Denmark. They had already missed the fast one.

'You remember they ceremonially reburied the Tsar and his family in St Petersburg after the pathologists and the geneticists had finally finished with them?'

'Yes.' Eusden could only assume Marty's response would ultimately lead to an answer to his question.

'St Peter and Paul Cathedral, seventeenth July 1998: the eightieth anniversary of the massacre at Ekaterinburg. The priests didn't refer to the deceased by name during the service, you know. They called them 'Christian victims of the Revolution'. The Orthodox Church never formally acknowledged that they were burying royalty. And none of the crowned heads of Europe turned up to see them do it. Anyway, last September, they got round to reburying Dagmar there as well. No one doubted who she was and she'd always said she wanted to be buried with her husband, Nicholas the Second's father, Tsar Alexander the Third. So, she was disinterred from Roskilde Cathedral — traditional resting place for Danish royals — and shipped off to St Petersburg. But there was a strange incident during the disinterment. A man rushed into the crypt and tried to stop it happening. As protests go it was pretty half-baked. He was arrested and later released without charge. It was never clear what he was protesting *about.* It probably wouldn't even have been reported in the papers but for the fact that he's a reasonably well-known artist. In Denmark, at any rate. Lars Aksden.'

'Never heard of him.'

'No. Nor had I. But Werner had. Lars Aksden, it turns out, is Hakon Nydahl's great-nephew.'

'Really?'

'Yes. Really. Nydahl's sister married into a Jutland farming family: the Aksdens. Lars is her grandson. His elder brother is Tolmar Aksden. Heard of him?'

'I don't think so.'

'Think again. Mjollnir, the Scandinavian conglomerate. Shipping, timber, hotels, electronics . . . Ring any bells now?'

'OK, Marty, you've had your fun. Of course I've heard of them. Mjollnir buys X; Mjollnir sells Y. It's difficult to flick through the business pages in the paper without seeing a headline like that sooner or later.'

'Tolmar Aksden is chairman and chief executive of the company. He owns it. He *is* Mjollnir.'

'So, I'm guessing he didn't appreciate his brother's antics at Dagmar's disinterment.'

'Probably not. No way of knowing for sure.

The guy's notoriously reticent. He lets Mjollnir's share price do the talking for him.'

'No good asking him for the lowdown on his great-uncle, then.'

'None. But other members of his family might prove more . . . talkative.'

'Any of them live in Århus?'

'As a matter of fact, yes. His sister still lives on the family farm, south of Århus. She and her husband run the place. Tolmar's son, Michael, is a student at the University of Århus. And Lars divides his time between Copenhagen and the farm. Well, farm's an understatement. More of a country estate, actually. Since his escapade at Roskilde, he's mostly been lying low there, apparently.'

'How convenient.'

'It's worth a try, isn't it? Werner will have his hands full for the next couple of days translating the letters and negotiating a price for them. We can steal a march on him.'

'*If* Lars or any of the others know what their great-uncle's secret was. And *if* they're willing to share it.'

'Don't be so pessimistic. My bet is Lars is itching to share it.' Marty grinned. 'We just have to ask nicely.'

★ ★ ★

They finished their beers and went out on to the walkway serving the steps down to the platforms. A clamour of PA announcements rose with the rumble of arriving and departing trains towards the station roof. Their train was up on the platform indicator, but had not yet pulled in. Marty lit a cigarette and leant on the railings, gazing down at the comings and goings.

'I love stations,' he remarked. 'Big ones, I mean, like this. Everyone going somewhere. Converging and diverging. North, south, east, west. Endless . . . possibilities.'

'How long will it take us to get to Århus?' Eusden asked.

'About six hours.'

'*Six hours?* Couldn't we have flown?'

'You're forgetting the real advantage of train travel, Richard: anonymity. As long as we don't stray outside the EU, nobody will ask to see our passports. Set foot in an airport and it's a different story. I'm not just thinking of my own problems, either. We're operating incognito now. So, the train makes sense. And stay off your mobile. Any calls you want to make, use a payphone. Better still, don't make any.'

'What about Gemma? Shouldn't we . . . '

'Keep her informed? Why would you want to do that?'

'She might be worried about us.'

'She should've come along, then, shouldn't she? Between you and me, I'm glad she didn't. I'm glad she sent you in her place.' Marty turned to look at Eusden. 'The question is: are you?'

'I think so.'

'Only *think?*'

'You *are* telling me everything, aren't you, Marty?'

'Everything I know.'

95

'Did Otto Straub have any . . . pet theory . . . about what Clem and Nydahl were up to?'

'According to Werner, he thought Clem must've been sent over to Copenhagen at some point in the nineteen twenties as part of a Buck Pal initiative to assist Nydahl in dealing with the fallout from Anna Anderson's claim to be Anastasia. The Queen Mother, Alexandra, was Dagmar's sister, remember. It'd be understandable if she wanted to help out.'

'Why Clem?'

'Well, Alexandra was in the royal party at Cowes regatta in August 1909. She was the queen then. Maybe she was impressed by how Clem thwarted the assassination attempt *and* kept his mouth shut about it.'

'But what was there for Clem — or Nydahl — to do? You said Dagmar wrote off Anna Anderson as an impostor without even meeting her.'

'Did I?' Marty looked troubled. 'That's not strictly accurate. Blame the tumour. Surprisingly enough, this is one of my good days.'

'Would you care to be 'strictly accurate' *before* we start rattling cages in Århus?'

'Cupboards, more like. With skeletons inside. All right. But it'll have to wait.' Marty nodded down at a train approaching the platform below them. 'That's ours, I think.'

★ ★ ★

Marty began his explanation as soon as they were settled aboard the train. He looked tired,

Eusden noticed in the watery sunlight that angled through the window as they left the station. He was struggling to concentrate. It was easy to forget how ill he really was.

'OK, where was I? Dagmar. The Dowager Empress. No dope, apparently. She realized that, if she admitted her son and grandson were dead, she'd have to choose an official pretender to the Tsardom from a squabbling bunch of cousins, inevitably causing a split in Romanov ranks. She solved the problem by steadfastly maintaining that the Tsar, Tsarina and all their children were still alive, somewhere in Russia, a convenient fiction that preserved family unity in her lifetime but ruled out the very possibility of acknowledging Anna Anderson as Anastasia. She didn't exactly ignore her, however. She sent her daughter Olga, who was living with her in Copenhagen, to visit Anna in hospital in Berlin, in the autumn of 1925. Olga seemed to agree the girl was Anastasia, only to change her mind when she got back to Copenhagen. Her trip had coincided with the death in England of Queen Alexandra, which sent Dagmar into a depression from which she never really recovered. It's hard to say what she might have done if she'd remained fit and well. But she never actually denounced Anastasia as an impostor. The so-called Copenhagen Statement, in which twelve members of the family, including Olga, formally rebutted Anna's claim to be Anastasia, was only put out after Dagmar's death. Straight after, as a matter of fact.'

'Surely Olga wouldn't have signed such a

statement unless she believed it? We're talking about her own flesh and blood.'

'We're also talking about Russian royalty of the nineteenth century. Virtually a separate species of humanity. There was a huge stumbling-block to accepting Anna's claim, one of Anna's own making. I don't mean her obstinate and prickly personality, though that didn't help, even if it did chime with people's memories of Anastasia. No, no. The real problem was her story of how she'd escaped the massacre.'

'They died in a hail of bullets in a cellar, didn't they? How did she get out of that?'

'She said she stood behind her sister Tatiana and was knocked out when Tatiana fell on top of her. She woke up in a farm cart being driven by the Tschaikovsky family, mother, daughter and son. The son, Alexander Tschaikovsky, had been a guard at Ekaterinburg and had rescued her from the pile of bodies when he realized she was still alive. They smuggled her out of Russia and took her to Romania. They settled in Bucharest, where she married Alexander shortly before giving birth to a son, in December 1918. The son wasn't Alexander's, though. She'd been raped by another guard while in captivity. She let Alexander's sister adopt the boy. Then, when her husband was killed in a street brawl, she decided to seek help from her family and set off for Berlin, where her aunt Princess Irene lived, accompanied by Alexander's brother, Serge. After they reached Berlin, Serge inexplicably vanished. She convinced herself he'd been

98

murdered and that she'd be rejected by her family, so she tried to end it all by jumping into a canal. She was rescued, hospitalized, then sent to an asylum suffering from amnesia and referred to as Fräulein Unbekannt — Miss Unknown. Gradually, she revealed who she really was and a fellow patient went public with the story when she was discharged early in 1922. Cue general hysteria and enduring controversy. But it's worth remembering that the truth, if it was the truth, was completely unacceptable — viscerally intolerable — to any right-thinking Romanov. A daughter of the Tsar couldn't bear a child to an illiterate peasant turned prison guard. It just couldn't happen.'

'But if she was raped?'

'It didn't matter. A daughter of the Tsar who told that story was by definition no daughter of the Tsar. She should have died rather than endure such shame. Therefore Anastasia must have died.'

'But you don't think she did, do you?'

'I don't know what to think. The counter-claim was that she was an uppity Polish factory worker who tried to drown herself when she realized her dream of becoming an actress, which had brought her to Berlin, wasn't going to be fulfilled. Then, ironically, it was fulfilled, thanks to the role she artfully assumed while in the asylum. That's what the DNA says. Mrs Manahan's DNA and that of a great-nephew of Franziska Schanzkowska are a perfect match. Maybe too perfect, since there's some evidence the great-nephew's grandmother was only a half-sister of Franziska, which would make such a close match impossible.'

'Proving the hospital sample was a fake.'

'It doesn't *prove* anything, Richard. Nothing does. I've turned myself into a *Mastermind* specialist on Anastasia these past few weeks and the only thing I know for certain about the case is that there *is* no certainty and probably never will be.' Marty yawned and flexed his arms behind his head, as if bored with the subject. Then he chuckled at some humorous thought that had occurred to him. 'But I did only say 'probably'. You never know your luck, do you?'

ÅRHUS

12

Eusden dozed for much of the journey, the late and anxious hours he had kept the previous night catching up with him as soon as the rhythm of the train asserted itself. Marty also slept — the deep sleep of a sick man.

The afternoon had given way to evening as they headed north through flat, snow-patched fields and wraith-pale stands of silver birch. Studying his friend, unconscious in the seat opposite, during one wakeful interlude, Eusden had noticed how much older and weaker and iller Marty seemed when his eyes were not open and twinkling, his voice not rising and falling. The search he had embarked upon was also a flight from his own mortality. In that sense, it could not succeed. At its end lay only a choice of ways to fail. It was a dismal truth to grasp as darkness fell across the Jutland sky.

★ ★ ★

Another station in another city. It was early evening in Århus, cold, dank and dark. Asked for a hotel recommendation, their taxi driver talked up the Royal on the grounds that it had a casino where he had once finished an evening in profit. They did not argue.

The Royal turned out to have advantages other than in-house roulette: comfortable rooms and a central location adjacent to the cathedral, in the old heart of the city. En route to their rooms aboard the geriatric lift, they agreed to go in search of supper once they had unpacked.

Eusden had observed Marty's ban on mobile usage, despite regarding it as an excessive precaution. But he did not intend to leave Gemma to imagine the worst. He called her on the phone in his room, was guiltily relieved when neither she nor Monica answered and left a message assuring her all was well and he was spending a few days with Marty before returning home. As far as it went, the message was accurate enough.

★   ★   ★

Marty had already changed some of his euros into Danish kroner and taken soundings on the local restaurant scene by the time Eusden met up with him in reception. He led the way down to the pedestrianized riverside, where there was a cluster of bars and brasseries, and selected the Argentinsk Bøfhus on the basis of its promise of the fattest steaks this side of Buenos Aires.

'Good to see you *sans* the suit, Coningsby,' he remarked as he sank his fork into a three-inch-thick slab of sirloin. 'Though, strictly speaking, you'd need an altogether grungier look than you've settled on to blend in where we're going.'

Eusden smiled at him tolerantly. 'I'll visit a charity shop in the morning if you're that bothered.'

'Too late. I'm talking about tonight. The part

104

of it left after we've devoured these mastodons.'

'You haven't got some crazy idea of hitting the night spots, have you, Marty? You can count me out if you have. And I'd advise you to count yourself out too.'

'I'm talking business, not pleasure, Richard. Take a look at this.'

Marty plucked a newspaper cutting from his pocket and unfolded it on the table. Above a splurge of Danish print was a grainy photograph of a young couple emerging from a bar. The young man was tall, thin and narrow-faced, piratically bearded and bandannaed but otherwise kitted out in fashionably ill-fitting military surplus. The young woman, whose posture suggested she might easily fall down if he took his arm from round her waist, was slight and pale, hair spikily blonde, eyes wide and unfocused, clothes black, shining like leather in the flashlight of the camera. Her companion was gesturing angrily at the photographer, but she did not seem to be aware of what was happening — or indeed of much at all.

'I spotted it while I was in Copenhagen in a tabloid someone left in a coffee shop. The girl's the daughter of an actor who's big on Danish TV. He's in a long-running police series. Their very own Inspector Mørse. Her boyfriend's the interesting one. That's Michael Aksden. And the place they're leaving is here in Århus. So, I thought we might . . . check it out.'

'D'you know where it is?'

'The receptionist at the Royal recognized it right away. And gave me directions.'

'And you're planning to . . . drop in?'

'Why not?'

'Well, for a start because Michael and the girl probably won't be there.'

'Come on, Richard. Get real. Students are creatures of habit. Don't you remember? When we were at Cambridge, what were the chances, on any given night, that you and/or I could be found propping up the bar in the Champion of the Thames?'

Eusden considered the point, then conceded it. 'Better than fifty-fifty, I guess.'

'Exactly. So, shall we try our luck?'

★ ★ ★

They walked back the way they had come, past the cathedral and a statue of King Christian X on horseback. The cathedral square was empty and silent. There was hardly any traffic on the streets, let alone pedestrians. The night was windless and catacomb-cold.

'Nice time of year you picked for this jaunt,' Eusden good-naturedly complained.

'I'd have waited till summer,' Marty replied, 'but there's a doubt about my availability.'

'Sorry.' However often Eusden reminded himself that Marty was dying, the reality never quite stuck. 'I just — '

'Don't worry about it. Gemma always used to say I was too short-term in my thinking. Well, it's come into its own now.'

★ ★ ★

106

Their destination lay a couple of blocks north of the cathedral: a cramped, crowded, smoky street-corner bar that might have looked drab in daylight but had enough candles and mirrors to confer a certain grotto-like glamour by night. Students comprised most of the clientèle, hunched and bunched over hookahs, laptops and games of backgammon. Marty ordered Belgian beer and he and Eusden squeezed themselves into a corner.

There was no immediate sign of Michael Aksden or his girlfriend, but the limited visibility and identikit appearance of most of the patrons meant it took them quite a while to be sure they were not there. Marty insisted patience was required. The night was young in the context of student drinking establishments. They needed to stick with it. He added the smoke of several Camels to the prevailing fug and began a nostalgic description of how much better he would feel if he could resort to something more exotic than alcohol and tobacco.

'What's stopping you?' asked Eusden. 'I'm sure somebody here'd be willing to help you out.'

'Doctor's orders, Richard. The old white stuff might start me fitting, apparently. When you haven't got a lot of time, it's amazing how much care you're prepared to take of it.'

'Are you sure we're not wasting a load of it sitting here?'

'Absolutely. Some of these girls are definitely worth studying at length, wouldn't you say? And you've got to — ' Marty broke off and pointed to

107

the door. 'Look what's just walked in.'

The newcomer was Michael Aksden, helpfully sporting the same outfit he had been photographed in. He was alone and looked none too happy about it, twitching and frowning as he surveyed the crowd. Then he caught sight of someone he knew and raised a hand coolly in greeting. He made no immediate move to join them, however, heading straight for the bar instead.

Marty was by his elbow before he had ordered a drink, with Eusden two steps behind. 'This one's on me, Michael,' Marty said, grinning broadly. 'What'll you have?'

Michael glared at him with a mixture of suspicion and hostility. 'Who are you, man?' He sounded far more American than Danish with his practised drawl.

'The name's Hewitson. Marty Hewitson.'

'Have we met before?'

'No. But I thought you might know the name. My grandfather was Clem Hewitson. Heard of him?'

'Never.'

'Your father probably has. Or your uncle. Good old Lars.'

'Are you friends of Lars?'

'Not exactly,' Eusden replied, drawing a sharp glance from Marty.

'I don't want to talk to you, whoever you are.' Michael shouted a request to the barman, then went on: 'Get it? Leave me alone.'

'No need to be like that, Michael,' said Marty. 'We're just trying to be friendly.'

108

'I don't want to be friendly.' The barman handed him a bottle of Tuborg Grøn. 'Piss off, will you?'

'Any idea why Lars pulled that stunt in Roskilde back in the autumn?'

'Didn't you hear what I said?'

'Only, we might know, y'see.'

Michael took a swig from his bottle and stared flintily at Marty. 'You're full of shit, man.'

'Sure of that, are you?'

The shadows around them suddenly deepened. Eusden became aware of a young man, tall and broad and blond enough to have stepped out of a Viking myth, standing at Michael's shoulder. The straining fit of his denim jacket, over a white T-shirt, implied a formidable quantity of muscle beneath. He and Michael exchanged a few words in Danish between menacing glares at Marty.

'Who's this, Michael?' Marty asked. 'Your backgammon partner?'

'He's a friend,' Michael replied, speaking slowly for the sake of emphasis. 'He wants to know if I've got a problem. I said no. 'Cos you and *your* friend are leaving. Right?'

'Wrong, actually. I was thinking of having another beer. Richard?'

'No, thanks,' said Eusden, nodding meaningfully towards the door, currently hidden from view by the muscleman's massive shoulderline. 'I think we ought to be going.'

'Really?'

'Definitely.'

'OK.' Marty grinned at Michael. 'We'll

obviously have to do this another time.'
'Fuck off, man.'

★ ★ ★

'What exactly did that accomplish?' asked
Eusden as they headed back to the Royal.
Marty chuckled. 'It's got the introductions out
of the way.'

13

Eusden was woken the following morning by the insistent ringing of the telephone. His first thought was that the caller must be Gemma. Then he remembered he had not told her where they were. By that time, he had picked up the receiver.

'Hello?'

'Mr Eusden. Reception here. Will you take a call from a Mr Burgaard?'

He was too fuddled by sleep to consider refusing. 'OK. Put him through.' Burgaard? *Who the hell was he?*

'Mr Eusden?'

'Yeah.'

'My name's Karsten Burgaard.' His English had less of an American accent than Michael Aksden's, though he did not sound much older. 'Can you meet me?'

'What?'

'Now, I mean. I'm in the Baresso coffee bar. By the bridge in Sankt Clemens Torv.'

'*Where?*'

'Ask at the desk. It's not far.'

'But . . . who are you?'

'I overheard your . . . conversation with Michael Aksden . . . last night. Then I . . . followed you back to your hotel.'

'You followed us?'

'Yes. But come alone, hey? Your friend is . . . rather loud.'

'I don't understand. What d'you want?'

'Come and find out.'

'Hold on. I — ' But Burgaard had not held on. The line was dead.

★ ★ ★

Eusden struggled to order his thoughts as he washed and dressed. Marty would insist on going along if he alerted him to what had happened. And Burgaard had a point. He could be loud. Eusden was still irritated by how blithely Marty had provoked Michael Aksden. Perhaps the time had come to demonstrate the merits of diplomacy and restraint. He headed out as instructed — alone.

★ ★ ★

Århusers were making their way to work in scarfed and muffled silence, exhaled breath pluming around them in the frigid dawn air. Eusden hurried the short distance to the Baresso Kaffebar and spotted Burgaard before he even entered, watching him through the window as he approached.

Burgaard was one of only two customers. The other was buying *latte* and a muffin to go. Several others had arrived, with the same to-go look about them, by the time Eusden had bought his coffee and joined Burgaard by the window.

'Thanks for coming, Mr Eusden,' said Burgaard, smiling nervously. He was a thin, slightly built, prematurely balding young man

112

with a round, boyish face and a skittering, uncertain gaze. His fingernails, Eusden noticed, were chewed to the quick. He was dressed anonymously in shades of brown and grey.

'Well, like you said, it wasn't far.'

'No. It's a small city.' Burgaard seemed to be scanning the queue at the counter over Eusden's shoulder. 'Too small, maybe.'

'Your home town?'

'No. I'm from Falster. I came here . . . to study. At the University.'

'What's your subject?'

'Economics.' As if to prove the point, Burgaard had a pink business paper folded open at his elbow.

'Uh-huh.'

'You probably don't remember seeing me last night.'

'You're right. I don't.'

'People generally . . . don't notice me.'

'How well d'you know Michael Aksden?'

'Better than he'd like.'

'What's his subject?'

'Economics also. Michael and I . . . started together. But I have my degree. I'm studying for a doctorate. Michael is . . . drifting.' Burgaard shrugged. 'It doesn't matter how long you take for a degree — or if you ever get one — when your father is Tolmar Aksden.' He swivelled the paper round and tapped a headline. Eusden noticed the word Mjollnir. 'It says 'Mjollnir shares break through new barrier'.'

'Own any?'

'Some. But not enough. Anyway, I'm not

113

interested in Mjollnir for investment, though maybe I should be. I'm interested in finding out why they do so well.'

'The secret of their success?'

'Exactly.' Burgaard lowered his voice. 'The secret.'

'Why don't you ask Michael?'

'I have. He tells me nothing. I think he knows nothing. I ask him to arrange for me to meet his father. No. I ask him to arrange for me to meet someone who works with his father. Again, no. This is for my thesis, Mr Eusden. I have worked on this nearly two years. Mjollnir is . . . a phenomenon. But no one understands it. I have tried. But, you see, they do not want anyone to understand. Tolmar Aksden does not give interviews. He does not . . . give anything.'

'Perhaps he's just a gifted entrepreneur.'

'His sort of entrepreneur normally likes to tell everyone how gifted he is. Not Tolmar Aksden. This paper calls him *Den Usynlige Mand:* the Invisible Man. Everyone admires him. But also everyone . . . distrusts him.'

'Do they?'

'Oh, yes, Mr Eusden. Just like you and your friend. What was that about last night? Mr Hewitson mentioned his grandfather . . . and Lars Aksden's arrest in Roskilde. You and Mr Hewitson . . . know something. And I . . . ' Burgaard's head twitched in a slight but palpable nervous convulsion. This was clearly the stage of their encounter he had been steeling himself for. 'I would be grateful if you told me what it is.'

Eusden took a sip of coffee to camouflage a

114

tactical pause, then smiled and said, 'Why would I do that?'

'Because I know things you don't.'

'Maybe we know it all.'

'No. If you did, you wouldn't have challenged Michael. And also . . . you wouldn't have agreed to meet me this morning.'

'Is that right?'

'Yes. I think it is.' Burgaard's calculations were sound, even though he projected little confidence in them. 'I propose . . . a trade.'

Another pause; another sip. 'Propose away.'

'I guess you've come to Århus because Lars is here. Near here, I mean. He has been ever since the . . . incident . . . in Roskilde. You've come to see him, haven't you?'

'Maybe.'

'I want to be with you when you do.'

'And you propose to buy your ringside seat with . . . information.'

'Yes.' Burgaard nodded. 'A lot of information.'

★ ★ ★

Tolmar Aksden was born at the family farm, Aksdenhøj, in 1939. He trained as an engineer, but worked on the farm for some years before setting up Mjollnir in the early 1970s. Mjollnir's ostensible business was plant hire, but from the very start, according to Burgaard, it seemed to be more of a general investment vehicle. Aksden began buying up disused industrial land in the Århus area and regenerating it as housing complexes and high-tech business parks. He was

115

always one step ahead of the economic trend. By the 1980s he had taken over a shipyard and an electronics factory, which both appeared defunct but were transformed under Mjollnir into leaders in the fields of containerization and micro-processing. In the 1990s came the big leap for the company: acquisition of a Swedish hotel chain, a large Norwegian fish-farming operation and a Finnish timber producer. Mjollnir's headquarters moved to Copenhagen and its reign as a pan-Scandinavian economic powerhouse began. Burgaard emphasized the shock element in this development. Aksden kept such a low profile that his competitors never saw him coming. His far-sightedness was envied, his ruthlessness feared. He was considered by many to be positively un-Danish in this regard, although ignorance of his true personality and the rarity of his sightings in public ensured criticism gave way to awe at his achievements and a certain mystique that attached itself to the Invisible Man of the Nordic business world.

His family life was similarly low-key. He married Pernille Madsen, a Mjollnir employee nineteen years his junior, when he was forty-two. Their only child, Michael, was born in 1983. They had subsequently divorced. His sister, Elsa, married a neighbouring landowner in Jutland, and seldom stirred from rural obscurity. His brother, Lars, was the odd one out, cultivating a larger-than-life image as an artist, womanizer and dabbler in politics. As a young man, he had participated in the establishment of the Christiania hippy commune in Copenhagen and had sedulously maintained his anti-Establishment credentials ever since. About the only thing he had in common with Tolmar was that they were both divorced.

In Norse mythology, Mjollnir was Thor's magical hammer, an instrument of destruction *and* creation. Tolmar Aksden had chosen the name for his company well. He had specialized in eliminating competitors and turning their failures into his successes. Nor was he finished yet. At sixty-eight, he gave no sign of slowing down. The consensus was that he had a strategy for further expansion, though where, and into what, was, as ever with the man, an open question. And it would remain so, until he chose to reveal the answer.

* * *

'What did you tell the guy?' Marty demanded as soon as Eusden had finished relaying what he had learnt from Burgaard about the life and times of Tolmar Aksden. They were in the hotel restaurant, where Eusden had found Marty having breakfast when he returned from the coffee bar.

'I told him I was helping you research your grandfather's mysterious dealings with Aksden's great-uncle, Hakon Nydahl. That was it. I said nothing about Anastasia — or Clem's attaché case.'

'How did he react?'

117

'I think he suspected I wasn't giving him the full story. But I think he also sensed I suspected the same of him.'

'What's he after?'

'Something to spice up his analysis of Mjollnir's success.'

'Which he reckons we can deliver?'

'He's betting on it. And I'm happy to let him. He knows where Lars is hanging out and he's willing to take us to see him. Today.'

'Mmm.' Marty frowned sceptically. 'How can we be sure he's not getting more out of us than we're getting out of him?'

'We can't. You think I should've turned him down?'

'I'm not saying that.'

'What *are* you saying, then?'

'Why did he insist on meeting you alone?'

'He's the shy, retiring type. He described you as 'rather loud'.'

'Bloody nerve.'

'I promised him you'd be on your best behaviour when we went to see Lars.'

'What the hell does that mean?'

'It means don't pick a fight with the man.'

'As if I would.'

'As if.'

'All right, all right. I'll be nice. But don't forget' — Marty pointed his fork at Eusden for emphasis — 'I'm in charge.'

14

Burgaard called for them at eleven o'clock, as agreed. He was clearly wary of Marty and the feeling was just as clearly mutual. They set off in Burgaard's battered old Skoda and little was said until they had left the city and were driving south through a snow-veiled landscape of farms and forests and empty roads.

'How many generations of Aksdens have farmed here?' Eusden asked, as much to break the silence as out of genuine curiosity.

'Many, I guess,' Burgaard replied. 'But Aksdenhøj was never a rich farm. Høj means hill. The ones with names ending in *dal* — valley — are where the best land is. So, we know why Tolmar did not stay on the farm.'

'But his sister stuck with it,' said Marty.

'Not exactly. She married Henrik Støvring. He owns Marskedal, one of the largest manor farms in east Jutland.'

'So, what's happened to Aksdenhøj?'

'They say Tolmar stays there occasionally. And Lars uses it as a studio.'

'Is that where we're going, then?'

'Yes. With luck, we'll find Lars there.'

★ ★ ★

After about ten miles on a main road, they turned off on to a narrower, winding side road.

119

The going was rougher over compacted ice, the snowbanks at the fields' edges higher as they entered rolling, hillier countryside. Off to one side, down a tree-lined drive, a large, half-timbered, terracotta-roofed manor house came into view.

'Marskedal,' Burgaard announced. 'Nice, yes?'

'Looks like Elsa Aksden married money,' said Marty.

'Or Henrik Støvring did. They say Tolmar's pumped a lot of cash into the estate.'

'What do they farm?'

'Pigs. Bacon's big business.' Burgaard pointed to a plain, blank-windowed structure on the other side of the road. 'There are probably several hundred pigs in there. Aksdenhøj used to be a sheep farm. Not so profitable.'

★ ★ ★

Another turn-off took them on to a lane that hugged the edge of a birch forest as it climbed into the hills. Aksdenhøj appeared ahead of them at the lane's end, a quadrangle of thatch-roofed stone buildings on a shoulder of land close to the crest of the hill, sheltered by the forest.

Burgaard beeped his horn as he drove into the cobbled yard. Smoke was climbing from a chimney in one of the buildings, next to which was parked an old Volvo estate. Someone was at home. And Burgaard evidently wished to give them ample warning of their arrival.

'How well do you know Lars?' asked Eusden.

'As well as he'll let me,' Burgaard replied with

measured ambiguity. He pulled up behind the Volvo and climbed out.

The chill of the hilly air hit Eusden as he emerged from the car. It was colder up here than in Århus and the snow had blanketed the world in silence. The farmhouse itself looked to be shut up. The smoking chimney was on one of the barns that formed the rest of the quadrangle. It clearly no longer served as a barn: high dormer windows had been added to its steeply sloping roof; lights, blurred by condensation, glimmered within.

One of the windows opened as Eusden gazed up at them. A man peered out: grey-haired, balding, ruddy-faced. He shouted something in Danish. Burgaard replied in kind. A shepherding gesture appeared to constitute an invitation to enter. They headed for the door.

The barn had been converted into a dwelling, disconcertingly modern in design and layout. A lobby opened into a large, well-appointed kitchen. Burgaard led the way straight up the wide stairs ahead of them to Lars Aksden's studio.

It covered the length and breadth of the building beneath the exposed thatch. A gigantic, rhythmically ticking radiator warmed the air, bringing out the pungent smells of oil paint and turpentine. Dozens of paintings — Expressionist nudes and vibrantly hued landscapes — were hung or easelled in view. Dozens more were stacked against the walls. There was an area set aside for relaxation, with couches and rugs, and at the far end, beyond a half-drawn curtain, an

121

unmade bed. A voice from Eusden's past was singing softly on a hi-fi somewhere in the jumble: Françoise Hardy. As music will, it plunged him into a memory: a trip to Paris with Gemma and Marty in the long hot summer of 1976. He saw a shadow of the same memory cross Marty's face. Then someone pressed the off-switch.

The floorboards creaked as Lars Aksden moved towards them. He was a big, heavy-footed bear of a man, clad in paint-flecked maroon, with a face like one of his own portraits: deeply scored and passionate. His voice, as he and Burgaard swapped a few more words in Danish, was a fractured growl; his laugh, when it unexpectedly followed, as loud as a roar.

'Karsten, you are a scheming little bastard.' Lars pinched Burgaard's cheek as if he were a naughty child. 'Introduce us.'

Burgaard did the honours. Handshakes were exchanged, a lingering one in Marty's case, as Lars murmured his surname and stared thoughtfully at him.

'Where do you come from, Marty?'

'England. The Isle of Wight. We both do.'

'And what's brought you here?'

'Family history. I've always wanted to know how my grandfather came to have a Danish friend: Hakon Nydahl. Richard's helping me . . . look into it.'

'Well, I tell you: I've always wanted to know that too.'

'Did you know Clem?' asked Eusden.

'I met him twice. He came to see us here when

I was a child, with Great-Uncle Hakon. And again, when I was older, on his own. That would have been around . . . '

'Spring of 1960?' suggested Marty.

Lars cocked his head and frowned at him. 'Ja. Around then.'

'We know he . . . was abroad at that time.'

'But I'm not going to be able to tell you how he met my great-uncle. That was never explained to me. Nor were his visits. My grandparents were expecting him, though. It was all . . . arranged beforehand.'

'Your grandparents? What about your parents?'

'They were dead by then. My mother died giving birth to my sister. My father was killed in an accident on the farm. Hard times, Marty. Did you have them?'

'Not as a child.'

'Lucky for you.'

'You really have no idea what Clem's connection with your great-uncle was?' asked Eusden.

'Idea? Oh, I've got several of those. But that's all they are. Ideas. Theories. Dreams.' And a dreamlike state was indeed what Lars seemed briefly to descend into. He moved across to one of the windows and gazed out for a moment, then rounded on them. 'You want a drink? Beer? Schnapps?'

'Why not?' said Marty. And Eusden saw no point in arguing. Beer all round was agreed. At a word from Lars, Burgaard headed down to the kitchen to fetch them.

'Karsten's a clever boy,' Lars confided in an undertone while he was downstairs. 'But not as clever as he thinks he is.'

'Who is?' Marty murmured reflectively.

'Ja. Exactly. Who is? Not me, for sure. Karsten first came to me saying he wanted my memories of Christiania. Y'know? Our little — well, not so little — flower-power utopia in Copenhagen. There's a famous photograph — you see it often — of some hairy guys putting a plank through the fence round the disused barracks. Day One of the commune. November thirteenth, 1971. I'm the one whose face you can't see. Tolmar says that's the only good turn I've ever done him: looking away from the camera that day.' He grinned.

'Your brother's a remarkable man,' said Eusden.

'Remarkably successful, for sure. And my brother' — Lars raised his voice as Burgaard rejoined them — 'is the Aksden my young friend really wants to know about. Isn't that right, Karsten? Tolmar. Not Lars and his paintings and his girlfriends and his dopehead memories.'

Burgaard looked sheepish as he handed round the bottles. Glasses were evidently not part of the deal. He said something in Danish.

'Speak English,' Lars growled, raising his bottle in a toast. '*Skål.*' They all joined in. 'Go on, Karsten. Tell them how it is.'

'I've already told them.'

'Only enough to keep them interested, I bet.'

'They think they know why you tried to stop the ceremony in Roskilde.'

124

'Is that right?' Lars grinned coolly at Eusden and Marty. 'You know, do you?'

'We were just trying it on, Lars,' said Marty. 'We haven't a clue. But why don't you tell us anyway? Put us all out of our misery.'

'Why should you care?'

'Hakon Nydahl administered Dagmar's affairs,' said Eusden. 'And you didn't want her reburied in Russia. Why was that?'

'It had nothing to do with Dagmar. I was protesting against the government's plans to close down Christiania. It was a high-profile event, that's all. An opportunity for an old revolutionary like me to make a point.'

'But you didn't make a point,' Burgaard objected. 'You never mentioned Christiania when you were arrested.'

'They didn't report me mentioning it, you mean. Tolmar got them to keep quiet to avoid embarrassment. He had some big deal going through at the time.'

'The Saukko takeover,' said Burgaard.

'That was it.'

'So,' said Eusden, 'it was just a coincidence that the ceremony involved Dagmar.'

'Ja. Just a coincidence.'

'Wait.' Burgaard looked thunderstruck. 'Coincidence. I should have thought of it. The Saukko takeover.'

'What's Saukko?' asked Marty.

'A Finnish bank. Mjollnir bought it last autumn. You'd call it a strange move by any other company. Banks are bought by other banks, not industrial conglomerates. But Tolmar

Aksden always knows what he's doing. That's what they said. That's what they always say.'

'Maybe you should shut your mouth, Karsten,' said Lars, his tone suddenly serious.

Silence fell. The atmosphere in the studio had become tense, almost electric. When the telephone began ringing, piercingly loud, Eusden started with surprise.

For several seconds, Lars made no move to answer it. Eventually, he grunted and lumbered off to the lounge area. The telephone stood atop a slew of newspapers and magazines. He grabbed the receiver. *'Hallo?'*

As the conversation proceeded in mumbled Danish, Marty sidled closer to Burgaard. 'What's the big coincidence, Karsten?' he asked in a whisper.

'I'll tell you later.'

'But you think Lars is lying about why he staged his protest?'

'For sure he's taken a long time to explain it.'

'Are we really getting anywhere here?' Eusden put in, reflecting his opinion that they had merely succeeded in antagonizing another member of the Aksden family.

'Maybe we could if you came out with everything you know,' Burgaard hissed.

'That cuts both ways,' Marty responded, smiling humourlessly at him. 'You've obviously been — ' He broke off as Lars slammed the phone down and strode back to join them.

'My sister,' he announced. 'Warning me about two Englishmen asking questions. They tried to frighten our nephew last night.'

126

'Is asking a few questions so very frightening?' Eusden responded, giving way to irritation despite knowing it would be counter-productive.

'You have family, Richard?' Lars threw back at him.

'Yes.'

'You must know how it is, then. You might think they're all shits. But you defend them against outsiders. Elsa says Tolmar wouldn't want any of us to talk to you. And she's right. She says I should throw you out.' He took a swig of beer and grinned at them, half-apologetically. 'So, I guess that's what I'm doing.'

15

They drove away from Aksdenhøj in a recriminatory silence. Eusden sensed Marty and Burgaard were engaged in a test of nerves: which of them would tell the other what they knew first? In his opinion, it made no difference. They would achieve nothing without collaborating.

A Range Rover was barrelling down the driveway of Marskedal as they passed. The thought occurred to Eusden, as he guessed it must have occurred to his companions, that this was Elsa heading out to confirm her brother had done as she asked. If so, she did not need to worry. Lars Aksden was as efficient an ejector of unwelcome guests as they came.

'Are we just going back to Århus with our tails between our legs?' Marty suddenly snapped.

'No,' Burgaard replied calmly. 'There's something I want to show you in the next village.'

'You could tell us about that coincidence now.'

'Not yet. First the show. Then the tell.'

★   ★   ★

The village of Tasdrup was consumed in wintry stillness. It gave every impression, despite the smartness of the houses, of being uninhabited. Burgaard parked by the church — small and plain, save for some fancy crenellations on the gables of its high, narrow belltower. They clambered out and Burgaard struck off into the snowy churchyard, Eusden and Marty slithering after him and rapidly falling behind.

He waited for them at the end of one row of graves, brushing snow off a memorial stone as they approached.

'Lars' parents and grandparents,' he explained, pointing to the inscription. 'Listed in the order of their deaths.'

HANNAH AKSDEN   † 14.10.1947
PEDER AKSDEN   † 23.3.1948
GERTRUD AKSDEN   † 29.8.1963
OLUF AKSDEN   † 1.9.1967

'Pretty bloody terse,' commented Marty.

'Yes,' said Burgaard. 'Even for Lutherans. And see — just the dates of death; no dates of birth; no ages at death.'

'So?'

'It's unusual.'

'Maybe they were paying by the letter.'

'Is there more to it, Karsten?' asked Eusden, confident there had to be.

'Oh, yes. Much more. But shall we talk in the car? It's cold out here.'

★ ★ ★

There was no argument about that. Eusden sat in the front with Burgaard. Marty took the back seat. Burgaard whirled round when he heard Marty fumbling in his pocket for his matches. There was already a cigarette in his mouth.

'Please don't smoke, Mr Hewitson. I am *astmatiker*.'

'Pardon me,' groaned Marty, dolefully replacing the cigarette in his pack.

'What are you going to tell us, Karsten?' Eusden prompted.

'One thing. And I expect one other thing in return.'

'We'll see,' said Marty.

'I want all information you have on your grandfather.'

'OK.' Marty's agreement sounded suspiciously airy to Eusden.

'All right. Saukko Bank. The coincidence. I found out everything I could about Hakon Nydahl when I realized he was Tolmar Aksden's great-uncle. As a courtier, I wondered if he'd . . . done Tolmar any favours. Nothing turned up. But there was a strange event . . . just before he died. Summer of 1961. He was in hospital by then. He never came out. While he was there, his housekeeper was arrested for stealing money from his apartment. He had a safe and she knew the combination. The papers got interested in the case because what she stole was . . . very unusual money. Finnish markkaa, nineteen thirties issue. She'd tried to change it for Danish kroner, but the notes were no longer legal tender. Also, she was trying to change a massive amount: several millions in kroner. She didn't realize how much the notes were worth — or would have been worth. No one could understand why Nydahl should have had all this out-of-date Finnish money. He was too ill to be asked for an explanation. But during the case they reported that the Bank of Finland had traced the serial numbers on the notes to a batch of currency supplied in 1939 to — '

'Saukko Bank,' said Eusden.

'Yes. Exactly. Saukko. Now owned by Tolmar Aksden.'

'You think that's why he bought it?'

'Somehow, yes. There's a connection. I just can't . . . work it out. But maybe I can . . . if I know all there is to know about Clem Hewitson.'

'It's possible,' said Marty. 'But here's the deal, Karsten. I'm expecting a call later today. I'm hoping it'll join up the dots in what we know about Clem's relationship with Nydahl.'

'Join up the dots?' Burgaard frowned dubiously at Marty over his shoulder. So did Eusden. What call? What the hell was Marty playing at?

'Once that's done, we should be in business. Know what I mean?'

'No. Just give me all you have so far.'

'No point. I don't want to run the risk of . . . unintentionally misleading you.' Marty's smile, doubtless intended to be reassuring, looked patently disingenuous to Eusden. 'By tonight, everything should be clearer. And I'll be happy to share it with you. Now, what about that gravestone?'

Burgaard's mouth tightened. 'Do you think I'm a fool, Mr Hewitson?'

'Of course not.'

'You get nothing more till I get something.'

'No need to be like that.'

'Yes, there is. You've cheated me. You promised me information.'

'And you'll get it.' Marty leant forward and looked Burgaard in the eye. 'Tonight.'

★ ★ ★

The journey back to Århus was a wordless ordeal. Burgaard drove fast and tensely, like a man simmering with resentment, as Eusden had no doubt he was. Eusden was feeling pretty resentful himself. Marty was stringing him along as well as Burgaard. This had always been the way of it, of course. Marty had never been able to resist playing the role of smart arse. Several of the more infuriating passages of their friendship replayed themselves in Eusden's memory as they sped through the Jutland countryside.

★ ★ ★

Eusden had assumed Burgaard would drop them at their hotel, but he noticed after they had entered the city that they were on a ring road, skirting the centre, and soon the university campus appeared to their right. Soon after that, they pulled into a car park behind a cluster of multi-storey red-brick accommodation blocks.

'I'll expect to see you tonight, then,' said Burgaard as they climbed out, his voice flat and expressionless. 'I'll be waiting for your call.' With that he plodded off towards the entrance of the nearest block.

'How are we supposed to get back to the

132

Royal?' Marty called after him.

'Take the bus. Or walk. I don't care.'

'Thanks a lot.'

Burgaard's answer to that was a V-sign, delivered without a backward glance. Eusden could hardly blame him. And even Marty seemed to consider further protest pointless. He lit a cigarette as they watched Burgaard vanish indoors.

'Why don't we try to track down a restaurant over there?' Marty nodded in the direction of the shopping street they had turned off a few minutes previously. 'We'll feel better after we've had something to eat and drink.'

Eusden looked at him unsmilingly. 'Why not?'

★ ★ ★

A dismal pizza parlour was the best they could find so far from the city centre. Eusden contained himself while food was ordered and beer delivered to their table, then let Marty have it.

'What the bloody hell do you think you're doing, giving Burgaard the runaround like that? The poor bloke's offering to help you.'

'It couldn't be avoided,' Marty replied, beaming at Eusden over his glass of Carlsberg.

'What's that supposed to mean?'

'Like I told him: I'm waiting for a phone call.'

'That was true?'

'Certainly.'

'You never mentioned any call to me.'

'You never mentioned your rendezvous with

clever clogs Karsten until after the event.'

'And that's how I'd have got to hear about the call?'

'Yeah. What's the problem?'

'Who's the call from?'

'You don't need to know just yet. I'm hoping for . . . some good news. Let's leave it like that.'

'You're not going to tell me?'

'I'd rather not. It'd be tempting fate.'

'Well, I'd *rather* you did. It's bad enough keeping Burgaard in the dark. I'm supposed to be your friend.'

'Calm down, Richard. You're ranting.'

It was true, in the sense that Eusden's voice had risen steadily during their exchanges. He noticed the waiter peering apprehensively round the kitchen blind. He tried to stifle some of the anger he felt.

'You reckon I'm handling Burgaard badly, do you?' Marty asked.

'Yes. There was more he'd have told us if you'd offered him something in return.'

'More of the same, in all likelihood. That stuff about Nydahl's cache of Finnish currency? Old news, I'm afraid.'

'You already knew?'

'Sure. It was about the only interesting fact I dug up on the man.'

'When were you planning to tell me about it?'

'I thought I had. In fact, I meant to congratulate you on acting dumb so convincingly.'

'You said you found out nothing about him.'

'Did I? Sorry. It must have . . . slipped my mind.'

'*Slipped your mind?*'

Marty shrugged. 'I'm not firing on all synapses.'

The blatant bid for sympathy was the last straw for Eusden. He should have remembered: there always came a time when Marty drove him beyond endurance. He shook his head ruefully and stood up.

'Going somewhere?'

'For a walk. I'll see you back at the hotel.'

'What about your pizza?'

'The way I feel at the moment, I think it might choke me.'

'Hold on. There's no — '

'Save it, Marty, OK?' Eusden held up a hand in solemn warning. 'Whatever you've got to say, I don't want to hear it.'

16

They had planned to potter round Bembridge
Harbour and The Duver before tea with Aunt
Lily at her cottage in St Helens. It was a hot,
windless day towards the end of August, 1971.
The tide was exceptionally low — low enough,
according to Marty, who claimed to have studied
the tables, for them to walk out through the
shallows to St Helens Fort. It was one of
Palmerston's Follies, a ring of forts on sea and
land around Portsmouth, built to defend the
home of the Royal Navy from attack by the
French. All had long since been abandoned. The
expedition was too tempting an idea to resist.
And they made it out there with some ease. But
a futile attempt to penetrate the fort delayed
their return journey and Marty tardily admitted
that he did not actually know when the tide was
due to turn. Beaten back by the inrushing sea
and lucky not to be drowned, they were
eventually rescued by a passing yachtsman as
darkness was falling.

It was an important lesson in a subject
Richard Eusden was to become an expert on: the
inherent unreliability of Marty Hewitson. Marty
was generous, but seldom repaid a debt unless
reminded of it. He was game for anything, but
often failed to turn up when the time came. He
was confident in everything he asserted or
proposed, but the confidence he inspired in

others was frequently misplaced. In short, he possessed charm in abundance. But even abundance can be exhausted.

The exasperation Eusden felt as he trudged down past the campus of Århus University towards the city centre was thus all too familiar to him. Burgaard had asked Marty if he thought him a fool and Eusden could well have asked the same question of himself. Except that he knew the answer, as Burgaard did not. Marty treated everyone in the same way, whether he thought them a fool, or a friend, or both. He was never going to change. Believing everything he said — or believing he had told you everything: that was foolishness.

Eusden went into a bar down by the riverside, where he ate a club sandwich, drank several beers and considered what he should do. Suspicion is a progressive disorder and he had started to wonder just how deceitful Marty was being. He could not have invented the whole thing. Werner Straub was real enough, as was Karsten Burgaard. They were on to something. But was it really connected with Anastasia? And was Marty really dying? Doubt had begun to weevil into Eusden's mind on every count.

★   ★   ★

By the time he returned to the Royal, he had half-decided to tell Marty he was bailing out and heading back to London by the first available flight. As it was, he never got the chance. A woman was waiting for him in the lobby. With

137

her iron-grey hair, raw-boned, weathered face and faintly old-fashioned outfit of loden and tweed, she looked like a well-to-do country-woman of sixty or so on a shopping expedition to the city. And that did not turn out to be a misleading impression, although shopping was not high on her agenda.

'Mr Eusden? I'm Elsa Støvring. I wanted to speak to Mr Hewitson, but he's not here.' This was slightly surprising. Eusden would have expected Marty to take a bus back into the centre and be at the hotel long before him. But there was, as he well knew, no legislating for Marty's movements. 'Could you spare me a few minutes? I need to speak to one of you. It really is rather urgent.'

★ ★ ★

Elsa Støvring was not a woman to be fobbed off and Eusden did not try. They walked across the square to a café for the urgent discussion she was clearly intent on having.

'I'm not sure what you and Mr Hewitson are trying to achieve, Mr Eusden, but you've certainly succeeded in upsetting several members of my family,' she began. 'My brother Tolmar is a very private person and I hope you'll agree he has a right to his privacy.'

'We haven't breached it as far as I know,' said Eusden. He could not decide whether to be defensive or conciliatory. He badly needed to establish where he stood with Marty, but he was going to have to see off Elsa first.

'You harassed my nephew in a bar.'

'We *spoke* to him.'

'You imposed on my brother Lars.'

'We paid him a visit and left when he asked us to.'

'Yes, well . . . ' Her dogmatic tone faltered slightly. 'Lars is not the best judge of his own interests.'

'But you are, no doubt.'

Elsa gave him a sharp look over the rim of her coffee cup. 'The world changes, Mr Eusden. I'd never met a Lithuanian until about ten years ago. Now my husband employs six of them to manage his pigs. My brother Tolmar probably employs many more, in Lithuania as well as Denmark. Oh yes, the world changes. But we have the past inside us. And that doesn't change. I never knew my parents. My mother died a few days after I was born. Blood poisoning. Five months later, my father died also. He cut an artery in an accident with a *segl*. What is it in English? A curved blade . . . with a handle.' She finger-painted a question mark in the air, minus the dot.

'A sickle?' Eusden suggested.

'Yes. A sickle. He was working alone a long way from the farm. He bled to death. So, blood killed both of them. I sometimes wonder if it really was an accident. Perhaps he couldn't live without my mother. We'll never know. Before I was six months old, they were both gone.'

'We saw the eloquently inscribed tombstone at Tasdrup church.'

The hint of sarcasm caused a pursing of Elsa's

139

lips and a stiffening of her tone. 'I want you to understand us, Mr Eusden. My grandfather was nearly seventy when my father died. He had to start running the farm again. Tolmar helped him as soon as he was able to. By the time he was sixteen, he was in charge. He has been ever since. The farm, the company, the family. He never really had a childhood. He's always had . . . responsibilities. He got his engineering qualifications through evening classes. Life was easier for Lars and me. Tolmar made sure it was. We owe him a lot. More than we can ever repay.'

'Do you remember Clem Hewitson visiting you at Aksdenhøj?'

'Yes. He was a friend of Great-Uncle Hakon. That's all I know.'

'Maybe Tolmar knows more. As head of the family.'

'Maybe he does.'

'About that load of pre-war Finnish currency Great-Uncle Hakon's housekeeper stole from him, for instance.'

'You shouldn't listen to Karsten Burgaard, Mr Eusden. He has no . . . sense of proportion. He had a nervous breakdown last year. Did he mention that to you?'

'No. But the story about the Finnish currency's true, isn't it?'

'I believe so.'

'So, why do *you* think your great-uncle had millions of markkaa stashed away?'

'I have no idea.'

'And why did Lars try to stop the disinterment ceremony at Roskilde?'

'It was a silly protest about Christiania. He can be very silly.'

'Karsten doesn't think that explanation stacks up.'

'Naturally.'

'Frankly, neither do I.'

'Why are you so interested? Mr Hewitson claims to be researching the history of his family. What are you doing?'

'Helping him.'

'And does that explanation . . . 'stack up'?'

It did not, of course, as Eusden was painfully well aware. What he said next was a reflex attempt to deflect the question. He regretted it as soon as the words were out of his mouth. 'I expect you and Lars — and Michael too — all have substantial shareholdings in Mjollnir. You must be pleased how well they're doing. I suppose that means Tolmar effectively employs you too — along with all those Lithuanians.'

Elsa carefully replaced her cup in its saucer. She treated Eusden to a contemptuous frown. 'You should advise Karsten Burgaard to drop his campaign against Tolmar. And I'd advise you to have nothing to do with it. If family history really is Mr Hewitson's motive, you should ask him how much it matters to him. Michael's probably told his father about you by now. Tolmar will phone me, asking what you're doing. I'd like to be able to tell him you're already on your way home.'

'You can say that if you want.'

'But will it be true?'

'I don't know. It's up to Marty.'

141

'Don't try to push Tolmar, Mr Eusden. He doesn't like being pushed.'

'What will he do if he is?'

'Push back. Harder.'

'He sounds a tough customer.'

'As tough as he needs to be.'

'But would asking a few questions about Great-Uncle Hakon's friendship with Marty's grandfather really count as 'pushing'?'

'He wouldn't welcome your questions, Mr Eusden. I can assure you of that. You appear to be a sensible man. Listen to what I'm saying. Don't try to contact my brother. Or any of us again. Leave us alone. And persuade your friend to do the same.'

'Well . . . ' Eusden cobbled together a non-committal smile. 'Thanks for the advice.'

* * *

They parted outside. After watching Elsa stride away across the square towards the shopping centre, Eusden wandered listlessly into the cathedral and sat down in the nave to think. According to the leaflet he had picked up at the entrance, the walls of the cathedral had been covered with frescoes until the Reformation, when they had been whitewashed over. Parts of several had been uncovered since and restored. He gazed around at the colourful scenes that had been exposed — fragments of illustrated tales, pieces of a greater whole. It was human nature to want the full story, the picture complete. But sometimes human nature had to give way to

142

worldly wisdom. And this, he sensed, was such an occasion.

★ ★ ★

The afternoon was growing colder as it faded towards evening. Eusden went back to the hotel and was told Marty had still not returned. He did not know what to make of his friend's continued absence, but there was nothing he could do about it. He went up to his room and lay on the bed, watching the sky darken over the cathedral. He rehearsed the argument he would present to Marty for heeding Elsa Støvring's advice. He convinced himself Marty would be forced to agree. And then, at some point, he fell asleep.

★ ★ ★

For the second time that day, he was woken by the telephone. His guess, as he picked up the receiver, was that Marty was calling him from his room. He was unsure of the time, but night had fallen outside. Marty surely had to be back by now.

But he was not. 'Reception here, Mr Eusden. We've had a call from the hospital. Your friend Mr Hewitson was taken there this afternoon after collapsing in the street. They say he's seriously ill.'

17

'Seriously ill,' the receptionist had said. And seriously ill was exactly what Marty looked, propped up in bed in a side ward of Århus Kommunehospital, attached to various drips, drains and monitors. According to the nursing staff, he had had a stroke, the severity of which only time could determine. He managed a smile when he saw Eusden, but it was a lopsided effort. The right side of his face was slack and it was his left hand he raised in greeting.

'Hello, Richard,' he said, his voice slurred as if he was drunk. 'Good to see you.'

'What the hell happened, Marty?'

'A stroke, but not of luck. I was crossing the road to the bus stop after leaving that pizza parlour and I suddenly had to bolt for it when some bloke in a van nearly ran me over. Don't let anyone ever tell you the Scandinavians are careful drivers. That one certainly wasn't. Anyway, I made it to the bus stop, but then this splitting headache came on. Literally blinding. Next thing I know, I'm on the deck. Somebody took pity on me and called an ambulance. I can't remember much about arriving here. They did a CT scan and found the tumour. The poor buggers assumed I didn't know about it. I got the full breaking-bad-news works. They've lost interest now they know I was expecting something like this to happen.'

'How bad is it?'

'Too soon to say. The paralysis is only partial.' Marty flexed his right arm feebly from the elbow. 'And there's a good chance it's temporary. I might be back in fair working order within twenty-four hours. Then again . . . I might not.'

Eusden sighed. 'I'm sorry we . . . parted the way we did, Marty.'

'Don't worry about it. You were right. I should've levelled with you. But better late than never, hey? I've got something to tell you.'

'Would it involve Vicky Shadbolt, by any chance?'

'Ah.' Another half of a grin. 'You know.'

'The hotel asked me to bring you this message.' Eusden handed Marty a sheet of paper on which was printed: *Mr Hewitson — Vicky rang. She has arrived safely and will wait for you to contact her.* 'Where is she?'

'Copenhagen.'

'Doing?'

'Me a favour. She has the attaché case, Richard. The real one, I mean. The one you took to Brussels was a ringer.'

'*What?*'

'Keep your voice down or they'll chuck you out for upsetting me. It was like this. I felt pretty certain Werner was planning to double-cross me, so I set a trap for him. Bernie mocked up an old case with Clem's initials on it. I'd never seen the original till Aunt Lily showed it to me, so I knew neither you nor Gemma were going to spot the difference. As for the contents, Bernie arranged with a Danish VAT fraudster he knows to have some letters written in old enough ink on old enough paper to pass muster. I don't know what's in them. The text of a few Hans Christian Andersen fairytales, I expect. Werner will have had the pleasure of reading them by now, so he'll be on the warpath. Which means we have to move quickly. Or, rather, you do. I'm obviously not going anywhere for the moment.'

'What exactly do you expect me to do?'

'Go to Copenhagen and collect the case from Vicky. She'll be staying at the Phoenix Hotel. Take Burgaard with you. Better still, get him to drive you there. He can translate the letters. It won't take much to persuade him. I wasn't sure about roping him in, but I haven't got much choice now.'

'Why didn't you get Bernie's Danish friend to translate them?'

'Because I don't know what's in them. Bernie's a good mate, but if he got the idea there was serious money to be made, he might be tempted to cut me out. He *is* a crook, after all. Tell Vicky I've gone back to Amsterdam. *Don't* tell her I'm languishing here or she'll be on the next train. I've been the man of her dreams since we first met in the visiting room at Guys Marsh Prison. Terminal illness seems only to have added to my romantic aura.'

'Not as far as I'm concerned, Marty. You've been stringing me along the whole time. It's only because you're a sick man I'm not holding you up against a wall and demanding an apology.'

'You can have the apology. I *am* sorry.'

'Why didn't you tell me what was going on

146

— what was *really* going on?'

'I was afraid you'd be so pissed off if you found out I'd used you as a decoy that you'd leave me in the lurch and jet back to your desk in Whitehall.'

'For the record, I'd decided to do just that this afternoon. We had a visit from Elsa. She gave me a sob story about how Tolmar held the family together after their parents died. She also gave me a stark warning against prying into his affairs.'

Marty closed his eyes and leant his head back against the pillow. He let out a long sigh. He had aged another few years in the course of the day. He was fading almost visibly and Eusden knew he was clinging to the mystery Clem had left behind him as he would to a life raft in a cold, cold sea.

'Are you all right, Marty?'

'Yeah. Just thinking.'

'She said I should ask you how much this really matters to you.'

'Nice one.' Marty opened his eyes, the lid on his right eye sagging pitifully. 'She doesn't know about the letters, though, does she?'

'No.'

'It's good to have an ace up our sleeve. I always preferred poker to bridge. Whereas you ... ' He rubbed his face like someone waking from a deep, dream-laden sleep. 'Sorry. Rambling. Which I mustn't do. How much does this matter? You tell me, Coningsby. If you want to walk away from it, you can. But wouldn't you like to find out what's in those letters?'

'Of course I would. But — '

'And we have to get Vicky out from under. So . . .'

'I'll go, OK?' Eusden shook his head in wonderment at his own foolhardiness. 'I'll go to Copenhagen.'

'Good man.'

'And I'll get Burgaard to translate the letters. Beyond that . . .'

'No promises?'

'None.'

'It's a deal. Fetch my bag from the hotel. There's a sunglasses pouch in it. The key's inside.'

'The key?'

'To the attaché case. Try to keep up, Richard, please. Help yourself to Werner's money and drop the bag off here. I'll need a few things from it. Then get yourself and Burgaard on the road to Copenhagen. Time, as you mandarins no doubt say on a Friday afternoon, is of the essence.'

★ ★ ★

Eusden called Burgaard from a hospital payphone. Marty's ban on using mobiles now seemed worryingly sensible. The conversation was brief and guarded.

'Hallo.'

'Richard Eusden here, Karsten. I have a proposal for you.'

'Don't say any more, Mr Eusden. Come round.'

'I'll be there in about an hour.'

'OK. Just you? What about Mr Hewitson?'

'He won't be coming.'

'Good. He makes me uncomfortable. See you later.'

★ ★ ★

Eusden had a lot to accomplish in the hour he had set aside. He travelled to the hotel by taxi and kept the cab waiting while he packed and checked out, then doubled back to the hospital to drop off Marty's bag. He had another question he wanted to put to Marty, but the duty nurse said he was asleep and not to be disturbed, so Eusden left the bag with her and headed for Burgaard's flat. He knew the answer to his question, anyway. Marty had sent Vicky Shadbolt to Copenhagen because that was where Mjollnir had its headquarters. He had had Tolmar Aksden in his sights from the very start.

18

'So, are you in?'

It was Eusden's concluding question after he had told Burgaard what they wanted him to do. The letters were waiting for them in Copenhagen: the letters that might reveal the secrets Hakon Nydahl and his friend Clem Hewitson had taken to their graves. It was unthinkable that Burgaard would spurn the chance to read them, but Eusden needed his explicit agreement. They were sitting in Burgaard's stuffy, overheated, under-furnished lounge, drinking coffee and eyeing each other uncertainly.

'I need a yes or a no, Karsten.'

'You're still not telling me everything, Mr Eusden.'

This was true. Eusden had omitted the Anastasia dimension altogether. If the letters touched on the subject, so be it. If not, it was an unnecessary complication. And he sensed simplicity was the key to securing Burgaard's assistance. He either wanted to read the letters or not. Everything else could wait.

'But I guess that doesn't matter. These letters could be the breakthrough I need.'

'Exactly.'

'Then I'm in, of course.'

'Good.'

'When do you want to leave?'

'Right away?'

'We don't need to do that. It's three hours to Copenhagen, whether you drive or take the train. If we leave now, we'll arrive in the middle of the night. This friend of Mr Hewitson . . . '

'Vicky.'

'Yes. Vicky. She'll wait till morning, won't she?'

'Well . . . yes.'

'OK, then. We'll leave at four. Catch her early. I'll drive us if you like. But I need to sleep first. You're welcome to use the couch. It folds out.'

This was not as Eusden had envisaged. But he could not push matters without revealing Straub might be on their trail. 'Thanks very much,' he sighed.

'Hold on.'

Burgaard rose and marched out to the kitchen with something decisive evidently in mind. Eusden glanced around the lounge. Apart from one framed print of a flat, wintry landscape — Burgaard's native Falster, perhaps — there was nothing in the way of decoration. The flat felt sterile and impersonal: a place to sleep and little else, its tenant a solitary obsessive, his existence pared down to the thesis that would give it meaning. Eusden was really not sure he wanted such a man for a travelling companion. But his wants were far from paramount.

Then Burgaard was back, with a bottle and

two shot glasses. 'Schnapps, to toast our . . . collaboration.'

The schnapps was poured, the toast drunk, the glasses refilled. Eusden sipped the second. It was a heavy, bitter concoction.

'I'm sorry Mr Hewitson is ill.' Burgaard's tone was singularly lacking in conviction.

'Me too.'

'Perhaps that's why he was so . . . abrupt.'

'Perhaps so.'

'When I told you about all that Finnish currency Nydahl had in his apartment, I got the feeling . . . Mr Hewitson already knew.'

'I'm impressed.' Eusden smiled. 'He did.'

'But you didn't.'

'No.'

'So, he doesn't trust you with everything.'

'He does now he's in hospital. He's got no option.'

'Are you sure?'

'Sure enough. The important thing is he's trusting me — *us* — with the letters.'

'Yes. The letters.' Burgaard moved to the uncurtained window and gazed out at the nightscape of the university: lights gleaming in laboratories and seminar rooms and halls of residence, scattered between gulfs of darkness. 'The letters must hold the answer, I suppose. *Men kan det nu have sin rigtighed?*'

'Sorry?'

'Excuse me. I said, 'Can that really be true?''

'Only one way to find out.'

'Yes.' Burgaard drained his glass. 'Only one way.'

After a frugal supper of pickled herring and cheese washed down with beer, Burgaard headed for bed, promising to set his alarm for 3.30. Eusden could hardly keep his eyes open by then. The couch was more comfortable than it looked and he plunged at once into a deep sleep.

★ ★ ★

He woke several times only to relapse into slumber before his dulled senses registered that daylight was streaming greyly through the window. Then he started violently awake, aware that it had to be a good deal later than 3.30. A glance at his watch told him a story he could not at first believe. It was nearly half past ten in the morning. He and Burgaard should by rights have arrived in Copenhagen several hours previously. Instead —

He was alone in the flat. His instincts told him as much even before he checked. Burgaard's bed had not been slept in. His coat, which had been hanging on a peg inside the front door, was missing. He had gone. Eusden's brain was still struggling to engage a functioning gear. A residuum of drowsiness was sapping his thought processes. He could not understand what had happened. Where was Burgaard? What was going on?

He immersed his face in a basin of cold water. That seemed to clear some of the fug and enable him to concentrate. He must have been drugged to have slept so long and so soundly, which explained why he still felt woozy. Burgaard had slipped something into his schnapps or his beer. But why? Only one answer sprang to mind: he wanted the letters for himself. Collaboration did not interest him. Eusden had told him where they were and he must have backed himself to be capable of talking Vicky Shadbolt into handing over the attaché case. Eusden checked his coat pocket. The key was still there. He had not mentioned it last night. That was a very small mercy, however. The locks on the case could easily be forced.

Maybe it was not too late to warn Vicky. Eusden raced to the phone and called the Phoenix in Copenhagen. They rang her room, but got no answer. They could not say whether she was in or out. He left a message which he could only hope she would heed: *Agree to nothing until I arrive — Richard Eusden.* But Burgaard had already had half the morning to implement whatever plan he had cooked up.

The flat comprised a lounge, kitchen, shower room and two bedrooms, one of which Burgaard had converted into a study. It contained his desk and computer, plus half a dozen cardboard boxes crammed with papers. Each box had a word scrawled on the side in felt-tip: *Mjollnir, Aksden, Saukko,*

154

Nydahl. Eusden wondered if he should look through them or try to access Burgaard's computer files in search of clues to his intentions. But every minute he remained was a minute lost in reaching Vicky. And Burgaard would surely have taken anything vital with him. There was simply no time to sift through his records.

As Eusden turned to leave the room, he noticed a chart stuck to the back of the door. It was a family tree for the Nydahl/Aksden clan, meticulously drawn up with names and dates. Eusden remembered Burgaard drawing their attention to the lack of birth dates on the Aksden tombstone at Tasdrup church. But here they all were. He must have gone to the registration authorities to obtain them.

'*Is there more to it, Karsten?*'

'*Oh, yes. Much more.*'

Eusden pulled the chart free of its blobs of Blu-Tack and rolled it up. He would study it later. Then he headed back to the lounge, grabbed his coat and bag and made for the front door. He had no idea of the times of trains to Copenhagen, but he would have to be on the next one. Stopping at the hospital to tell Marty what had happened was not an option. Let him believe his old friend was in control of the situation, at least for a little longer. His recovery was not going to be aided by knowing Burgaard had outwitted them.

Eusden was halfway out of the door when the

155

telephone rang. After a moment's hesitation, he hurried back to answer it.

'Hello?'

'Karsten?' A male voice, probably Danish, with an edge of suspicion — or anxiety.

'No. He's . . . not here. Who's calling?'

'Henning Norvig. Who's that?'

'Richard Eusden.'

'Are you a friend of Karsten's?'

'Er . . . yes.'

'Do you know where he is? He was supposed to be here an hour ago. I've tried his mobile, but it's switched off.'

'Where's 'here'?'

'I'm in a coffee shop. The one he said.'

'In Copenhagen?'

'Of course in Copenhagen.'

'What are you hoping to discuss with Karsten?'

There was a pensive pause before Norvig replied. 'Who did you say you were?'

'Richard Eusden. A friend . . . from England.'

'Where's Karsten?'

'I don't know.'

'What are you doing in his flat?'

'I've . . . been staying with him. But listen. Were you hoping Karsten could give you some information about . . . Tolmar Aksden?'

Norvig's tone suddenly became flat and defensive. 'I don't know what you mean. Ask Karsten to call me if you hear from him.'

'You'd better give me your number.'

'He's got my number.'

'Give it to me anyway. Just in — '

But Norvig was giving nothing. He had rung off.

★ ★ ★

Eusden could not decide if Burgaard's no-show for his rendezvous with Norvig was good news or bad. It suggested his plans had misfired in some way. Maybe Vicky had proved a tougher nut to crack than he had anticipated. Maybe — But all speculation was idle. He had to get to Copenhagen pronto and head off whatever Burgaard had in mind. There was nothing else he could do.

★ ★ ★

He struck lucky with the buses on the main road and made it to the railway station with ten minutes to spare before the next train to Copenhagen. He managed one payphone call to the Phoenix before boarding and this time Vicky's number was engaged. He did confirm his message had been delivered, however. And clearly she *was* there. He consoled himself that his effort had not been entirely in vain.

★ ★ ★

As the train eased out of the station, Eusden unrolled Burgaard's family tree of the Nydahls and Aksdens. It was nothing if not precise, printed out, presumably, from one of his computer files.

157

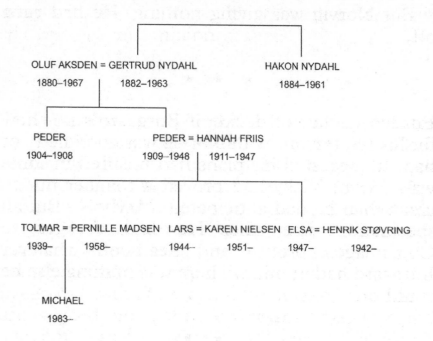

OLUF AKSDEN = GERTRUD NYDAHL
1880–1967   1882–1963

HAKON NYDAHL
1884–1961

PEDER
1904–1908

PEDER = HANNAH FRIIS
1909–1948   1911–1947

TOLMAR = PERNILLE MADSEN   LARS = KAREN NIELSEN   ELSA = HENRIK STØVRING
1939–   1958–   1944–   1951–   1947–   1942–

MICHAEL
1983–

So, there had been two Peder Aksdens. One had died in infancy. Then the new child had been given his dead brother's name. There was nothing particularly unusual in that. But the first Peder did not feature on the Tasdrup gravestone, which was odd. He must have a separate grave, which Burgaard had not shown them. Eusden stared long and hard at the chart. Nothing else of significance leapt out at him. Eventually, he rolled it up again and stowed it in his bag.

Then he checked his coat pocket to confirm the attaché case key was still there, which of course it was. He sat back and tried to calm himself. Vicky Shadbolt was a level-headed young woman. There was no reason why she should fall for whatever story Burgaard had cooked up. There was no reason, in short, why

158

the day should end as badly as it had begun. Once he was in Copenhagen, he could put everything back on track. And in three hours he would be there.

KØBENHAVN

19

Copenhagen central station was the disorientating mix of stairways, walkways, neon-lit signs and swirling crowds to which Eusden was now becoming inured. He had been to the city once before, in the summer of 1989, with Gemma and her niece, Holly, who had begged to be taken to see the Little Mermaid on her home turf (or surf) after repeated viewings of the Disney film. Holly had enjoyed herself, undismayed by the modest scale of the Mermaid's statue and revelling in the carnival delights of Tivoli Gardens. Unfortunately, she was the only one who had a good time, Gemma and Richard's relationship having entered a fractious phase which wonderful, wonderful Copenhagen had proved powerless to resist.

At least, however, it had been warm and sunny. The afternoon into which Eusden emerged from the station was bleak and grey and sleety. An entrance to Tivoli met his gaze on the other side of the street, but the park was closed for winter. He was alone. Squabbling with Gemma did not seem such a bad memory when set against his problems of recent days. And the queue for a taxi looked long and cold.

★　★　★

The Phoenix was at the smart, sophisticated end of town, near Kongens Nytorv and the royal palace. Gleaming marble and glittering chandeliers greeted the weary traveller. Eusden supposed Marty had stayed there during his research visit, true to his policy of dying in comfort. It was hard to imagine Vicky Shadbolt feeling at ease in such opulent surroundings, but love, especially the hopeless, unrequited kind, works many a wonder, as Eusden well knew.

Nor, as it dismayingly transpired, had Vicky lingered long in four-star luxury. 'Ms Shadbolt checked out earlier, sir,' the receptionist announced.

★   ★   ★

Eusden booked himself in because he was, for the moment, too frustrated and confused to know what else to do. His top-floor room, set in the mansarded roof, gave him a wide-ranging view of numerous other roofs, but nothing else. The panorama of louring sky, domes, gables, slates, gutters, chimneys and fire-escapes was a metaphor for his plight. He could see a lot, but none of what really mattered.

He had no choice now but to contact Marty and tell him the worst. Where Vicky might be he had no idea. What had become of the attaché case he did not care to ponder. The situation was about as bad as it could be.

But putting Marty in the calamitous picture was far from straightforward. Århus Kommunehospital did not connect callers with its patients at the caller's say-so. A message would be passed. Hr Hewitson, if he was well enough and *if* he wanted to, would phone him back. The urgency of the message was noted. But nothing could be guaranteed. Hr Hewitson was, for the record, 'reasonably well'.

★ ★ ★

Nearly an hour passed, during which Eusden raided the minibar, flicked through innumerable brain-rotting TV channels and stared out at the slowly darkening roofscape. Then the telephone rang.

'What gives, Richard?' Marty asked, sounding disconcertingly chirpy.

'She's not here, Marty. I've lost her.'

'I know. Because what you've lost I've found.'

'Sorry?'

'Vicky's here. With me. Well, not with me at the moment, as it happens. She's gone to find a hotel. But she'll be back.' Marty sighed. 'I have her word on it.'

'Vicky's in Århus?'

'When neither of us showed up this morning in Copenhagen, she phoned the Royal again. They told her where I was. As I predicted, she reacted by rushing straight to my bedside. Chairside, I should say. I'm feeling — and moving — a lot better today.'

'You sound better too.'

'Yeah. Which is quite some achievement, considering I've had to worry all day about what the hell you've been up to. What kept you?'

165

'Burgaard. He slipped me a Mickey Finn and left me to sleep it off at his flat. I assumed he'd planned to drive here and try to persuade Vicky to hand over the case. Hasn't she seen him?'

'Nope.'

'That doesn't make any sense. He knew she was here and he had a head start on me. What was the point of drugging me otherwise?'

'I don't know. But we'll obviously have to find a new translator. I told you Burgaard was a wrong'un.'

Eusden could not actually recall any such warning, but he was in no mood to argue. He was merely relieved that chance and circumstance had somehow contrived to rescue them. 'What do we do now, Marty?'

'We keep our heads, Coningsby, that's what we do. Everything's under control, thanks to my powers of foresight. Vicky deposited the case, as per my instructions, with a lawyer in Copenhagen I primed before I left. I'll phone him and say you're authorized to collect it on my behalf.'

'Why the hell didn't you tell me that before I set off?'

'Because I reckoned the less there was for you to let slip to Burgaard the better. And I reckoned right, didn't I? Now, listen. The lawyer's name is Kjeldsen. Anders Kjeldsen. He's got an office in Jorcks Passage, off Strøget. Y'know? The main pedestrian street through the centre.'

Eusden sighed. 'I know it.'

'Right. Wait till the morning. I might have trouble raising him this afternoon. Then pick up the case and sit tight till I arrive. Book me a

166

room at the Phoenix.'

'You're coming here?'

'Why not? The doc seems to think I should be well enough to leave by tomorrow. Besides, they know there's nothing they can do for me. I'm a model of mobility for someone thirty years older and I'm back elocuting like a BBC announcer. I'll get Bernie to order Vicky home and then I'll train it to Copenhagen. Oh, and I'll ask Kjeldsen to recommend a translator. We need to make up for lost time.'

'Aren't you supposed to be taking it easy?' Marty's buoyant tone was beginning to worry Eusden. He sounded positively exuberant, like a man given a second chance — or a last one.

'Don't worry about me, Richard. I'll be fine.'

★ ★ ★

But Eusden *was* worried. And not just about Marty. The thrill of the chase was wearing thin. Every step they took to uncover Clem's secret past seemed to leave them just as far from doing so as they had always been. He could not justify extending his absence from the office beyond a week, even to humour a dying friend. Despite Marty's disdain of his Civil Service career, there actually were working commitments he had to honour. It was already Thursday and he could not devote more than another couple of days to Marty's escapade. An end, of some kind, was fast approaching.

★ ★ ★

167

Until the next day, however, there was nothing for Eusden to do but wait. He struck out into the Copenhagen dusk on foot, hoping to walk off his fretfulness. He had to maintain a stiff pace just to stay warm. His route took him through the palace square, where Holly had hooted with laughter when he was bawled out by one of the guards for trespassing over the chain round the statue of yet another Danish king on horseback (Frederick V, this time), and out along Amaliegade to the waterside park where the Little Mermaid was to be found, perched on her rock. The fountain at the entrance to the park, where they had lazed in the sun, was frozen solid and the moat round the old citadel further in was iced over. Flecks of snow were drifting down from a darkening sky. It was cold enough to deter all but the hardiest.

A couple of joggers were nonetheless doing circuits of the citadel's protective earth rampart. Eusden set out to walk a circuit himself before returning to the city centre. As he progressed, he noticed another man walking behind him, keeping pace with him more or less exactly. Casting his mind back, he realized he had seen the same man loitering in the palace square while he had read the plaque on the plinth supporting Frederick V's statue. He was a stockily built fellow of thirty-five or so, dressed in jeans, leather jacket and woolly hat. Eusden told himself the idea that he was being followed was absurd, but when he stopped to gaze out over the harbour, so did his shadow. When he moved, the shadow also moved.

168

Disquieted but still keen to believe it amounted to nothing, Eusden cut short his circuit and hurried back out of the park. On his way in he had spotted a ferry heading across the harbour from a nearby jetty, so he took a hopeful turn in that direction as he left and was rewarded by the sight of another ferry easing in towards the jetty. He quickened his pace.

Turnaround was swift on the 901 harbour bus, destination — for Eusden — immaterial. He paid his thirty kroner and took a seat. There were only two other passengers aboard, a couple of tourists in day-glo parkas. But a breathless latecomer joined them at the last minute.

The man pulled off his woolly hat as he sat down and glanced round at Eusden. His hair was short-cropped blond, his face wide, eyes blue and watchful, jaw square. He slid a rolled newspaper out from his jacket and began to study a front-page article. It was the same pink business paper — *Børsen* — that Burgaard favoured. Eusden glimpsed a familiar name — Mjollnir — in a headline.

The ferry made two stops on the other side of the harbour in Christianshavn, before crossing back again, to Nyhavn. If Eusden stayed on beyond Nyhavn, it meant a longer walk back to the Phoenix. He debated with himself what to do, then yielded to impulse. 'I'm getting off at the next stop,' he said, tapping his shadow on the shoulder. 'What about you?'

The man turned and looked at him with an ironical tilt of one eyebrow. 'The same,' he said softly.

'You've been following me.'

'Have I?'

'Yes.'

'OK.' The admission was casual, as if the fact was self-evident. 'I have.'

'Why?'

'I thought you might be meeting Karsten.' There was a brittleness in his voice Eusden felt sure he recognized. 'I'm Henning Norvig, Mr Eusden. We talked earlier. And now we need to talk again.'

20

The river bus moved away from the jetty through a slush of half-formed ice and headed south. Eusden and Norvig stood watching it go, Eusden's mind racing to calculate what he should or should not admit. Norvig smiled at him, as if sensing his indecision.

'*For fanden, jeg fryser.*'

'What?'

'You don't speak Danish, Mr Eusden?'

'No.'

'I said I'm fucking freezing. Why don't we talk over a drink?'

★　★　★

The Nyhavn canal was lined with bars and restaurants — a colourful, crowded scene in summer, as Eusden well recalled, with diners and drinkers massed at outdoor tables, admiring the elegant yachts tied up along the quay. A cold late afternoon in February provided a different, bleaker scene, relieved only by the reds and yellows of the house fronts and the enticingly twinkling lights of those bars that were open for business. They went into the first one they came to after leaving the jetty.

'This morning, Karsten was supposed to be here in Copenhagen, but wasn't, and you weren't supposed to be in Århus, but you were,' Norvig

171

opened up as they settled at a table. 'Now he's still not here. But you've arrived instead. What am I supposed to make of that?'

'How did you know who I was?' Eusden countered, aware that this was to be a game of who could learn more from the other.

'Karsten said he had to meet a woman at the Phoenix this morning before coming on to meet me. When I still hadn't heard from him this afternoon, I went there to see if they knew anything. The name Burgaard meant zip to them. But Eusden? That was different. You left while I was standing at reception. The guy on the desk pointed you out to me.' Norvig lit a cigarette, proffering the pack to Eusden, who waved it away. 'So, I've answered your question. How about answering mine?'

'Well, like you say, Karsten's gone missing. I'm . . . trying to track him down.'

'Because . . . '

'He's a friend.'

'Yeah. Right.' The barman approached. Norvig ordered a beer. Eusden nodded his assent and he made it two. 'How'd you meet him?'

'Economics conference . . . at Cambridge . . . last year.'

'Uhuh. And since then you've become . . . an item?'

'An item?' Belatedly, Eusden caught Norvig's drift. 'No. I — '

'Karsten's bøsse, Richard. Gay. I'm surprised you didn't know that. As a friend of his.'

'How do you know?' It was the best retort Eusden could manage.

'We've met a few times. It was obvious.'

'Maybe you're just his type and I'm not.'

'Stop fucking me about, Richard. Where's Karsten?'

'I don't know.'

'Well, that makes two of us, doesn't it?'

'Yes. It does.'

The arrival of the beers imposed a brief truce, which Norvig extended by sitting back in his chair to savour his first swallow and following it with a thoughtful pull on his cigarette. 'What do you do for a living, Richard?'

'I'm a civil servant. I work at the Foreign Office in London.'

'The Foreign Office?'

'That's right. What about you?'

'Freelance journalist.'

'Were you meeting Karsten . . . about a story?'

'Yes. I was.'

'Did it involve . . . Tolmar Aksden?'

Norvig smiled. 'There it is. That name. Tolmar Aksden. The Invisible Man. Yup. He was on the agenda, all right. Are you interested in him . . . officially?'

'Officially? No. I'm on leave.'

'Which you're spending with your not very close friend Karsten Burgaard in Århus. In the middle of winter. That's great. That's so likely.'

Eusden did not react. He was beginning to feel he might actually win out in the trading of points. 'Have you written about Aksden before?'

'Most Danish journalists have. Tell me, Richard, do you ride?'

'What?'

'Do you ride? Horses, I mean.'

'No.'

'Well, I do. And when I was a boy I worked weekends at a stable. It means I know what horseshit smells like. So, stop shovelling it in my direction, OK? Karsten told me two Englishmen had shown up in Århus with access to highly sensitive information about Tolmar Aksden. The sort of stuff that might knock a couple of digits off Mjollnir's share price for starters. I'm guessing you're one of those two Englishmen. Let me finish before you deny it. Karsten's given me titbits about Mjollnir quite a few times. It's his specialty. He made it clear this was something big, something . . . shattering. He needed to collect some documents from a woman staying at the Phoenix. Then we were to meet. He never showed. Now, I don't know what you had going with him and I don't necessarily care. If you've got the documents, I might be in the market for them, no questions asked. You understand?'

Eusden stared Norvig down as calmly as he could before responding. 'I don't have the documents.'

'Do you know where they are?'

'I — '

A phone began ringing in one of Norvig's pockets. '*Skide*,' he said, pulling it out. '*Unskyld Hallo?*' His face was a mask during the conversation that followed, to which he contributed little beyond *ja, nej, okay* and *tak*, interspersed with sighs suggesting that something other than unalloyed good news was being

174

conveyed to him. He said nothing at first after ringing off, gazing at a point in the middle distance somewhere over Eusden's shoulder. Then he murmured, 'Karsten's dead.'

'*What?*'

'He hit the wall of a flyover on the motorway near Skanderborg early this morning. High-speed crash. No other car involved. Apparently.'

The shock was followed for Eusden by the sickening realization that if Burgaard had not decided to go it alone, they would have been together in his car. 'What do you mean — 'apparently'?'

'It was around four thirty. Empty road. No witnesses.'

'You're suggesting . . . he was run off the road?'

'Did I say that? Fuck, this is serious.' Norvig contemplated just how serious over several nervous drags on his cigarette. 'No, no. They wouldn't. It must have been just . . . an accident. Maybe there was ice. Maybe he was . . . careless.'

'But you don't think so.'

'*I don't know.*' Norvig grabbed his phone again, as if intending to make a call. Then he thought better of it and clunked it down on the table. 'You got here safely, didn't you?' He glared accusingly at Eusden as he stubbed out his cigarette.

'Look, I know nothing about this. I came by train.'

'Who's the woman at the Phoenix?'

'She's gone.'

'What's her name?'

175

'It doesn't matter. *She* doesn't matter.'

'The other Englishman, then. Who's he?'

'Marty Hewitson. He *is* a friend.'

'Where is he now?'

'Århus. But he'll be here soon. Probably tomorrow.'

'OK, Richard. Let's be cool. Accidents happen. Business is business. You get these . . . documents. You have them in your hand. They deliver what Karsten promised. Then I'm interested. Anything less — any more horseshit — forget it.' Norvig scribbled a number on a corner of the front page of *Børsen*, tore it off and passed it to Eusden. 'Call me. *If* there's something to talk about. If not, we never met. Understood?'

'Understood.'

★   ★   ★

They left separately, at Norvig's insistence. Eusden would actually have been glad of his company, rattled as he was by the news of Burgaard's death. An accident was credible enough. He had probably been speeding, his head full of plans to smooth-talk Vicky into handing over the case. Or maybe he had just fallen asleep at the wheel. Oh, yes, an accident was the obvious explanation. And yet . . . And yet.

Eusden walked up Nyhavn to Kongens Nytorv, the broad square at the eastern end of Strøget. He was in no hurry to return to his cramped room at the Phoenix. He knew he ought to eat something but had no appetite. His senses were alert, his nerves jangling. He felt exposed and helpless and foolish for feeling so. Marty needed to be told what had happened, but there was no way Århus Kommunehospital was going to put a call through to him at this hour. Eusden was trapped between the urge to act and the certainty that for the moment there was nothing he could do.

He remembered there was a quaint old bar on the square where he had passed a carefree hour one summer's night back in 1989: Hviids Vinstue. He went in, found it reassuringly unaltered and drank several glasses of the house schnapps. Alcohol soon began to take the edge off his anxiety. Burgaard had killed himself in a car crash. That was all there was to it. There was no second car, no van speeding past, then swerving in, causing Burgaard to swerve and skid. It was —

A van. Marty had nearly been run over by one before collapsing at the bus stop. Maybe there really was a plot. And maybe the plotters had banked on Eusden being in the car as well. Maybe they had only just — or still not — learnt that Burgaard had left him behind. His mouth dried as he found himself actually crediting the possibility.

He decided to go back to the Phoenix. Cramped or not, his room promised safety if nothing else. He finished his schnapps and left.

★ ★ ★

A short distance round the square was Copenhagen's grand hotel, the d'Angleterre, where he and Gemma had taken Holly for tea one afternoon, earning the girl's highest accolade: 'Ace.' Eusden paused to gaze in at the hotel's warmly lit windows. It was to occur to him later in the evening that if he had lingered at Hviids just a little longer or alternatively pressed straight on in that instant, he would not have been standing there when a couple emerged from the d'Angleterre into the chill night air.

The woman was fur-coated and -hatted, amply proportioned in height *and* girth, dark-skinned and statuesquely poised. She stopped, instantly aware of Eusden's astonished gaze and that the cause of his astonishment was not her, but her companion, a tall, middle-aged man in a dark-green overcoat. 'Do you know this gentleman, Werner?' she asked in a lilting American accent. 'He certainly seems to know you.'

'Oh, yes.' Straub gave Eusden a wintry smile. 'We know each other.'

21

'Richard Eusden. Regina Celeste.' Straub managed the introductions with measured aplomb. Eusden had already guessed that the lady was the moneybags from Virginia Straub had been planning to sell the contents of the case to. What he could not guess was who he planned to say Eusden was. But he did not have to wait long to find out. 'Richard's a friend of Marty Hewitson's.' This was a surprise. Did he propose to continue by explaining how he had treated Marty? No, of course not. 'Is he here with you in Copenhagen, Richard?'

'It would be *so* convenient if he was,' said Regina as Eusden hesitated over an answer. 'The man's been leading us quite a dance.'

'Has he really?'

'I'm afraid it's the kind of thing I've gotten used to since I became an Anastasian.'

'A what?'

'A true believer in the Grand Duchess. Anastasia Manahan. Maybe you don't call yourself that over here. But I guess you must be one if you're a friend of Mr Hewitson's. So, where's he hiding himself?'

'I . . . don't really know.'

'What has brought you to Copenhagen, then?' asked Straub.

'The same as you, perhaps.'

'Why don't you join us for dinner, Mr

179

Eusden?' Regina trilled. 'We were on our way to a restaurant. Close by, you said, Werner?'

'Very.'

'We could talk there. And from what Werner tells me, we have plenty to talk about.'

'Indeed,' said Straub. His guarded expression revealed some scanty hints of alarm mixed with determined opportunism. He obviously did not want Eusden to tell Regina what he had done to Marty, though it was equally obvious he would merely utter a horrified and doubtless credible denial. But nor did he want Eusden to melt away into the night. Happenstance had given him the chance to probe his opponent's defences, albeit vicariously. But it was a chance that cut both ways.

'I'd be delighted to join you,' said Eusden.

★ ★ ★

The Restaurant Els was indeed close by, only a short step away across the square, a candle-lit haven of mirrors and murals presided over by the prominently mounted head of the eponymous elk. Or, as Regina described him, 'My Lord, a moose.'

They were settled at a table and supplied with menus. Aperitifs were declined on the grounds that champagne had already been quaffed at the d'Angleterre. Eusden was happy to go along with this. His head was clear despite the amount he had already drunk, but he needed to keep it that way. He and Straub had embarked on a battle of wits, with Regina

180

as unwitting referee. Predictably, Straub sought to seize the initiative, by creatively refashioning the circumstances of their acquaintance for Regina's benefit.

In this version of events, Eusden had been visiting Marty in Amsterdam after hearing of his friend's illness, and had accompanied him to Hamburg at the time of Marty's initial discussions with Straub about selling his grandfather's archive of Anastasia-related documents. 'I had intended we would both meet you in Frankfurt, Regina,' Straub continued, 'but Marty was too ill to travel. Then came our great surprise, Richard. When we arrived at the Vier Jahreszeiten yesterday, we found you and Marty had left.'

'Destination unknown,' put in Regina, who had discarded her furs to reveal a helmet of tightly curled gold-grey hair, a dramatically cut purple dress and an extravagant amount of cleavage. With her huge eyes and vast, ever-present smile, she seemed cast as cheerleader for Straub's artfully ad-libbed cover story. He had clearly done a lot of thinking on his feet over the past couple of days. And now it was Eusden's turn to do the same.

Supplied with extra thinking time by the taking of food orders and Straub's theatrical agonizing over the wine list, Eusden embarked on what he reckoned was the least implausible of many improbable explanations for his presence in Copenhagen. 'Marty persuaded me to go home on Tuesday. He said he was feeling a lot better and I had work commitments to deal with in London, so it seemed to make sense. I booked a flight and set off for the airport. But I had the impression Marty was trying to get rid of me. I don't know why. It worried me. In the end, I couldn't go. I thought he might be sicker than he was letting on. So, I doubled back to the hotel. To my surprise, they said he'd just booked out. The porter said he'd put him in a taxi to the central train station. I headed off there. It's a big place, as you know, Werner. Logically, I stood no chance of finding him. But, as it happened, I *did* spot him, boarding a train to Copenhagen. It pulled out before I could make it to the platform. I had no idea what he was up to. I still haven't. I followed by the next train. I've been trawling the hotels since I arrived, trying to track him down. So far, without any luck.'

'You've rung him, of course,' Straub prompted.

'No answer. It's very strange. I'm seriously concerned about him.'

'Of course.' Straub nodded sympathetically. 'I was annoyed, I must admit, that he left Hamburg without warning, but from what you say he may be in some . . . difficulty.'

'What kinda difficulty might that be?' asked Regina. It was undeniably a good question.

'Who can say, my dear?' Straub took on an air of stoic puzzlement. 'We must be grateful, however, that chance has come to our aid so . . . remarkably. Perhaps we will be able to reach an agreement with Marty after all.'

'It's certainly remarkable that you decided to come to Copenhagen,' Eusden observed.

'I insisted,' said Regina, sailing once more in

her full-rigged fashion to Straub's rescue. 'I couldn't pass up the chance of taking a look at Hvidøre.'

'The Dowager Empress's home in Klampenborg.' Straub shot Eusden a triumphant little smile. 'We plan to visit it tomorrow.'

'You might like to come along,' said Regina. Eusden was beginning to sense she thought he could prove a more agreeable companion than Straub. 'How'd that be, Werner?'

'It's up to Richard. He may have . . . other plans.'

'I'm not sure,' said Eusden, thinking rapidly ahead. 'Could I let you know?'

'It'd be great if you could make it,' said Regina. 'I've read such a lot about the place. There's a tower on the roof where they say Dagmar used to sit and look out to sea — east, towards Russia. So much scheming and intriguing went on there. It's where all those grand dukes and duchesses put their treacherous heads together and signed the Copenhagen Statement denying Anastasia her birthright. I see the month of Dagmar's death — October 1928 — as the turning point in the whole conspiracy against my cousin. Wouldn't you agree, Werner?'

'I would,' Straub replied, breaking off from a carefully considered appraisal of the wine.

'By your cousin,' Eusden began, 'you mean . . .'

'Anastasia. Well, cousin-in-law, I guess I oughta say.'

Regina set off without the need of further encouragement on an animated but not always coherent account of the intertwined genealogies of the Bonaventures of North Carolina (Celeste was merely her married name) and the Manahans of Virginia that carried them through their starters and some of the way into their main courses. Eusden eventually deduced that much of her vagueness about assorted aunts, uncles and cousins once, twice or thrice removed was designed to obscure the year, indeed the decade, of her birth. The impression she gave of her age fluctuated bewilderingly. Sometimes she seemed no older than forty, sometimes no younger than sixty. Exactly when she had married her late husband, Louis Celeste, of Celeste Ice Cream Parlors fame, was far from clear. What was clear was that she had applied her well-funded widowhood to a pursuit of proof positive that Anna Anderson, late-life bride of her distant cousin Jack Manahan, was in truth Her Imperial Highness the Grand Duchess Anastasia Nikolaievna.

'I had the pleasure and honour of attending her eightieth birthday party, in June 1981, and her very last birthday party, two years later. There never was a doubt in my mind she was who she said she was. You know true royalty when you meet it.' (Eusden idly wondered how extensive Regina's experience of true royalty actually was.) 'I had my suspicions about the whole DNA thing right from the start, let me tell you. The Martha Jefferson Hospital finds a sample in a jar of Anastasia's intestine they'd supposedly had standing on a shelf in a cupboard since an operation back in 1979. We don't have any way of knowing how securely it'd been stored over the intervening decade and then some, but there surely were strange things going on in Charlottesville in the fall of 1992, when the hospital came out and said they had no sample, then changed their mind and said they did after all. I dug out a report in the *Daily Progress* of a janitor at the hospital being knocked cold by an intruder one night in November of that year, a few weeks before the change of mind. Now, what do you make of that, Richard?'

'That's the *Charlottesville Daily Progress*,' Straub smilingly clarified.

'Poor cousin Jack was dead by then, thank the Good Lord,' Regina proceeded, sparing Eusden the need to say what he made of anything. 'If he hadn't been, I reckon the rank injustice of that whole proceeding would have finished him. The Romanovs saw their chance to foist that Polish peasant identity on Anastasia and they grabbed it. You can't deny their thoroughness. They must have thought they had her right where they wanted her for all time. But now we *might* be able to turn the tables on them. If we can find your friend Marty Hewitson, Richard.'

'You've no idea where he is?' pressed Straub.

'None at all, I'm afraid. I'll just have to . . . keep looking.'

'He didn't happen to open the case in front of you, did he?' asked Regina.

'No such luck. I actually know less about the contents of the case than I imagine you two do.'

'There will come a time to put that right if you

can locate it,' said Straub, holding Eusden's gaze.

'Amen to that,' said Regina, gulping some wine. 'It could be the answer to our prayers.'

★ ★ ★

Regina ordered a dessert after the main courses were cleared, then adjourned to powder her nose. It was a moment Eusden had been preparing himself for, when he and Straub could drop the pretences they had both been maintaining. And Straub had obviously been preparing for it as well. The second the door leading to the loo had closed behind her, he launched in.

'Are you about to repay me the ten thousand euros, Richard?'

'What do you mean?'

'Marty did not leave the money at my mother's apartment. Therefore he accepted it. But he did not deliver his side of the bargain. Where is the *real* attaché case?'

'I don't know.'

'You expect me to believe that?'

'Not really. But it *is* true. He told me the real case would be waiting for him in Amsterdam and he encouraged me to go back to London, just like I told you. But I'd been put through so much by then, thanks to the tricks the pair of you were playing on each other, that I decided, after setting off for the airport, to go back and demand a slice of whatever the contents of the case were worth. I reckoned I was owed that.'

Straub's expression suggested he found this credible. Eusden was gambling that a confession of greed on his part would be more convincing than anything else. 'I've been ripped off by Marty a good few times over the years. The ten thou is obviously nothing to what he and you think the letters will fetch. So, why shouldn't I get a cut of the action?'

'It is a . . . an understandable point of view, I would have to admit.' Straub's tone hinted at relief. He was comfortable with venality. He knew how to deal with it.

'I thought I'd be able to catch up with Marty at the station, but he wasn't waiting for the Amsterdam train. It was pure luck I was in the right place at the right moment to see him leaving for Copenhagen.'

'And where was that place, Richard?' The question, apparently trivial, was actually a vital piece of fact-checking. Straub knew Hamburg central station as well as a native of the city would.

'I was on the walkway above the platforms. The train had pulled out before I could get down there. I came after him by the next train. I think it's pretty clear he had the case sent here, not Amsterdam, don't you?'

'It would seem so, certainly.'

'If I can find him, I'm sure I can persuade him to rope me in. But into what? He's a dying man, Werner. I doubt he has the energy, the resources or the contacts that you do. In other words, I doubt he can get such a good price as you can.'

A smile flickered around Straub's mouth. 'Are

you proposing some kind of deal, Richard?'

'I'll track him down sooner or later. When I do, I'll contact you. After all, you're the one with the buyer in place, aren't you?'

'True. And here she comes.' Straub dropped his voice to add: 'Very well, Richard. We are agreed. But find Marty soon, no? The quicker the better, for all of us.'

'You two are looking kinda conspiratorial,' said Regina, as she shimmied back into her seat. 'Should I be worried?'

'Not at all,' Straub replied. 'Though perhaps disappointed. Richard has decided he cannot visit Hvidøre with us. He must continue his search for Marty.'

'That's a real shame. But . . . I guess I understand. Lord knows, we want you to find him.'

'We do,' Straub glanced intently at Eusden. 'Indeed we do.'

22

Eusden woke early the following morning. He made some coffee and drank it gazing out at the roofs of Copenhagen, wondering whether it was better to wait for Marty to call, or try his luck again with the Århus Kommunehospital switchboard. There was a lot Marty had to know before he arrived in Copenhagen. *If* he arrived in Copenhagen. The news that Straub was lying in wait for him might put him off the idea altogether.

In the event, Marty rang before Eusden had finished his coffee. 'I'm getting out of here today whatever the sawbones says,' he announced. 'I spoke to Kjeldsen yesterday. He's expecting you at eleven o'clock. I also spoke to Bernie. He's going to insist Vicky returns to London. When he snaps his fingers, his daughters jump, so that's a problem solved. I guess it'll be mid- to late afternoon before I make it to Copenhagen. No need to come to the station. I'll meet you at the Phoenix.'

But that was not a good idea, as Eusden set about explaining. And Straub's presence in the city was not the only cause of concern. Eusden also had to report Burgaard's fatal so-called accident. Marty was singularly unfazed, however.

'You're getting better at this, Richard. You seem to have played Werner like a fish on a line. Well, you're right, of course. The Phoenix is

189

obviously out. I'll tell you what. There's a Hilton at Copenhagen airport. I'll book myself in there. It's only a quarter of an hour from the centre and it's the last place Werner would think of looking; he knows I won't be coming or going by plane. He'll be out at Klampenborg with Regina when you collect the case and you can take a taxi to the Hilton later. I'll call you when I know what time I'll be arriving. As for Burgaard, good riddance. It's bloody lucky you weren't in the car. But don't overreact. It sounds like it was an accident to me: cocky Karsten putting his foot down when he should've been watching out for black ice. Serves the treacherous little bastard right. No sense getting paranoid at this stage, hey?'

'There's a big difference between paranoia and commonsense cautiousness.' Marty's unquenchable optimism was beginning to worry Eusden. Did the doctors have him on happy pills? 'What about Straub's hired heavy? Shouldn't we be asking ourselves if he might start tailing me now his boss knows I'm in town?'

'He was Hamburg muscle, Richard. Werner will have paid him off long since.'

'You're sure of that, are you?'

'OK, OK. Keep a look out for a bald-headed seven-footer built like a wardrobe. You see what I'm saying? He was taken on for enforcement, not surveillance. You'd spot him a mile off. Werner would have to buy in local talent and he can't do that while he's got his hands full with the widow Celeste. Everything's going to be fine. I'm feeling heaps better and Kjeldsen's going to

190

give you the name of a reliable and discreet translator. We've got this in the bag, Richard. All we have to do is hold our nerve.'

★　★　★

It sounded simple and straightforward as Marty put it. Eusden could not decide whether it was merely the pessimistic nature Marty had always attributed to him that accounted for his suspicion that the day would somehow turn out otherwise.

Marty would certainly not have been surprised that he arrived absurdly early for his appointment with Kjeldsen — and without a single glimpse of a mountainous German dogging his footsteps. Jorcks Passage was an old, narrow arcade of shops, with offices on the floors above, linking Strøget with Skindergade. A board at the Strøget end listed the occupants, among them Anders Kjeldsen, *advokat*. Eusden whiled away half an hour in a nearby coffee shop, then went up in a tiny wheezing lift to the lawyer's third-floor lair.

The door was ajar. Eusden tapped and pushed it further open. A heavily built man clad in a baggy grey suit was standing by the window of a disorderly, paper-strewn office, smoking a cigarette and gazing down into the arcade. He had long hair matching the colour of his suit tied back in a ponytail and a doleful, jowly, pockmarked face. The creak of the door seemed to catch his attention where the tap had not.

'Mr Eusden?' His voice was gravel mixed with treacle.

191

'Yes. Hr Kjeldsen?'

'Yes. I am Kjeldsen. Come in.' He moved to a desk piled high with paperwork, propped his cigarette in an ashtray and turned to offer his hand. They shook. 'Sit down. Please.'

Eusden sat as directed. Kjeldsen flopped into the chair on the other side of the desk and shaped an awkward smile. His manner suggested they were meeting to discuss a divorce or the death of a close relative. Eusden smiled himself, seeking to lighten the mood. 'Marty spoke to you yesterday?'

'Yes.' Kjeldsen gave an exaggerated, donkeyish nod. 'He did.'

'So, can I have the case, please?'

'Do you have ID?'

'Sure.' Eusden pulled out his passport.

'*Tak.*' Kjeldsen examined it briefly. Then his face crumpled into an apologetic grimace. 'There is a problem, Mr Eusden.'

'What kind of problem?'

'A serious one. I do not have the case.'

'Sorry?'

'*I* am sorry.'

'What are you saying?'

'Last night . . . ' Kjeldsen broke off for a drag on his cigarette, then began again. 'Last night, someone came in here, opened the safe' — he waved a hand towards the safe in question, which stood, stout and apparently secure, in a corner — 'and stole some money, some jewellery I was storing for another client . . . and Mr Hewitson's case.'

Eusden was at first too shocked to respond.

Apart from anything else, there was no sign of a break-in or of any damage to the safe. For this at least Kjeldsen was swift to supply an explanation.

'As I told the police, it is obvious who is responsible. I had to dismiss my secretary last week. She had become . . . unreliable. She knew the combination of the safe. She must have made a copy of the keys. So, she stole the money and the jewellery and took the case . . . hoping it contained something valuable. I did not mention the case to the police. I wanted to speak to you or Mr Hewitson first. Did it, in fact, contain something valuable — something easily converted into cash, I mean?'

'Not easily, no.' Eusden shook his head at the thought of how he was going to break this to Marty.

'Then, she will probably get rid of it. She has probably already got rid of it. She knows I will send the police after her. Do you want me to tell them about it?'

'Why not?' Eusden threw the question at Kjeldsen like an accusation, though technically the only thing he could accuse him of was poor choice of secretarial staff.

'There are sometimes reasons why people do not wish such things to be told to the authorities. But I will make sure the police know about the case, now that you have . . . cleared up the matter.' Kjeldsen shrugged helplessly. 'Though, as I say, she will almost certainly have thrown it away by this time. A canal; a skip: anywhere. There is nothing to say who owns it, so — '

'How do you know that?' The Foreign Office had honed Eusden's analytical nature even if it had stifled his soul. There was a flaw in Kjeldsen's logic. And he sensed it might be significant.

'Know what . . . Mr Eusden?' Kjeldsen asked, blatantly prevaricating.

'How do you know there's nothing to say who owns the case? Your former secretary will have broken it open before discarding it, won't she? How do you know Marty's name and address aren't inside?'

'I believe . . . ' Kjeldsen resorted to his cigarette to win further thinking time, but it had burned down nearly to the filter and he was obliged to content himself with a protracted stubbing-out. Then: 'I believe Mr Hewitson said so. Or perhaps it was . . . Ms Shadbolt.'

The man was lying. That was clear. But just how big was the lie? 'Where does your ex-secretary live, Hr Kjeldsen?'

'I cannot tell you that, Mr Eusden. It is . . . a police matter. But they have promised to be in touch. And I will contact you as soon as I hear from them. You are staying at the Phoenix, yes?'

'Yes.'

'Well, wait for news, then, Mr Eusden. I am sorry. I am . . . professionally embarrassed. For such a thing to happen is . . . awful. I blame drugs. I suspect my secretary had . . . an expensive habit. Employing the right people . . . is so difficult.'

'That's certainly true.' Eusden looked Kjeldsen

194

in the eye, letting him understand exactly what he meant.

'Please give my . . . personal apologies . . . to Mr Hewitson. All we can do now is . . . hope the police get lucky.'

'You'll let them know about the case?'

'Most certainly.'

'What's the name of the officer handling the inquiry? I'd like to speak to him myself.'

Kjeldsen smiled unreassuringly. 'Why would you want to do that?'

'To make sure every effort to find the case is being made.'

'You can leave that to me, Mr Eusden. I am sorry to say many of our police officers speak rather poor English. There would be confusion, miscommunication. I will ensure they do everything they need to do. And I will keep you informed of progress.'

'If there is any.'

'Let us say *when* there is any.' Kjeldsen's smile remained fixed in place. 'We must try to be positive.'

23

Eusden was angry and frustrated. Angry because he was convinced it was Kjeldsen, not his phantom former secretary, who had stolen the case. Frustrated because he could hardly go straight to the police and confirm they had received no report of a burglary in Jorcks Passage, then lodge a complaint against Kjeldsen, since Marty had made it very clear police involvement in his activities was something he wished to avoid at all costs. Kjeldsen probably knew that and was trading on it. He must have broken into the case and judged he could make a lot of money out of the contents. *How* was an open question; how *soon* the more pressing issue.

Eusden had to speak to Marty. That at least was certain. But he would not be able to do so for several hours. A message was waiting for him at the Phoenix. *Catching 11.54 train. Meet you at the hotel 4 p.m. Marty.* Marty had been phoneless since Straub had stolen his mobile and would probably have kept it switched off even if he still had one. It would be mid-afternoon before Eusden could speak to him, out at the airport Hilton, a long way from Jorcks Passage.

That could not be helped. Or could it? Eusden suddenly realized there was a way to bring forward their meeting by an hour or so. Marty would have to change trains at Copenhagen

196

central station and Eusden could be waiting for him when he stepped off the 11.54 from Århus.

That still left him with time to kill, which he resolved to put to good purpose by harassing Kjeldsen. He returned to Jorcks Passage and phoned the slippery lawyer on his mobile while loitering in the entrance to the arcade.

'Any news from the police, Hr Kjeldsen?'

'I regret not, Mr Eusden. But it is only . . . just over an hour . . . since we met. These things take time. Have you spoken with Mr Hewitson?'

'Not yet. He's arriving in Copenhagen later today. I'm sure he'll want to hear your explanation of what happened in person.'

'Bring him to see me, then. What time will he be arriving?'

'We could be with you by five.'

'I will expect you then.'

★   ★   ★

Eusden continued to loiter and was rewarded, twenty minutes later, by the sight of Kjeldsen emerging from the entrance to his office's stairway at the other end of the arcade, muffled up in loden coat and scarf. He ambled off along Skindergade and Eusden followed at a discreet distance. There were enough shoppers about, and office workers taking their lunch breaks, for him to blend into the background. Kjeldsen appeared wholly unconcerned about the possibility of being tailed. An Italian restaurant in a small square nearby turned out to be his destination.

197

There was a café opposite, where Eusden nabbed a table with a suitable eyeline and washed a toasted sandwich down with a couple of Tuborg Grøns while monitoring Kjeldsen's activities. He emerged from the restaurant after forty minutes or so, patting his stomach contentedly like someone who had put away a *table d'hôte* lunch with expeditious relish. Eusden had already settled up and exited with the lawyer still in view. Kjeldsen popped into a secondhand bookshop for a few minutes on his way back to Jorcks Passage, rounding off an entirely convincing performance in the role of a man going about his customary lunchtime routine.

Eusden had learnt nothing of the remotest value. He decided to head for the station.

★ ★ ★

The 11.54 from Århus, it transpired, ran through to the airport. Marty would not be getting off; Eusden would be getting on. He eked out an hour sipping Americanos in a coffee shop, watching the sky darken over Rådhuspladsen. Sleety rain began to fall. Eventually, the time came for him to return to the station.

He bought his ticket and went down to the platform. The Københavns Lufthavn train rolled in on schedule at 3.20. He did not catch sight of Marty as the carriages decelerated past him, but there were lots of people rising from their seats to disembark. He would find him soon enough.

The train had an eight-minute lay-over before

proceeding. Eusden waited to see if Marty would get off for a smoke. He did not. Eusden boarded at the front and started working his way through the carriages. He reached the other end before the eight minutes were up. Marty was nowhere to be seen. He started retracing his steps. The train left the station. Still he could not find Marty.

It was a twelve-minute run to the airport. Long before the train arrived, Eusden knew what he could not quite bring himself to believe: Marty was not aboard.

★ ★ ★

He lingered in the foyer of the airport Hilton until gone four o'clock, clinging to the frail hope that Marty would still turn up. He did not. And it became bleakly obvious to Eusden that he was never going to. He phoned Århus Kommunehospital, who confirmed Marty had discharged himself earlier in the day; he was no longer any concern of theirs.

But he remained of great concern to Eusden, who could think only of sinister explanations for his friend's failure to make it to Copenhagen. He phoned the Phoenix. There was no message for him, from Marty or anyone else. But Marty's earlier message had been clear. *Catching 11.54 train.* Yet he had not caught it. Or if he had, he had got off somewhere along the way. Why would he have done that? He had been intent on reaching Copenhagen that day. Hence his insistence on leaving the hospital. He would surely not have got off the train unless compelled to do so.

Eusden thought about the van that had nearly run Marty down and the car crash that had killed Burgaard. He wondered, chillingly, if he had made it to Copenhagen himself only because whoever had run Burgaard off the road thought he was in the car as well. That made his survival an oversight, a discrepancy to be corrected as soon as it was deemed convenient.

He walked out of the hotel into the airport, his legs rubbery, his mind scrambled. He felt like a ghost, drifting through the bustling crowds of travellers: the businessmen, the tourists, the family groups. Everyone was going somewhere, except him. He gazed up at the departures board. Every destination offered him an escape route. He could return to London. He could jet off to Bangkok or New York or . . . anywhere he chose. He had the means. He had the opportunity. And he had the reason. All he needed to do now was walk up to one of the airline desks, flash his credit card . . . and fly away from all this.

But the only ticket he bought was back into Copenhagen. He would face down Kjeldsen and offer him a stark choice: surrender the case, or answer to the police. And then . . . he did not know. But he did know it was time to act.

★   ★   ★

It was only just gone five when he reached Jorcks Passage. Night was falling, icy cold and

200

cellar-damp. He hurried up the stairs to Kjeldsen's office, unwilling to wait for the lift. The door was closed and locked. There was no answer to his knock. He was barely late for their appointment. But Kjeldsen was gone — probably long gone.

Eusden hammered on the door and shouted the lawyer's name. It made no difference. There was no response. He stood on the drab, dully lit landing, breathing heavily, sweating despite the chill of the air. He was enraged as well as frightened. He either fought back now or he fled. It was as simple as that. And for Marty's sake, if not his own, there was really no choice.

But he stood little chance of accomplishing anything on his own. He needed help. And he needed it fast. He pulled out his phone, squinted at the number written on the scrap of pink newspaper in his hand and stabbed at the buttons.

24

'Tell me again what's in the case,' said Henning Norvig.

They were sitting in Norvig's car in a quiet residential street in the well-to-do suburb of Hellerup, parked in the deep shadow of a silver birch tree a short distance from the large semi-detached house where Anders Kjeldsen lived alone, following the break-up of his marriage. Norvig was, as Eusden had hoped, very well-informed. Though not quite as well-informed as he would clearly have liked.

'I'm only helping you because you promised me dirt on Tolmar Aksden, Richard. So, are you sure you can deliver?'

'Doesn't the fact that Kjeldsen's stolen the case prove the contents are hot stuff?' Eusden responded, coughing in the stale, smoky air. Norvig had worked his way through half a pack of Prince cigarettes since they had stationed themselves outside Kjeldsen's house. The lights were on and the lawyer's Volvo was parked in the drive, but of the lawyer himself there had been no sign. His telephone number had been engaged on the two occasions Norvig had dialled it, suggesting he was not passing an idle evening in front of the television. Beyond that, Norvig had nothing to go on but what Eusden had told him. And it was cold, dark and late.

'Hot stuff,' he murmured. 'But can it burn Aksden?'

'The case contains letters, sent to Marty's grandfather before the War by Aksden's great-uncle. Who else but Aksden *could* such letters damage?'

'I don't know. And you don't know.'

'But Kjeldsen knows.'

'*Ja*. I guess so. And he's what I'd call . . . *hensynløs*. Without scruple.'

'How in God's name did Marty come to choose him?'

'He advertises in the *Copenhagen Post* — the English language paper. Plus he's cheap.'

'How do you know so much about him?'

'He works for people I write about.'

'And what sort of people are they?'

'Crooks in suits — cheap suits, naturally.'

'Who hire a lawyer to match?'

'Exactly.'

'What's he up to, do you think?'

'Agreeing a sale. Negotiating. Fixing a price.'

'Who with?'

'Someone who doesn't like Tolmar Aksden. A rival. An enemy. There's quite a queue.'

'What can we do?'

'Nothing. Until he moves. It could be a long wait.'

'Why don't we just knock on his door?'

'Because if he doesn't have the case with him, we're fucked. OK?'

'OK.'

Eusden sighed and stretched his neck back against the headrest. Fatigue had sucked all the fury and much of the anxiety out of him. There was a chance — a reasonable one, given his track record — that Marty had simply changed his plans without telling him. And there was an even better chance that Norvig could turn the tables on Kjeldsen. Local knowledge was a precious commodity. All that was required to deploy it effectively was patience. He took out his phone and reread the message he had found on it earlier. *Phone me asap*, timed a few hours ago. It was terse even by Gemma's standards. Presumably she wanted to rebuke him for keeping her in the dark about what he and Marty were up to. Actually, he thought, she ought to thank him. But putting her right on that, like so much else, would have to wait.

'What do you know about Mjollnir's takeover of Saukko Bank, Henning?' he asked, determined to learn as much from Norvig as he could.

'Not as much as I would if Karsten had made our meeting, I reckon. The deal didn't seem so big when it happened, but it's . . . kind of grown since. Saukko's St Petersburg subsidiary gives Mjollnir a slice of more Russian companies than anyone realized at the time. That's partly why their share price has gone up like a rocket. First Scandinavia. Now Russia. They just keep expanding. There's no stopping the Invisible Man. But anyone can read that in the papers. Every fucking day you can read it. What I need is — ' Norvig broke off. Eusden sensed his sudden tension. '*Look*.'

A pair of headlamps threw their light into the street from the driveway of Anders Kjeldsen's house. The lawyer's Volvo eased into view, took a stately right turn and moved away from them. Norvig started up and followed at a cautious distance.

'He's heading for the main road. Going back to his office, maybe?'

'Why would he do that?'

'To pick up the case. I'm guessing it never left the safe. I doubt he had anywhere so secure at home. The question is: why pick it up now?'

'Because whoever's buying it won't wait until tomorrow?'

'Has to be. But they'll meet on neutral ground, for sure, so we should be able to catch Kjeldsen on his own at Jorcks Passage. Easy, no?'

'If you say so.'

'I do, Richard, I do. Trust me.'

★   ★   ★

Eusden had no option but to trust Norvig. Kjeldsen joined the main road, as predicted, then followed a link road to the expressway into Copenhagen. Traffic was thin, visibility good. Keeping the Volvo within sight but hanging far enough back to avoid attracting the driver's attention was a straight-forward task. It became more complicated when they neared the city centre, with its light-controlled junctions. But Norvig knew what he was doing, judging any stops behind Kjeldsen perfectly so as to keep to the shadowy stretches between streetlamps.

205

Besides, as he pointed out, the lawyer had no reason to think he might be followed. He was probably confident he had thoroughly outwitted Eusden.

* * *

But confidence can easily become complacency. Kjeldsen steered an undeviating course for Jorcks Passage, driving down past the old university buildings and the cathedral to Skindergade, then turning into the service yard next to the northern entrance to the arcade.

Norvig drove blithely by, glancing into the yard as he went. He pulled over a short distance further on and stopped. 'Wait here for my signal,' he ordered, then climbed out and jogged back along the pavement. Eusden turned round to watch him.

Norvig slowed as he neared the turning into the yard. Hugging the wall, he peered cautiously round the corner, then waved for Eusden to follow and vanished from sight.

* * *

Norvig was standing with his back against the service door into the building, holding it open, when Eusden caught up with him. The yard was full of shadow and silence, broken only by the tick-tick-tick of the Volvo's cooling engine. Norvig smiled, his teeth gleaming ghostly pale through the gloom.

'Kjeldsen was in a hurry,' he whispered. 'He

left the door to swing shut and didn't wait to check. Come on.'

They took the stairs two at a time to the third floor. The landing was in darkness, but light glimmered at the edges of the lawyer's office door.

'I doubt he's locked himself in.' Norvig's fingers curled cautiously round the handle. 'Shall we join him?' Without waiting for a response, he jerked the handle down and flung the door open.

Kjeldsen looked up in alarm from behind his desk. His mouth dropped open. The only light in the room was from a green-shaded reading lamp to his right that turned his face into a pantomime-mask of horror. In front of him, on the desk, stood a battered old leather attaché case. The lid was half-raised, casting towards them a crooked shadow that began to waver in time to the trembling of Kjeldsen's hand.

'*Skide*,' he said numbly, staring at Eusden. Then he let go of the lid. It fell shut. And on it, revealed by the light from the lamp, Eusden could see the stencilled initials CEH.

25

Kjeldsen flopped down into the chair behind his desk and spread his hands in a gesture of helpless admission. 'What can I say, Mr Eusden? I know this . . . looks bad.'

'It looks what it is,' said Eusden, advancing across the room. 'Theft. Which you're not going to get away with.'

Kjeldsen started to say something to Norvig in Danish, but the journalist cut him short. '*Speak English.*'

'If you prefer.' He smiled uneasily. 'Norvig and I know each other, Mr Eusden. We've met . . . in court.'

'And we'll be meeting in court again after this.' Norvig smiled back at the lawyer. 'You're in deep shit, my friend.'

Kjeldsen shrugged, as if he regarded that as an open question. 'You know what the case contains, Mr Eusden?'

'Letters from Hakon Nydahl to Clem Hewitson, written in the nineteen twenties and thirties.'

'Ever seen them?'

'Not till now.' Eusden raised the lid. There they were in a slewed stack, resting on the faded green baize lining of the case: cream notepaper, filled with black-inked writing in a copperplate hand, the separate sheets of each letter held together with old paper clips that had begun to

208

rust. Eusden picked up the topmost letter. There was an address: *Skt Annæ Plads 39, København K, Danmark*; a date: *den 8. marts 1940*; and a salutation: *Kære Clem*. Beneath, sentences in Danish swam across his gaze. It was bizarre but self-evidently true. Clem could read Danish.

'That's the most recent,' said Kjeldsen. 'The first one's at the bottom. They cover fourteen years.'

Eusden shuffled through the stack to check. He glimpsed dates in receding order through the thirties and twenties until he came to the first: *den 3. januar 1926*. The handwriting was slightly more precise than fourteen years later, the strokes of the pen slightly stronger. But Nydahl and Clem had been on first-name terms from the start. That had not changed. *Kære Clem* . . .

'You've read them?' asked Norvig.

'*Ja*.' Kjeldsen nodded. 'The whole lot.'

'What are they about?'

'*Who* are they about, you mean.'

'OK. Who?'

'Peder Aksden. Tolmar's father. The letters are a record of his life, from sixteen to thirty.'

'A record?'

'*Ja*. Everything about him. What work he did on his parents' farm. The girls he dated. The books he read. His hobbies. His opinions. His health. His . . . personality.'

'That's crazy. Why would Peder Aksden's uncle write letters about all that to a retired British policeman?'

'They're not really letters to a friend, Henning. They're reports. For posterity.'

'Why should . . . posterity . . . be interested in Peder Aksden?'

'Good question. Listen to this.' Kjeldsen gestured to Eusden for permission to handle the letters. He was behaving meekly and contritely, like someone who accepted that the game was up — or like someone secure in the knowledge that he had the ace of trumps up his sleeve. 'Is it OK . . . if I read to you from one?'

'Go ahead.'

Kjeldsen eased out a letter from the stack, checked the date, then pulled it free. 'November, 1938. Nydahl is worried about Peder's engagement to a local girl. This is what he says. Henning can translate for you, Mr Eusden.'

Kjeldsen read the words in Danish, pausing at intervals to allow Norvig to catch up in English. 'He is determined . . . to marry Hannah Friis . . . in the spring . . . Oluf and Gertrud are worried . . . and want me to decide . . . if I should stop him . . . I remember you and I discussed . . . the problems a family might cause . . . and whether we should ever allow him . . . to have one.' At that Kjeldsen stopped reading and slid the letter back into place.

'What 'problems' is he talking about?' asked Eusden.

Kjeldsen smiled thinly. He seemed to be growing more confident, despite the lack of obvious cause.

'They emerge when you work your way through the letters,' he replied enigmatically.

'Why don't you just tell us?' demanded Norvig.

'There's not enough time.'

'Bullshit.' Norvig leant across the desk and looked Kjeldsen in the eye. 'We've got all night.'

'No. I'm supposed to meet the buyer in less than an hour. I'm already supposed to have phoned him to find out where.'

'Bad luck.'

'For you also, Henning. And for you, Mr Eusden. Very bad luck. I'd be willing in the circumstances to share the proceeds with you.'

'There's not going to be a sale,' Eusden declared, reaching for the case.

But Kjeldsen was quicker. He grasped the handle tightly and declared bluntly, 'Twenty million kroner.'

For a second, no one moved or spoke. Kjeldsen looked at Norvig, then at Eusden. He moistened his lips with his tongue.

'Twenty million kroner,' he said softly. 'A little over two million pounds at the current exchange rate. That's the price I've agreed. So, what do you say, gentlemen? Is it still no sale?'

'Who's your millionaire buyer?' demanded Norvig.

'It's safer if you don't know.'

'It's never safer for me not to know something.'

'In this — '

The burbling of Kjeldsen's mobile, which lay on the desk next to the case and began circling on its axis as it rang, cut him off. He looked enquiringly at Norvig and Eusden.

'My buyer must've got tired of waiting for me to call.'

'Let him go on waiting,' said Eusden. He pushed the lid of the case down and let his hand rest on the rim, a few inches from Kjeldsen's grip on the handle.

'If I don't answer, he'll send his people to look for me.'

'Answer it,' said Norvig.

Eusden glanced round at him suspiciously, wondering for the first time whose side the journalist was on. Norvig shrugged.

Kjeldsen picked up the phone. '*Ja?* . . . No, there's nothing wrong.' He was speaking English, Eusden noticed, not Danish. Perhaps that meant his buyer was not Danish. 'OK.' Kjeldsen let go of the case, grabbed a pencil and scrawled something — a single word — on a notepad. 'OK . . . Yes, I can find it . . . I understand . . . See you there.' He rang off and glanced at his watch. 'I'm due to meet them in half an hour.'

'You can meet them whenever you like,' said Eusden. 'But you're not taking this with you.' He swung the case round and grasped the handle.

'Hold on.' Norvig slammed the flat of his hand down on the lid of the case. 'Let's all just . . . take a moment.'

'Good idea,' said Kjeldsen, sounding like the very embodiment of honey-toned reason. 'Twenty million kroner in cash is something to take a moment to think about, no? A lot of problems solved. A lot of pleasures bought. Ours to share three ways.' He glanced at Norvig. 'Or two.'

'This case belongs to Marty Hewitson,'

Eusden declared. 'There's no — '

'What do the letters tell us, Anders?' put in Norvig. 'What exactly do they tell us?'

'A secret. With a twenty million kroner price tag on it. Ten for you. Ten for me. The clock's ticking, Henning.'

'I'm taking this,' said Eusden, tugging at the case. 'Don't try to — '

The blow took him unawares. Norvig's fist landed sideways under his jaw, jerking his head back. He staggered away from the desk, the case no longer in his grasp. Before he had recovered, Norvig was between him and the desk.

'I can't let you fuck this up for me, Richard,' he shouted, pushing him against the wall. 'Twenty million's too much to say no to.'

'The case isn't yours to sell,' Eusden gasped. He was pinned by the shoulders and unable to move. Norvig was evidently stronger than he looked. 'You agreed to help me.'

'I am helping you. Give it up, Richard. Take your share.'

'I don't want a *share* of anything.'

'Then take nothing. It's up to you.'

'*You bastard.*'

'Karsten's dead. Your friend Marty's probably dead too. It's time to get smart. Time to cash in.'

'*Let go of me.*'

'OK.' Norvig released him. 'OK.' The journalist took a step back. He was breathing through gritted teeth. A rivulet of sweat was trickling down his temple. There was sorrow in his gaze. But it was not enough. Every man has his price. And Norvig's was on the table. 'Like

213

you say, Richard, I agreed to help you. But now I'm helping myself. Don't try to stop me.'

'Give me that case.' All Eusden could cling to was a stubborn assertion of his rights as Marty's representative. He lunged towards the desk. Kjeldsen grabbed the case and jumped up from his chair.

Suddenly, Eusden's leading foot was whipped from under him. Norvig added a shoulder barge to the trip. Caught off-balance, Eusden fell. He glimpsed the shadow-etched rim of the desk, closing fast, as he pitched sideways. Then . . . nothing.

26

Eusden was swinging gently in a hammock. His head ached. A glaring sun threatened to dazzle him if he opened his eyes. He did not know where he was, except that it was pleasanter by far than the alternative he sensed he would become aware of if he roused himself. Something was pushing him, setting off the sway of the hammock. His head throbbed. The threatening sun turned cold. His recent memories began to reassemble themselves into a more or less coherent knowledge of time and place. Then full recollection flooded into his mind like blood into a starved limb. He opened his eyes.

A slightly built, sad-faced Asian man in a boiler suit, wearing a baseball cap with the New York Yankees logo on it, stopped nudging him with the toe of his grubby trainer and stared down at him. He said something in oddly accented Danish. Eusden could only respond with a groan.

He pushed himself up on one elbow and blinked about him. They were on the landing outside Kjeldsen's office. There was the door to his right, firmly closed, and the sign: A. KJELDSEN, ADVOKAT. Pallid overhead light fell on the bare walls and floor and the nervous expression of the man in the boiler suit — the office block's caretaker, presumably — who repeated what he had just said, to no more comprehensible effect.

'Do you speak English?' Eusden asked, in a slurred voice he hardly recognized as his own. There was a smell of whisky in the air and it seemed to be coming from him. His gaze drifted to an empty bottle of Johnnie Walker lying by his elbow. It looked like Kjeldsen had raided his filing cabinet supply of the hard stuff to set him up as a drunken intruder. No doubt his appearance fitted the bill. He raised a hand to what felt like the epicentre of his headache. The area around his left eyebrow was damp and tender. The dampness, he saw as he withdrew his hand, was blood. A hazy memory of being dragged to where he now lay floated to the surface of his turbid thoughts. He looked at his watch, focusing on the dial with some difficulty, and was surprised to see that only twenty minutes or so had elapsed since Norvig had turned on him. 'Do you speak English?' he asked again.

'Yes.' The caretaker frowned down at him. 'You should not be here.'

'I expect you're right there.' Eusden levered himself slowly and painfully to his feet, the caretaker taking an apprehensive step back as he did so.

'I must phone the police if you are not leaving now.'

Eusden stooped forward as a wave of nausea swept over him. It did not return as he stood upright again. But his head throbbed painfully. Anger stirred within him. He had been as stupid to trust Norvig as Marty had been to trust

Kjeldsen. They were both as treacherous as each other. And they had played him for a fool. They were at the rendezvous now, waiting for their fat pay-off, dreaming of how they would spend the money. If only he could catch up with them, he might still retrieve the situation, though how he could not imagine. Besides, he did not know where the rendezvous was. There was nothing he could do. Except —

'Please go, mister. I'm not wanting any trouble.'

'Nor me. But I've got it. In spades.'

'I cannot help you.'

'Actually, you can. I need to get into this office.' Eusden pointed to Kjeldsen's door. 'I bet you've got a pass key.'

'I cannot let you in there.'

'Sorry . . . ' Eusden bent down, picked up the empty whisky bottle by the neck and smashed it against the wall. The caretaker jumped in alarm. Glass scattered across the floor. 'I'm going to have to insist.' He was between the other fellow and the stairs. He had blood on him and reeked of alcohol. He probably looked like a man it was unwise to defy. 'Open the door.'

'I cannot do that. I will be losing my job.'

'Better than losing your life.' Eusden held the broken bottle in front of him like a weapon. He could not believe he was behaving like this. But he would achieve nothing with politeness and appeals to reason. The caretaker was frightened. And his fear was Eusden's only hope. 'Open the door.'

'Please, mister. I — '

217

'*Open it.*'

'OK, OK.' The caretaker gestured submissively and fumbled in his pocket. Out came a massive bunch of keys. He sorted through them with trembling hands, sweating and breathing shallowly as he did so. Eusden hated himself for putting the man through such an ordeal. But it had to be done.

'*Hurry up.*'

'OK, OK. I have it.' The caretaker moved to the door, unlocked it and pushed it ajar.

'Switch on the light and go in.'

The poor fellow obeyed. Eusden followed him into the room and pulled the door shut behind them. Stark fluorescent light made the office look different. But the biggest difference was that Clem's attaché case was gone from the desk.

'What's your name?'

'Wijayapala. They call me . . . Wij.'

'OK, Wij, just do as I say and you'll be fine. Is that clear?'

'Please, mister. Don't hurt me.'

'I won't. If you do exactly what I tell you.'

'Yes, yes, I will.'

'Go over to the desk and sit down in the chair.' Eusden prodded Wij between the shoulderblades and he started moving.

They reached the desk. Wij walked slowly round behind it and sat down.

'Turn on the lamp.'

Wij reached up and engaged the switch. A pool of mellower light spread across the desktop.

The notepad was where Kjeldsen had left it. And he had not bothered to tear off the sheet he

218

had written on. Careless of him — and considerate. Eusden did the tearing off instead. Marmorvej was the word Kjeldsen had scrawled. 'Yes,' he had said, 'I can find it.' So, the location had not been instantly familiar to him. And to confirm that, lying on the desk where it had not been lying before, was a Copenhagen street atlas. Eusden slapped the sheet of paper down in front of Wij. 'Find that street in the atlas,' he ordered, hardening his tone as well as his heart.

Wij's general state of alarm turned the exercise of consulting the index and finding the right page into an agony. But Eusden could not do it himself without putting down the bottle, at which his captive kept casting anxious glances, so he had no choice but to stick with it. Eventually, after several long, uncertain minutes of searching and squinting, Marmorvej was located. Wij's trembling finger pointed to the spot: a dockside street away to the north, beyond the Citadel.

Eusden snatched the atlas and shoved it into his pocket. Marmorvej was probably no more than a couple of miles off but he certainly did not have time to walk there. 'How do you get here from home?'

'Sorry?'

'*How do you travel?*'

'Oh, on my . . . my scooter.'

'Where is it?'

'Down in the yard.'

'Give me the key.'

'Oh, mister, no. I need that scooter badly.'

'You'll get it back. I'll leave it there for you to

219

find.' Eusden pointed to the piece of paper with the word Marmorvej written on it. 'Now, give me the key. And hand over your mobile phone as well.'

Wij undid a couple of buttons on his boiler suit and reached into an inner pocket for his mobile and the scooter key. He laid them on the desk and Eusden picked them up.

'I'll need the key to the door as well, Wij. I'm afraid I'm going to have to lock you in here. Sorry, but there it is. You'll be able to call for help from the window in the morning. Oh and unplug Kjeldsen's phone.' He pointed to the landline receiver. 'I'll also have to take that. I'll leave it downstairs with your mobile.'

'Why you doing this, mister? You don't look . . . like a crazy man.'

'I don't have time to explain.'

'I got no money for a new scooter.'

'Don't worry. I'll ride carefully. Believe it or not, I am sorry.' Eusden sighed. 'This isn't the start to the weekend I had planned.'

27

Eusden's most recent experience of two-wheeled transport lay many years in the past and even then it had not been motorized. His wobbly ride through the mercifully empty streets of Copenhagen on Wijayapala's scooter would ordinarily have been a nightmarish ordeal. As it was, its hazards and difficulties paled into insignificance compared with the other anxieties his mind was grappling with. Marty had vanished and Clem's attaché case had been stolen. It had very possibly already been sold to a sinister and anonymous buyer. Certainly Eusden's chances of preventing the sale were negligible. Logically, there was no point even trying to prevent it. So far, the attempt had involved behaving despicably as well as criminally. And he was still breaking the law by riding without a crash helmet — not to mention jumping a succession of red lights.

He could not simply give up, however. An admission of defeat at this stage would be more painful than pressing on until he had done everything he could, even if it was to no avail. The blow to his head had scrambled his thought processes and he was aware he might be acting irrationally, but he felt helpless in the grip of his determination to hit back at Kjeldsen and Norvig. One had cheated him. The other had betrayed him. He could not simply let them get away with it — and pocket their ill-gotten half shares of twenty million kroner.

★ ★ ★

The docks were separated from the city centre by a dual carriageway and a railway line. The route into them by road involved a double-back after passing Nordhavn S-tog station. This brought Eusden out on to one of the harbour basins, with a vast warehouse complex between him and Marmorvej. He left the scooter there, conscious that he could not afford to advertise his arrival with the mosquito-whine of its engine, and jogged along the narrow road between the warehouse and the dual carriageway.

Beyond lay another basin, with a huge car ferry moored at a jetty on the far side. Marmorvej was the quay to his left and he heard the thrumbling note of a boat's engine as he turned on to it. A launch was moving away from the quayside, heading out into the harbour. And two men were walking towards a car parked in the lee of the warehouse. Widely spaced security lights cast a jumble of deep shadows and shallow reflections across the snowmelt-puddled wharf and the launch's ghostly wake. For a second, Eusden could not be sure what he was actually seeing. His perceptions were sluggish, his reactions slow. Then the scene became clear and obvious in his mind.

The two men were Norvig and Kjeldsen. They were walking towards Kjeldsen's Volvo. The lawyer was carrying a case that was marginally

222

the wrong size and shape to be Clem's. They had handed his over, of course, in exchange for this case, containing their pay-off. The buyer was leaving in the launch. Eusden was too late. It had always been likely he would be. His heart sank. He strode forward, unsure of what he meant to do but set on doing something to sour the pair's victory.

Clunk, clunk: the doors of the Volvo slammed shut as Kjeldsen settled behind the wheel and Norvig in the passenger seat beside him. The engine coughed into action. The headlamps flared. The car was facing towards the sea, so they would not yet be able to see him. As Kjeldsen forwarded and reversed into a multi-point turn, Eusden broke into a run.

Almost at once, however, he stopped, confused by other movements and noises intruding on his senses, swifter than the manoeuvring car, louder than its muffled engine — or that of the departing launch, which by now had left the basin. An unlit motorbike sped into view round the seaward flank of the warehouse. Its rider and his pillion passenger were black-leathered, sleek-helmeted shadows. The machine closed on the Volvo, fast and dark. Eusden guessed Kjeldsen and Norvig were unaware of its approach. And he also guessed its approach spelt danger for them. '*Look out!*' he shouted.

The warning was in vain. Time was about to slow yet accelerate in front of him. Kjeldsen had reversed towards the warehouse wall as the motorbike reached them. It braked sharply. Its rear light bled into the night. The pillion passenger jumped off as the bike halted, wielding what looked like a gun in his hand. Doubt on the point was snuffed out by the sharp cracks of repeated shots. Glass splintered. The gunman yanked open the driver's door and unloaded more shots. Six, seven; ten, twelve: they came in rapid succession. The car horn blared. Eusden glimpsed slumped figures behind the windscreen. The gunman leant into the car. He pushed one of the figures aside. The horn died. Then the engine stopped. And the headlamps faded. Several more shots followed, less rapidly. They sounded calm and deliberate: a fail-safe guaranteeing of a specified result. The gunman recoiled from the car, holding the case, and climbed aboard the bike.

The flight response kicked in belatedly for Eusden. It was only now that he turned and ran. As he did so, he separated himself from the stationary shadows on the quay. To flee was also to become visible. He heard a shout from behind him, in a language that was neither Danish nor English. The motorbike engine revved, then roared. They were coming after him. At best a witness, at worst a confederate of the men they had just killed, he could not be allowed to escape.

Granted more time, Eusden would have cursed the instincts that had brought him to this place. If he had not been so obsessed with striking back at Norvig and Kjeldsen, he might have foreseen that they too could be double-crossed. But murder? The clinical executions he had just watched? His foresight would never have stretched so far. There was more at stake than he could ever have envisaged. And now that included his own life.

He turned the corner into the narrow road that led back to the other quay, where he had abandoned the scooter. A glance over his shoulder confirmed he would be overtaken before he got there. He was running to the end of a short leash. He had nowhere to go and nowhere to hide.

Then he saw the gate in the fence. It gave on to a path that led to a footbridge over the dual carriageway. They could not use the bike to pursue him over that. He dodged through the gate and sprinted for the steps, not daring to look behind him.

He ran up the steps and out along the span of the bridge. There was enough traffic on the road below to blot out the noise of the motorbike. He let himself believe for a moment that they might have given up the chase. But a sharp ping against the parapet of the bridge told a different tale. He crouched forward as he turned on to the steps down, ducking and dodging as he descended. He thought he heard a second shot, then a third.

There was a subway ahead of him, leading under the railway line. It was a brightly lit tunnel in which he would be a clear target. But only to someone at ground level. His pursuers would have to cross the footbridge to reach such a position. He could not afford to hesitate. He plunged along it, bracing himself for the jab of pain that would herald the shot that did not miss.

It never came. He emerged from the subway on Østbanegade, the road he had ridden along earlier before entering the docks. He risked a backward glance as he jinked right. There was no one coming after him. Maybe they had given up after all.

A short distance up the road was the bright-red hexagon of the S-tog station. Eusden did not know when the trains stopped running. If one happened to be due, it would be as quick and safe a getaway as he could hope for. But it was a big if. On the other side of the road there were apartment blocks and residential streets where he could hope to lose himself. Maybe they were the better bet. He stood on the pavement debating the point with himself as he panted for breath. His heart was thumping. Blood was singing in his ears. He did not know what to do. He took a chance with another glance into the subway. It was still empty. It was beginning to look as if —

Then he heard the familiar growl of the motorbike. He whirled round and saw it heading towards him down Østbanegade. They had taken the road route out of the docks, calculating — correctly — that they could cut him off. He had delayed too long. They would be on him in a matter of seconds.

To retreat along the subway was to become a rat in a maze. Eusden's only chance of escape was to make it to the street opposite and pray one of the residents would open their door to him. He launched himself across the road.

He heard the blast of its horn before he saw

the lorry thundering towards him from the left. He had forgotten Østbanegade was one-way at this point. But he could not stop now. He lowered his head and lunged on, reaching the pavement in a vortex of rushing air as the lorry swallowed the space behind him, its horn still blaring, its brakes squealing.

In the same breath there was a screech of tyres and a deafening thump of metal crunching into metal. Eusden shrank from the sound, stooping so far forward that he lost his footing and fell to the ground in three stumbling strides. The sound grew and extended itself into a yowl of squealing rubber and crumpling steel as he tumbled against the nearest wall and looked back, winded, into the road.

The lorry had struck the motorbike with crushing force as it crossed in front of it. The rider must have gambled on making the turn before the lorry could shield Eusden from the gunman. But he had misjudged fatally. Now, as the lorry slewed to a halt, jack-knifing slowly across the road in the process, the bike was a twisted shape juddering beneath the cab, the rider and passenger broken dolls bouncing and rolling to rest along the pavement ahead of it. The case had broken free and been split open. Fistfuls of kroner were whirling like autumn leaves in a gale.

The bikers did not move once they had come to rest and the lorry was thirty or forty yards away by the time it stopped. The driver pushed open the door of his cab and commenced an awkward clamber out, moving numbly, like a man in shock. Eusden could see the gun lying in the gutter, glimmering coldly in the lamplight. He rose unsteadily to his feet and edged back into the shadows as the lorry driver looked vaguely in his direction. A Transit van was braking to a halt as it approached. Windows were opening in the apartments nearby. Soon the alarm would be raised.

Eusden headed down the side street, away from the scene, moving as fast as he dared without breaking into a run. He did not know where the street would lead. But it did not matter. It led away. It led to safety.

28

What the night porter at the Phoenix had thought of his bloody-browed and dishevelled appearance Eusden could not imagine. Waking in the morning after several hours of unconsciousness that could only technically be called sleep, he could remember little of his return to the hotel. He had not even undressed and was aching in every limb. His head throbbed painfully with every movement, he had developed a black eye overnight and generally felt as if he was engaging with the world through a thick curtain of delayed shock.

He showered, put on some clean clothes and headed out to a nearby seven-eleven for antiseptic and plasters. He suspected he should be checked by a doctor for the effects of concussion, but he also suspected drawing attention to himself in such a way would be unwise to put it mildly. Wijayapala had probably given a description of him to the police by now and they were bound to tie him to the carnage out at Nordhavn because Kjeldsen was among the dead. The only sensible thing he could do was lie low until he left Copenhagen. And he should leave soon. The longer he remained, the greater his chance of being dragged into a murder inquiry.

But he could not simply scuttle back to London and abandon Marty to an unknown

229

fate. He had to find out what had become of his friend, even though that friend had been responsible for transforming his comfortable and predictable life into a raw struggle for survival. 'Fuck you, Marty,' he muttered several times under his breath as he plodded back to the Phoenix through the gnawing chill of a bleak Copenhagen morning. It was a sentiment he had often expressed before, of course. And one he had never quite succeeded in drawing the obvious lesson from.

★   ★   ★

He had banked on a quick ascent to his room, with a breakfast delivery to follow, strong black coffee being the self-prescribed medicine he proposed to dose himself with. But he was intercepted halfway across the marbled lobby by an unexpected visitor: Regina Celeste.

'There you are, Richard. I guessed it might be worth waiting to see if you'd be back soon. Well, where are you gonna go on a morning like this, after all?' She seemed even louder in manner and dress by day than night. Or perhaps, Eusden thought, he was simply more vulnerable. 'Say, what happened to you? Get in with the wrong crowd last night? That's quite a shiner.'

'I slipped in the bath.'

'Really?' She looked understandably sceptical.

'What brings you here, Regina? I'm afraid I've still no news of Marty.'

'You haven't?'

230

'No. Like I told Werner, I'll let you know as soon as I do.'

'But that's just the point, Richard. Werner has heard from Marty.'

'What?'

'I think you'll agree with me: we need to talk.'

★ ★ ★

They found a café over the road on Bredgade that had just opened for business and was only otherwise being patronized by a group of Japanese tourists intent on photographing their breakfasts. Eusden contented himself with coffee. While Regina fussed over the infusion of her herbal tea bag, he wondered just how monstrously Marty had misled him with his carefully presented plan to evade Straub. For misled him he surely had. It was only a question of scale. Regina's announcement had struck a chord in him that was wearily familiar. It seemed Marty had taken him for a ride yet again.

'Where's Werner now?' he asked.

'That's just it, Richard. I don't know. He was gone when I surfaced this morning. He left this note for me at reception.' She took a sheet of Hôtel d'Angleterre notepaper out of her portmanteau-sized handbag and passed it to Eusden.

Dear Regina,
I am sorry to leave without warning. Marty has contacted me. I am going to meet him. I hope to get answers to all our questions. Wait

for me here. I will call you later today. We will settle our business in Hanover as soon as possible after I return.
Best wishes,
Werner.

'Best wishes, my sweet behind,' Regina continued as she retrieved the note. 'He must have known last night he was gonna take off like this. The only reason he didn't tell me then was that he knew I'd insist on going with him. Or at the very least on being told *where* he was going. I don't like being strung along, Richard, especially not by a lounge lizard like Werner. Know what I mean?'

'Yes. I certainly do.'

'Everything was sugar and sunshine when we went to Klampenborg yesterday morning. Hvidøre's been turned into a conference centre, but he'd fixed it for us to have a proper guided tour of the place. You could imagine the rooms as they'd have been in Dagmar's day, stuffed with clumpy furniture and kitschy statues and dusty aspidistras. It gave me a real feel for the old lady, let me tell you. Especially the turret room she's supposed to have spent so much time in, looking out to sea. Anyhow, Werner couldn't have been a much more attentive host short of offering me his hand in marriage, resounding 'no' though he'd have got if he had. We had a nice lunch at a restaurant just up the coast road from Hvidøre, then we went on to Rungsted to visit the Karen Blixen Museum. Well, it was too good a chance to miss. I just loved that movie, didn't you?'

There came into Eusden's mind a memory that was both alluring and painful of going to a cinema in Guildford with Gemma some time in the mid-1980s to see *Out of Africa*, the film Regina had proclaimed her love for. He had been a contented husband then, Gemma a secretly discontented wife. Time, he often thought, was more of a tormentor than a healer.

'Werner got a call on his cell while we were looking over the exhibits. He came over kinda coy and went outside to take it. Told me when he came back the call had been from his mother, which I didn't buy for a second. But what's a girl to do? He was different after that. Edgy. Distracted. All the way through to dinner back at the d'Angleterre. Excused himself straight after. Said he needed an early night, which seemed way out of character. I didn't know what to make of it.' She smiled grimly. 'I do now, of course. The scheming weasel.'

'What time did he take the call?'

'Not sure. Around . . . three, I guess.'

Three o'clock was tantalizingly close to the time when Marty was supposed to have arrived in Copenhagen. Though what the timing signified — if anything — Eusden did not know.

'Any inspired thoughts?'

'I'm afraid not. I'm sorry, Regina. I've no idea what Marty's up to. Or Werner.'

'Cooking up a private deal between themselves, that's what.'

'I . . . suppose so.' Regina was right, of course. Nothing else made sense.

'The question is: are you and I going to let

them get away with it?'

'What else can we do?'

'Pool our resources for starters.' That did not sound like a good idea to Eusden, though he did not propose to say so. He certainly had no intention of volunteering any details of his recent activities. 'Do you really have no idea what Clem Hewitson's archive contains?'

'None at all.'

'That's kinda . . . disappointing.'

'What's your 'business in Hanover'?' Eusden asked, keen to switch topics.

'Well, I guess I may as well tell you. Werner's forfeited all confidentiality rights with this little escapade as far as I'm concerned. He's been negotiating with a collector of Nazi curios in Hanover called Hans Grenscher for the purchase of a cache of Gestapo documents supposedly including something crucial about Anastasia. She lived in Hanover throughout the Second World War, at the Gestapo's insistence. They didn't want her wandering around the country for some reason. She was taken to Berlin on one occasion, though, to meet the Führer. What Hitler had in mind for her is unclear. Maybe he saw her as a potential bargaining chip in his dealings with Stalin. Anyhow, I don't rightly know what Grenscher has on her, but Werner claims it can be matched with something Marty's grandfather preserved to prove Anastasia truly was Anastasia. Evidently, Grenscher isn't willing to split his hoard. We have to buy the whole lot for the sake of the one Anastasia-related item. In fact, I've already had to put up a hefty deposit just to get first refusal on it.'

Eusden could not help wondering if Regina's deposit was the source of the money with which Straub had tried to buy off Marty. It seemed typical of the man to use someone else's cash rather than his own — assuming he had any. It also seemed typical of him to strike side deals whenever he needed to: with Regina, with Marty and, in all likelihood, with Grenscher too. 'How can Werner be sure this matching whatever-it-is is amongst the stuff Marty inherited from his grandfather?'

'Beats me, Richard. But he's been adamant on the point the whole way along. That's why I flew over here. Because he was so confident we could nail that DNA lie about the lady I met in Charlottesville being nothing but a Polish peasant once and for mercy's sake all. Now I'm wondering if Werner didn't overstate how much money we had to put up front to fix himself up with negotiating capital. You see where my thoughts are leading? Maybe he plans to put this proof together for his own profit. Write a book, sell the film rights and freeze me out. I might be nothing more than the cash cow he plans to milk in the meantime. Well, this is one cow that can do more than swish her tail, let me tell you.'

'What have you got in mind?'

'A trip to Hanover. A one-on-one with Hans Grenscher. I can do my own negotiating if I have to.'

'I'm sure you can.'

'But I need to know what's happening this end while I'm away. That's where you come in.'

'It is?'

'Werner's bound to turn to you when he gets back here and finds I've flown the coop. Well, I want you to point him in the wrong direction. Say I've vamoosed to St Petersburg to catch up with Dagmar — pay my respects at the last resting place she now shares with the Tsar, the Tsarina and *some* of their children. I reckon he'll swallow that considering how tearful I came over during our visit to Hvidøre. Well, I'm an emotional person, Richard. I'm sure you appreciate that. But the emotion I'm in closest touch with right now is suspicion. So, I also want you to figure out if you can *exactly* what he and Marty are up to — and to let me know. What do you say?'

Now was definitely not the time to mention that the clinching document Clem's archive supposedly held — along with the archive as a whole — was conclusively out of reach of all of them and that no amount of intrigue and double-dealing could retrieve it. Eusden doubted if he would still be in Copenhagen when Straub returned. But he could not explain why to Regina Celeste. He regretted having to deceive her on the point, but there were other things he regretted far more. He gave her a reassuring smile. 'I'll certainly do my best, Regina.'

★ ★ ★

Eusden finally made it to his room at the Phoenix half an hour later. He patched himself up and ordered breakfast, then lay down on the bed to await its arrival. He was too tired to ponder the full depth and meaning of Marty's latest abuse of their friendship. All he knew was that it marked a new low — and an end of his involvement in Marty's tangled affairs. It was time to cut himself loose.

He checked his mobile to confirm there was no apologetic or exculpatory message on it from Marty. Since, as far as he was aware, Marty did not even have the number, it was even more unlikely than would otherwise have been the case. But Eusden felt obliged to give him the benefit of the negligible doubt.

Sure enough, there was no message from Marty. But Gemma had phoned again. To *Phone me asap* had been added *Very urgent*. Eusden relented and rang her, despite his reluctance to face questions about what he and Marty had been doing for the past few days. He was at least relieved when Gemma, not Monica, answered.

'It's me.'

'Christ, Richard, why haven't you called before now? I've been going out of my mind.' She certainly sounded distraught, though Eusden could not begin to imagine why.

'What's the matter?'

'What do you mean, 'what's the matter'? You're in Copenhagen, aren't you?'

'Yes.' Even as he replied, Eusden wondered how she knew that.

'So, why didn't you tell me? Why did I have to hear it from a Danish policewoman?'

'Hear what?'

'About Marty, of course.'

'What about Marty?'

'Are you playing games with me, Richard?'

'No. Marty isn't with me. I'm not sure where he is at the moment, to be honest.'

'Of course he isn't with you. He's . . . ' She broke off.

There was a heavy silence. Dread formed a cloud in Eusden's mind.

'Gemma?'

'You really don't know?'

'Know what, for God's sake?'

'Oh Christ.'

'*Know what?*'

'I'm sorry, Richard.'

'Sorry? What the hell — '

'Marty's dead.'

29

'You'll miss me when I'm gone.' Looking back, Eusden was surprised Marty had not said this at some point during their few days together in Hamburg and Århus. Perhaps he had not needed to. Perhaps he had thought it self-evidently true. And so it was, though there had been several occasions when Eusden would vehemently have denied it. But all the grudges and resentments and irritations, even the numerous breaches of faith, fell away in the face of death. And it was the face of death that Eusden looked into when he gazed down at Marty on the mortuary slab at Roskilde Amtssygehuset later that morning: a cold, pale, vacant face — no longer really Marty's at all.

A hovering administrator was anxious to establish whether Eusden would be arranging Marty's removal — to a local undertaker or back home to Amsterdam or England. Eusden prevaricated. He could not afford to commit himself to remaining in Copenhagen for the week or more he suspected such arrangements would take. He was going to have to offload the responsibility on to Gemma. And he was going to have to find a way to explain that to her.

But he could not summon the effort to concentrate on such stark practicalities as he left the hospital and wandered towards the centre of Roskilde, past the railway station where he had arrived from Copenhagen a couple of hours earlier. The death of his childhood friend was like the amputation of a limb he had not realized until then he possessed. He kept remembering Marty's most characteristic expression, by which all his mischief and humour and daring — his ineluctable spirit — were magically conveyed. Eusden could see it now, clear and golden in his mind's eye. Richard would jump off the bus from Newport at the Fountain Arcade in Cowes on a Saturday morning and Marty would be waiting for him, chewing gum and smiling and assuring him, just by the look on his face, that life for the next few hours was going to be fun. Some trace of that had still been there when Eusden pulled the tape off Marty's mouth at Frau Straub's flat in Hamburg. *'Good to see you, Coningsby.'* And the feeling, despite everything — the forfeited surety, the rivalry for Gemma, the disputes and deceptions — had been mutual. It always had been. But it never would be again.

There was an old cemetery next to the station that had been turned into a park. Eusden had the benches to himself, thanks to the dank chill of the day. He sat and gazed towards the red-brick gables and copper-tiled spires of Roskilde Cathedral, its shape blurred by the tears that were in his eyes. According to the information Gemma had been supplied with, Marty had collapsed in the cathedral at about 3.30 the previous afternoon and been pronounced dead on arrival at the local hospital. Cause of death was a massive stroke. He had not been carrying a passport and had been identified from a prescription in his pocket issued by the pharmacy at Århus Kommunehospital. He had recorded Gemma as his next of kin on admission there. The oncologist had evidently strongly advised him not to discharge himself specifically because of the likelihood of a second stroke, but Marty had insisted. And Eusden knew just how insistent he could be.

The 11.54 train Marty had said he was catching from Århus would have got him to Roskilde just before three o'clock, the time of his supposed telephone call to Straub. Half an hour later, he walked into the cathedral — but did not walk out. The unanswerable question was why he had got off at Roskilde at all. He must have changed his mind about travelling through to Copenhagen for some reason. Regina Celeste would say it was to fix a rendezvous for his covert meeting with Straub. But that rendezvous was clearly not Roskilde. Straub's note had implied somewhere farther flung. Eusden preferred to believe Marty had sent Straub off on a wild-goose chase so he would not be in Copenhagen when Marty arrived there after a strategic stop-over in Roskilde — only for sudden death to prevent him carrying through his plan. If Eusden was right, Marty had died while trying to protect both of them.

★   ★   ★

Eusden had been to Roskilde once before with Gemma and Holly, to visit the Viking Ship

241

Museum. The cathedral had played only a bit-part in the day's entertainment, though Holly had enjoyed hunting for the tomb of Harold Bluetooth. Dagmar's tomb must have been somewhere in the crypt then, but Eusden had not gone looking for it. It was no longer there, of course, so exactly what had drawn Marty to the cathedral was hard to say. He was an avowed atheist and no fan of ecclesiastical architecture. A mausoleum catering for umpteen centuries of Danish royalty would ordinarily have elicited little more from him than a shrug of indifference.

But gone there he had. And Eusden followed. He stepped into the entrance porch and was greeted by a volunteer guide. When he explained he was a friend of the man who had died there the day before, he was directed to the woman behind the sales desk. She, he was told in hushed tones, 'knew all about it'.

This, it transpired, was because it was in the porch, rather than the main body of the cathedral, that Marty had collapsed. The sales lady, a kindly middle-aged woman with a ready smile, identified by her badge as Jette, had seen it happen.

'He had just come in and bought a ticket and a guidebook. He asked me about Princess Dagmar, mother of the last Tsar of Russia. She was Danish, you know, and was buried here. Until last September, that is, when she was moved to St Petersburg. He wanted to know where her coffin had been. I showed him on the map inside the guidebook. We have postcards of it.' She plucked a card from the rack and showed it to Eusden. Dagmar's large, handsomely carved wooden coffin was pictured in its appointed corner of the crypt, flanked by icons and glowing candles. 'He bought one of these also.'

'How did he seem?'

'A little . . . shaky. I noticed he was . . . sweating, although it was really quite cold. And he kept rubbing his head, as if it ached. But he had a lovely smile. You knew him a long time?'

'From childhood.'

'Oh dear. You must be very upset.'

'Yes. I am.'

'Is your name Coningsby?'

'Sorry?'

'He wanted to send a message to someone called Coningsby. It was the last thing he said, while he was lying there.' She pointed towards the door into the nave. 'He had only gone a few steps from here when he stopped and bent his head. He reached out as if he was trying to find something to hold on to. But the wall was too far away. I realized he was not well and went to help him, but he fell on to the floor before I could get to him. Some other visitors came over to help also. We held up his head. I'm not sure he could see us. His eyes were . . . strange. And it was difficult for him to speak.'

'But he did speak.'

'Yes. He asked us to give a message to Coningsby. Then he . . . died.'

'I'm Coningsby. It's not my name. But . . . it's what he sometimes called me.'

'Then the message is for you.'

'Yes.' Eusden nodded. 'What is it?'

' 'Tell Coningsby the babushka was right.' '

The babushka. Of course. Eusden had forgotten all about her. Until now.

'Does it mean something?'

'Oh, yes. It certainly does.'

30

September, 1976. The burnt-out end of a blazing
summer. Gemma suggested a trip to Paris as an
enjoyable way to fill the gap between their
holiday jobs and the start of the Michaelmas
term at Cambridge. She roped in a schoolfriend
of hers called Pamela and made all the
arrangements. They were to meet at Portsmouth
and catch the ferry to Le Havre.

The day before setting off, Richard accompanied his mother, for want of anything better to
do, on one of her monthly shopping trips to
Southampton. Browsing in Gilbert's Bookshop,
a multi-floored repository of literary riches to
which he always gravitated, he made, as usual, an
impulse buy. *The File on the Tsar* by Anthony
Summers and Tom Mangold, hot off the press.

Marty picked up the book whenever Richard
put it down during the Channel crossing and rail
journey to Paris. Soon they were both talking of
little else, much to Gemma's annoyance.
Foot-slogging round the Louvre at Pamela's
insistence, they were taken to task for neglecting
the artworks in favour of arguing about whether
the women of the imperial family could have
been secretly evacuated from Ekaterinburg to
Perm, as the authors suggested, before the night
of the alleged massacre.

Marty rapidly developed a conspiracy theory
fingering Lord Mountbatten as orchestrator of a

245

plot to deny Anastasia her inheritance: millions of pounds supposedly salted away in the Bank of England by the Tsar. He was excited to discover that Mathilde Kschessinska, the elderly ballerina who had been the Tsar's mistress prior to his marriage and had subsequently married one of his cousins, lived in Paris. She had given an interview on French television in 1967, when she was ninety-five, supporting Anna Anderson's claim. Gemma, forced to read the relevant passage in the book, pointed out that if Mathilde was still alive she would have to be well over a hundred, but Marty was undaunted in his enthusiasm for tracking down the old lady.

Gemma had earmarked their last morning in Paris for a visit to Les Invalides, but Marty had other ideas. In the end, the girls went to see Napoleon's tomb on their own, while he and Richard headed for Little Russia, the area around Alexander Nevsky Orthodox Cathedral where Russian exiles had settled after the Revolution. There was nowhere better, according to him, to ask after surviving Romanovs and gauge opinion.

The results were disappointing. The haughty proprietor of a Russian bookshop informed them that the 'Grand Duchess Mathilde' was dead. He cast a scornful eye over their by now dog-eared copy of *The File on the Tsar* and said there were 'many, many lies' told about the imperial family. Marty had also failed to check the opening times of the cathedral. They had come on a day when visitors were not admitted.

Recrimination threatened to break out as they

stood in front of the cathedral, gazing at its golden domes and firmly closed door. Then Marty noticed an old woman dressed in threadbare clothes pinning up an advertisement on the noticeboard attached to the wall of the diocesan office. She was clad entirely in black. Her face, peering out from a tightly fastened headscarf, was lined like a dried riverbed. Her advert was in Russian and French. It offered her services to the local community as a clairvoyant. Marty tackled her in English to no avail, but he and Richard managed to communicate with her eventually in rudimentary French. Had she known the Grand Duchess Mathilde? Yes. Also Mathilde's son, her husband and assorted cousins. Did she know anything about the woman who claimed to be Anastasia? Yes again. She knew much, which she was willing to share with them — if they were willing to stand her a meal. She was poor, hungry, neglected — and a fount of information.

Information the babushka, as Marty later dubbed her, undeniably possessed. And she purveyed a great deal of it while slurping soup and sipping vodka in a nearby bar, where she was clearly viewed with well-entrenched suspicion by the staff. Unfortunately for Marty and Richard, the portion they could actually understand of what she said added little to the sum of their knowledge. Mathilde's husband, the Grand Duke Andrei, had also expressed his belief in Anna Anderson and that was good enough for the babushka, who had once shaken his hand and held it long enough to sense, as she

247

had informed him, that his son would betray him. Sure enough, the son, Vladimir — '*la vipère Vova*', as she called him — had gone over to the other side and denounced Anna as an impostor. Why? '*Pour l'argent. Toujours pour l'argent.*' It was, she flatly declared, the real ruin of the Romanovs. '*La cupidité.*' Greed. 'Thanks for the startling insight,' murmured Marty as she downed another vodka.

Sensing perhaps that she had inadequately repaid their generosity, the babushka concluded by offering to read their palms. Richard declined, but Marty submitted gleefully. He was rewarded with vague predictions of good fortune and wealth which so dissatisfied him that he demanded to be told how long he was going to live. Longer than her, the babushka cutely replied, adding, almost as an afterthought: '*Vous mourrez dans un endroit sacré.*'

Marty laughed at the idea that he would die in a holy place. Gemma, when told the story later, remarked that he would be lucky to be buried in a holy place, let alone die in one. They were at the top of the Eiffel Tower at the time, admiring a smudge on the horizon that Pamela insisted was Chartres Cathedral. 'I hate cathedrals,' Marty whispered to Richard, 'and now I've got the perfect excuse to avoid them.'

★ ★ ★

Eusden walked out of Roskilde Cathedral into the cold grey Danish afternoon. But his mind lingered in the dazzling sunshine of Paris thirty

248

years ago. He saw Marty smiling at him across a café table in Montmartre. He felt the heat flung back at him from the stone wall above the quay on the Île St-Louis. He heard the past calling to him. And he could not answer.

'Mr Eusden?'

A chubby, shaven-headed man in a grey suit, white shirt and navy-blue tie was standing in his path. Behind him, a gleaming black Mercedes was parked at the roadside. Eusden's thoughts were suddenly wrenched back to the present. 'Yes,' he said weakly.

'I have instructions to drive you to Mjollnir HQ.'

'What?'

'Mjollnir. Birgitte Grøn wants to see you.'

'Who?'

The chauffeur smiled wanly. 'My boss.'

'I don't know her. And I don't think I want to meet her.'

'Hold on, please.' The chauffeur took out his phone and made a call. He spoke a few words in Danish, then passed the phone to Eusden. 'It's her.'

'Hello?' said Eusden cautiously.

'Richard Eusden?' The voice was clipped and brittle enough to hint at impatience.

'Yes.'

'I am Birgitte Grøn, CFO of Mjollnir. We need to talk.'

'What about?'

'Things that cannot be discussed on the phone. Jørgen will bring you to my office.'

'Maybe I don't want to be brought.'

249

'And maybe I don't want to be here on a Saturday afternoon, Mr Eusden. But I am. And you'll come and talk to me. Because, if you don't, the police will get a name to put to the description they have of a man they wish to question about the murders last night of a lawyer called Anders Kjeldsen and a journalist called Henning Norvig. My office is much more comfortable than an interview room at police headquarters. And nobody will be recording what you say. So, I suggest you get in the car. I'll expect you shortly.'

31

An entire second city appeared to be under construction south of Copenhagen. Eusden gazed out through the tinted window of the Mercedes at the office complexes and apartment blocks rearing up between clusters of cranes and mountains of earth where their neighbours were soon to be. This was the future. And at its heart, raised like a finger pointed to the sky, was what Jørgen informed him was called *Det Blå Tryllestav* — the Blue Wand: an ultramarine-louvred tower of glass housing Mjollnir AS.

Jørgen drove straight into the underground car park and escorted Eusden to the lift. An ear-poppingly high-speed ascent took him to the top of the tower. The lift doors opened to a scene of deserted open-plan workstations through which strode a snappily trouser-suited woman who greeted him as she approached. 'Mr Eusden. I'm Birgitte Grøn.'

She was small and slightly built, about forty-five, with shortish blonde hair, a sharp-featured face and slender letterbox-framed glasses. Beneath her pink shirt she wore an austerely wrought platinum necklace. She looked brisk and business-like and spoke in a tone that suggested their meeting was no different from half a dozen others she might expect to manage in an average day.

'Come through to my office,' she said after a

perfunctory handshake. 'We have the place to ourselves this afternoon. Mjollnir doesn't encourage weekend working. But this is an emergency.'

'Is it?'

'Yes. For us as well as you.' She marched back the way she had come and Eusden followed. 'I wouldn't be here otherwise.'

They entered a large glass-walled office carpeted and furnished in restful pastels and pale wood. A man was waiting there for them, dressed in a black suit and open-necked white shirt. He looked about fifty, balding and neatly bearded, with a melancholic blue-eyed gaze.

'Erik Lund, CSO,' said Birgitte.

Eusden shook the man's hand. Lund's grip was strong, his expression unsmiling.

'What does the S stand for?'

'Security,' said Lund.

'Ah.'

'Would you like tea or coffee, Mr Eusden?' asked Birgitte.

'Coffee would be nice. Black. No sugar.'

'A man of your own tastes, Erik,' said Birgitte. 'Pour him a cup, would you? Nothing for me. Let's sit.'

They sat at a broad maple conference table angled towards a corner of the building and commanding a chevroned view of the vast construction site that stretched away towards the centre of Copenhagen.

'Please accept my condolences for the death of your friend.'

'Am I supposed to take that seriously?'

252

'I said it seriously.'

'You'll be telling me next Karsten Burgaard's death really was an accident.'

'As far as I know, it was.' Birgitte gave him a faintly sympathetic smile that hinted at a vivacious persona she left at home every morning. 'You've had twenty-four rough hours, I think. That looks nasty.' She acknowledged with a nod the combined effect of the plastered gash on his forehead and the black eye below it. 'You look tired. And a little desperate. If you don't mind me saying.' Lund delivered the coffee and sat down next to her. 'Maybe that'll help.'

'Maybe.' Eusden took a sip. And it did help — a little.

'If you have any questions . . . '

'I'm sure you're going to tell me why I'm here soon enough.'

'I am.'

'Then this'll do to be going on with: where's Tolmar Aksden?'

'Helsinki.'

'Saukko Bank taking up a lot of his time, is it?'

'No more than he expected.'

'But he's . . . authorized this meeting?'

'He trusts me, Mr Eusden. I act with his authority.'

'Is that a yes or a no?'

Lund muttered something in Danish which Birgitte appeared to ignore. 'This is what you need to know,' she proceeded. 'The police have already matched the bullets found in Kjeldsen and Norvig with the gun found near the bodies of two motorcyclists killed in a collision with a lorry on Østbanegade late last night. The motorcyclists themselves haven't been identified yet. They were carrying millions of kroner in cash. The lorry driver thinks they were chasing a man who ran across the road in front of him. Earlier, a caretaker was locked in Kjeldsen's office at Jorcks Passage by a man he thinks was English and who said he was going to Marmorvej — the quay where Kjeldsen and Norvig were shot dead. The police don't have a very good description of this man. Their chances of finding him are poor. He probably left his fingerprints in numerous locations. But I doubt they're held in the Europol database, so, unless they're given a name . . . '

'You've made your point.'

'Good.'

'What do you want from me?'

'Help.'

'*My* help?'

'Yes. We have a . . . situation . . . we need to deal with.'

'What kind of situation?'

'We've been contacted by the people we believe employed those two motorcyclists to kill Kjeldsen and Norvig and take back the money they'd been paid. We don't know who these people are. Let's call them . . . the Opposition. They have material that could damage our CEO and therefore the company . . . quite severely. They're willing to sell it to us. And we're willing to buy it. Frankly speaking, we have no choice. We face . . . a potential disaster.'

'What is the material?'

'Don't you know, Mr Eusden?'

'Maybe I do. Maybe I don't.'

Another Danish mutter from Lund elicited a tight frown of irritation from Birgitte. 'We're not here to discuss the nature or detail of the material. We believe it originated from your late friend's grandfather, Clement Hewitson. Is that correct?'

'Yes.'

'Marty Hewitson left it with Kjeldsen for safekeeping. Kjeldsen stole it and contacted Norvig, a journalist who has written several articles hostile to this company. Between them, they set up a deal with the Opposition, who then double-crossed them. Is that how it was?'

'More or less.'

'You were lucky to survive, Mr Eusden.'

'I know.'

'And that's lucky for us. Because you've seen the material. You know what it looks like in its original form. Yes?'

'Yes. So?'

'The Opposition may try to sell us fakes. They've already demonstrated they can't be relied on to deal fairly. We need someone who can authenticate the material. We need you.'

'I may have seen it, but I haven't studied it. I wouldn't necessarily know whether it was all there.'

'You'll have to do the best you can. We have no one else we can use.'

'You mean you have no one else you can blackmail into taking the risk that these people may do what they did to Kjeldsen and Norvig all over again.'

'That's unlikely. Kjeldsen and Norvig were selling. We're buying.'

'Nice distinction.'

'An important one. Besides, the Opposition won't want to lose any more men. I doubt last night's . . . exposure . . . will have pleased them.'

'It didn't exactly please me.'

'We appreciate that, Mr Eusden. You have my personal apology for involving you. I regret there's no alternative.'

'There is for me. Maybe I'd rather take my chances with the police than a faceless bunch of hoodlums from who knows where.'

'I wouldn't advise it. Think of your career, Mr Eusden. Think of your pension. Think of the months of uncertainty about what charge you'd face — or what sentence if convicted. We're offering you a much better deal.'

'It doesn't sound like it.'

'That's because I haven't finished. We're not asking you to pick up the material on a deserted quayside in the middle of the night. Everything will be done in controlled surroundings. There'll be no danger.'

'So you say.'

'To prove it, we're sending someone with you.'

Eusden looked doubtfully at Lund. 'Who?'

'Not me,' growled Lund.

'Mjollnir can't be linked with this, Mr Eusden,' said Birgitte. 'We have to have . . . deniability.'

Did Tolmar Aksden know what his subordinate was doing? Eusden was still uncertain on

256

the point. Birgitte Grøn had been at pains to emphasize that it was Mjollnir's interests she was serving. Maybe she saw a crucial distinction between them and those of the company's founder. 'I suppose this conversation isn't actually taking place.'

'You suppose correctly.'

'Who are you sending with me, then?'

'Pernille Madsen.'

'Tolmar's ex-wife?'

'Yes.'

This was a surprise, to put it mildly. And one which only heightened Eusden's suspicion that Tolmar Aksden himself had been left out of the loop. 'Why her?'

'Interesting question. It suggests you really haven't studied the material. The damage would be to all members of our CEO's family, particularly his son. Pernille is a loving mother. She wants to protect her child.' Birgitte delicately cleared her throat. 'I would do the same in her position.'

'And what exactly is it you expect her — expect *us* — to do?'

'Pernille has been fully briefed. She'll tell you all you need to know *when* you need to know it.'

'Marvellous.'

'Erik has pointed out to me that we need to minimize the possibility of third-party involvement.'

'What does that mean?'

'Straub,' said Lund, in a tone that suggested it was Danish for a drain blockage.

'He flew to Oslo this morning,' said Birgitte.

257

'Do you know why?'

There seemed no point pretending not to. The effort of deciding how much to reveal and how much to conceal had already exhausted Eusden. 'I knew he'd left, but not where he'd gone. As to why, I think Marty agreed to meet him there, but I doubt he meant to keep the appointment. It was a way of getting Straub off our backs until we could reclaim the . . . material . . . from Kjeldsen.' He shrugged. 'A lot of things went wrong.'

'Straub's American friend, Mrs Celeste, has also left Copenhagen.'

'She's not important.'

'We'll have to take your word for that. But you'll agree Straub is — or could be — a nuisance.'

'Not in Oslo.'

'He'll be back soon, though, won't he? And he'll expect you to explain why Mr Hewitson didn't show up. So, we need you to be . . . out of his reach. We'd like you to phone the Phoenix Hotel and tell them you're sending someone to collect your belongings and settle your bill. We'll supply the someone.'

'Where am I going?'

'Tonight, Stockholm. Jørgen will drive you to the airport. You'll catch the train there. You have to change at Malmö, where your belongings will be waiting for you. We've booked you into a hotel in Stockholm. Pernille will drive up tomorrow and meet you there. You'll be travelling with her on the overnight ferry to Helsinki.'

'*Helsinki?*'

258

'Yes. The exchange will take place there on Monday.'

'But Tolmar's in Helsinki.'

'Yes. The threat is clear. If we don't meet the Opposition's terms, they'll give the material to the Finnish media. That would put our CEO — and us — in an impossible position.'

'Shouldn't you warn him to leave?'

'The deal requires him to stay.'

'He doesn't know, does he?'

Lund plucked an envelope out of his pocket and slapped it down on the table. 'Your travel documents,' he said baldly, as if that was the only kind of answer to his question Eusden could expect.

'The documents include a Finnair club-class ticket for a flight from Helsinki to London on Tuesday,' said Birgitte. 'Our business will have been safely concluded by then.'

'How confident are you of that?'

'Very.'

'Really?'

'Really.'

Eusden sighed and looked down at the envelope, then up at Birgitte. 'I wish I was.'

'We're grateful for your cooperation, Mr Eusden.' She treated him to another of her fleeting smiles that was like a shaft of sunlight through a blanket of cloud. 'And now . . . we need to make a start if you're going to catch that train.'

STOCKHOLM

32

'It's me.'

'Richard? I've been waiting for you to call all evening. What's going on? Your hotel said you checked out this afternoon.'

'That's true.'

'Where are you now?'

'Stockholm.'

'What?'

'I can't explain, Gemma. I had to leave Copenhagen. I *will* explain, when I'm back in London. But I can't now. The thing is — '

'How could you leave Copenhagen just like that? What about Marty?'

'There's nothing I can do for him.'

'Of course there is. There are arrangements to be made. Aunt Lily is desperate for news. She wants to know how and when he's going to be flown to England. She's hoping he can be buried on the Isle of Wight.'

'Maybe he can. I don't know.'

'But you're on the spot, Richard. Or you *were*. What did you tell the hospital?'

'Nothing.'

'*Nothing?*'

'Marty died in a cathedral.'

'I know that. What — '

'Just like the babushka predicted.'

'The who?'

'The babushka. Don't you remember? The old

263

woman we met at the Orthodox Cathedral in Paris in September seventy-six.'

'Never mind that. It's the here and now that matters.'

'If only it was so simple.'

'For God's sake pull yourself together, Richard. Why have you gone to Stockholm?'

'Orders, I'm afraid.'

'Orders? What the hell are you — '

'I can't talk any more, Gemma. Whatever arrangements need to be made, you'll have to make them. There's nothing I can do.'

'Don't be ridiculous. This is — '

'Sorry.'

Eusden stared at the telephone for a minute or more after putting it down, then rose and crossed the room. He slid the glass door open and stepped out on to the balcony. The night was still and cold, the lights of Stockholm bright and clear in the motionless air. He knew he should have handled the conversation with Gemma better. But fatigue and grief and anger had fed his reluctance to offer her anything by way of justification for his behaviour. He would make his peace with her in due course. He would have to. Meanwhile . . .

The cold had done its numbing work. He stepped back into the room and closed the door. He had dozed fitfully on the train and knew he would not sleep if he went to bed now, tired though he was. He decided to head down to the bar. The only way to cope with the night that lay ahead of him, alone in an anonymous hotel,

264

mourning a friend and cursing his misfortune, was to blot it out as best he could.

* * *

Sunday dawned cloudless and icily cold. Squinting through the thick double glazing of his hotel room as he nursed a cup of black coffee and a headache that thumped away behind the gash over his eye, Eusden rehearsed all the ways in which he could have avoided the situation he now found himself in. The surest one was never to have left London, of course. But it hardly helped to know it.

* * *

Pernille Madsen was due to arrive an hour or so before the Helsinki ferry sailed at 4.45. That left Eusden with half a day to kill. He could have seen the sights if he had been in any mood for sightseeing. Stockholm looked beautiful in the white and gold of a winter Sunday. The harbour was frozen and people were out strolling on the ice. Eusden heard their laughter when he left the Sheraton and crossed the bridge into Gamla Stan. He saw the gilded light falling on the ochre-plastered house fronts of the old town. But sights and sounds barely registered in his mind. He had dreamt of Marty in the night, Marty alive and well and youthful, rejecting the report of his death as a mischievous rumour. But the day contradicted the night. The rumour was

265

true. And the truth of it sat like lead in Eusden's heart.

★ ★ ★

After more than an hour of aimless walking, he was cold and tired enough to be glad the bars were open. He went into one that was more Irish than Swedish and sat sipping a Danish beer while an ice hockey match proceeded largely unwatched on a widescreen television. He steeled himself to check his phone for messages, expecting Gemma would have slept on her indignation, woken to find it undiminished and sought to remind him of his responsibilities. Surprisingly in the circumstances, she had not called. But Bernie Shadbolt had, leaving his mobile number and a peremptory demand that Eusden ring it, which he had no intention of doing.

The other message was less easy to shrug off. He had forgotten giving Regina Celeste his number and now regretted it. At the time it had seemed unimportant. But every judgement had become provisional: they could all be overtaken by events.

'Hi, Richard. This is Regina. As you'll deduce, I've gotten myself a cellphone that actually functions on this continent, so can you call me? I need an update on the Werner situation. Also you might like to know what I've accomplished so far on my Hanoverian expedition. If I don't hear back soon, I'll try your hotel. So long.'

He slowed down the beer intake and tried to

266

do some cool rational thinking. Maybe it was actually a blessing he had given Regina his number. If she rang the Phoenix and learnt he had checked out, she might hurry back to Copenhagen and start looking for him. Worse still, she might go back into partnership with Straub. The less either of them knew of what he was really up to the better. It was safer by far to keep Regina in ignorance. Less than half an hour had passed since her call, so it was a safe bet she had not yet called the Phoenix. He decided to make sure she did not need to.

★ ★ ★

'Hi, Richard. Thanks for calling back.'

'No problem.'

'What's happening your end?'

'Nothing. There's been no sign of Werner.'

'Nor Marty, I take it?'

'No.' Eusden steeled himself to speak the words in a casual tone. 'No sign of Marty either.'

'So, you're basically twiddling your thumbs, right?'

'Sort of.'

'Well, fortunately, one of us has been busy. Werner and Marty have got a nasty surprise coming their way. Thanks to little old me.'

'What do you mean?'

'I've gone ahead and bought Hans Grenscher's collection of Gestapo documents. As soon as the money hits his bank account tomorrow morning, they'll be in my hands. Which means I'll have in my possession the only

267

item I'm actually interested in: a record of Anastasia's fingerprints, taken by the Hanover police in 1938 on orders from Berlin. *That's* the magical matching item Werner made such a big thing of. And no wonder, if it really can be matched.'

'I don't understand. *Matched?*'

'With Anastasia's pre-1918 fingerprints. Don't you get it, Richard? That's what Marty's grandfather must have got hold of. How, I can't imagine. But somehow. Her fingerprints must have been taken during the imperial visit to Cowes in 1909. And Clem Hewitson must have hung on to them.'

Was it possible? Clem claimed to have met Anastasia aboard the imperial yacht. He had gone aboard to be thanked by the Tsar and Tsarina for preventing the assassinations of Anastasia's elder sisters, Olga and Tatiana. Where and how could fingerprinting figure in such an encounter? The science had surely been in its infancy in the Edwardian period. It was probably completely unknown in Russia in 1909 — a point Regina had clearly been pondering.

'Sounds crazy, doesn't it? Isle of Wight bobby taking a Russian princess's dabs. I can't begin to imagine how that could've come about. But let's say it did. Let's say PC Hewitson was bragging about how scientifically advanced British police methods were, spotted Anastasia with ink on her fingers — she was always said to be a messy girl — and laid on an impromptu demonstration of how to take her prints. And let's also say he kept them as a memento of his brush with Russian

268

royalty. If they match the 1938 prints . . . we've struck the mother lode.'

If they matched. Unfortunately for Regina, Eusden knew she was never going to have the chance to find out whether they did or not. And a murkier issue still was troubling him. Where did Tolmar Aksden come into this? What connected him to Anastasia? How *could* Hakon Nydahl's letters to Clem all those years ago be so damaging to him?

'So,' Regina breezed on, 'Werner can cut any kind of deal with Marty he likes. Sooner or later, they're going to have to deal with me. We'll both have what the other needs to make out the case for Anastasia's recognition. Fingerprints trump DNA any day of the week. But only the matching pair of sets will do the job. We're going to have to come to some kind of an agreement. Unless, of course, you can prevail on your childhood friend to freeze out Werner altogether. It's nothing less than the man deserves, after all. What do you say, Richard? Willing to give it a try?'

★ ★ ★

Eusden could not remember, after Regina had rung off, exactly how he had answered her question. Some prevarication had sufficed, thanks to her blithe assumption that he was now her eager assistant. She would be heading back to Copenhagen, where she believed him to be waiting, as soon as her transaction with Grenscher was complete. Alas for her, another transaction hundreds of miles away was going to render her possession of Anna Anderson's fingerprints irrelevant. No match was ever going to be made.

★ ★ ★

Futile though curiosity was bound to be, Eusden could not entirely suppress it. He returned to the Sheraton to wait for Pernille Madsen and retrieved his bag, which he had left with the concierge after checking out. He went into the bar and ordered a coffee, opened the bag and took out Burgaard's family tree of the Nydahls and Aksdens. He had remembered Anna Anderson's claim to have given birth to a son in December 1918 and wanted to remind himself that Peder Aksden could not have been that son. It was true. According to Burgaard, who could certainly be trusted to have checked his facts, Peder Aksden was born in 1909. There was no fudging a nine-year age gap. He was not Anastasia's son. And hence Tolmar was not her grandson. There was no connection between them. And yet there was. There had to be. But what it could possibly be he —

'Richard Eusden?'

The softly inflected voice belonged to a woman standing beside his chair. He had not heard her approach. She was dressed in a black coat and boots, with a peacock-patterned scarf round her neck. There was nothing of the blonde Scandinavian about her. Her hair and eyes were dark brown, her face pale, her features delicate, her pink-lipsticked mouth opened in a hesitant smile even as her brow furrowed into the slightest of frowns.

'I'm Pernille Madsen.'

33

'Where did you get that from?' Pernille asked. She pointed at the sheet of paper in Eusden's lap. 'And why is my name on it?'

'See for yourself.' Eusden rose and handed her the sheet. 'Heard of Karsten Burgaard?'

'Yes.' She said no more than that. After scrutinizing the family tree for a moment, she returned it. 'His work?'

Eusden nodded, then, belatedly, offered her his hand. Her smile broadened by a cautious fraction. They shook. 'Want some coffee?'

'Yes. It's been a long drive.' She took off her coat and scarf to reveal another layer of black — woollen cardigan, jumper, skirt and wide shiny belt. The only colourful note was struck by a peridot necklace that she fingered as they sat down.

The waitress was already approaching with the coffee. Eusden signalled for her to deliver it to Pernille and ordered another for himself.

'Does it hurt?' Pernille asked, gesturing with her eyebrows at the wound on his head.

'Only when I laugh. And I haven't been laughing much lately.'

'Birgitte told me about your friend. I'm sorry.'

'Thanks. What else did she tell you?'

'Everything I need to know.'

'And now you're going to tell me everything *I* need to know.'

She sipped her coffee, then gave him a long, strangely soothing look of scrutiny. 'We'll be met in Helsinki by a former Mjollnir employee, now retired: Osmo Koskinen. He's arranging the handover. That's as much as I know.'

'Surely not.'

He knew from Burgaard's family tree that she was in her late forties, but already she had looked both younger and older than that. There was vulnerability as well as strength in her, insecurity as well as self-control. Marriage to Tolmar Aksden had been an experience that had left its mark.

'I've no idea what Hakon Nydahl's letters to Clem Hewitson reveal about your ex-husband, but you must have. It's why you're here.'

'Not exactly.'

She broke off as the second coffee was delivered. Eusden studied her skittering glance around the room as the waitress came between them. She was frightened, though precisely what of he sensed he would not discover. Perhaps, it occurred to him, she had been frightened for a long time.

The waitress departed. She compressed her lips, then looked back at him. 'All I know is that the . . . material we're to collect . . . would ruin Tolmar if it reached the media. I don't know how. I don't want to know. Michael, our son, matters to me more than . . . all my troubles with Tolmar. Do you have children, Richard?'

'No.'

'Maybe you're lucky. Maybe it's best not to . . . care so much, so very, very much . . . about

273

this person who ... grows and changes and ... sometimes seems to hate you. But that's how it is to be a mother. I worry about Michael all the time. He isn't strong like his father. He couldn't cope with ... pressure. He plans to join Mjollnir. He thinks Tolmar is ... a great man. He wants to be like him, even though he can't be. If Tolmar is ruined, I don't know what would happen to Michael. And I don't want to find out.'

'Perhaps it would be the making of him.'

'No. It wouldn't. I'm sure of that.'

'You're taking quite a risk for his sake.'

'For my sake as well. Tolmar ruined ... would be a dangerous man. Besides, Birgitte said there's no serious risk. These people ... just want money. And Mjollnir have plenty of that.'

'How much are they paying?'

'That's something else I don't know and don't want to know. Koskinen will deliver the money to us and we'll deliver it to the people Birgitte calls the Opposition in a safe, secure setting. They'll deliver the attaché case, you'll check the contents and the exchange will be complete. Then we'll go our separate ways. And you and I can get on with our lives.'

'Sounds simple.'

'Why shouldn't it be?'

'Doesn't it worry you that Tolmar doesn't know about any of this?'

'Birgitte Grøn is a better judge of his interests than he is himself. She's calm and calculating. Tolmar ... gets angry if he's threatened. And then ... ' Pernille took another sip of coffee and

274

fingered her necklace again. 'It's better this way,' she said softly, as if addressing herself rather than Eusden. 'Much better.'

⋆ ⋆ ⋆

It was a short drive to the Viking Line terminal at Stadsgården. The sinking sun was casting long shadows across the harbour ice as they crossed to Gamla Stan. When Pernille lowered her visor, Eusden noticed a photograph of a fair-haired, smiling boy of twelve or thirteen taped to the back of it: Michael, as his mother preferred to remember him, waiting to greet her whenever the sun shone.

⋆ ⋆ ⋆

Pernille brought her BMW to a gentle halt in the queue for the ferry. The bluey greyness of dusk was creeping over the harbour. She took a folder containing their tickets out of the door pocket and checked the contents, then dropped it back into place. She seemed nervous now their departure was drawing closer.

'I'll stop here on the way back and do some shopping,' she said. 'Treat myself . . . to some normality.'

'Good idea.'

'You'll be back in London by then. Your life will be normal again as well.'

'I suppose so.'

'You sound doubtful.'

'To be honest, I'm finding it difficult to

remember what normal life is like.'

'How did they persuade you to help them? Mjollnir, I mean. I'm here for my son. Why did you come?'

'They left me no choice.'

'I thought they couldn't have.' She ran her hands round the steering-wheel. 'I used to work for Mjollnir. That's how I met Tolmar. On the surface, they're a . . . perfect employer. Good pay and conditions. Health insurance. Childcare. Pension. Everything you could ask for.'

'And beneath the surface?'

'They organize things so that . . . people have no choice . . . except to do what Mjollnir wants.'

'Or what Tolmar wants.'

'It's the same thing.'

'Not this time.'

'Apparently not.'

'Why did you marry him?'

'I was young. He was . . . powerful and wealthy and attractive. Very attractive, actually. I loved him. And I persuaded myself he loved me.'

'When did you find out he didn't?'

'When Michael was born. That's what Tolmar wanted from me. A son and heir. Once he'd got it, he . . . blanked me out of his life.'

'Well, you're back in it now. Even if he doesn't know it.'

★ ★ ★

The sun had set, but its glow was still lighting the western sky when the M/S *Gabriella* eased away from the pier and headed out into the

276

shipping lane that curved ahead of it like a dark grey snake through the matt white expanse of ice. Eusden lingered among the hardy souls on deck, watching the cityscape slowly change as the ship moved across the harbour. Pernille had gone to her cabin. They were to meet later for dinner. He wondered if she felt as he did: that it was better to be two than one on the journey they were taking; better by far.

ÖSTERSJÖN — ITÄMERI

34

Pernille toyed with the salmon on her plate and sipped some wine. She did not seem to have much of an appetite — for food or conversation. Eusden suspected uncertainty about what lay ahead of them was a likelier explanation than seasickness. Neither had any way of knowing whether the planned exchange of attaché case for Mjollnir money would really be the swift, simple and above all safe affair others had predicted. Those others would not be there when it happened.

'For what it's worth, Pernille,' he ventured, 'I think it'll all go very smoothly.'

She smiled fleetingly. 'That's not what you said this afternoon.'

'I've thought it over since.'

'Have you? Well, so have I. And I'm sure you're right. The Opposition want money. Mjollnir want the material. We're just the . . . mellemmœndene — the middlemen. There won't be a problem with the handover.'

'With something else, then?'

'It's what you said at the terminal. I'm back in Tolmar's life, even if he doesn't know it. But he will know. Eventually. He finds out everything in the end.'

'Surely it won't matter by then.'

'You don't know him. It always matters.'

'I get the feeling . . . you're frightened of him.'

'That's what my psychotherapist said.'

'Is it true?'

'Oh yes.' She smiled and shook her head in wonderment at the obviousness of the truth. 'The question is whether the fear is about something else ... in me. That's what my psychotherapist thinks.'

'I guess that's the sort of thing they always think.'

She laughed. 'How would you know? You've never had one.'

He was forced to laugh himself, discovering in the process that he had been right: the wound above his eye throbbed painfully. 'How can you be sure of something like that? You hardly know me.'

'It's obvious. Look at yourself, Richard. White, male, middle-aged, well-paid, heterosexual Englishman. Nice family. Good education. Comfortable life. What would you talk to a psychotherapist *about?*'

'Divorce maybe. You didn't mention that.'

'I bet it was very ... civilized.'

'Wasn't yours?'

'On the surface, yes.'

'What does that mean?'

'It means Tolmar pays me a generous allowance and leaves me alone. And it means I think he might be standing there, with that ... look on his face I remember so well because I ... see it in my dreams ... every time I answer the doorbell.'

'Is he a violent man, Pernille?'

'He never hit me. Not once. But I knew ... if

it happened . . . it only ever would be once.' She swallowed some wine. 'I don't know why I'm telling you all this. I don't normally . . . open up. Neither do you, I guess.'

'Maybe there's nothing for me to open up about.'

'There's always something. Plenty, according to my psychotherapist.'

'Have you ever considered . . . remarrying?'

'Once. A few years ago. He was a good man. But it didn't work out.' A brief silence fell. Then she went on. 'Are you going to ask me what went wrong?'

'If you want me to.'

'He died. In a car crash. At night.' She looked Eusden in the eye. 'Remind you of anything?'

'Are you saying . . . '

'Tolmar told me, when he agreed to the divorce, that I shouldn't . . . get into a permanent relationship again. I thought he was . . . giving me advice. But when Paul died, I . . . remembered that Tolmar always means exactly what he says.'

'Good God.'

'There's no evidence it wasn't an accident. I can't prove a thing. But I . . . wouldn't want another death on my conscience.' She laid her knife and fork neatly down. 'I can't eat anything else. We could finish the wine in my cabin if you like. Mjollnir booked me a suite. We may as well use the space.'

★ ★ ★

Pernille's suite was an elegant contrast with Eusden's cramped single cabin. Mjollnir treated their CEO's ex-wife and an outsider very differently. Sloping windows, across which the curtains had not been drawn, looked out over the bow into the still, cold Baltic night. The comfortably furnished lounge was large enough to hold a party in and came complete with complimentary champagne, the bottle standing forlornly in a bucket of water that had once been ice.

'I'm sorry if I rushed you out of the restaurant,' Pernille said as she topped up their wine glasses. 'I suddenly thought I was . . . saying too much . . . in a public place.'

'Afraid someone might've recognized you?'

'No. But . . . ' She cradled the glass against her throat and gazed out into the darkness. 'One of the reasons I drove to Stockholm was to make sure I wasn't followed. I know the signs. I know them well. Tolmar has no spies aboard. He doesn't know what we're doing. Even so . . . '

'How long have you been taking such precautions?'

'Since Paul died.'

'And how long's that?'

'Seven years.'

'Sorry.'

'What for?'

'Your loss. Your . . . anxiety. Being divorced from Tolmar Aksden doesn't sound like a lot of fun.'

'It's better than being married to him. You can take my word for that.'

'When did it end?'

'When he sent Michael away to a . . . *kostskole*. You know? A school where the children live as well as learn.'

'Boarding school.'

'That's it. Michael was twelve years old. The school was near Aalborg, up in the north of Jutland. We'd only just moved from Århus to Copenhagen. Everything changed around then. Tolmar got . . . harder.' She smiled. 'I think he finally decided what he wanted to do. And I was . . . irrelevant.'

'What *did* he want to do?'

'I don't know. He has a lot of secrets, Richard. He collects them. He *enjoys* them.'

'Everyone seems to think what we're buying is . . . the biggest secret of all.'

'Maybe it is.'

'You must know it involves his father.'

'Yes. There's always been a . . . mystery about the family. Only Tolmar knows what it is. Lars would like to. Elsa would prefer not to. But only Tolmar knows. Though one day, I imagine, he'll tell Michael.'

'As his son and heir.'

'Yes. And that frightens me also. Michael becoming . . . the next keeper of the family secret.'

'There's a Russian connection. You must know that too.'

'Of course,' she said sadly. 'The last house I lived in with Tolmar was at Klampenborg. From the garden, you could see across to Hvidøre. Lars said Tolmar had chosen the house *because* you could see Hvidøre from it. He told me

285

stories about his great-uncle, Hakon Nydahl, the courtier. He thought I could get more out of Tolmar than he was able to. But I wouldn't have, even if I'd tried. No one gets more out of Tolmar than he wants to give. And that isn't much.' She drained her glass and set it down on the table. 'Would you like to go on deck? I need some fresh air after all this . . . talk about the past.'

'It'll be freezing up there.'

She smiled and nodded at him. 'Good. That'll be how I like it.'

* * *

It *was* freezing. And no one else was braving the conditions. The sky above them was scattered with more stars than Eusden could ever recall seeing. The cold was intense, almost tangible. The ship's engine rumbled below their feet. And sea ice stretched away, blue-grey and ghostly, on every side.

'It all seems so simple out here,' said Pernille, her breath frosting in the air as she gazed upwards. 'The stars and the sea and the moving ship. But it can't stay like this, can it? Tomorrow, we *will* reach Helsinki.'

'Have you ever been there before?' Eusden asked.

'No. Tolmar often went to Helsinki for business. But he never took me with him. He has an apartment there. It's his only base outside of Denmark.'

'Does he still have the house in Klampenborg?'

'No. He moved out to the country after the divorce. He bought himself an estate near Helsingør. A lovely place — they tell me. I could have been . . . lady of the manor . . . if I'd stayed with him.'

'You don't wish you had, though.'

'Never. I like my . . . small apartment in the city. It's close to the shops. And to where I work.'

'And where's that?'

'I'm HR director of a charity called Uddanne Afrika. We ship educational equipment to . . . wherever it's needed in Africa. Which is all over, really. Have you ever been there, Richard?'

'Does Cape Town count?'

'No.'

'Then, I haven't.'

'You should. I've stood in schoolrooms in Burkina Faso and looked at the children's faces and realized . . . I was doing something really worth doing . . . at last.'

'It sounds like a good feeling.'

'It is. You ought to try it. Birgitte said you work at the Foreign Ministry in London, yes?'

'For my sins.'

'How long for?'

'Nearly thirty years.'

'We could use someone with your experience at Uddanne Afrika.'

'Are you offering me a job?'

'I'm offering you the chance to change your life. But maybe . . . you don't want to change it.'

'I think I do, actually. I think I want to quite badly.'

'Then, you should give me a call . . . when this is over.'

★ ★ ★

They parted at the door to Pernille's suite with subdued goodnights. Eusden headed down to his lower-deck cabin light-headed with fatigue and fragile hopefulness. Pernille Madsen was, as she had made clear to him, a dangerous woman to become emotionally attached to. There was no reason to regard her proposition as anything more than an opportunity to switch career paths. But the elation he felt at knowing that their acquaintance need not end tomorrow was undeniable. He doubted it was shared. But that made it no easier to stifle.

HELSINKI

35

Helsinki was white from recent snowfall, the shoreline dividing the city from the snow-carpeted sea ice hard to discern. The sky was a featureless dome of bruised cloud. There were no shadows in the thin winter light. Even sounds were subdued in the Finnish winter morning. The *Gabriella* docked at ten. By 10.30 Eusden and Pernille Madsen had checked into the Grand Marina Hotel, a stylishly converted warehouse a short distance from the Viking Line terminal. Waiting for them there was Mjollnir's man on the scene, Osmo Koskinen.

He was seventy or so, with a sad, drooping face and rheumy eyes offset by an eager smile. He had grey, slicked-down hair and a bowed air of lifelong dutifulness. His flapping brown suit appeared to date from a time when he had carried more weight. This, his pasty complexion and a faint tremor in his hands and voice implied he might not be in the best of health. Nevertheless, as a former senior employee of Mjollnir's Finnish subsidiary, he was, Eusden assumed, deemed to be the perfect combination of detachment and reliability required for the job in hand.

Koskinen lightly acknowledged as much over coffee in Pernille's harbour-facing suite. 'Birgitte Grøn has asked me to look after you, Ms Madsen. And you also, Mr Eusden. I am retired now, but Mjollnir still use me for . . . special business . . . from time to time. I do not know what dealings they have had with the people you will meet later. I do not need to know. But I have made all the arrangements Birgitte asked me to make. First, though, my apologies. You should be staying at the Kämp. It is Helsinki's finest and most historic hotel. And I should be showing you the sights of the city. I have lived here all my life. But they tell me we must be . . . discreet. A hotel near the ferry terminal and no unnecessary movement. Those were my instructions. So, I am sorry. But I fixed it like I was told.'

'Don't worry about it, Hr Koskinen,' said Pernille, gazing past him through the window. 'We're not here to enjoy ourselves.'

'No. It's a pity. But I understand.'

'What are the arrangements?' asked Eusden.

'Of course. The arrangements. The payment will be made in US dollar bearer bonds. I do not know the value. Again, I do not need to know. I will collect them from the bank Birgitte is using at two this afternoon. I will deliver them to you here at two thirty. They will be in a secure combination-locked case. The exchange will take place at three thirty at my house in Munkkini-emi. The address is Luumitie twenty-seven. I have marked it for you.' Koskinen spread out a street map of Helsinki on the table between them. A red X marked the spot in a north-western suburb. 'This is where we are now.' He pointed to the location of the hotel, out on the Katajanokka peninsula, on the other side of the city. 'Erik Lund is supplying security and a

292

lawyer to supervise the exchange. His name is Juha Matalainen. He will travel with you. The combination of the case will be phoned through to him when you have inspected the material delivered by the other side, Mr Eusden. Ms Madsen will take charge of the material. The other side will take their money. The exchange will be complete. Everyone leaves.' He smiled. 'Then I will return home and cook my dinner.'

'It's kind of you to let your house be used for this,' said Pernille.

'Oh, I am pleased to help. It is really Mjollnir's house, to tell the truth. I would probably be in a one-room apartment if they had not been so . . . generous to me. A good employer is as important as a good wife, they . . . ' Koskinen broke off, apparently reflecting on Pernille's status as his former boss's former spouse. He coughed awkwardly. 'Well, there it is. Everything should be . . . very straightforward.'

'Exactly what sort of security is . . . Erik Lund . . . laying on?' asked Eusden, catching Pernille's eye. She seemed amused by Koskinen's discomfiture.

'Enough, Mr Eusden, I assure you. You will be able to see for yourself when you arrive at the house.'

'I'm sure it'll be more than enough,' said Pernille. 'These people only want the money, after all.'

'Yes.' Koskinen smiled. 'Exactly.'

'And until two thirty?'

'I have to ask you to stay here, Ms Madsen.

293

Your husband — I mean, Hr Aksden — is in the city. Birgitte told me we must . . . be careful.'

'Of course.'

'But there is a trip for you to take, Mr Eusden.'

'Really?'

'Matalainen's office. To sign a . . . confidentiality agreement. To say you will . . . never talk about the material you will see this afternoon.'

'Is that necessary?' asked Pernille. There was an edge of irritation in her voice.

Koskinen gestured helplessly with his hands. 'It is not my decision. Do you . . . object, Mr Eusden?'

'What if I do?'

'Then we have . . . a problem.'

Eusden took a slow walk to the window and back to mull the point over. The reason Birgitte Grøn had said nothing about such a formality was obvious. The less warning he had, the less likely he was to argue. Once the material was in Mjollnir's hands, nothing he said about it could be proven anyway, even supposing he gleaned anything at all from letters written in Danish, which was doubtful in the extreme. His signature on a piece of paper was more or less irrelevant. A refusal to supply it would only complicate matters that all concerned wanted to keep as uncomplicated as possible.

'Do we have a problem, Mr Eusden?'

'No, no. I'll sign on the dotted line. When's Matalainen expecting me?'

★   ★   ★

The answer was that Koskinen proposed to take Eusden to Matalainen's office straight away. He said he would wait for him in reception and took his leave.

'Birgitte should have told me about this,' said Pernille as soon as the door had closed behind him.

'It doesn't matter,' said Eusden, finishing his coffee. 'What matters is that the handover goes smoothly. The set-up sounds good to me. What do you think?'

'Yes. It sounds good.'

'So, I'm the lucky one. I get a morning stroll while you stay cooped up here.'

'Call me when you get back. I'm going to take a bath. It'll help me stay calm.' She sighed and ran her fingers down over her face. 'I think I might need to get drunk tonight, Richard. Want to join me?'

Eusden smiled. 'It's a date.'

★ ★ ★

It was a short taxi-ride from the hotel into the city centre. Koskinen plied Eusden with a tourist commentary as they went. 'Uspenski Orthodox Cathedral.' (Eusden gazed up at snow-capped onion domes.) 'The presidential palace.' (They passed a colonnaded and pedimented mansion.) 'Senate Square.' (Another cathedral, Lutheran this time, loomed wedding-cake white above them.) 'The Bank of Finland.' (More colonnaded grandeur.) 'Most of what you see was built when Finland was under Russian rule, Mr

Eusden. In little more than a hundred years after taking over from the Swedes, they gave us a city to be proud of. What did we do to thank them? Revolt as soon as we could after they deposed the Tsar. Clever, no?'

'Very. And I gather Saukko Bank have maintained the tradition.'

'What . . . do you mean?'

'Dealing cleverly with Russia.'

'Ah, yes, I suppose . . . you could say that.'

'Isn't that why Tolmar Aksden bought them out? To acquire their Russian holdings?'

'I . . . do not know. It — ' Koskinen looked round with grateful alacrity as the taxi drew to a halt. 'Ah, we are here.' He opened his door and climbed out.

Eusden exited on the offside, checking for traffic as he did so. There was none close behind. The nearest vehicle, another taxi, was still some way off, driving slowly. He glanced towards it as he slammed the door and rounded the boot. The passenger was sitting in the front. His eyes met Eusden's in an instant of recognition. Then he looked away and said something to the driver, who flicked on his indicator and turned abruptly right.

Eusden heard Koskinen shout to him as he ran towards the side street. Pursuit was futile, he knew, but the knowledge did not stop him. What did was skidding on a patch of ice that had spread around a pipe draining a roof somewhere above him. He hit the pavement with a shoulder-jarring thump that set his head wound throbbing. By the time he had recovered his

296

senses and picked himself up, the taxi was taking another right at the far end of the side street, its brake lamps blinking fuzzily red in the thin grey light.

'Are you all right, Mr Eusden?' Koskinen panted as he caught up.

'Yes. I . . . thought I recognized the passenger in the taxi.'

'What taxi?'

'The one that just . . . ' Koskinen's uncomprehending gaze did not encourage fuller explanation. What would he say, after all — what *could* he say — if Eusden put a name to the face he had glimpsed? The presence of Lars Aksden in Helsinki was disturbing enough. The fact that he had been following them moved beyond disturbing into downright sinister. But what did it mean? What did it portend? All Eusden was sure of in that instant was that Osmo Koskinen would be of no help in finding out. 'Never mind. I must've been mistaken. Let's go in.'

36

Juha Matalainen's office was a shrine to Finnish minimalism, with a wide-windowed view of surrounding roofs and a narrow glimpse of the domes of the Lutheran Cathedral. Matalainen himself was kitted out in slim-lapelled chocolate-brown suit and collarless cream shirt. He was a lean, angular man with tight-cropped dark hair and a beard reduced to virtual pencil lines around his jaw and mouth. His gaze was steady and curious and had rested on Eusden for several minutes on end.

Eusden had supposedly spent those minutes perusing the tersely worded confidentiality agreement Matalainen had slid across the flawless surface of his desk for him to sign. The English version was flanked by one in Danish and one in Finnish. The agreement amounted to an undertaking never to disclose to any third party any information which he came into possession of at Luumitie 27, 00330 Helsinki, Finland, on this twelfth day of February, 2007. It had taken him only a few seconds to establish that much. His thoughts had then drifted to the host of questions raised by his sighting of Lars Aksden in the street below. And it was anxious contemplation of those that no doubt caused him to frown and shake his head.

'Is there a problem, Mr Eusden?' Matalainen asked.

'What?'

'A problem? With the agreement?'

'No. I . . . ' Eusden raised an apologetic hand. 'Sorry. I just . . . ' He exerted himself to focus his thoughts. 'The agreement's fine. I'm happy to sign it.' Then some instinct told him not to be *too* cooperative. 'I can't read Danish, of course.'

'I assure you they are exact translations.' Matalainen's gaze narrowed as the point struck home. 'Surely you can't read Finnish either, Mr Eusden.'

'No. I can't.'

'But you specified Danish.'

'I wasn't talking about these documents. I meant the ones we'll be collecting later. They're all in Danish. So, how could I learn anything from them I might reveal later? The agreement caters for an impossible contingency.'

Matalainen smiled thinly. 'In that case you lose nothing by signing it.'

Eusden returned the smile. 'Quite so.' He picked up the proffered pen and signed.

Koskinen added his signature as witness. Matalainen gathered up the trilingual versions of the documents, gave Eusden a copy and stood up, signalling that their meeting was at an end. '*Näkemiin*, Mr Eusden,' he said, extending a hand and bowing faintly. 'I'll see you later.'

★　★　★

'Matalainen reminds me of my dentist,' said Koskinen as they descended in the lift.

'You should change your dentist.'

'Ah, no. He is very efficient. I just don't want to go fishing with him. But I always need a drink after visiting him. You want one?'

'I want several. But one will do.'

★ ★ ★

Koskinen took him to the Café Engel on Senate Square. Their window table kept the Lutheran cathedral in view, this time front-on across the snow-covered square. Trams rattled by in the street. Early lunchers maintained a jumble of conversation.

'*Kippis*,' said Koskinen, starting on his beer. 'Your good health, Mr Eusden.'

'Call me Richard. How long have you worked — did you work — for Mjollnir, Osmo?'

'Not so long really. They bought me with VFG Timber. But they were good to me. Another company might have . . . moved me on.'

'So, Tolmar Aksden's a good man to work for?'

'He asks for a lot. He gives a lot.'

'You got to know him well?'

'Not well, Richard, no. He has a saying: 'Don't bring your family to work.' He never brought his. Besides, he was most of the time in Copenhagen.'

'Ever meet his brother Lars?'

'No. I have heard about him. He paints, I think. But, no, I have never met him.'

'Would you know him if you saw him?'

Koskinen frowned. Eusden's line of questioning was beginning to puzzle him. 'Probably not.'

300

'Have you seen Tolmar during his latest visit to Helsinki?'

'No. He has been very busy, according to the newspapers. That is all I know now I am retired: what I read in the papers.'

'And what do you read about him?'

'Oh, there are some messy politics now he has brought Saukko Bank. They are full of it.'

'What do they say?'

Koskinen's smile was more of a wince. He had been drawn into a subject he was clearly uncomfortable with. 'It looks like not everybody is happy with the scale of Saukko's Russian investments now the takeover has brought them to their attention. Commercially smart, but politically . . . sensitive.' He shrugged and took a swig of beer, then glanced through the window, squinting as if focusing on something in the distance. 'We Finns always worry about Russia. Either it is too strong or too weak. But always it is our neighbour.' He looked back at Eusden. 'Excuse me, Richard. This talk of weakness has gone to my bladder.'

Koskinen rose with a scraping of his chair, and ambled off to the loo, leaving Eusden to dwell once more on the mystery of Lars Aksden's presence in Helsinki. Should he tell Pernille? The moment of decision was fast approaching. He was also aware he needed to phone in some fresh — or warmed-over — excuse for his no-show at the Foreign Office now a new working week had begun, though his life there felt more like a false memory of someone else's. In search of distraction, he grabbed an abandoned newspaper from an adjacent table.

Helsingin Sanomat forecast minus temperatures in double figures and cloudy conditions for Helsinki. 'Great,' Eusden muttered to himself, leafing through page after page of impenetrable Finnish headlines. 'Just great.' Then he saw the magic word: Mjollnir. And then . . .

A photograph adjoining an article in the business section of the paper analysing, as far as he could tell, Mjollnir's performance since its takeover of Saukko Bank, showed two smiling besuited captains of commerce in a wood-panelled conference room. The caption beneath identified them as Arto Falenius and . . . Tolmar Aksden.

Falenius was a debonair middle-aged figure in pinstripes, with a spotted tie and a matching handkerchief billowing from his breast pocket, greying hair worn daringly long, handsome face tanned enough to suggest he spent a sizeable chunk of the Nordic winter in sunnier climes. His status was unclear to Eusden. Saukko's CEO, perhaps, celebrating a synergetic merger? The photograph might not be contemporary, of course. It could easily date from the previous autumn.

There was certainly no doubt, however, that Aksden was the dominant partner. He was taller than Falenius by several inches, older by a couple of decades and altogether more serious. His suit and tie were unpatterned, his smile cooler, his gaze harder. There was a bulk about him, of muscle and intellect. He looked a lot like his brother, but without as many visible ravages

302

of self-indulgence. Instead, there was calmness and certainty in his face, confidence edged with something like defiance in his expression. Or was it contempt? Yes. There was a hint of that in his bearing and demeanour: an ingrained knowledge of his own superiority.

A movement at the door suddenly caught Eusden's eye. He looked up just in time to see Koskinen exiting the café, shrugging on the overcoat he had retrieved from the hatstand as he went. He moved fast, without looking back.

'Osmo!' Eusden called. But he was too late. The door had already closed. He stood up, baffled and dismayed. What was the fellow playing at? He headed after him.

But the waiter intercepted, clutching the bill. There was a flurry of confusion and misunderstanding. Eusden wasted precious minutes offering Danish, then Swedish, kroner in payment before pulling out some euros. By the time he reached the street, Koskinen had vanished. He swore, loudly enough to offend a woman walking by, and asked himself again what Koskinen's game could possibly be. His behaviour was inexplicable.

Then Eusden remembered him looking out of the window just before excusing himself. What had he been looking *at*? The cathedral was the obvious answer. It dominated the view across the square. Had someone on the steps leading up to it signalled to him? Had the time shown on its clock triggered his move?

In one sense, it did not matter. The fact was that he had gone. Eusden shivered, realizing as

303

the chill bit into him that he had left his coat in the café. He turned back.

A man was standing directly in his path dressed in a black cap and dark casual clothes. He was tall and muscular and stony-faced. For a second, Eusden gaped at him. And the man stared expressionlessly back. Eusden heard a vehicle pull up at the kerb next to him, skidding in the ice-clogged gutter. Then the man kneed him in the groin with such force that he doubled up, his eyes misting with pain. He was seized about the shoulders. A heavy hand descended on to his neck. He was pushed and pulled backwards, his heels dragging on the pavement.

Suddenly, he was on the floor of a Transit van, the door sliding shut as it accelerated away. There were two men above and around him, lurching with the motion of the van. He heard the sound of tape being peeled from a roll. He tried to sit up, but was shoved back down. His hands were yanked round behind him. The tape was wound tightly round them and his ankles simultaneously. Within seconds, he was trussed and helpless.

'For God's sake,' he gasped. 'What do you — ' Then a strip of tape was slapped over his mouth as well.

'Change of plan, Mr Eusden.' Eusden twisted in the direction the voice had come from and saw Erik Lund smiling at him through the grille from the passenger seat. 'For you.' He felt something sharp jab into his left arm. 'My advice is to stop struggling.'

Eusden had no intention of taking Lund's

advice. But within seconds he had no choice in the matter. The jolting of the van merged with waves of wooziness that swept into his brain. The figures around him blurred into monochrome — then merged into blackness.

37

For a second, when he woke, Eusden believed he was in bed at home in London, the pounding in his head and the stiffness in his limbs attributable to a serious hangover. But no. Reality pounced on his thoughts with the force of a nightmare. He was still in the van, alone now, alone and cold and enveloped in darkness.

A trace of light was seeping in from somewhere, however, enough to cast shadows within the van. He crawled on to his knees and looked about him as best he could. A shutter was rattling somewhere outside the vehicle, but no other sound reached him. How long he had been wherever he was he had no way of knowing. His wristwatch was out of sight. Why he had been left there was equally impenetrable. 'Change of plan for *you*,' Lund had said, as if this had always been the plan as far as Mjollnir were concerned. Koskinen's behaviour confirmed as much. A trap had been laid for him. But *why*?

He had to break free. For the moment, that was all he could think of. A conjunction of shadows towards the front of the van revealed a tear of some kind in one corner of the grille sealing off the cab. He worked his way over for a closer look. The frame was dented and several wires had sprung out of their sockets. The loose ends were stiff and sharp. He turned round, stretched his arms up behind him and felt one of the wires against the heel of his hand. He manoeuvred so that it snagged on the tape, then sawed away until the tape split.

Within a couple of minutes, he had released his hands. He teased the strip off his mouth, sat down and peered at his watch. It was a few minutes past two. Koskinen should be in the process of collecting the caseload of bearer bonds around now. He must already have given Pernille some cooked-up explanation of Eusden's disappearance. He felt in his pocket for his phone. But they had taken it. No surprise, really. He unwound the strips binding his ankles and prised at the handle of the side door. Locked. That was no surprise either. He stood up and moved to the rear doors. Also locked. There was no way out. He thumped pointlessly at the nearest door panel, then lowered himself to the floor, flexing fruitlessly at the handle as he sat there, staring glumly into the shadows. God, it was cold. Did Lund mean him to freeze to death?

As much to warm himself as with any realistic hope of getting out that way, he went back to the dented grille and tried to pull it further loose. No more wires budged. Apart from a gash to his finger, he achieved nothing. He slumped down on the floor, sucking the wound, cursing Lund and Birgitte Grøn — and Marty for dragging him into all this.

Unmeasured minutes passed while he contemplated the horrifying nature of his plight. The invisible shutter went on rattling. The cold began to gnaw at him. He started to shiver. 'Fucking hell, Marty,' he said aloud, 'how could you — '

A sound deeper and farther away than the rattling shutter reached his ears. It was a car engine. It stopped and was succeeded by a burble of human voices. There was the creak of a door opening. The light strengthened marginally. Through the grille and the windscreen beyond, he could see shadows moving on a brick wall. A switch was flicked and a fluorescent lamp pulsed into life overhead. A key turned in the rear door of the van. One of them swung open. Then the other.

Eusden blinked as his eyes adjusted to the harshness of the light. A squat, bull-necked, shaven-headed man in jeans and windcheater stared in at him. Then another man appeared at his shoulder: taller and thinner, dressed in a dark overcoat with the collar pulled up. He had a round, soft-featured face, a mop of ginger hair shot with silver and matching stubble round his fleshy jaw. His small blue-green eyes studied Eusden through circular-lensed glasses.

'You're Eusden?' His voice was pure west-coast American.

'Yes.'

'Let's get the party going, then. Come on out.' His squat companion took something from inside his windcheater and pointed it at Eusden: a gun. 'We're not about to take no for an answer.'

The two men stepped back as Eusden stood up slowly, moved to the end of the van and climbed out. They were in some kind of workshop, sealed by a ceiling-high shutter-door

308

and a smaller wicket-door set within it. There were no windows, just three blank walls, along one of which ran a bare bench. A third man was leaning against the bench, staring, like his companions, at Eusden. He was tall and heavily built, with black hair and beard, a hawkish nose and dark, simmering gaze. He wore a long black leather coat and was chewing gum vigorously. Beside him, on the bench, stood Clem's attaché case.

'Who are you people?' Eusden asked, looking straight at the chatty one and trying not to sound as frightened as he really was.

'I'm Brad. The guy with the gun is Gennady. The guy with the gum — who also has a gun, by the way — is Vladimir. Sorry I couldn't keep the alliteration going. They speak English when they need to, but they usually communicate in other ways.'

'What do you want?'

'You, sport. The guy who offed our very good buddies Ilya and Yuri a few nights back.'

'That was an accident.'

'You're probably right. You don't look capable of getting the better of them. And Yuri? He was always a hell-rider. But let's not allow the facts to get in the way of a good grudge. There's nothing Gennady would like better than putting a bullet in your brain — *after* kicking the shit out of you. A friend dies. A stranger pays. Old Ukrainian tradition. That's where they're from. They always like me to point out that they're not actually Russian. They just look and sound as if they are. And get tetchy when they haven't swallowed a

309

gallon of vodka recently. For the record, they're stone cold sober today. Draw your own conclusions. While you're at it, tell me what your role is in Mjollnir's organization.'

'I don't have one.'

'Why'd you come to Helsinki, then?'

'They blackmailed me.'

'Ah, right. So, what did they say they wanted you to do? I'm assuming they didn't mention they were planning to hand you over to us.'

'I was to . . . authenticate the letters.' Eusden nodded towards the attaché case.

'Strictly non-essential, sport. We faxed them copies of the whole lot. But I guess it sounded plausible to you. Fact is, though, we stipulated your head on a platter *plus* the big fat pay-off right from the get-go. And they never batted an eyelid. I got the feeling they didn't mind us rubbing you out one little bit. Now, why might that be?'

'They seem to think I know too much.'

'What about?'

'Tolmar Aksden.'

'Ah. The Invisible Man. Well, do you?'

'I know he has a secret.'

'Don't we all?'

'Mjollnir wants his kept quiet at any cost.'

'Of course they do. That's why they're buying it from us at a price that makes it well worth our trouble cutting out the original buyer *and* compensates us for leaving twenty million kroner blowing in the Copenhagen wind, not to mention Ilya and Yuri splattered across an unlovely stretch of highway. So, working on the basis that it might, just *might,* persuade us not to kill you, why don't you tell us what that secret is?'

'You must know if you have the letters.'

'Well, there's the weirdest thing. I never did learn Danish while I was growing up in California. Spanish, right on. French and Italian? I can get by. I've even picked up enough Russian to understand Vladimir's jokes on those rare occasions when he cracks one. But Danish? Somehow I let it slip past me. Careless, I know. But that's the way it is.'

'We should have kept Olsen alive,' Vladimir growled.

Brad grinned. 'Don't you just love an after-the-event wise guy? Bet you're wondering who Olsen was, sport, so I'll put you out of your misery. He was our original buyer's very own Danish representative. We were hired for the hands-on side of things. When we decided to sound out Mjollnir as an alternate buyer, Olsen tried to phone his boss. We had to cut him off, if you know what I mean. Unfortunately, he hadn't quite got round to telling us what the letters were all about when that happened, so we're . . . looking to you to fill us in.'

Eusden swallowed hard. Making the little he knew about the contents of the letters sound tantalizing enough to persuade them to let him live was a next to impossible task. But it was his only hope. 'They chronicle the early life of Tolmar Aksden's father, Peder, on a farm in Jutland.'

'A farm in Jutland, huh?' sneered Brad. 'Why

311

isn't my pulse racing at the thought?'

'I can't read Danish either. But I know Tolmar's secret has something to do with . . . Anastasia.'

'Really? You're sure he's not Elvis Presley in disguise? The age would be about right.'

'I don't pretend to understand it. But it's true.'

'You're saying Tolmar Aksden is related somehow to the daughter of the last Tsar?'

'Yes.'

'The one some mad old bat made a small fortune out of claiming to be?'

'Anna Anderson. Yes.'

'Anna Anderson. That's right. Didn't I catch some crappy mini-series about her on cable a few years back? Jane Seymour in the title role, maybe?'

'Jane Seymour,' said Gennady, sounding cheered by the mention of the name. '*Dr Quinn, Medicine Woman*. I love her.'

Brad rolled his eyes. 'You know what? We don't have time for this, we really don't. Anastasia doesn't push any buttons for me, sport. I think we'll bypass the kicking-the-shit-out-of-you phase and cut straight to the bullet in the brain.' His affable features suddenly twisted into something tight and vicious. He pulled a gun out of his coat pocket, stepped forward and pointed it at Eusden's head. 'Now is the moment to give me one good reason not to pull this trigger. Believe me, there won't be another.'

'F-Fingerprints.' Eusden heard the stammer in his voice from some strange detached place where death was imminent and imaginable and not quite the disabling horror he had always supposed it would seem in such a situation. 'You should have . . . found a set amongst the letters.'

Brad shook his head slowly and emphatically. 'No fingerprints.'

'They must be there.'

'But they're not.'

'Hidden in the case maybe.'

'Check it out, Vlad.' Vladimir opened the case and turned it over. The letters fell out on to the bench and slewed across it. 'Whose fingerprints are we looking for, sport?'

'Anastasia's. Taken in 1909, when she was eight years old. I'm in contact with a genealogist from Virginia who's bought a set of Anna Anderson's prints, taken in 1938. If they match, it would prove she really was Anastasia.'

Vladimir was tapping the case and peering at it like a sceptical theatre-goer invited to inspect the conjurer's top hat. '*Nichivo*,' he muttered, which Eusden suspected meant *Nothing* in Russian or Ukrainian — or both.

'The proof would be worth a lot of money,' Eusden pressed on, willing Brad to listen to him — and to believe him. 'It'd be a worldwide sensation. You could name your own price.'

'Sounds great. Just a pity we don't have that proof.'

'It's got to be there somewhere. Let me look.'

'Stay where you are. Vlad?'

Vladimir had laid the case on the bench and was prodding at the insides of the lid and base. He shook his head ominously.

'It's looking bad for you, sport.'

'For God's sake, let me — '

'Wait,' said Vladimir. 'I think, yes, I think there *is* something.' He flicked a knife out of his pocket and cut a slit in the lining of the lid. A creamy white envelope slid out into the body of the case. He stared down at it in a mixture of awe and amazement. Then, slowly and deliberately, he crossed himself.

'What the hell is it?'

'*Tsarski piriot.*'

'What?'

'See.' Vladimir held up the envelope. The front was blank. But when he turned it round, there, clearly visible, embossed on the flap, was the black double-headed eagle of the Romanovs.

38

The envelope was unsealed. Inside was a single sheet of vellum notepaper. At its top was the same black double-headed eagle clutching an orb and sceptre. Beneath, neatly arranged, was a full set of fingerprints in red ink, left hand, then right. Below the prints, in black ink, someone had written *A.N. 4 viii '09.*

'What exactly is this, sport?' demanded Brad. He held the sheet of paper up. He had put his gun back in his pocket, but Gennady still had his trained on Eusden.

'The fingerprints of the Grand Duchess Anastasia, taken aboard the imperial yacht off Cowes on the fourth of August 1909.' It was true, then, though Eusden could scarcely believe it. The prints were clearly those of a child and the date was right. A.N. was Anastasia Nikolaievna. Nearly a hundred years had passed since Clem had entertained the Tsar's precocious youngest daughter with a demonstration of the British police's most recent advance in the science of detection. Eusden could almost see the sunlight sparkling on the wave-tops in Cowes Roads and hear the blue-blooded little girl's gleeful laugh. Clem had always had a way with children. *'This is how Scotland Yard keeps a track of those infernal anarchists, Your Highness. First one finger. Then the next.'* 'They were there for the regatta. The Tsar, the Tsarina and all their children. The King and Queen came down to — '

'Fuck the King and Queen. You're serious about this?'

'Absolutely.'

'And you can get a set of Anna Anderson's prints to match with these?'

'Yes.'

'How soon?'

'Regina will already have them. She's in Germany. It's just a question of — '

'Phone her.' Brad tossed Eusden his mobile. 'Phone her now and get her to come here.'

'What about Mjollnir?' asked Vladimir.

'We agreed terms with them for the letters. This is something else. This, boys, is what's known as a bonus. And, hell, haven't we earned one? Make the call, sport.'

'OK. I'll try.'

'Do more than try.'

'The number's in my wallet.'

'Get it out.'

Eusden took his wallet from his jacket and found the piece of paper with Regina's number written on it. It was unfair to involve her, of course, but he had no choice. This was his only chance of survival. He placed the call. And started praying she would answer.

She did. 'Hello?'

'Regina, this is Richard Eusden.'

'Richard. Hi. I didn't recognize the number. I tried to call you earlier.'

'Sorry. Stupidly, I've mislaid my phone. I've had to borrow one. Where are you?' There was a blur of sound in the background. He caught the ding-dong of a PA system.

'Hanover airport. They should be calling my flight to Copenhagen any minute.'

'You've got the 1938 fingerprint record?'

'You bet. Any news for me your end?'

'Yes. I have the matching record from 1909, Regina. I have it in front of me.'

'You're joshing me.'

'No. It's right here.'

'But . . . how did you get it?'

'I'll explain when we meet. It's . . . complicated.'

'OK. Well, I should be able to make it to your hotel by around three thirty.'

'Three thirty? That's only . . . ' Belatedly, Eusden remembered that Finland was an hour ahead of Germany and Denmark. 'Actually, Regina, I'm no longer in Copenhagen. I'm in Helsinki.'

'*Helsinki?*'

'Like I said, it's complicated. Can you join me here?'

'I . . . guess I could try to book a connecting flight before I leave.'

'Meeting here's much the safer bet. Werner's sure to come looking for us in Copenhagen sooner or later.'

'OK. Point taken. I'll do it.'

'Call me on this number when you know what time you'll be arriving. I'll meet you at the airport.'

'Will do. Hey, Richard, have you been holding out on me? This has all happened very suddenly.'

317

'I'll tell you the whole story when you get here. See you soon. 'Bye.'

'Nicely played, sport,' said Brad as he retrieved his phone. 'I guess you've negotiated yourself a stay of execution.'

'We should kill him here,' said Vladimir.

Brad sighed heavily. 'We don't know what the Virginian genealogist looks like, Vlad. And she's expecting Eusden here to meet her. So, we'll keep him on ice. Time?'

'Less than an hour till we meet Mjollnir.'

'OK. One more call, then we head out.' Brad punched a number into his phone. While he waited for an answer, Eusden wondered queasily what 'on ice' actually meant. Then: 'Bruno? Brad . . . Yuh . . . I have something for you. How are you with fingerprints? . . . Excellento. Haven't I always said Orson Welles was way out of line with that crack about cuckoo clocks? . . . Talking of clocks, there's one ticking on this job. We need you tonight . . . Helsinki . . . Yuh. Slip into your thermals before you leave. It's the Ice Age here . . . Got you. ETA to follow. Understood . . . Of course, Bruno, of course. Standard fee. Standard percentage. When have I ever let you down? . . . OK. *Ciao,* good buddy.' He ended the call and shot Eusden a smile. 'Bruno will give us an authoritative yes or no on whether the prints match. If they do, we're in business. If not . . . ' Brad's smile remained in place just a little too long. Eusden knew they would keep him alive only as long as he was useful to them. And his usefulness was likely to expire once Regina had arrived with the other fingerprint sample. But

318

airports were crowded, public places. There had to be a good chance he could escape once they were there, taking Regina with him. If all else failed, he could probably get himself arrested; Regina too. Until then, there was nothing for it but to do Brad's bidding in every particular.

'Let's get moving.' Brad pulled out his gun again. 'Fetch the car, Gennady. Reverse it up to the door and pop the trunk.' Gennady nodded and lumbered out through the wicket-door, leaving it open behind him. 'Put the letters back in the case, Vlad.' As Vladimir started on that, a car engine coughed into life outside. The rear of a silver Mercedes saloon eased into view. The boot sprang open. 'You're travelling in the trunk, sport. Can't risk your Mjollnir buddies spotting you. Climb aboard.'

★ ★ ★

Eusden had only the briefest glimpse of the industrial wasteland Lund had dumped him in before the pressure of Vladimir's hand on the back of his head told him to clamber into the boot of the thrumbling Mercedes.

'Carpet and loads of leg room,' said Brad, meeting his backward gaze with a smirk. 'Gennady grew up in Kiev with four brothers in less comfortable and capacious surroundings.'

'When do I get out of here?'

'When we need you. Don't worry. We'll know where to find you.' He reached up to close the boot, then stopped. His phone was ringing. He pulled it out of his pocket and read out the

319

number of the caller. 'Means nothing to me. You, sport?'

'Regina.'

'You'd better take it.' He handed Eusden the phone.

'Regina?'

'Hi, Richard.' She sounded breathless. 'I've got to make this quick. I'm on my way to the gate. I'm booked on a flight from Copenhagen to Helsinki that gets in at seven twenty. Finnair six six four.'

'Six six four at seven twenty. Got it. I'll see you then.'

'Likewise. 'Bye.'

Eusden passed the phone meekly back to Brad. 'Would it do any good to tell you I suffer from claustrophobia?'

'Not a bit. But, hey, it's not like we're going to forget about you. We'll be checking on you regularly.' Brad frowned thoughtfully, as if reviewing his tactics for the pending encounter at Koskinen's house. He drummed his fingers on the boot lid, then plucked the envelope containing the fingerprints out of his pocket and slid it inside the lapel of Eusden's crumpled jacket. 'Look after that for me, sport. Like your life depends on it.' Then he slammed the lid shut. And Eusden was plunged into darkness.

39

The boot smelt nine parts of carpet fibre and one of diesel. There was no light of any kind. Eusden spent some minutes trying to find a manual switch for the internal lamp before giving up. Gennady drove like a chauffeur for a wealthy old widow: smoothly and slowly. The car accelerated and decelerated, turned and straightened. Beyond the steady hum of the engine, sound was muffled and distant: horns, air brakes, tram bells and pneumatic drills drifting in and fading away as the Mercedes threaded through the Helsinki traffic towards its destination.

Eusden could not stop himself wondering — and doubting — whether his plan to escape his captors' clutches at the airport would work. Brad would surely anticipate such an attempt and seek to forestall it. He had to pin his hopes on Brad's greed skewing his judgement and he did not know the man well enough to assess how likely that was.

The consoling fact remained, however, that he had talked them into sparing his life so far and stood a good chance of outwitting them if he held his nerve. He would be outwitting Mjollnir into the bargain, since Lund no doubt assumed he was already dead. What had Koskinen told Pernille? he wondered. How had they accounted for his sudden disappearance? Whatever lie they had concocted, he intended to ram it down their throats once he was free. Pernille must think he had deserted her. He would make it his business to ensure she did not go on thinking that. She would be at Koskinen's house now, with Matalainen, waiting and worrying. There was nothing he could do to help her or to explain his absence. But he promised himself she would know the truth — and others would be held accountable for that truth — before he was finished.

He smiled at the irony that Brad had given the envelope containing the fingerprints to him for safekeeping. He tried to retreat into a fanciful recreation of events aboard the imperial yacht that August day in 1909 as a means of distracting himself from the grimness of his situation. But Clem in his Isle of Wight constable's uniform and the Grand Duchesses in their white, lace-fringed dresses were figures from a dream. The sunshine he imagined had no warmth, the voices no strength, the smiles no permanence. He was where he was. And they were far away and long ago.

★ ★ ★

The car stopped, as it had several times. Then the engine stopped. This was different. They had arrived at Luumitie 27. The exchange was about to take place.

A minute or so passed. Then a door slammed. And then another. Brad and Vladimir had left the car. Something whirred and clicked close to

322

the boot. The aerial, he guessed. Gennady had switched on the radio. He wanted music while he waited, though he evidently thought he should play it low. No sound reached Eusden. The silence of the suburban residential side street was total.

More minutes passed. Five. Ten. Fifteen. The preliminaries must be over by now. Matalainen would be comparing the letters with the faxed copies. Soon, he would express his satisfaction. Then the combination of the case Koskinen had delivered to Pernille would be phoned through. Brad would open it up, check the bearer bonds and express his satisfaction. And then —

★   ★   ★

The noise hit him in a shock wave of air. His dark, cramped, silent world was split open by sound and light. The car rose and crashed back down as if struck by an earthquake. Something large and heavy crunched into the lid of the boot, driving in a deep dent to within an inch of Eusden's face. As it did so, the lid jolted open. He was dazzled and deafened simultaneously and could only cower from the violent, roaring force of an event he could not comprehend.

Then sight and hearing and understanding rushed in on him. Fragments of masonry were raining down, hitting other parked cars as they fell, bouncing from roofs, chipping windows, sinking into the snow piled in the gutters. And smoke was billowing across the street in

323

dust-laden clouds. He pulled a handkerchief from his pocket to shield his nose and mouth as he scrambled out over the sill of the boot.

The house that had once stood on the other side of the street was a wreck of flame and smoke, of sundered walls and splintered glass. The roof had caved in and between the surviving gables was a chaos of rubble. Pernille's BMW stood in the driveway piled with debris, its windows smashed, and a toppled chunk of gatepost, with the number 27 screwed to it, lay on the pavement. Smaller pieces of debris were still pattering down as Eusden stared at the scene in horror. The smoke began to clog his lungs. He retreated.

As he did so, the driver's door of the Mercedes opened and Gennady fell out on to the snow-covered verge, blood streaming from a gash across his head. A windowful of shattered glass fell with him. He looked up at Eusden and moaned. His eyes rolled up under his lids. Then he went limp.

In the next instant one of the gables gave way and crashed down into the wreckage. Smoke and dust mushroomed into the air. Eusden was forced back still further. A middle-aged woman appeared in the front yard of a house behind him. She shouted something to him in Finnish.

'Phone for an ambulance,' he shouted back. 'There are people in there.'

'What happened?'

'I don't know. Some kind of explosion.'

She gaped past him, her mouth slack with

324

shock. She started to cough.

'Phone for help. *Now.*'

'OK. Yes.' She ran back into the house.

Eusden stood where he was, squinting through the spreading haze of smoke. Luumitie 27 looked as if it had been hit by a bomb. And that, he knew, was precisely what had happened: a bomb. No one inside could have survived such an explosion. It had demolished the entire building, shattering walls and floors, crushing flesh and bone. Brad, Vladimir, Matalainen *and* Pernille must all be dead.

Eusden suddenly realized how badly he wanted to believe Pernille could still be alive, despite all evidence to the contrary. In simple truth, there was no hope. But he could not accept that. He *would* not accept that. He started across the street.

He was stopped in his tracks by the blare of a horn and a squeal of brakes. A pick-up truck juddered to a halt a few yards from him and two men in overalls jumped out. They shouted at him in Finnish.

'There are people trapped in there.' He gestured towards the wrecked house. 'Help me check if they're still alive.'

The two men stared at him incredulously. Then the older of the two said, 'Too dangerous. Anyone inside's dead for sure.'

'We've got to try.'

'Don't do it. There could be — '

A loud bang triggered a gout of flame from somewhere in the wreckage. Fragments of rubble flew into the air. One smashed into the windscreen of the pick-up. The two men turned and fled.

'Get back,' the older one shouted to Eusden over his shoulder.

Then the second gable gave way. And with it went the last of Eusden's defences against reality. He retreated, his eyes stinging, his lungs straining. Dust and smoke rose and rolled in the air. Fire crackled behind him.

He reached the Mercedes, his thoughts focusing now on a single resolve: someone must be made to suffer for this. He knelt by Gennady's motionless body and felt inside his coat for the gun. Suddenly it was in his hand: an automatic of the kind he had seen many, many times in films but never in the world he had inhabited until a week ago. It was too large and heavy to carry in his jacket. He tugged Gennady's woollen scarf from around his neck, wrapped the gun in it, stood up and set off along the street.

Other residents were out by now, gaping at the devastation that had once been Osmo Koskinen's house. They paid Eusden no attention, their gazes fixed on the burning, smoking ruin of number 27. He upped his pace.

As he neared the end of the street, he saw a big black Saab SUV pull over as it passed the junction. Its driver stared keenly along Luumitie towards the plume of smoke and a faint smile crossed his face.

The driver was Erik Lund. He was alone in the car and he seemed wholly unaware of Eusden's presence. He looked straight past him, seeing nothing but what he expected to see. The pedestrian crossing the road in front of him was a mere shadow.

All that changed when Eusden yanked open the passenger door and jumped in the car.

'*Hov! Hvad* — ' Lund's expression froze. He clearly could not believe what he saw: a man he confidently supposed dead sitting right next to him — and holding a gun.

40

Several long, silent seconds passed as they stared at each other. Then Lund swallowed hard and said, 'Don't shoot. Please.'

'Why shouldn't I? You set me up, you bastard. You expected them to kill me, didn't you?'

'I was . . . following orders.'

'Go on doing that and you might live. Drive.'

They started moving. 'Where are we going?'

'Head for the airport.'

'Listen, Eusden, I — '

'*You* listen. Just answer my questions. OK?'

'OK.'

'Did Tolmar Aksden know this was going to happen?'

Lund nodded. 'Yes.'

'He knew everything from the start?'

'Yes.'

'What were his instructions?'

'Destroy the case. Force the Opposition to back off with a show of overwhelming strength. And get rid of you.'

'As well as Pernille?'

'Yes.' They turned on to the main shopping street of Munkkiniemi. A fire engine was speeding towards them, light flashing, siren wailing. Another siren was wailing further in the distance. 'He always says . . . a problem is an opportunity.'

'You killed Burgaard as well, didn't you?'

328

'We've killed no one. Everything is . . . contracted out.'

'How very businesslike.' The fire engine roared past. 'Hold on. What about the security you were supposed to supply?'

'I had two men in the house. They were there to reassure Pernille she'd be safe.'

'And you just . . . sacrificed them?'

'I did what had to be done. I don't know how you got away, Eusden, but I promise I won't tell Tolmar you did.' A rivulet of sweat was trickling down Lund's temple. 'The airport is a good choice. You can fly to England tonight. No one will find out.'

'Of course they will, Lund. You'll tell them.'

'No.'

'Just keep driving. And go on answering my questions. Did Koskinen know what was going to happen as well?'

'Not the details. But he does as he's told. Like me.'

'Where is he now?'

'He's gone to stay with his brother.'

'Address?'

'I don't know.'

'Don't give me that.'

'I swear I don't. I could make something up, couldn't I? How could you tell? Truthfully, I don't know.'

A police car swept past them. Then another.

'What about Tolmar? Where's he?'

'Out of town.'

'When will he be back?'

'Tonight. Tomorrow. I'm not sure.'

'Where's his apartment?'

'Mäkinkatu six. But you won't get to him there. It has state-of-the-art security.'

'Was Birgitte Grøn in on all this?'

'No. She wouldn't have cooperated if she'd realized what Tolmar had decided to do. She thought he was going to pay as agreed.'

'So, there is someone in Mjollnir with a conscience, is there?'

They were leaving the centre of Munkkiniemi now and approaching a big interchange. Lund joined the queue at the lights for a left turn on to the main road heading north.

'You have no idea how it works, Eusden. You can't imagine. The money. The luxuries. The things he sees you want and gives to you . . . in exchange for other things. You're in too deep to get out before you know it.'

'Is that your excuse?'

'I just do what I'm told to do.'

'In this case, help Tolmar murder his ex-wife.'

'There's been no murder. The explosion was caused by a gas leak.'

'I know better.'

'I'm only saying what I think the Finnish police will say in the end. A terrible accident. Why Pernille was there . . . Who knows?' Lund accelerated on to the main road. The light was beginning to fail, the sullen sky filling in from the east. The afternoon was fading fast. 'You can get away clean, Eusden. Tonight. I won't tell Tolmar. Truthfully. It would look bad for me if I admitted you got away.'

'You really are a heartless bastard, aren't you?'

'I'm a realist. Pernille's dead. You're alive. You should do everything you can to stay that way.'

'What will Birgitte do when she finds out you deceived her?'

'Nothing. She's a realist also.'

'Where does Lars Aksden come into this?'

'He doesn't.'

'But he's here in Helsinki. Why?'

Lund shook his head. 'I don't know what you're talking about. Lars isn't here.'

'I saw him with my own eyes. Near Matalainen's office. This morning.'

'Koskinen didn't say anything about that.'

'He didn't see him. I did.'

'Maybe you were . . . mistaken.'

'No. It was him.'

'Then, I don't know. It doesn't make any sense. He shouldn't be here.'

'Maybe he wants to find out what the family secret is.'

'He never will.'

'But you could enlighten him, couldn't you? You and Birgitte read the faxed copies of the letters.'

'No. The number they were faxed to was Tolmar's. Only he read them. Everything we told you and Pernille . . . he instructed us to tell you.'

'Because we'd have refused to go through with it if we'd known Tolmar was in charge. So, we had to be suckered into believing you were going behind his back.'

'Exactly.'

'Throwing me to the wolves was one thing,

331

Lund, but Pernille? How could you do that to her?'

'It was stupid of her to think she could just walk away from Tolmar. She should have known he wouldn't let her treat him like that.'

'And that's your rationale, is it? Do what he wants or suffer the consequences.'

'It's how it is.'

'My God.'

Silence fell between them. Eusden had no questions left to ask and no words to describe the disbelief he felt that any man could live by such pitiless rules. They had joined a dual carriageway by now, tracking north and east. The airport symbol had appeared on signs beside the road. There were only seven kilometres to go. Eusden's thoughts drifted to how it must have been at Koskinen's house, less than an hour ago: Pernille, Matalainen, Brad and Vladimir seated round a table, with Lund's two security men in the background; the wary discussions; the telephone call; the rotation of the combination cylinder on the case Pernille had brought with her; the release of the —

Eusden was flung forward as Lund slammed on the brakes. He had forgotten to fasten his seat belt. He got his hands up just in time to prevent his head hitting the windscreen, but the gun slipped from his grasp and clunked to the floor. The car swerved to the side of the road and skidded to a halt a few inches from a crash barrier. Lund made a dive for the gun and had his fingers on the butt when Eusden's reactions caught up with him. He stamped on the Dane's outstretched hand. Lund cried out in pain. Then Eusden grabbed him by the nape hair, yanked his head up and punched him hard on the nose. As Lund fell back, Eusden bent forward and retrieved the gun.

Blood was welling from the Dane's nostrils. He was breathing heavily through his mouth and clutching his nose with one hand while he shook the other to ease the pain in his fingers. He cowered away from the gun as Eusden pointed it at him. 'I'm sorry,' he panted. 'Sorry.'

'Get out of the car.'

'What?'

'Give me your phone and your wallet and get out of the car.'

'Look, I'll drive you to the airport. It's OK. I won't — '

'*Get out!*' Eusden edged the barrel of the gun closer to Lund's face. 'Or I swear to God I'll do the human race a big favour and put an end to your miserable, morally bankrupt life here and now.'

41

Night was falling by the time Eusden reached Vantaa airport. He left the Saab in one of the car parks, with Lund's wallet locked inside. He had only taken it to slow the man down. He had no faith in Lund's promise to say nothing to Tolmar Aksden. He tossed the key into some bushes next to the car park. Using the Saab again would be too risky.

Not that he had any clear idea of what he was going to do from this moment on. How much to tell Regina Celeste was the first problem he had to confront. She would soon realize all was not well with him. He cleaned himself up as best he could in the airport toilets, but his reflection in the mirror told its own story. He looked haggard and distraught. He looked like a man whose resources were failing him.

They undeniably were. The grief he felt for Pernille Madsen, a woman he scarcely knew by all logical criteria, had shocked as well as sapped him. Her death cut off a future he had just begun to dare to imagine. It had stripped him of hope. What remained was an urge to avenge her. He had come closer to killing Lund than the Dane probably imagined and certainly closer than he himself would ever have expected. If Tolmar Aksden had been in the car instead of Lund, Eusden would have pulled the trigger. He had no doubt of that. And he still had the gun.

★ ★ ★

He used a wad of euros from Lund's wallet to buy a warm coat from one of the airport shops. It had pockets large enough to conceal the gun and made him look rather less like a man who has recently been roughed up by gangsters. He checked the arrivals board for news of Regina's flight. It was expected in on schedule. Then he noticed another flight due in a quarter of an hour earlier, from Zürich. He remembered Brad's reference to the Orson Welles jibe about cuckoo clocks and wondered if Bruno the fingerprint expert would be on board. If so, there would be no one waiting to meet him. Unless Eusden did the honours.

★ ★ ★

There were several limo-drivers holding up name cards when the first of the Zürich passengers made it to the arrivals hall. Eusden loitered among them, with BRUNO blazoned on the lid of a box he had cadged from a fast-food kiosk.

The man who approached him was short and tubby, clad in well-cut tweed and a python of cashmere scarf. Groomed dark-brown hair, clipped moustache and tortoiseshell-framed glasses gave him the appearance of a vain and fussy professor.

'Who are you?' he demanded in Italian-accented English.

'A friend of Brad's.'

'Name?'

'Marty Hewitson.' Recourse to Marty's identity as a pseudonym was so instinctive that Eusden was surprised when he heard himself say it.

'Brad's never mentioned you. Why isn't he here?'

'Unforeseen circumstances.'

'I should have had a message if there was a change of plan.'

Eusden shrugged. 'Sorry.'

Bruno pulled out his phone with a put-upon harrumph and stabbed in a number with a cocktail-sausage forefinger. The response did not please him. He tried again, with the same result. 'There's something wrong. Brad's phone is dead.'

'Look, Bruno, I — '

'My name is Stammati. I am Bruno to my friends. You I have never met.'

'OK, Mr Stammati. Sorry, I'm sure. Now, as you know, Brad wants you to confirm a match between two sets of fingerprints. I have one set with me. The other's arriving with a Mrs Celeste on a flight from Copenhagen due in very shortly. Any objection to casting your eye over them while we wait for word from Brad?'

Stammati looked as if he did object, but was constrained by his obligation to Brad. His moustache twitched querulously, then he said, 'I will wait in that café' — he pointed to a coffee-bean logo in the middle distance — 'for one half-hour.' And with that he bustled off.

★ ★ ★

Eusden decided against following Stammati. He suspected attempts to charm the man would prove disastrous and was not equal to making the effort anyway. He did not have to stick it out long in the arrivals hall, although Regina was not among the first clutch of Copenhagen passengers to emerge from Customs. Delayed by collection and trolleying of a gigantic suitcase, she finally appeared with only five minutes of Stammati's allotted half-hour remaining.

'I expected a triumphant greeting, Richard,' she said, looking him up and down. 'What in the world's happened to you?'

'It's been a stressful day.'

'So I see.'

'I have a not-so-tame fingerprint expert parked nearby, Regina. He's liable to walk out on us if we don't step on it.'

'Who needs an expert? You and I are perfectly capable of judging whether two sets of fingerprints match. And match I'm confident they will.'

'Me too. But we may as well get a neutral opinion while it's available.'

'All right, all right. Just let me catch my breath. And steer this for me, would you?' She swung the handle of the trolley towards him. 'Then we'll go see this so-called expert. Where'd you find him?'

'It's a long story.'

'Can I at least take a peek at what you have before we meet him?'

Eusden took the envelope from his pocket and showed it to her. At the sight of the double-headed eagle of the Romanovs, her eyes rolled.

'Be still, my beating heart,' she gasped.

* * *

The pastelly plasticated decor of the Café Quick appeared to have done nothing to soften Stammati's temper. He broke off from glaring grumpily at his pseudo-espresso to announce, 'Brad has not phoned me.'

Eusden synthesized a smile. 'Mr Stammati, this is Regina Celeste.'

'Pleased to meet you, I'm sure,' trilled Regina, extending a hand.

Stammati's Italian genes belatedly kicked in. He rose and clasped her hand in both of his. *'Buonasera, signora.'*

'Which part of Italy are you from, Mr Stammati?' Regina asked as they settled at his table.

'The Swiss part, *signora.'*

'Oh, really?'

'How, may I ask, do you know Brad?'

'Who's Brad?'

'A mutual acquaintance,' Eusden cut in. 'Why don't we look at what we've got?'

'This is an exciting moment for me, Mr Stammati,' Regina enthused, opening her hand-bag and pulling out a square brown board-backed envelope.

'Please, *signora,* call me Bruno.' The southern belle was evidently chiming with him. 'Two sets of fingerprints require matching, I believe.'

'Oh, they match, Bruno. You can rely on that.' She opened the envelope and slid the contents out on to the table: two record cards, yellowing at the edges, one headed RECHTE HAND and the other LINKE HAND. There were squares filled with the prints of each finger and thumb and a larger square below where the palm and fingers had been pressed down together.

Stammati peered at the details typed at the base of the cards. 'Prints of a Frau Tschaikovsky, taken in Hanover, ninth July 1938. A long time ago. Is this lady still living?'

'Sadly, no. She passed away more than twenty years ago. But we're about to restore her to life in a sense, aren't we, Richard?'

'*Richard?*' Stammati frowned suspiciously at Eusden. 'I thought your name was Marty.'

'Marty's a nickname,' said Eusden, pressing his knee against Regina's under the table.

'And a silly one too,' Regina laughed, casting him an intrigued sidelong glance. 'I never use it.'

'The other set of prints,' Eusden hurried on, taking the sheet of paper out of the double-headed-eagle envelope and placing it next to the two cards.

Stammati looked at it closely. 'Fourth of August 1909,' he murmured. 'Even longer ago.'

'When she was a child.' Regina's tone suggested she had a vision of the child in her mind's eye as she spoke.

'That does not matter,' said Stammati, his gaze switching from the sheet of paper to the cards and back again. 'The prints acquire their uniqueness in the womb. They never change.'

339

'Is that so?'

'Yes. It is. Now . . . ' Stammati glanced reproachfully at the ceiling. 'The light is not good. *Tuttavia* . . . ' He opened the briefcase that appeared to be his only luggage and removed a small leather pouch, from which he slid a magnifying glass. He squinted through it at the fingerprints and a couple of minutes slowly elapsed. Then he sighed and laid the magnifying glass down on the table. 'Who is A.N., may I ask?'

'They're Frau Tschaikovsky's maiden initials,' Regina replied.

'I think not, *signora.*'

'What do you mean by that?'

'I mean that these are not matching prints. A full ridge count is unnecessary. One set is looped, the other whorled. They are, obviously and undoubtedly, the fingerprints of two different people.'

42

Regina had been forced to accept Stammati's verdict after examining the contrasting loops and whorls of the two sets of prints through his magnifying glass for herself. Eusden needed less convincing. Even to his naked eye the differences were clear once they had been pointed out to him. He replaced the sheet of paper in the envelope and put it back in his pocket while Stammati made further futile efforts to contact Brad by phone and Regina sat staring into space with an expression of undisguised stupefaction on her face.

'I am sorry if I have disappointed you, *signora*,' said Stammati, when he had given up again. 'I assure you I also am disappointed to travel so far for so little.' He glared at Eusden. 'Since no one is able or willing to explain this ... fiasco ... I shall check into whatever the Finns have supplied in the way of an airport hotel after booking a seat on the first flight back to Zürich tomorrow morning.' He closed his briefcase and rose to his feet with a grunt. '*Buonanotte* to you both.'

★ ★ ★

'How in the name of sweet reason can this be?' Regina asked after Stammati had bustled off.

'Anna Anderson wasn't Anastasia,' Eusden

341

listlessly replied. 'It's as simple as that.'

'But she was. I know she was.'

'The fingerprints say otherwise.'

'There's got to be some mistake.'

That was a considerable understatement. If Anastasia's survival of the Ekaterinburg massacre was not part of Tolmar Aksden's secret, then what had Hakon Nydahl's letters been about? And why had Clem stored Anastasia's fingerprints with them? Marty must have discovered the envelope when he first examined the attaché case. Otherwise how could Straub have known it contained prints that could be compared with the Hanover set? Why had Marty never told Eusden about them? Why had he kept the secret back? What game had he really been playing when death interrupted him? Eusden's thoughts reeled as the unanswered questions swirled in his mind.

'We're both tired, I guess,' Regina continued. 'I need to think this through when I'm properly rested. You look bushed yourself.'

'That I am.'

'Let's get out of this place. Where are you staying?'

'The Grand Marina.'

'I booked myself into the Kämp. They tell me it's Helsinki's finest. And I need all the comfort I can get after the day I've had. Shall we share a taxi? You promised me a full explanation of how you came by those fingerprints, remember. Well, you can deliver over a drink in the hotel bar.'

★　★　★

Regina was silent for the first mile or so of the taxi ride, immersed in her own dejected thoughts. Then, suddenly, she declared, 'I believe I've seen through it,' and grasped Eusden's forearm. 'They aren't Anastasia's fingerprints, Richard. Don't you see? Grenscher tricked me.'

'I'm not sure I do see,' Eusden responded wearily.

'Werner must have guessed I'd try to deal direct with Grenscher and primed the grotesque little man to sell me a forgery. It was the date that convinced me the record cards were genuine. July ninth 1938 was the day Anastasia was summoned to police headquarters in Hanover to meet the brother and sisters of Franziska Schanzkowska. Typically, they disagreed among themselves about whether she might be their missing sister. But it's still much the likeliest occasion for the police to have fingerprinted her.'

'Are you saying you doubt now they ever did?'

'No. I'm saying Grenscher still has the real record cards. He denied receiving a deposit from Werner, you know. A deposit *I* paid. But the more I think about it the more certain I become he *had* been paid. It's just that sending me off with a smile on my face and a set of fake prints in my purse is what he'd been paid to do.'

'Well, I suppose — '

'But Werner's slipped on his own trail of slime, hasn't he? Because now we have the 1909 record. Which means he's going to have to do business with us whether he likes it or not. And I can personally assure you that the first item in

343

our negotiations will be reimbursement of the substantial sum of money I paid over to his counterfeiting co-conspirator in Hanover. With interest — at a punitive rate.'

★ ★ ★

Regina had convinced herself Anna Anderson's fingerprints did not match Anastasia's because they were not her fingerprints. Eusden remained sceptical, though he did not bother saying so. He believed Straub had used Regina's deposit to bribe Marty. Grenscher, grotesque or not, was probably a genuine dealer. The fingerprints were a dead end.

For clues to what the truth really was — and a way to strike back at Tolmar Aksden — he had to look elsewhere. When they reached the quietly opulent Hotel Kämp, Regina headed up to her room to 'unpack a few things and shower away three airports' worth of grime' before they met for a council of war in the bar. And Eusden did not propose to waste the hour or more this sounded as if it would take.

The man on the desk readily lent him a copy of the Helsinki phone book. He sat in reception and started ringing his way through all the Koskinens listed, using Lund's mobile. It was a laborious exercise. Koskinen was not an uncommon name. Only with the thirteenth who actually answered did he strike lucky.

'*Hei?*'

'Can I speak to Osmo Koskinen, please?'

'Who's calling?'

'Are you his brother?'

'Yes. I am Timo Koskinen. Who — '

Eusden pressed the red button and scribbled down the address, then went back to the desk. 'Thanks,' he said, returning the phone book. 'Can you tell me where this is?' He held out the note.

'Certainly, sir.' A map of the city was produced and the index consulted. Then: 'Here it is. In Kulosaari.' It was clearly a taxi ride away.

'Thanks again.'

Eusden wandered off towards the bar, then stopped and looked at his watch. It was nearly ten o'clock. Time, as Marty would have reminded him, was of the essence. And there was one sure way to solve the problem of what to tell Regina. He turned and headed for the door to the street.

43

The temperature had plummeted with nightfall. The cold was an invisible and hostile presence surrounding Eusden in the stillness and silence of the Kulosaari side street. He pressed the button beside the name KOSKINEN on the panel in the entrance porch of the anonymous apartment block where the taxi had delivered him and stamped his feet for warmth as he waited for a response.

A minute or so passed. Then there was a click from the entryphone grille. And a voice: '*Hei?*'

'Timo Koskinen?'

'*Kyllä.*'

'We spoke earlier. My name's Richard Eusden. Your brother knows me. We need to talk.'

'*Who* are you?'

'I'm sure Osmo's told you all about me. So, why don't you let me in? If you don't, I'll have no choice but to go to the police.'

There was a laden pause. Then: 'Wait, please.'

Another, longer pause followed. Eusden imagined an anxious conference between the two brothers. It ended in a loud buzz abruptly signalling the release of the entrance lock.

★ ★ ★

The apartment was a functionally furnished and faintly dowdy bachelor residence. Timo Koskinen was a thinner, older, grimmer version of his brother, guardedly inexpressive. Osmo himself had imploded from affable ease into anguished distraction, his hair awry, his clothes crumpled, the tremor in his hands more pronounced. There was a sheen of sweat on his upper lip and a slack-mouthed, blank-eyed look of helplessness about him. A bottle of vodka stood prominently on the coffee table in the cheerless lounge, with just the one tumbler beside it, cloudy with finger smears.

'Got anything to say to me, Osmo?' Eusden asked, taking off his coat and hanging it up carefully in the hall before entering the lounge. Timo followed him in.

Osmo squirmed in his armchair and avoided Eusden's gaze. 'I . . . didn't know . . . what they were going to do.'

'But you knew Pernille and I were being set up.'

'Yes. But . . . killing people? I never . . . imagined . . . '

'Did you think I was dead too?'

Osmo rubbed his face, as if trying to force some clarity into his thoughts. 'Yes.'

'And maybe you reckoned that was best. No one left to come after you. Well, here I am. And I want answers.'

'There's nothing . . . I can tell you.'

'You're going to have to come up with something. I won't be leaving until you do.'

'Please, Richard, I . . . ' Osmo looked at him for the first time. 'You have to understand . . . He can destroy any of us . . . if he wants to.'

'Or if you let him. He's gone too far. I mean to

stop him. And I need your help.'

'I can't — '

'Go and make some coffee, Osmo,' Timo cut in, stepping between them. 'We'll talk to this man. We have to. You know we do.'

Osmo struggled to his feet. 'Timo,' he began, 'we should . . . ' He switched suddenly to Finnish, lowering his voice as he did so.

Timo's response was a decisive shake of the head. 'The coffee,' he repeated.

With a defeated shrug, Osmo headed unsteadily for the kitchen.

Timo watched him go, then gestured for Eusden to sit down on the sofa. He took the other armchair, opposite him. 'He really didn't know what they planned, Mr Eusden. He didn't ask. He will tell you that's the way to do well at Mjollnir: ask no questions. Have you met Erik Lund?'

'Oh yes.'

'Lund gave Osmo the case. It was already locked. It was supposed to contain bearer bonds, yes?'

'Yes.'

'Well, Osmo took the case to Ms Madsen at the Grand Marina Hotel. Then she and the lawyer, Matalainen, drove away, heading for Osmo's house. He came here, as instructed. About an hour after he arrived, he got a call from the police. They told him about the explosion. They wanted to know who was in the house when it happened. He said Ms Madsen had asked him if she could use it for a meeting. Who with and what about . . . he didn't know.'

'Did they buy that?'

'Probably. Why not? They've no reason to suspect he was lying. My brother is a respectable man.'

'Yeah. Like all the other people I've met who do Tolmar Aksden's bidding.'

'He doesn't like what's happened, Mr Eusden. And not just because his house has been destroyed. Mjollnir will compensate him for that. They'll probably buy him a bigger and better one. No, the problem is Osmo's conscience. He's tried to drown it.' Timo nodded towards the vodka bottle. 'But it keeps coming to the surface.'

'Then, he should go to the police and tell them the truth.'

'Would you be willing to go with him?'

'Of course I would.'

'You'd be making a big mistake. It's probably just what Tolmar Aksden wants you to do.'

'We can't go to the police, Richard,' Osmo said as he shuffled back into the room, carrying a large cafetière and three mugs on a tray. He set the tray down on the table and subsided into his armchair. 'It would be our word against Aksden's. There's no proof of anything. We would end up as the suspects, not Tolmar. I was seen at the hotel. We were both seen at Matalainen's office. You signed the confidentiality agreement. I witnessed it. It would look like we did the setting up, not Mjollnir.'

'Sounds to me as if you're just making excuses for keeping out of it,' snapped Eusden.

'I guess I would say the same in your position.'

349

Osmo stretched forward and pushed down the plunger on the cafetière. 'I am sorry, Richard. Lund said they wouldn't harm you. And Pernille? I never thought for a second she was in danger.'

'How did you explain my disappearance to her?'

'I said you had gone when I came back from the toilet at the Café Engel. There was no time for her to ask me any questions. She and Matalainen had to leave right away.'

'Christ.' Eusden had to look away for a moment. Confirmation that Pernille must have concluded he had run out on her was even harder to bear than he had expected.

Timo leant across the table and poured their coffees. There was silence for a minute or two as they each contemplated the awfulness of what had occurred that day. Then Osmo said, 'When the police spoke to me, they had no idea what caused the explosion or even how many people were killed. There's a man in hospital who they think might be involved, but he has a serious brain injury. They're not sure he's going to survive. There's also a man they're looking for who they think was in the street when the explosion happened. The neighbours said he left in a hurry.'

'Me,' said Eusden dolefully.

'If I was you, I think I would fly home to England and pretend you were never here.'

'I can't do that.'

'But what can you do if you stay?'

'Make Tolmar Aksden pay for what he's done.'

'You'll fail,' said Timo, sipping his coffee.

'Maybe. But that's better than not trying. That's better than . . . living with his heel on your neck.'

The two brothers exchanged an eloquent glance. Timo cleared his throat. 'What do you want to know?'

'Tolmar Aksden's secret.'

'We don't know it,' said Osmo. 'No one does.'

'Not quite no one,' Timo corrected him. 'Arto Falenius knows, I'm sure.'

'Falenius? Head of Saukko Bank?'

'Yes. Grandson of the founder, Paavo Falenius.'

'Timo used to work for Saukko,' said Osmo.

'You did?'

'Forty-two years, Mr Eusden. Eighteen to sixty. Paavo Falenius was still alive when I started there in 1949. It's a long time ago. Some of the senior staff had been there from the beginning.'

'And when was the beginning?'

'1899. But it was just called the Falenius Bank then. The name Saukko wasn't used until the nineteen twenties. In English, *saukko* is an otter.'

'Why the change?'

'Paavo never explained. He had a reputation for not explaining things. But it wasn't the only change. The bank expanded greatly at that time. It was quite a small business until about 1920. Then, suddenly, it was big, rivalling Union Bank, Finland's oldest joint-stock bank. That took capital. A lot of capital. And no one really knows where Paavo got it from. But everyone who

351

worked for him benefited from how profitably he used it, so . . . '

'Is that the secret? Paavo Falenius's money?' Eusden remembered the cache of pre-war Finnish currency at Nydahl's apartment in Copenhagen. 'Ever heard of Hakon Nydahl?'

'Yes.' Timo looked surprised. 'I have. He was one of our customers. A very special customer.'

'In what way?'

'His account was managed personally by the chairman, Eino, Paavo's son, Arto's father. Everything relating to it had to be referred to Eino. The only other customer who ever got treated like that . . . was Tolmar Aksden.'

'So, they're all tied together in some way. Hakon Nydahl, Tolmar Aksden and the Faleniuses.'

'Yes.'

'And what *is* the connection?'

'Like Osmo said, we don't know. But . . . '

'But what?'

Osmo interrupted in Finnish before Timo could reply. There was a flurry of exchanges between the two brothers. Though Eusden could not understand a word, he had the impression that an argument they had had several times before was being repeated. Eventually, it petered out. And Osmo made a gesture with his hands that looked like a concession of kinds.

'There is a man I know, Mr Eusden,' Timo said, slowly and carefully. 'His name is Pekka Tallgren. Twenty years ago he was a history lecturer at Helsinki University. He planned a book on revolutionaries active in Finland before the First World War. Lenin, obviously, but there were many others, mostly Russian. Tallgren came to us — to Saukko — for information about Paavo's links with these people. Paavo had been dead many years by then, of course. Tallgren said he had evidence that Paavo had provided several revolutionary groups with funds. He asked if we had records of these dealings. We referred his request to the chairman. Arto had only recently taken over the chairmanship from his father. He was . . . embarrassed, it seemed to me. He told us Tallgren was to be given no information of any kind. Tallgren soon realized he was getting nowhere. He stopped asking his questions.'

'What happened to his book?'

'It was never published. Several years later, after I retired, I met Tallgren in Observatory Park. He was not in a good state. He told me his publisher cancelled his book contract soon after he approached us. Then one of his female students complained he had molested her. He denied it, of course. He was suspended. He started to drink heavily. He never went back to the university. In the end, even though the student later withdrew her complaint, he was dismissed.'

'Arto Falenius arranged all that?'

'Or Eino did. He was still a powerful man even after he handed the chairmanship over to Arto. Tallgren told me it was when he asked Arto about one revolutionary in particular that his troubles began.'

'Who was that?'

'I can't remember the name. But Tallgren will

353

remember for sure.'

'You know how I can contact him?'

'I felt sorry for him, Mr Eusden. So, I gave him a little money and helped him find somewhere decent to live. He sobered up, I'm glad to say. Later, I . . . recommended him for a job. Do you know Suomenlinna?'

'No. What is it?'

'A small group of islands out in the harbour. The Swedes constructed a fortress called Sveaborg on them in the mid-eighteenth century to defend their eastern frontier against the Russians. Later, the Russians took it over. And, later again, we Finns. It's a tourist attraction now. It includes a museum where you can learn about the history of the fortress. That's where I helped Tallgren get his job. He works as a curator in the Suomenlinna Museum. And he lives out there, in an apartment block on one of the islands. I think . . . if I asked him . . . he would speak to you. Yes, I think he would.'

'Then, ask him.'

'You're sure you want me to?'

Eusden nodded. 'I've never been more sure of anything in my life.'

44

It was gone midnight when Eusden reached the Market Square pontoon, but a couple more ferry crossings to Suomenlinna were still to be made. The cold had become more intense than he had ever experienced. The sea ice moaned and creaked. His breaths were plumes of frost in the still, deeply sub-zero air.

The few passengers, Suomenlinna residents bound for home, huddled in the cabin as the ferry chugged out through the broken skin of ice on its channel across the harbour. Eusden sat staring at their reflections in the windows, including his own — gaunt, drained and hollow-eyed. He spun Lund's phone in slow circles on the table, wondering if he should call Gemma and tell her . . . But since he did not know what he should or could tell her, he made no call.

He scrolled idly through Lund's contacts list. Tolmar Aksden was there; so, too, was Arto Falenius. He was tempted to call one of them — or both. He wanted them to know, even though he was well aware it was better they did not, that he was coming after them. They had overreached themselves. This time, he willed them to understand, there would be a reckoning.

★ ★ ★

The tower above the main gate of the fortress loomed through the chill mist that hung over Suomenlinna as Eusden stepped ashore. A single figure was waiting on the quay, wrapped in a parka with a huge Arctic-standard hood. 'Richard Eusden?' he enquired, pulling off a mitt to offer his hand. 'I'm Pekka Tallgren.' They shook. 'Cold night for a boat trip, no?'

'Thanks for agreeing to talk to me, Mr Tallgren.'

'Call me Pekka, Richard. OK?'

'OK.'

'I bet you're thinking: why does the crazy man live out here on this frozen island?'

'Timo said you work here.'

'I do. But sometimes . . . it feels a bit like Alcatraz, with San Francisco across the bay. Anyway, let's not stand here, freezing our balls off. I brought the car with me.' Tallgren turned and led the way towards a tiny old Fiat. 'It's not far to my place. But everywhere's a long way on a night like this.'

'Sorry it's so late.'

'Don't worry. I don't sleep so good.' They clambered into the car. Tallgren threw back his hood, revealing a bearded, heavy-featured face. He started the engine and skidded away along a sparsely gritted strip through the surrounding blanket of snow and ice. 'I've got interested in astronomy since I came here. You can see so much more this far from the lights of the city. Not when it's like this, of course. You're not keeping me from my telescope, that's for sure.'

They rumbled over a narrow bridge to an

356

adjoining island and turned left past a high stone wall. 'How long have you lived here, Pekka?' Eusden asked.

'Nine years. Some exile, hey? But, truthfully, I like it. I'm near Helsinki but not in it. That suits me. It keeps my memories at just the right distance. Timo told you all about my . . . troubles, no?'

'Yes. He did.'

'He helped me a lot. More than he needed to. So, I owe him. Which is lucky for you. I don't normally talk to anyone about Saukko.'

'I know. I'm grateful.'

'Maybe you shouldn't be. Knowing this stuff . . . can be unhealthy.'

They crossed a second bridge to a further island and slewed to a halt in a courtyard flanked by barrack blocks converted into apartments. Most of the windows were in darkness and a profound silence closed about them as they climbed from the car.

'Welcome to my world, Richard,' said Tallgren.

⋆ ⋆ ⋆

The apartment was small and felt smaller still thanks to the crammed bookshelves lining every spare wall and the piles of books and papers that had overflowed on to the floors beside them.

Stripped of his mitts and parka, Tallgren looked just what the domestic disorder might have led Eusden to expect: untidily dressed, grey hair overdue for a trim — a middle-aged

357

academic content in his own shambolic environment. Except that he was an academic no longer.

'I set some coffee going before I left,' Tallgren said as Eusden hung up his coat in the tiny hallway. 'You want some?'

'Fine.' Eusden would have preferred a stiff drink, but he knew better than to ask for one.

'Come into the kitchen. It's the warmest room.'

An aroma of coffee had filled the kitchen in Tallgren's absence. An electric percolator stood ready on the crumbstrewn worktop. He grabbed a couple of mugs and waved Eusden to the table opposite, where a crumpled copy of *Helsingin Sanomat* lay, folded open at the page in the business section Eusden had seen earlier, with the photograph of Tolmar Aksden and Arto Falenius. Tallgren pushed it aside as he delivered their coffees.

'Black OK? I'm out of milk.'

'No problem.'

'And cream.' Tallgren nodded down at the newspaper. 'Looks like they got it all.'

'Do you regret tangling with them?'

'You bet.' Tallgren took a reflective sip of coffee, then sat down and folded the paper back on itself. The faces of Aksden and Falenius obligingly vanished. He smiled. 'I've seen enough of that pair.'

'What can you — '

'Hold on.' Tallgren raised his hand. 'This is how it's going to work, Richard. You give me the full story of what brought you here. The whole thing. Then, if I'm convinced you're not

. . . some kind of spy for those bastards . . . I'll tell you everything I know. You're sitting here with me because of Timo. No other reason. I don't know you. He says I can trust you. OK. But that's a two-way street. And you've got to trust me first. Do we have a deal?'

★ ★ ★

It was a relief in many ways to have no choice but to share everything he knew with somebody else. Tallgren sipped his coffee and smoked his way through a couple of roll-ups while Eusden recounted the events that had brought him to Suomenlinna. He took out the double-headed-eagle envelope and showed Tallgren the piece of paper with the fingerprints on it. He talked about Marty and Clem and all the people he had met in the course of one desperate week. He held nothing back. He laid it all on the line.

★ ★ ★

When he had finished, Tallgren topped up their coffees and said, simply, 'It's worse than I thought.'

45

'I'll assume you know as much Finnish history as the average non-Finn, Richard, which is zero,' said Tallgren. 'So, I'll try to keep it simple. Sweden surrendered Finland to Russia in 1809, but Tsar Alexander the First granted the Finns self-government. He knew he'd have too much trouble with us otherwise. The Grand Duchy of Finland, as it was called, was part of the Russian Empire, but not part of Russia. It ran its own affairs. That made it a haven for anti-Tsarist revolutionaries — Bolsheviks, Mensheviks, anarchists, nihilists — in the years before the First World War. It became Lenin's second home. He and Stalin met for the first time at a Bolshevik conference in Tampere in 1905.

'I set out to write a full study of the revolutionaries active in Finland during that period. It was a fascinating subject. I never thought it was dangerous as well. The Falenius Bank, as Saukko was called back then, was mentioned in a lot of correspondence as a source of loans to such people. Well, Arto Falenius was willing to admit his grandfather lent money to revolutionaries, though he denied they were gifts in effect, never repaid. He also denied Paavo sheltered mutineers who took part in a short-lived Red uprising here on Suomenlinna in 1906. It was odd. The evidence was clear and I couldn't see a problem. Paavo Falenius was a

360

socialist sympathizer. Good publicity, I'd have thought.

'Then I came across some other information that confused the picture. Lots of new stuff was leaking out of the Soviet Union around then thanks to *glasnost*. It turned out from some of it that Lenin suspected Paavo Falenius was a double agent, feeding information about the revolutionary groups to the Tsarist government in St Petersburg. True? I never found out for sure, because that was when I really got Arto's attention, by probing his grandfather's relationship with a shadowy character called Karl Vanting.

'Vanting was Danish, born in Copenhagen in 1884. He moved to Helsinki in 1905 specially to offer his services to Lenin as an active revolutionary. He played a big part in organizing the 1906 mutiny and a general strike the same year. The story was that he was a bitter enemy of the Romanovs because he was an illegitimate son of Tsar Alexander the Third. It could be true. There was supposed to be a resemblance. And my researches showed his mother worked as a maid in the Danish royal palace of Fredensborg. She was dismissed in December 1883. Karl was born five months later. Pregnancy was probably the reason for her dismissal. The Tsar and the Tsarina, Dagmar, went to Fredensborg with their children every summer to visit their Danish relatives. So, the timing fits. Karl's mother married a Copenhagen shopkeeper called Vanting in 1885 and the boy took his stepfather's name.

361

'The same material that quoted Lenin as suspecting Paavo Falenius of working for the other side mentioned Vanting as his alleged confederate. This is where it gets murky. Vanting left Helsinki in 1909, destination unknown. It took a lot of work to follow his tracks. He dropped out of revolutionary politics altogether and turned up on the Caribbean island of St Thomas, working as a clerk for the aide-de-camp to the Governor of the Danish Virgin Islands. The aide-de-camp's name was Hakon Nydahl. Denmark sold their Virgin Islands colony to the United States in 1917 and Nydahl went home. Vanting didn't go with him. He stayed on, working for the new American administration. Then, in the spring of 1918, he got himself attached to a US regiment sent to intervene in the Russian Civil War. He spoke quite good Russian and they were short of interpreters.

'The Russian Civil War was the Whites against the Reds — crudely speaking, Tsarists versus Bolsheviks — in the aftermath of the Revolution, complicated by parts of the old Empire trying to break away and British, French, German and American forces trying to grab territory and/or stop the Reds winning. Plus rescue the Tsar — if they could. Finland declared independence from Russia at the end of 1917 and then had its own Reds against Whites Civil War. Unlike in Russia, the Whites won, with a little help from the Germans. It was all over by May 1918. Thousands had died. And thousands of Reds had been taken prisoner. This is where they were

362

held. Here on Suomenlinna. The fortress became a prison.

'What's this got to do with Karl Vanting? Well, one day in October 1918, two people arrived in Suomenlinna in a small boat they said they'd rowed across the Gulf of Finland from Russia. One of them was Vanting. The other was a lad in his early teens. Vanting didn't say anything about serving in the American army and he claimed he didn't know what had been happening in Finland. Unfortunately for him, the prison commandant remembered him as a Red revolutionary. He and the lad — whose name wasn't recorded — were locked up.

'Conditions here in 1918 were terrible. Over-crowding. Disease. Famine. Vanting couldn't have chosen a worse place to land. But he wasn't here for long. After a few weeks, he and his companion were released on the recognizance of Paavo Falenius. And then . . . they dropped out of sight.

'It gets even murkier now. Like Timo told you, the big unanswered question about Saukko Bank is where their influx of capital in the early nineteen twenties came from. Well, what you've found out fills in the gaps in a theory I thought was really off-the-wall when I first developed it, but now . . . fits together like Lego. A Danish invention, no? *Lege godt.* To play well. And they did play it well.

'Paavo Falenius was a double agent. Not much doubt about it. Maybe the best kind. The kind both sides trust so completely you have to ask: which side was he really on? He was born in

1869. Studied law at St Petersburg University. One of his fellow students was Peter Lvovich Bark, who also went into banking and was the Russian Minister of Finance from 1914 until the Revolution. He fled to England afterwards, where he became *Sir* Peter Bark, a director of the Bank of England. Strange, no? But consider. Bark acted as executor for the Tsar's estate after his presumed death. Only he knew how much money there was and where it was. Falenius was an old friend of his. I found photographs of them together in a university rowing team and later at banking dinners in Helsinki *and* St Petersburg.

'I think I know what it all adds up to. The assassin your friend's grandfather saved the Grand Duchesses Olga and Tatiana from in Cowes in August 1909 was Karl Vanting. It was hushed up because Tsar Nicholas the Second knew he was his illegitimate half-brother. Vanting was banished to the Danish Virgin Islands in the hope he could be reformed. It sort of worked, at least for a while. But in 1918 he went to Russia with the American army — and vanished. Then he turned up in Finland with a young companion who was never officially identified. Well, I think that companion was — or became — Peder Aksden. I think Sir Peter Bark used some of the Tsar's money to buy the young man a new life in Denmark and to buy the silence of those people who thought they knew who he really was.

'And who were those people? Falenius gave us a clue when he changed the name of his bank. *Saukko.* Otter. Tolmar Aksden went to Norse mythology for the name of his company. Mjollnir. Thor's magic hammer. I think he followed the example of the man who gave him the capital to start Mjollnir. But what's the mythical significance of an otter? In Finnish myth, Tuonela is the land of the dead, from which no traveller returns. The only exception was the hero Vainomoinen. He crossed the river marking the boundary of Tuonela and was greeted by Tuonetar, goddess of the dead. She offered him some of the wondrous ale of Tuonela. He drank his fill. Then, while he slept it off, Tuonetar's son built an iron net across the river, so that Vainomoinen couldn't leave and would be trapped for ever. But, when he woke and saw what had been done, Vainomoinen changed himself into an otter and swam through the net back to the land of the living.

'In 1918, Russia was the land of the dead. Vanting's young companion escaped by changing himself into someone else. Hakon Nydahl persuaded his sister to take the young man in as a kind of replacement for the child she'd lost, supplied false records of his birth in Jutland and money for his new family. The money came through Falenius Bank, later Saukko, from the Tsar's secret accounts controlled by Sir Peter Bark. Paavo Falenius skimmed off some for his own use. Some of the rest ended up in Mjollnir. And some in Nydahl's safe at his apartment in Copenhagen. The markkaa his housekeeper stole were 1939 issue, right? Well, the signs were growing all through 1939 that Stalin would invade Finland. Falenius probably sent a large chunk of money to Nydahl because he was afraid the Soviets would overrun the country and close him down. He must have thought they'd send him to a gulag if his double dealing was found out.

'As it happened, the Soviets were never able to conquer Finland. The Germans got involved again. And Field Marshal Mannerheim saved the country, as every Finnish schoolboy knows. So, Paavo Falenius lived on. And so did his bank. He died in 1957. He has a very fine tomb in Hietaniemi Cemetery. Poor Peder Aksden was dead by then, of course. An accident with a sickle, his daughter said? I can believe it. Sharp blades are dangerous things for haemophiliacs to handle.

'You see now, Richard? The Tsar's money. The nameless young man from Russia. The change of identity to slip through the net. Hakon Nydahl's sister thought she was adopting the Tsar's haemophiliac son, Alexei. Crazy, no? But they were crazy times. No one knew for sure what had happened to the family. Rumour, rumour, rumour. But nothing certain. Vanting told some tale of rescuing the boy to atone for trying to kill his sisters. Did Falenius believe him? Maybe. More likely he reckoned he could persuade others to believe him. Was that how he extracted the money from Bark? By threatening him with a convincing impostor? Or by convincing him the young man *wasn't* an impostor? Dagmar, the Dowager Empress, was still in the Crimea at the time. She didn't leave until spring 1919. So, Bark had to act without consulting her. And he had to stick by his actions. Maybe, if he believed Vanting's story, he thought it was better to let the Tsarevich heal his body and mind in the seclusion of the Danish countryside and to keep his survival secret — even from his grandmother — in case the Soviets sent assassins after him. The young man may have had no clear memory of who he was or what had happened to him. If he *was* Alexei, he'd been through a traumatic experience. But, then again, maybe Bark never believed the story for a moment. Maybe he paid up to avoid the damage a false Alexei, manipulated by Falenius, could do. The same goes for Nydahl. He knew Vanting from his days in the West Indies. What did he think he was getting himself involved in? Or was he just following orders from Dagmar's nephew, King Christian the Tenth of Denmark, to bury the problem before the old lady came home? The possibilities are endless. We'll never know now.

'Whatever the truth behind it was, the plan worked well. But then a young woman showed up in Germany claiming to be Alexei's sister, Anastasia. And many people believed her, including several members of the Romanov family. If she was formally acknowledged, she'd get control of her father's estate and find out where a lot of his money had gone. So, she had to be stopped. And what better way could there be of doing that than supplying a set of fingerprints that proved she couldn't be Anastasia? Bark had made powerful friends since arriving in London. I think he arranged through them to send Clem Hewitson to Copenhagen at some point in 1925, probably the autumn, with the fake prints he was instructed to claim he'd taken on board the imperial yacht in August 1909. He and Nydahl were going to travel to Berlin, where Anna Anderson was in hospital, fingerprint her and expose her as a fraud.

'But something went wrong. Maybe Hewitson started to think Anna was genuine and wasn't willing to cheat her out of her inheritance. Or maybe he found out from Nydahl what was really going on. Bark's friends in the British Establishment wouldn't have known about his arrangement with Falenius. If Hewitson exposed *that*, there'd have been a big rethink. In the end, though, it would still have been hushed up. The fingerprint plot against Anna Anderson would have been abandoned, but Bark's other deal would have been quietly overlooked. The Tsar's unclaimed deposits at the Bank of England, which Bark controlled, bought a lot of silence. Anyway, Anna Anderson never did win acknowledgement as Anastasia, did she? They wore her down over the years.

'Clem Hewitson, the English policeman, and Hakon Nydahl, the Danish courtier, must have trusted each other after that more than they did their superiors. I think they decided to keep a record of everything that happened, which they could use to defend themselves if they ever needed to. I think that's what the letters were all about: insurance. I doubt Nydahl ever told his relatives he'd written them. It was a clever idea: documents in Danish, stored in England; as good as a secret code. If you could read them,

368

you'd know whether Nydahl believed Peder Aksden truly was the Tsarevich. If he didn't, then you'd also know some of the Tsar's money, intended for his children, was stolen by a Finnish banker and used by a Danish businessman to create his own empire. Tolmar Aksden: Tsar of all the enterprises. If I'm right, he badly needed to destroy those letters. And now he has. All that's left are the fake fingerprints. On their own, they prove nothing.

'I'm sorry, Richard. But that's how I see it. It all ends in nothing.'

46

'I'm not going to let them get away with it,' said Eusden, breaking the silence that had followed Tallgren's bleak conclusion.

'Brave words, Richard.' Tallgren smiled at him. 'I would have spoken them myself once.'

'But it's worse than theft and fraud, Pekka. They've killed people, including Tolmar's ex-wife. Pernille was actually trying to help him, for God's sake.'

'She should have known better.'

'Is that all you can say?'

Tallgren looked surprised by the flare of anger in Eusden's voice. '*Anteeksi.* I forgot you knew her. What was she like?'

'A fine and brave person.'

Tallgren sighed. 'I *am* sorry. But . . . they've always been ruthless. Consider what happened to Karl Vanting in the end.'

'What *did* happen?'

'He was found shot dead at his lodgings in Hakaniemi on New Year's Eve, 1925. It was a poor area of the city then. Whatever money Paavo Falenius gave him, he must have lost it. Then, perhaps, he asked for more. The police decided it was suicide. Maybe it was. Maybe it wasn't. I saw the television news this evening. They interviewed the officer in charge of investigating the explosion at Osmo's house. He talked about a gas leak as the likeliest explanation.'

370

'They'll find traces of explosive.'

'Will they? I guess that depends how thorough they are. Even if they do, what evidence do you think they'll find that Tolmar Aksden had anything to do with it?'

'None,' Eusden admitted.

'Let me show you something.' Tallgren rose stiffly to his feet and left the room, patting Eusden consolingly on the shoulder as he passed.

There was the sound of a filing-cabinet drawer being slid open and of papers being shuffled. Then Tallgren was back in the kitchen, carrying a bulging file. He placed it carefully on the table. On the cover was a single word written in felt-tip capitals: WANTING.

'The fruit of my research. Not very sweet, I'm afraid.'

'Wanting is . . . Vanting?'

'Ah. The spelling. Yes. The name's probably German originally. The W is pronounced like a V, of course. In English, it makes a sick kind of joke, doesn't it? He wanted a lot. Revenge. Wealth. Success. He didn't get any of it.' Tallgren flicked the file open. 'My notes are all in Finnish. There are some documents in Danish and Russian also. So, nothing for you to read. But something for you to see.' He slid out an A5-sized photograph, glossily printed, though the picture itself was grainy and indistinct, a black-and-white shot of a crowd of people on some steps. In one of the margins was written *Helsingin Sanomat 11 Huhtikuu 1957.* 'This shows some of the mourners leaving Helsinki

Cathedral after Paavo Falenius's funeral. Take a look at those three particularly.'

Tallgren pointed to a short, middle-aged man near the top of the steps, who seemed to be conversing with two other men, one older, one much younger. All three were dressed in dark overcoats. The youngest man was bare-headed, but the other two wore dark Homburgs, the brims pulled down so that only the lower halves of their faces could be seen.

'Eino Falenius, Hakon Nydahl and Tolmar Aksden. There they are, Richard. Caught together, for once. They say Eino looked a lot like his father. He was in his forties then. Nydahl was in his seventies. And Aksden was . . . just eighteen.'

Eino Falenius was a sleek, elegantly tailored businessman running to fat, with a smudge of moustache and a confidential air. He had his hand on Hakon Nydahl's shoulder. The elderly Dane was thin and straight as a pencil, a walking cane clutched in front of him, his gaze fixed inscrutably on Falenius. Tolmar Aksden, meanwhile, was barely recognizable as the bulky, assertive figure he was to appear in the pages of the very same newspaper forty years on. He was tall and slim, a boyish lock of hair falling over his unlined brow, his face clear and open, yet also watchful, studying Falenius with the faintest of frowns, concentrating on something that was being said — or something he had noticed.

'What was a teenager from a farm in Jutland doing at an eminent Finnish banker's funeral, eh? And not just in the congregation, but conversing afterwards with the banker's son? This was long before he set up Mjollnir or did business with Saukko. The official version of Tolmar Aksden's life has him pulling sheep out of ditches in 1957, not fraternizing with Helsinki money men. So, what's it all about? I asked Arto Falenius that. I asked him how he explained it. Do you know what he said? 'I don't have to explain it to someone like you.' And he smiled when he said it. Such a smile. I wish now I'd punched him in his smiling face. Well, it couldn't have gone any worse for me if I had, could it? Someone like me, Richard. Someone like you. They don't have to account to us.'

'We'll see about that.'

'What do you intend to do?'

It was a good question. And the answer was only just beginning to form in Eusden's mind. Run away? Give up? Write it all off as Marty's folly that he had no stake in? He could not do it. The rest of his life would diminish into an apologetic murmur if he did not at least try to bring Pernille's murderers to justice. 'Do you have a tape recorder?'

'Yes.'

'Can I borrow it?'

'Sure, but — '

'Do you know where Arto Falenius lives?'

'Yes. He owns a villa near Kaivopuisto Park. The embassy district. Very smart. His father and grandfather lived there before him. The Villa Norsonluu, in Itäinen Puistotie. You're thinking of going there?'

'Tolmar Aksden's out of town. So, it has to be

373

Falenius. He's probably the easier of the two to crack anyway.'

'Crack?'

'I'll make him explain to someone like me. On tape.'

'He'll never agree to do that.'

'I don't propose to give him a choice in the matter. Do you know anything about firearms?'

'Well, I did my eight months in the army. They made me fire a rifle. Plus take it apart and put it back together again.'

'That's more than I've ever done. I've got a gun, you see. An automatic pistol. In my coat. I've no intention of using it. But I need to look as if I know how to. And I don't want any accidents.'

'You're going to force a confession out of Falenius at gun-point?'

'Exactly.'

'Are you crazy?'

'Probably.'

'Even if you could, it wouldn't . . . prove anything legally.'

'I don't care about that. I'll have it. And I'll make what use of it I can.'

'You *are* crazy.'

'I'm not asking you to go with me, Pekka. Just give me the tape recorder and show me how the gun works. Then wish me luck.'

★ ★ ★

Eusden slept for a few hours on the sofa in Tallgren's lounge, his sleep the dreamless

374

unconsciousness of utter exhaustion. He woke before dawn, reluctantly ate some porridge and less reluctantly drank a mug of strong black coffee. Then Tallgren drove him over the bridges of Suomenlinna through the frozen twilight to the quay in time for the first ferry of the day. Tallgren had done his best to explain the mechanics of the gun and the intricacies of his tape recorder. Beyond that he only ventured the opinion that what Eusden was doing was madness. An admirable kind of madness, perhaps, but madness nonetheless.

'I fear you're about to make the biggest mistake of your life, Richard,' he said as Eusden climbed out of the car.

'I don't think so,' Eusden replied with a wry smile. 'A bigger mistake would be to do nothing.'

47

The cream gables of the Villa Norsonluu would have glowed warmly in summer sunshine, bowered in greenery, doves cooing peacefully. Late winter dawn revealed a different place. Snow obscured most of the roof, coated the branches of the leafless trees and blanketed the garden in white. There was no sound or movement from the dovecot that Eusden had seen through the boundary hedge, nor from the house behind it.

Now that he was standing there, alone, surrounded by silence, Eusden began to wonder if what he had embarked on was indeed an act of madness. He looked down the road and saw in the distance the Tricolour and the Union Jack flying over the French and British Embassies. Of all the places in all the world for him to do what he was about to do, this had to be potentially one of the most scandalous, the most ruinous, most irresponsible of all.

And what, when it came down to it, was he going to do? He had forgotten to ask Tallgren if Falenius lived alone. The size of the house suggested not. Was he married? Did he have children? Did Eusden seriously intend to force his way into some scene of domestic normality, brandishing a gun, issuing demands, crossing a line he could never step back over?

The entrance to the villa was sealed by a high

locked gate. There was no camera in sight, though there might of course be one on the house, ready to record any incursion he made. He stood in the lee of the hedge, willing himself to act, facing down the doubts and fears that swarmed in his brain. The railing-topped wall behind him was scaleable, the hedge penetrable. It was the only way to get in. He had to attempt it. And soon. The longer he delayed, the likelier he was to be spotted.

Suddenly, there was a sound, breaking the silence. A door was opening, electronically operated. Eusden peered through the hedge, but could see nothing. Then a car engine started in a throaty growl. And in the same instant the gates at the entrance whirred into operation, swinging back on their expensively automated hinges. There was a rumble of fat tyre on gritted snow. A shape, low, pale and metallic, moved somewhere beyond the hedge.

Falenius was leaving. And Eusden had to stop him. He ran to the gate and reached into his pocket for the gun. The driveway curved out of sight towards the house. He stood waiting for the car to come into view, waiting and wondering what he should do. Then it appeared: a Bentley, silver-grey and sleekly profiled, nosing round the corner. A glimpse of the driver was enough. It was Arto Falenius.

If Eusden drew the gun, what, he asked himself, would Falenius do? Stop? Or accelerate towards him? Could that raked and tinted windscreen possibly be bullet-proof? There had to be another way, one that was safer for both of them. He dropped to his knees and sprawled across the pavement, blocking the entrance.

The Bentley came to a halt in the gateway. Falenius gave the horn two short blasts. Eusden did not move. All he could see of the car from where he lay was the headlamp array, the number plate and the radiator grille, with the distinctive Bentley B above it. He heard the engine cooler roar, then the driver's door slam. Arto Falenius, pinstripe-suited as in his newspaper photograph, strode towards him, gleaming brogues crunching on grit and ice. He said something in Finnish that sounded impatient. Eusden made a show of struggling to his feet.

'Sorry,' he mumbled. 'I must've slipped.'

'Are you OK?' Falenius asked, with little obvious concern.

'Yes. Fine, thanks. But you aren't.' Eusden pulled the gun from his pocket and pointed it at Falenius's midriff. 'Do exactly as I say.'

'What is this?' Falenius looked shocked and angry and alarmed in equal measure.

'What do you think?'

'You want . . . money?'

'No. I want a ride. And a talk.' Eusden kept the gun trained on Falenius as he walked to the passenger door of the Bentley and opened it. 'Get in. We're leaving.'

'You can't do this.'

'But I am doing it. Get in. Now.'

Falenius was breathing rapidly as he moved to the car. Eusden lowered himself carefully into the passenger seat as Falenius settled behind the wheel. The doors clunked shut, sealing off the chill of the morning.

'Drive to the seafront.'

'Who are you?'

'Richard Eusden.'

'I've . . . never heard of you.'

'Really? Well, your good friend Tolmar Aksden *has* heard of me. And it's him we're going to talk about. Start moving.'

★ ★ ★

Traffic on the seafront road was light and none of it was stopping to admire the view of the frozen harbour, covered with snow and differing in appearance from Kaivopuisto Park on the other side of the road only by being flatter. When Falenius turned off the engine of the Bentley, his shallow breathing became audible in the muffled interior of the car. He did not look directly at Eusden, staring out instead through the windscreen at the grey hummocks of islands scattered across the white-carpeted sea. He moistened his lips and asked hoarsely, 'What do you want to know?'

'The truth.' Eusden propped the recorder on the dashboard between them and switched it on. 'In your very own words.'

'The truth . . . about what?'

'Your relationship with Tolmar Aksden.'

'He's the new owner of Saukko Bank. We're business associates. And friends. That's it.'

'Listen to me, Arto. I already know what you're going to tell me. But I need to hear you say it. On the record. So, don't lie to me. The consequences could be fatal. You understand?'

Falenius swallowed hard. 'I understand.'

'Good. Now, I'll ask you some questions. All you have to do is give me honest answers. Are we clear?'

'Yes.'

'You're Arto Falenius, son of Eino Falenius, grandson of Paavo Falenius, the founder of Saukko Bank. Correct?'

'Correct.'

'Where did Paavo get all his money from — the huge influx of cash in the early nineteen twenties that no one seems able to account for?'

'He . . . attracted some big investors.'

'Was one of them Sir Peter Bark, investing on behalf of Tsar Nicholas the Second?'

Falenius sighed and bowed his head, as if oppressed by the fulfilment of his worst fears. '*Kristus!* Not this. Please not this.'

'Did Bark pump the Tsar's money into Saukko Bank?'

'I don't know.'

'*You don't know?*'

'It's true. My father never trusted me enough to tell me the whole story. And Tolmar always says I'm better off not knowing. The Tsar's money? That could be it. If you say it was, then, OK, it was. Is that good enough for you?'

'No.'

'I didn't think it would be. So, go ahead. Ask about my grandfather, this man Bark, Hakon Nydahl, Karl Wanting. Ask me and tell me what I'm supposed to say. Then I'll say it. I'm too young to have met any of them. But apparently I have to live with their ghosts.'

'You must know your grandfather channelled money to the Aksden family through Nydahl.'

'Yes. I know that. But not why. Not really. You don't keep Tolmar as a friend by poking your nose into his affairs. Or as a boss. He owns Saukko now. I'm just one of his employees.'

'Why did you sell?'

'The sale was planned years ago. Tolmar's basically owned us ever since I became chairman. He struck a deal with my father. I was part of it.'

'And what did the deal require you to do?'

'Build up stakes in a range of key Russian businesses so that Tolmar could move into the Russian market without anyone noticing.'

'They've noticed now.'

'They were bound to eventually. Anyway, that's Tolmar's problem. I just do what he tells me.'

'Why do I keep hearing that phrase?'

Falenius managed a wintry smile. 'Because he's good at persuading people to obey him.'

'What do you know about the explosion yesterday at Osmo Koskinen's house?'

'What I hear on the news. Gas leak, maybe?'

'You are aware Pernille Madsen, Tolmar's ex-wife, was among those killed, aren't you?'

'Truly?' Falenius's expression was authentically shocked and baffled. It seemed he genuinely had not known. 'Pernille?'

'Yes.'

'I never thought he'd . . . ' Falenius shook his head. 'I don't know what to say.'

381

'He's made you a party to murder, Arto. How does that make you feel?'

'Sick. To my stomach. But you must understand. I knew nothing about it.'

'Because you didn't want to know.'

'OK. You can say that. But still . . . ' Falenius stared pleadingly at Eusden. 'You've got the wrong man. I'm not to blame. You should ask Tolmar your questions. Not me.'

'I would if I could.'

'I can tell you where he is.'

'Oh, yes?'

'He's hiding. Now I know what from. We've . . . done some dirty things over the years, but . . . never murder.'

'Where is he hiding?'

'We have a *kesämökki* — a summer-house — up on Lake Päijänne. He's gone there. He often goes there. To relax. To think.' Falenius appeared to believe he was winning Eusden over. 'I can tell you . . . exactly where it is. He'll be alone. At this time of the year, *very* alone.'

'You don't need to tell me where it is, Arto. You just need to take me there.'

'No. I can't leave Helsinki. I'll be missed. It's a . . . two-hundred-kilometre drive.'

'We'd better get going, then, hadn't we?' Eusden stretched forward and retrieved the recorder. 'You're right. There's nothing more to be said. We'll leave Tolmar to do all the talking.'

PÄIJÄNNE

48

It was early afternoon when they came within sight of the Falenius family's *mökki* on one of the many inlets along the shore of Lake Päijänne. The first half of the journey had been a fast motorway cruise, constrained only by Eusden's insistence that Falenius keep within the speed limit; he could not risk attracting the attention of the police. Since leaving the main road, however, the going had been slowed by snow and ice. Forests had closed around them. Traffic had thinned and vanished. They were alone, in a wintry world of stillness and grey light and blanketing white. The bumpy track they had followed off the last surfaced road emerged from snow-heavy pine and spruce into a stretch of skeletal ash and maple as the frozen surface of the lake, dead flat and matt white, appeared before them. And there, beside a snow-covered meadow, was the *mökki* — a simple wooden chalet, with smoke rising from its chimney and a Range Rover parked behind it, next to a log-store.

Falenius pulled up next to the Range Rover and turned off the engine. He looked drained and desperate. The long drive, during which Eusden had said little, leaving him to imagine the worst, had taken its toll.

'He must have heard us,' the Finn said

hoarsely. 'Why doesn't he come out?'

'Let's go and see. But, first, give me the key to this thing.'

Falenius pulled it out of the ignition and handed it over. 'What are you going to do to us?'

'I told you. I want the whole story on the record. If you give me that, we'll all leave here alive and well.'

'I'm cooperating, OK? Remember that. Any problems you have with Tolmar, they're not with me.'

'I'll remember. Let's go.'

★ ★ ★

They climbed out of the car. The stark reality of the place they had come to disclosed itself in the cold, misty air. If Tolmar Aksden had wanted to hide, he had chosen the right place. No one would come looking for him here unless they badly needed to find him.

Eusden gestured for Falenius to lead the way. They walked slowly round to the front of the chalet. The roof extended down to cover a planked veranda. Between the chalet and the shore was the snow-hummocked shape of a rowing boat. A landing stage jutted out beyond it into the lake. Falenius called out Aksden's name as he approached the door. There was no response.

'Look inside,' said Eusden.

Falenius opened the door and stepped in, calling out again. Eusden stood behind him in the doorway. Warmth from a stove wafted out to

386

meet him. There was a large table and some chairs, a sofa, armchairs and a rug in front of the stove. To his right was a well-equipped kitchen area. A couple of doors led off to other rooms out of his sight. There were books, papers and a laptop on the table, as well as a coffeepot and mug. Falenius touched the pot and looked back at Eusden. 'Still warm.'

'He can't be far, then. We'll — '

Two short blasts on the Bentley's horn burst through the silence. Eusden retreated from the veranda and strode to the corner of the chalet. A tall, bulky figure in a quilted parka and flapped cap was standing by the open driver's door of the car. He slammed it, revealing as he did so the rifle he was carrying, and stood where he was, staring at Eusden with cool curiosity.

'Where's Arto?' The voice was gruff, the tone peremptory. He must have been able to see the gun in Eusden's hand, but he paid it no attention.

'Here,' Eusden replied, stepping back to let Falenius pass.

'I told you not to come here, Arto,' said Aksden.

'This guy gave me no choice, Tolmar.' Falenius hurried eagerly towards his friend, as if he would give him the protection he needed. 'He says — '

'Let him speak for himself.'

Eusden followed Falenius at a cautious pace. Aksden held the rifle loosely and unthreateningly. Yet still it was a weapon. Eusden's advantage had been cancelled out. 'Do you know who I am, Tolmar?'

Aksden nodded. 'Oh yes. Lund told me you were still alive. Why have you come here?'

'I want the truth.'

'That's a large thing to want, my friend.'

'And a dangerous one, it appears.'

Aksden looked at Falenius with an expression of weary disappointment. 'You shouldn't have brought him here, Arto. It was a stupid thing to do.'

'He threatened me with a gun.'

'An empty threat, you fool. He's no killer. Are you, Eusden?'

'Maybe you've turned me into one.'

'I don't think so.'

'Are you going to put it to the test?' Eusden challenged Aksden with his gaze, but saw no hint of weakness in the Dane's steely blue eyes.

'If I have to.'

'Surely we can sort this out,' pleaded Falenius.

'I doubt it. It's not as simple as either of you think. Were you followed, Arto?'

'Followed? No. Of course not.'

'We weren't followed,' Eusden declared. He was confident on the point, though curious as to who Aksden thought might have done the following. 'Police on your tail, Tolmar?'

'Not that I know.' Aksden gave him a tight, ironical little smile. 'Check under the car, Arto.'

'Check for what?'

'Anything that looks different.'

Falenius knelt and peered under the Bentley. Something caught his attention. He bent lower. '*Kristus*, what's that?'

'What does it look like?'

'A box. With a . . . flashing red light.'

Aksden tossed back his head and sighed. *'Satans også.'*

'What is it?' demanded Eusden.

'A tracking device, I expect. Probably attached some time yesterday. You only had to look, Arto, and you'd have seen it. But you never *see* anything, do you?' Aksden glanced suspiciously towards the trees. 'We should go indoors.'

'Who's tracking me?' asked Falenius as he stood up. 'What — '

The bullet took him in the back. It knocked all the breath out of him. He looked first surprised, then mildly pained. He fell to his knees, swayed for a moment, and slumped forward on to the ground.

'Run,' shouted Aksden.

Eusden was already running, making for the shelter of the chalet. A bullet pinged off the bodywork of the Range Rover. Then another shattered one of its windows. Eusden made it to the veranda, blind-sided from the direction of the shots. Aksden lunged after him. The firing stopped.

'This is your fault, Eusden,' Aksden gasped. 'You ought to understand that, you piece of . . . ' He broke off and shook his head. 'I only needed another twenty-four hours. That's all. Just twenty-four hours.'

'I don't know what you're talking about. Who's shooting at us?'

'You think I know his name? He's a hunter. And I'm his prey. He'd probably have got me if

389

Arto hadn't stood up when he did.' Aksden engaged the bolt on his rifle, craned round the corner of the chalet and let off a shot, then jumped back.

'Can you see him?'

'No. He's hiding in the trees. That was just to keep him there.'

'Who sent him?'

'Did the American tell you about Olsen?'

'The American? If you mean Brad, yes. He killed Olsen, right?'

'Right. The Opposition didn't like that. They lost a man they trusted and the dirt on me they expected him to deliver. Also they thought I'd arranged it. So, they took out a contract on me to force me to negotiate with them. Clever tactic. We talked. They agreed to cancel the contract if I killed Brad as a demonstration of my good faith, with a commercial partnership to follow. A better deal for me than I'd have got any other way, but it only takes effect when they get confirmation that Brad and his crew are dead. All I had to do was stay out of their hit man's reach until then. Which I would have done, but for you and Arto leading him right to me.'

'Who are these people — the Opposition?'

'Businessmen, Eusden. The Russian kind. I'm beginning to win their respect for standing up to them. *Pokkers også*, now it looks like it might be too late.'

'You think I'd care if this man killed you?'

'No. But you should care about yourself. He'll kill you too just for being here.' Aksden pulled off his cap and blinked several times as if trying to clear his sight, then stepped to the corner of the chalet and fired another shot. 'I saw something this time,' he said as he moved back. 'I think he's edging closer.'

'Can we phone for help?'

'It would take hours to arrive. But go ahead — try.' Aksden pulled a phone from inside his parka and tossed it to Eusden. 'Dial one one two.'

'There's no signal.'

'As I expected. The tracker incorporates a jammer. He's a professional, Eusden. Don't you understand? He knows we're trapped. He'll wait for us to make a run for the car. Then he'll take us both. *For Guds skyld*, why did you come here? Why didn't you just thank your stars when you escaped from the American and go home to England?'

'I couldn't let you get away with killing Pernille. You'll burn in hell for that, Tolmar.'

'You and Pernille?' Aksden frowned at him, as if considering a point that had only now crossed his mind. 'I should have guessed.'

'You murdered her.'

'I didn't force her to go to Helsinki. She went because she thought she'd get her hands on the letters. She's always wanted to know my secrets.'

'She went for Michael's sake.'

'Hah!' Aksden reached out as if to grasp Eusden by the throat, his size and bulk suddenly intimidatingly apparent. But Eusden had the gun up between them pointing at his chest. Aksden stopped and took half a step back. 'Listen to me,' he said, running his hand across his mouth.

'While that sniper's out there in the trees, we have to help each other. Together, we stand a chance. It's the only one we're going to get. Do you want to live or die, Eusden? It's that simple.'

49

There could be only one answer to Tolmar Aksden's question. 'What do you suggest we do?' asked Eusden. He eyed the older man doubtfully. His strength, of mind and body, counted for nothing in the cross hairs of a telescopic rifle sight. But in Aksden's steady gaze and braced posture there was no hint that he was about to admit as much.

'I can take him, Eusden. How far is he away? A hundred metres or so? I've taken elk at further. I need glasses to read. But at distance . . . I don't miss. I have to see him first, though. I have to have a clear shot.'

'You think you'll get one?'

'Not unless we draw him out. You have to do that, my friend. It's the only way.'

'I'm not your friend, Tolmar.'

'Until that sniper's dead, you are. And I'm yours. It's about survival, Eusden. Him or us. You've got to make him show himself.'

'How?'

'Go to the other end of the veranda and run to the wood-store. The cars will cover you most of the way and there are trees behind you. He'll take a shot at you. He's bound to. But at that range with you moving fast and plenty of cover, he'll miss. I won't, though. Not a chance. We'll have him.'

'You expect me to go out there and get shot at?'

'Yes. Unless you're better with a rifle than I am.'

Eusden struggled to calculate the odds on being hit. He suspected they were much less favourable than Aksden claimed. But there was no alternative. Doing nothing was not an option. That at least was certain.

'We need to do this now, Eusden. He'll work his way closer and closer. He'll cut down the margin of error until there isn't any. We have to make our move.'

★   ★   ★

Eusden looked round the corner of the chalet at his route. It was as Aksden had said. He really should be able to make it. But he was aware that the judgement hinged on the hit man's accuracy and alertness. All he could do was trust to luck. It had to be done. There was no way round it. And the longer he hesitated, the slenderer his luck would grow. He looked over his shoulder at Aksden and nodded. Aksden nodded back. It was time to go.

He stepped off the veranda, jogged alongside the wall of the chalet, then put his head down and ran for it, focusing on the log-store and the shelter he would find behind it. It was not far. It was close, in fact, very close. He heard a shot and the whine of a bullet somewhere behind him. He was going to get away with it, no question. When would Aksden fire? When —

The bullet struck his leading foot. He fell as if tripped, pain slashing up through his leg. He hit the snow and, glancing down, saw blood welling from his ankle. He heard another shot. There was a distant cry, at once cut off. He tried to rise. The side wall of the log-store was only a few feet away. But the ankle would bear no weight. His shriek of agony was so immediate that it seemed to come from someone else. He fell again and started crawling forward.

'He's down,' Aksden shouted from the far side of the chalet. 'Stay where you are while I check.'

Eusden reached the corner of the log-store and propped himself up against it. He was panting for breath. His lower leg felt hot from the blood leaking out of him. There was a trail of it in the snow behind him. He saw Aksden striding across the meadow towards the trees, clutching the rifle in front to him. There was a slumped figure by one of the maples. Aksden had got his man.

Aksden slowed as he approached his victim and stopped a few yards from him. He raised the rifle to his shoulder, took steady aim and fired. The figure jerked from the impact. Then Aksden stepped forward, pushed the sniper's rifle clear of him with his foot and stooped to pick it up.

He started walking slowly towards Eusden. A minute or so passed. Then he called out. 'Did he hit you?'

'Yes,' Eusden shouted back. 'My ankle.'

'Too bad. I guess you won't be able to walk.' Aksden was moving more slowly with every stride. 'Or run.' He stopped, laid his rifle carefully on the ground and grasped the sniper's weapon in both hands.

'What are you doing?'

'What I have to, Eusden. This way it will look like he finished you before I finished him.'

'Don't come any closer.' Eusden pulled the gun from his pocket and pointed it. He wondered if the tremor in his hand was caused by fear or weakness — and whether Aksden could see it from where he was.

'I don't need to be closer. I can kill you from here.'

'Drop the rifle or I'll shoot.'

'Fine. Shoot. You'll miss. But go ahead anyway. Prove me right.'

He *was* right. Eusden knew that. He also knew that once he started firing, Aksden would not hesitate to respond. He lowered the gun. 'Wait,' he shouted.

'What for?'

'There are things you need to know.'

'True, my friend. But I doubt you can tell me any of them.'

'What's your brother doing in Helsinki?'

'Lars isn't in Helsinki.'

'Yes, he is. I saw him there yesterday with my own eyes.'

'You're lying.'

'No. He was there. He followed Koskinen and me to Matalainen's office. Didn't Lund mention that? I certainly told him. I'll tell you what I think, shall I? I think Lars was doing what you accused Pernille of: trying to get his hands on the letters. You haven't shared the secret with him, have you? Not all of it, anyway. You guard it jealously. Even from your own family. Why is

396

that, Tolmar? Why can't you bring yourself to trust them?'

'My family is none of your concern, Eusden. Prying into our affairs is why you're going to die here in the snow, a long way from home.'

'Kill me and you'll be making a big mistake.'

'And you're going to explain why, of course.'

Yes. He was. He had to. His brain raced to fill the gaps between what he knew and what he needed to guess — correctly. 'Do you really believe your father was the Tsarevich, Tolmar? I mean, *really*? I think you do. I think you've always wanted to believe it. That's why you're carving out a business empire in Russia. To make up for the real empire you reckon was your birthright. I imagine that information would come as an unpleasant surprise to your new friends over there. Of course, it could all be bullshit, couldn't it? Who did Karl Wanting find in Siberia? A haemophiliac peasant with a passing resemblance to Alexei? A lie for him and Paavo Falenius to sell to your family so they could help themselves — and ultimately you — to the Tsar's money? Or was your father the real thing — the one true Alexei? He must have told you.'

'You don't know what you're talking about.'

'He didn't, did he? That's it. That's your problem. He never said. You were too young when he died. Your grandfather didn't let you into the family secret until years later. Maybe he waited until Paavo Falenius was dead too. Wanting was long gone, of course. But your grandfather only knew what they wanted him to know — and to believe. It's not the same as certainty. Rock solid certainty. One way or the other. Well, I can give you that if you want it. If you have the guts to face it.'

'You can give me that?' Aksden's question was an admission of weakness. Eusden had found a way under his defences.

'Not everything was destroyed in the explosion. Brad kept back one item to sell later to the highest bidder. What else would you expect? The guy was a scumbag.'

'What item?'

'Two sets of fingerprints, taken by Clem Hewitson sixteen years apart. The first aboard the imperial yacht off Cowes in August 1909. The second at Aksdenhøj in October 1925. They prove — once and for all — whether your father was the Tsarevich. If he was, the two sets have to match. If not . . . '

Aksden raised the rifle to his shoulder. 'Where are they?'

'One set's in my pocket. The other's in a safe at the Grand Marina Hotel in Helsinki, accessible only to me.'

'Show me what you have.'

Eusden took out the envelope and held it up. 'You won't be able to see the insignia from there, Tolmar, so I'll tell you what it is: the double-headed eagle of the Romanovs. Want a closer look?'

'Throw your gun away.'

'OK.' Eusden tossed the pistol into the snow a few feet from him. 'Now what?'

'Don't move.'

Aksden walked slowly towards him, the rifle

398

held in front of him. The expression on his face was intent and watchful. But something else burned in his gaze. It was more than curiosity, more than desire for certainty. It was obsession.

He stopped a yard or so short and levelled the rifle at Eusden. He looked at the double-headed eagle for a second, then said, 'Show me what's in the envelope.'

Eusden fingered up the flap, slid out the sheet of paper and turned it for Aksden to see. There was an intake of breath. Aksden stared at the red-inked fingerprints and the writing beneath them: *A.N. 4 viii '09.*

'A.N.,' he murmured. 'Alexei Nikolaievich.'

The rifle was still pointing at Eusden, but Aksden's attention was fixed on the letter, held out to one side. It was the opportunity Eusden had gambled on getting. It was, in truth, his only chance. He slid forward, swivelled on his hip and lashed out with his uninjured foot. The Dane cried out and fell backwards as his leg was whipped from under him. The rifle went off, but the shot flew harmlessly skywards. As Aksden landed on his back with a thump, Eusden rolled the other way and lunged for the gun. The pain in his ankle counted for nothing now. He grabbed the gun, pushed himself up and turned in the same instant.

But Aksden was already sitting up himself, his eyes blazing, his mouth twisted in fury. He swung the rifle towards Eusden. His finger curled around the trigger. Eusden brought his arm down straight, in line with Aksden's face. And there was a roar as both weapons fired.

50

The sky, stared at long enough, seemed to turn from grey to palest blue. And the silence, once the ears had adjusted, gave way to tiny stirrings of wind and the distant cawing of crows somewhere in the forest. Only the gnawing chill of the air above and the snow beneath stirred Eusden from his reverie, which could have lasted several seconds or many minutes — he had no way of knowing. When he tried to sit up, the pain in his right side was sharp and deep. Blood had soaked through his jacket. He could not tell how serious this second wound was. But he was certainly alive. At least, he thought he was.

He propped himself up on his elbows and saw Tolmar Aksden's body lying a few feet away, the rifle across his chest, one hand still clutching the butt. His expression was a frozen mixture of anger and surprise. There was a sickeningly neat bullet-hole above his left eyebrow and blood on the snow behind his head.

Eusden felt weak, light-headed and curiously contented. Nothing he saw or felt was entirely real to him. He assumed this was some kind of trick being played on him by his brain, a defence mechanism designed to ease the onset of death. It did not dull the pain he was in, but somehow divorced it from him, as if he was watching himself from a place of warmth and safety and disinterested ease. It made the idea of lying back down and continuing to stare at the sky very appealing.

'Don't lie down, Coningsby,' said Marty.

The voice seemed to come from behind him. When he turned his head, there was no one there. Yet he had the sense that someone had been. It was like the quivering of a leaf after a creature has fled into undergrowth: a sign without a sighting.

'This is all your fault,' Eusden said aloud. 'You know that, Marty, don't you?' There was no rancour in his tone. It was more in the way of a friendly reproach. 'Thanks for landing me in it. One last time.'

'Don't lie down, Coningsby.'

'What do you expect me to do?'

'Deliver a touching eulogy at my funeral.'

'And for that I need to be there, of course.'

'It's customary.'

'Yeah. So it is.'

Eusden tried to sit up. There was a jab of pain in his side. The bullet had probably smashed a rib. What other damage it might have done he did not care to consider. Certainly standing up did not seem to be an option. He could not phone for help. He was closer to the jammer now than when he had failed to get a signal on the veranda. Theoretically, he could drive to where help might be found if he could make it to the Bentley. He had the key in his pocket. But theory was a long way from practice. Moving presented itself to his mind as a task best deferred, while another part of his mind insisted that deferral would be fatal.

401

He straightened his arms. It was like plunging into an ice-cold bath. He began to shiver and noticed the sheet of paper with the fingerprints on it lying close to his hand, beside the fallen gun. There they were: the unique traces of a human's existence on this planet. *A.N.* Anastasia Nikolaievna. Or Alexei Nikolaievich. 'Or A.N. bloody Other, Clem, eh?'

'*You've been checking up on me, boy? Well, we'll make a detective of you yet.*'

'Seems you've succeeded. Much good that it's done me.'

Eusden remembered asking Clem once how he had survived four years in the trenches without being killed or injured. And now he heard again the answer the old man had given him. '*You had to think ahead to survive, boy. If you didn't, you were finished.*' (Pause for puff on pipe.) '*'Course, if you thought too far ahead, you were finished as well.*' (Another puff.) '*I used to reckon five minutes was just about right.*'

'Five minutes? OK, Clem. I'll try it.' Eusden grabbed the sheet of paper, folded it as best he could and thrust it into his trouser pocket. The gun he left where it was. He rolled on to his hip and began to work his way towards the Bentley, sawing at the snow with his functioning leg. His shivering became a wild juddering, his breathing a panting wheeze. Pain ballooned inside him. But he did not stop. He felt suddenly and preposterously hot. Sweat started out of him. But still he did not stop.

He reached the car and rewarded himself with a few moments' rest. The pain ebbed. Then he stretched up to open the door. He managed to do so by about an inch. Pulling it fully open seemed impossible. It felt immensely heavy. He pressed himself close to the side of the car, forced his arm inside the door and pushed with all his failing strength. It was just enough.

An unmeasurable segment of time passed while he rested his chin on the soft leather of the driver's seat and contemplated, as if it were some abstruse problem he had no personal stake in, the difficulty of levering himself into the car. In the end, no easy answer presented itself. He counted down from ten to one and, after two false starts, simply hauled himself in, gripping the steering-wheel like grim death, an expression he felt in a moment of startling clarity he fully understood for the first time.

He lifted his injured leg in after him, and then nearly fell back out of the car as he pulled the door shut. The warmth that had built up during the drive from Helsinki folded itself round him like a duvet. It would have been easy, so very easy, to surrender to it and fall asleep. But he knew, if he did, he would never wake. He pushed the key into the ignition and turned it. The engine responded with well-tuned vigour. He shifted the stick into drive and eased down the accelerator. The car started moving. He steered it in a slow, wide circle past the body of Arto Falenius, out over the meadow and back on to the track they had arrived by. Every ridge of compacted snow, every minor undulation, sent pain stabbing through his body. But the Bentley rolled softly with the bumps. He knew it could

403

be a great deal worse. And he began to think that he really was going to get through this. He drove slowly along the track, away from the *mökki* and the bodies lying nearby, into the forest, towards the main road — and survival.

* * *

The Bentley essentially drove itself. All Eusden had to do was steer it. His concentration began to falter, his vision to blur. He wondered if dusk was setting in. There was a vagueness to the world beyond the windscreen, a fuzzying at the edges of his vision. The track wound ahead through the snow-stacked trees. He kept his foot on the accelerator, his hands on the wheel. He just needed to keep going. He just —

There was a jolt, a violent lurch. Suddenly, the Bentley was heading down a short slope straight into a mass of trees. He must have mistaken the line of the track somehow. He stamped down on the brake. The car skidded and slewed to the left. But there were as many trees waiting there as dead ahead. And the car slammed straight into one.

Eusden had forgotten to fasten his seat belt. It was far from a high-speed impact, but still he was thrown against the wheel, setting the horn blaring. He lay across it, watched with detached curiosity the steam rising from the crumpled radiator and the shower of snow and pine needles pattering down on to the bonnet.

Eventually, he pushed himself back into the seat. The horn fell silent. All the breath seemed to have been knocked out of him. He found it difficult to organize his thoughts into initiating any kind of action at all. He wondered how much blood he had lost. And how much more he could afford to lose. Then he stopped wondering. He would find out soon enough, after all. Until then . . .

He forced himself to focus. He engaged reverse and pressed down the accelerator. The tyres spun, but did not grip. The Bentley was going nowhere. And neither was Eusden. He turned off the engine.

Tranquillity descended. And a shaft of sunlight, the first he had seen in Finland, turned the surrounding curtain of snow from greyish white to granular pink. He sat back and savoured the beauty of it. The forest felt holy in that instant. And he would be warm inside the car for a while yet. He could always turn the engine back on.

'I'm offering you the chance to change your life,' Pernille had said to him on the ferry from Sweden. Eusden smiled gently at what struck him now less as a tragedy than an irony. If only they had known. In truth, neither of them had had any future to shape or alter. They had both been voyaging to their deaths.

'Pull yourself together, Coningsby. You should've let me drive. I was always better than you. Now, for God's sake phone for help and get us out of the mess you've got us into.'

Eusden did not bother to point out that the jammer had travelled with them. There would still be no signal. Even if it had been

405

conveniently knocked off, the closely packed trees would probably do as good a job. He pulled Lund's phone out of his pocket and pressed the green button. It was as he had expected. No signal. 'Sorry, Marty,' he murmured.

It was a relief in some ways. There was nothing more he could do now. He could stop struggling. He did not need to think, even five minutes ahead. He closed his eyes. And the darkness received him like a loyal friend.

JYVÄSKYLÄ

51

Forty-eight hours had vanished into a black hole. They existed as a memory, but one too dark and dense for Eusden to access: a singularity in more ways than one, since being alive confounded his last recollected expectation.

He had been lucky, according to the quietly spoken doctor who succeeded the nurses who were the first to greet him when he resumed meaningful engagement with the world. He had lost consciousness in the car and, thanks to the angle it was resting at, had slumped forward across the steering-wheel, setting off the horn again. The noise had failed to rouse him, but, in the absence of much other noise, had attracted the attention of an engineer repairing a power line half a kilometre away, who had recognized it for what it was. Eusden had been brought to the Central Hospital in Jyväskylä, the regional capital, where he now was, with smashed ankle reset and broken ribs realigned, wounds cleaned and stitched, lost blood replaced, vital organs checked. Neither of the bullets had lodged in his body or caused irreparable damage. And the tube in his chest denoted nothing more sinister than a minor pneumothorax in his right lung, caused by one of the fractured ribs. The doctor's prognosis was that he should make a full recovery, though not necessarily a speedy one. 'Your body has been through a lot, Mr Eusden. It will tell you how long it needs to get over it.'

The doctor's tone altered when he went on to inform him of the police's interest in his condition. There was an officer sitting outside the room whose superior was anxious to talk to Eusden at the earliest opportunity. 'I will have to inform him that in my opinion you are now well enough to be questioned.'

That seemed undeniable, though Eusden soon had cause to doubt it. 'We have the media in the car park,' the doctor added. 'The death of Tolmar Aksden . . . in these circumstances . . . is very big news.' Then he said something which Eusden had to ask him to repeat and even then could not quite believe he had heard, something so joyously unexpected and wholly astounding that he thought it must be a delusion on his part, until the doctor assured him it was not. 'It has been difficult for Ms Madsen to come to the hospital. The reporters and photographers will not leave her alone.'

★ ★ ★

Pernille was not dead. The doctor, of course, did not know why Eusden was so overwhelmed by his reference to her. Nor was he able to answer the seemingly obtuse question, 'How can she be alive?' The simple fact, self-evident to him, was that she was. And she was just as anxious to see Eusden as Inspector Ahlroos.

It was Ahlroos, however, who arrived first. A

410

slightly built, dark-haired man with a profession-ally guarded expression and the apparent ability never to blink, he was accompanied by a burly junior who prowled round the room and did a lot of gum-chewing and window-gazing while his boss asked the questions. And he had a lot of questions to ask.

The inspector might have anticipated caution or evasion from his interviewee. It was clear to Eusden that he must be an actual or potential murder suspect. He supposed the most prudent course of action would be to say nothing at all until he had taken legal advice. As it was, however, he was so euphoric at the news that Pernille was not dead that he told Ahlroos everything he wanted to know and probably more, which even so was less than the whole and multi-faceted truth. All he sought in return was an answer to the question he had put to the doctor in vain: 'How can she be alive?'

His persistence eventually won him an explanation of sorts. 'Ms Madsen was never at the house in Munkkiniemi, Mr Eusden. She told us she let Lars Aksden take her place. He was killed in the explosion. For why they swapped, you must ask her.'

★ ★ ★

Eusden's chance to do that came a couple of hours later. When Pernille entered the room, she stopped in the doorway and they smiled disbelievingly at each other. Then she walked

411

across and kissed him on the cheek and sat down on the chair beside the bed. She was dressed in the same black outfit she had worn when they first met in Stockholm. She looked tired and stressed — and wonderfully alive.

'I thought you'd run away,' she said, still smiling at him.

'And I thought you were dead.'

'I'm happy we were both wrong.'

'The police said Lars took your place.'

'Someone inside Mjollnir tipped him off about what was happening. He refused to tell me who it was and now I suppose we may never know. He saw his chance to find out what the family secret really was and I was so . . . disappointed . . . you'd quit on me I . . . didn't try to talk him out of it. We met halfway to Koskinen's house. I got out of the car and he got in. Matalainen had no choice about going along with it. There wasn't time for him to argue. They drove away — to their deaths. When I heard about the explosion, I realized Tolmar had double-crossed us — and killed his brother by mistake in the process. I moved to a different hotel so no one would know where I was and tried to decide what to do. In the end, I went to the police. They didn't believe me, of course. Then the news came from here that Tolmar and Arto Falenius and another man had been found dead — and that you were in hospital. It was the last news I was expecting.'

'The Opposition sent a hit man after Tolmar, who shot Falenius by mistake. Then Tolmar shot

412

the hit man. And then . . . ' Eusden searched Pernille's face for some clue to what she thought he had done. 'It was him or me.'

'I'm glad it wasn't you.'

'I don't suppose Michael will be. How is he?'

'Not good. He's lost his uncle as well as his father. He's . . . ' She shrugged. 'You can imagine.'

'I'm trying to.'

'I left him in Helsinki with Elsa.'

'Thanks for coming to see me. It . . . can't have been easy to get away.'

'I've been several times.'

'So I gather. And you've had to fend off reporters to do it, apparently.'

'I can handle them. I'm more worried about the police. What did they want to know?'

'Everything. And that's what I told them. Now I should tell you everything as well. About what happened by the lake.'

'It can wait. The doctor says you need plenty of rest. You also need a lawyer. I can help with that.'

'I'm just going to keep on telling the truth, Pernille. It's about all I feel capable of doing.'

'They've arrested Erik Lund.'

'Good.'

'And poor Osmo Koskinen. But I expect they'll let him go soon. I think it's going to be all right. But still you should have a lawyer.'

'OK. If you say so.'

A silence fell briefly between them, strangely lacking in awkwardness. Then Pernille said, 'I met your American friend, Regina Celeste, in

413

Helsinki. She asked me to tell you that Werner Straub has turned up there.'

'He's wasting his time. Sooner or later, he'll realize that and go home.'

'She also asked me to tell you that you owe her an apology.'

'I seem to owe quite a lot of people one of those.'

Another fleeting silence was broken this time by Eusden.

'I'm sorry about Lars, Pernille. He seemed a decent man.'

'He was. I never should have let him go . . . instead of me.'

'I'm glad you did.'

She sighed. 'It's not going to be easy . . . to find a way through this. Michael is so angry. He doesn't believe what I've told him about his father. He'll have to in the end. But then . . . '

'Maybe I can help.' Eusden reached out towards her and she took his hand.

'Maybe we can help each other,' she said softly.

★   ★   ★

Lying in bed that night, gazing up at the shadows on the ceiling and listening to the sounds of the hospital around him, Eusden wondered if he and Pernille really were alive, or if this frailly hopeful future that seemed now to be possible was merely a consoling fantasy devised by his brain to render the process of freezing to death in a Finnish forest more tolerable. Maybe it was, he

414

decided. But as consolations went, it was mightily effective. There was nothing to be gained by fighting against it. Time would tell whether it was real or not. He closed his eyes. And the darkness received him like a loyal friend.

COWES

52

The sky over Cowes is cloudless azure, the still air cool, the noon sun warm. It is a Wednesday in mid-September, yet there is no tinge of autumn in the late summer light. The warmth and stillness have certainly been a blessing for the occupants of the motorboat now approaching one of the jetties along the Parade. Richard Eusden and Gemma Conway are returning from a shared last act of mourning for their friend and in Gemma's case ex-husband, Marty Hewitson: the scattering of his ashes in the indulgently calm, gently lapping waters of the Solent.

The owner of the motorboat puts them ashore, acknowledges their thanks and heads out again. The two people who knew Marty best in the world watch the departing vessel for a while, then walk slowly away, their savouring breaths of the ozoned air blended with full-hearted sighs. The sunlight sparkles on the wake of a Red Jet ferry as it accelerates out of the harbour, bound for Southampton. Eusden tracks its progress from the corner of his eye, knowing he will soon be leaving the Isle of Wight himself, crossing the water where he has just bidden a final farewell to his friend of nearly forty years.

As they turn away from the sea into Watchhouse Lane, Gemma breaks the silence that has hung between them since leaving the boat. 'I'm glad we were able to do this at last,

Richard. Just you and me. And Marty.'

'Same here. I hated missing his funeral. This has . . . made up for it in a way, I guess. Even though . . . '

'Yes?'

'I should have been there. To say a few words. To tell everyone . . . I loved him.'

'I told them for you. They all understood you couldn't make the journey. Even Bernie Shadbolt.'

'And Vicky?'

'Her too, I think. They had lots of questions, of course. Questions I couldn't answer.'

'I'm not sure I'd have been able to either.'

'Able? Or willing?'

Eusden smiles ruefully. 'A bit of both.' They reach the High Street end of the lane and stop by the entrance to the Union Inn. It is a pub he and Marty frequented in their time, as did Marty's grandfather, Clem Hewitson, though never at the same time. 'Can I buy you a drink, Gem?' His use of the diminutive form of her name appears to surprise her almost as much as it does him. He wonders if this is the first occasion he has used it since their divorce. And he wonders if she wonders also. 'Unless . . . ' He is aware she is not an entirely free agent. Their long postponed joint adieu to Marty has been arranged as part of a pre-term holiday Gemma is spending on the Island with Monica, who has diplomatically absented herself, though not, Eusden suspects, for long.

'All right.' Gemma smiles awkwardly. 'Just a quick one.'

They enter the pub, stepping down into the cosy old bar that has changed little over the years. Eusden orders a pint of bitter for himself and a spritzer for Gemma. They sit by the window and toast Marty's memory, the urn that held his ashes sitting in a bag at their feet.

'I should've known Marty would die young,' says Gemma. 'He never stuck at anything.' At that they manage a laugh. 'You know, Richard, I've missed him more these past six months than I ever did in all the years we were apart.'

'That's because you could've talked to him if you'd really wanted to. But now . . .'

'I can't. Ever again.' She draws a deep breath. 'It feels like the three of us have been heading downriver in a boat and Marty's got out and stood on the bank, while we sail on, looking back at him as he slowly fades from view.'

Eusden pats her hand. 'I'll miss him too.'

'He so wanted his life to . . . add up to more than it did. I suppose that's why he wouldn't leave the mystery Clem bequeathed to him in that attaché case alone. It gave him . . . a high to go out on.' She half-turns in her seat to look at Eusden. 'All those things you told me when I visited you in Finland . . .'

'What about them?'

'Were they really true?'

'I didn't lie to you, Gemma. I can assure you of that.'

'No, but . . .' She opens the small rucksack that doubles as her handbag and takes out a newspaper cutting, which she unfolds and lays on the table between them. 'Did you see this?'

Eusden looks down at the *Guardian* headline from a few weeks ago. BONES FOUND BY RUSSIAN BUILDER FINALLY SOLVE RIDDLE OF THE MISSING ROMANOVS. He remembers it well, as a *Guardian* reader himself. He was wandering out of his local newsagent's in Chiswick one Saturday morning in late August when he opened the paper and saw the faces of the Romanovs staring at him from a 1915 photograph: the Tsar and Tsarevich in imperial navy uniform, the Tsarina and her daughters in the dresses of a bygone age, all solemnly unsmiling, as if oppressed by fore-knowledge of what history had in store for them. The two bodies missing from the burial site near Ekaterinburg had finally been found, the article declared, by a local builder on a speculative weekend root-around; case closed at long last. 'I saw it,' Eusden says quietly.

'So, this proves Tolmar Aksden's father *wasn't* the Tsarevich.'

'Does it?'

'Well? What do you think?'

'Not sure. But I can tell you what Marty would say.'

'Go on, then.'

'First, DNA isn't all it's cracked up to be. Second, the *Guardian's* man in Moscow falls for the Russian claim that the missing sister was Maria, whereas all the neutral pathologists agreed at the time it was Anastasia. Third, we're supposed to believe this guy with a prodder found what a whole team of archaeologists failed to find in years of systematic digging. Fourth, the

422

1991 excavation was patently a put-up job, so you'd have to reckon this was too. Fifth, it comes within months of Tolmar Aksden's death, unpublicized details of which could conceivably have reached the ears of those who arrange such things in Russia. And sixth, only people who know none of the details — which is more or less everybody, of course — would be convinced this settles a damn thing.'

Gemma smiles at him. 'I thought you'd say something like that.'

'I said it's what *Marty* would say. I don't have an opinion.'

'There speaks the civil servant.'

'Not any more.' He grins.

'Sorry?'

'I've resigned. I finished at the end of August.'

Gemma looks genuinely astonished. 'You're having me on.'

'No. I quit. Handed in my security pass. Cleared my desk. Sloughed off my Whitehall gravitas.'

'Why?'

'I got a better offer.'

'Doing what?'

'I'll be working for an aid organization in Denmark called Uddanne Afrika. I start next week.'

'In *Denmark*?'

'That's right.'

'Well, I . . . ' Gemma shakes her head in wonderment and sips her spritzer. 'Congratulations.'

'Thanks.'

'Does this . . .' She frowns thoughtfully. 'Does this have anything to do with Pernille Madsen?' She carries on before he can devise an evasive answer. 'It does, doesn't it? This isn't just about a job.'

'Maybe not.' He shrugs diffidently. 'We'll see.'

Gemma's astonishment has by now turned to delighted disbelief. She smiles broadly. 'In that case, I wish you all the luck in the world.'

★ ★ ★

Two hours later, Eusden is sitting alone in a coffee shop in the Fountain Arcade, sipping an *americano* and watching the quayside world go by before boarding the Southampton ferry. Gemma is long gone. There is nothing to keep him here now, on this island where he and Marty were born. He will return occasionally, of course, to visit his sister and her family. Or maybe *they* will visit *him*, wherever he may be. Either way, it will be a long time before he is here again. That much seems certain.

A bus from Newport pulls in as he gazes through the open doorway. The past does not arrive with it. His boyhood self does not step off into the mellow sunlight. And Marty is not waiting for him, chewing gum, hands in pockets, lolling against the nearest pillar. The memory of those times is so close he can almost touch it. But it will never be quite close enough. That much is also certain.

The ringing of his phone plucks him back to the present. He takes it out of his pocket and

424

smiles when he sees who the caller is.

'Pernille?'

'Hi.'

'Hi, yourself.'

'Where are you?'

'Fountain Quay. Waiting for the ferry.'

'So, it's done?'

'Yes. It's done.'

'Did it . . . go well?'

'Yes. I think it did.'

'Good.'

'I'm looking forward to seeing you tomorrow.'

'I'm looking forward to seeing you too.'

'Is everything all right?'

'Everything's fine. Though . . . '

'What?'

'I have some news for you. It's not urgent. It can wait until tomorrow if you like.'

'Not sure I could bear that. What is it?'

'Something Michael found while he was sorting through Tolmar's things. I was happy he finally did it. And I guess I should be happy he wanted to share this thing he found with me.'

'And this thing is?'

'A telegram. A very old telegram. Kept in a locked drawer of the desk in Tolmar's study. It was sent to Paavo Falenius in Helsinki from somewhere in Russia. I can't read the name of the place. It's in the Russian alphabet. But the message and the sender's name are in English. It's dated twenty-fifth September, 1918. Falenius must have given it to Tolmar as . . . some kind of proof, I guess. Though it doesn't prove anything actually.'

'Is it from Karl Wanting?' Eusden asks, knowing already there really is no one else it could be from.

'Yes. It is.'

'What's the message?'

'Just one word. And the sender's name. *Found. Wanting.*'

AUTHOR'S NOTE

None of the universally acknowledged facts concerning the ultimate fates of Tsar Nicholas II, his wife and their children have been misrepresented in this novel. The same is true of the life of the woman who later claimed to be their daughter, the Grand Duchess Anastasia. Readers who care to consult the archives of the *Isle of Wight County Press* will find a contemporary report there of the visit of the Russian imperial family to Cowes in August 1909. As to what really happened at the Ipatiev house in Ekaterinburg in the early hours of 17 July 1918, the most accurate statement that can be made is that those who believe they know the course of events for certain can surely never have seriously attempted to learn what the course of events truly was.

I am indebted to Andrew Roberts for suggesting it was time I tackled the subject of this novel. For help generously given to me while I was planning and writing it, I am very grateful to my good friends Susan Moody and John Donaldson, to their good friend Iver Tesdorpf and to my wonderful Danish translator, Claus Bech (whose family secret regarding Tsar Alexander III's walking stick I have vowed to keep). Thanks to them, location research was not merely fruitful, but a lot of fun into the bargain. *Skål!*

We do hope that you have enjoyed reading this large print book.

Did you know that all of our titles are available for purchase?

We publish a wide range of high quality large print books including:

Romances, Mysteries, Classics
General Fiction
Non Fiction and Westerns

Special interest titles available in large print are:

The Little Oxford Dictionary
Music Book
Song Book
Hymn Book
Service Book

Also available from us courtesy of Oxford University Press:

Young Readers' Dictionary
(large print edition)
Young Readers' Thesaurus
(large print edition)

For further information or a free brochure, please contact us at:

Ulverscroft Large Print Books Ltd.,
The Green, Bradgate Road, Anstey,
Leicester, LE7 7FU, England.
Tel: (00 44) 0116 236 4325
Fax: (00 44) 0116 234 0205

NAME TO A FACE

Robert Goddard

It began with a shipwreck in 1707; a secret mission thirty years later; a fatal accident during a dive to the wreck in 1996 and an expatriate's return home years afterwards. All these events are mysteriously linked and set in motion a chain of intrigue, deceit, greed and murder. A conspiracy of circumstances is about to unravel. And with it, the past.

NEVER GO BACK

Robert Goddard

Harry Barnett is in England following the death of his mother. Whilst settling her affairs he meets two old acquaintances from his National Service days in the RAF. A lavish reunion has been organized to mark their fiftieth anniversary at the Scottish castle where they spent three months acting as guinea pigs in a psychological experiment. But en route to Aberdeen, they are rudely interrupted by the apparent suicide of one of their number. Later at the castle another of the old comrades dies in suspicious circumstances. The dark turn the weekend has taken suddenly becomes inky black, and Harry finds himself plunged into a struggle for their very survival.

PLAY TO THE END

Robert Goddard

When actor Toby Flood arrives in Brighton whilst on tour with a Joe Orton play, he is visited by his estranged wife, Jenny, now living with wealthy entrepreneur Roger Colborn. Jenny is worried about a strange man who has taken to hanging around outside her shop in the Lanes. Roger has dismissed her concerns and she hopes instead that Toby will be willing to get to the bottom of the man's behaviour. Next day, Toby confronts the man. Derek Oswin blames Colborn for his father's death from cancer, on account of dangerous practices at the defunct plastics factory run by Roger and his late father. Before he fully understands the risks he is running, Flood finds himself entangled in the mysterious — and danger-ous — relationship between the Oswins and the Colborns . . .

SIGHT UNSEEN

Robert Goddard

1981. The peace of a summer's day at the ancient stone circle of Avebury is shattered by the abduction of two-year-old Tamsin Hall and the violent death of her sister Miranda. One of the witnesses, Ph.D. student David Umber, was waiting at the nearby pub to meet a man called Griffin who claimed he could help him with his researches into the identity of Junius, pen-name of the famous and mysterious eighteenth-century letter-writer. But Griffin never showed up. Nine years later, notorious paedophile Brian Radd confessed to Tamsin's murder and the case was closed. However, in 2004, retired Chief Inspector George Sharp seeks Umber's help in reopening his inquiry. He has never believed Radd to be guilty. And he has received a letter reproaching him for botching the original investigation — signed Junius.

DAYS WITHOUT NUMBER

Robert Goddard

Michael Paleologus, retired archaeologist and supposed descendant of the last Emperors of Byzantium, lives alone in a remote house on the Cornish bank of the River Tamar. A ridiculously generous offer has been made for the house, but he refuses to sell despite the urgings of his children, for whom the proceeds would solve a variety of problems. But the stalemate is soon tragically broken. Only then do Nick and his siblings discover why their father was bound at all costs to reject the offer. Their desperate efforts to conceal the truth drag them into a deadly conflict with an unseen and unknown enemy. Nick realizes that the only way to escape from the trap their persecutor has set for them is to hunt him down . . .

PAST CARING

Robert Goddard

Martin Radford, history graduate, disaffected and unemployed, jumps at the chance to visit Madeira at the invitation of an old university friend who is running the local English language newspaper. Luck continues to run for him when he is offered a lucrative commission to research the mysterious resignation and subsequent obscure retirement on Madeira of Edwardian cabinet minister Edwin Strafford. However, his investigation triggers a bizarre and inevitably violent train of events which remorselessly entangles him and those who believed they had escaped the spectre of crimes long past but never paid for.